The Big Book of Bootleg Horror

~

Volume II

A HellBound Books LLC Publication

www.hellboundbookspublishing.com

Printed in the United States of America

The Big Book of Bootleg Horror

~

Volume II

Compiled and Edited by Mitch Workman

A HellBound Books Publishing LLC Book
Houston TX

The Big Book of Bootleg Horror Vol. 2

Dedication

We dedicate this mighty tome to each and every one of the authors who made it possible by entrusting HellBound Books with their precious offspring.

A million thanks, one and all, for joining us on this incredible journey!

Foreword

Well, here we are again, Dear Reader, another superlative volume of the dark, nefarious and downright evil.

It's often asked of we horror writers – heck, of everyone who writes – *'where do your ideas come from?'* It is a loaded, and ill-advised question to be sure.

I guess there's no easy, nor straightforward reply to this, since many of us are actually at a genuine loss as to precisely where our ideas come from. There was a great quote from a British comedy double act (*Reeves and Mortimer* – look 'em up!) when asked this very question in a TV interview –

"From our heads."

And therein lies the scary part. In every writer's brain – that grey/pink slop that remains mostly a mystery to those who study such things – there are random thoughts, ideas and snippets of prose darting around, just screaming to be let out. Now, the majority of those products of neurotransmitters, bioelectrical impulses and uncountable synapses can be traced back to things we've experienced, seen, heard and read across our lifetimes, but there is a tiny fraction of those haphazard thoughts that appear to have come from nowhere…

It is those ideas, Dear Reader, that keep us awake at nights, that drive many a writer to the bottle, or even to the end of a rope – those thoughts that skulk deep within the creases and folds of the creative brain, random scenarios of death, destruction, madness and the otherworldly creatures from which nightmares are made, thoughts that might just have come from another place entirely…

So, as you enjoy this journey into the darkest planes of existence – and enjoy it you will – please do spare a thought for the poor, tortured minds who have sweated blood and tears in order to write out their nightmares, although not specifically for your delectation – but because they really do have no other choice.

HellBound Books

CONTENTS

Petronomicon
Leo X. Robertson

When my project leader told me Olav would be flying out to the Loki A platform to inspect the new freshwater package they'd installed as part of the Svindal Tie-in Project, and he'd specifically requested I go with him, the office landscape blurred. I might have made a noise like 'Dur' or drooled. Honestly, I don't even remember, which just shows what a disservice I do globally to the other four gay process engineers.

Joking. There is in all likelihood six in total, if we count Olav.

Oh, man, the adventure of going to an offshore platform for the first time. Just the pair of us, stuck on this little block of metal in the middle of the ocean with nothing else around; him, to my knowledge, having visited several times and so holding all the keys to my survival should something unexpected happen?

I accepted. Only because I'd been assisting with a project on a connected platform, Loki T, and thought it would be good for my understanding. To go for any other reason would be unprofessional and stupid.

#

We arrived on Loki A in a Super Puma helicopter, clad in matching orange survival suits. Beaming lights around the helipad's perimeter fired with all their might against the approaching night. Olav got out first and I followed, blasted by a fierce lateral wind.

After we registered at the reception, he ushered me towards the lift shaft and said, "I'm going to my room to take this suit off."

"I'll come with you then," I said. "I-I can't leave your sight this whole trip. I have to speak with the platform manager and return this form to reception before they'll let me wander around alone." I gestured with a limp piece of paper in my sweaty hand.

"That's only for when we leave the living quarters and explore the platforms." He looked at my keycard. "I see you're on the third floor. I'm on the fifth. Why don't I meet you down at the changing room?"

I stood, frozen, staring behind him at a watercolour of a demon horse with eight legs.

He forced air out his nose. "Just come back to this floor once you've gone to your room."

#

"I haven't been to the gym in months," Olav said as we took luminous boiler suits out of our designated changing room closets and put them on. "Fat bastard."

Sure enough, he had expanded a little since I'd last seen him. Through his t-shirt I saw he had that softness about him that makes an ellipse from a previously well-defined bellybutton.

I cocked my head at him. "It suits you better."

"Because you're gay I'm supposed to accept that?"

"How 'bout because I'm a human with eyes whose opinion you trust?"

He smiled. "Follow me."

We walked out into the November wind that seemed to circle the platform. Stumbling along metal walkways, up precarious external sets of stairs, he took me to the top of Loki A, and we worked our way back down, examining the round-ended cylinders of separators on top. Compressors a floor below that churned out a constant noise Long, tank-like manifolds took up the entirety of a room, the legs of its black piping snaking up and out through dark passages. Finally, we took the walkway to a less windy side of the platform and stood looking down the hollow cuboid of Loki T's cable-laden bridge.

"Can we go take a look?" I said.

"I think it's best if we stick to one platform tonight. Besides, I don't know Loki T that well." He placed a hand on my shoulder. "Hey, can we go back inside?"

This is it, I thought, he'll explain why I'm here. I'm ashamed to say my next thought was whether or not there were any rules about "bed sharing" offshore.

We were soon back in the changing room. He took off his boots, unbuttoned his suit, and I did the same.

"Listen," he said. "I'm going to stay up and talk to the controllers about my project. In Norwegian."

I'd been all too accommodating about his lack of confidence with English when we were both at university in Glasgow, waiting patiently for his answers, introducing him to my friends, explaining complicated engineering definitions to him in plain language over the phone late on Friday evenings. Now that I was the foreigner, on this mostly Norwegian platform, the favour wasn't going to be repaid.

"Don't mind me," he continued. "I just get this feeling when I'm out here that I need to work the whole time. If you're lucky enough not to feel like that, don't worry about it. You know how to get back, right?" he said.

I'd forgotten what floor we were on. And I was staying on the third floor of the living quarters, right?

"Sure," I said.

"Let's meet for breakfast at half six."

"Seriously?"

"You're offshore. The working hours are different here. But hey," he continued, "I'm sure you brought a book with you, right? I rarely saw you without one."

It was meant to sound like an affectionate remembrance, but it just came off as patronising.

"They took our phones," I said. "How do you wake up?"

"There's an alarm clock in the room."

"Oh. Is it set to the right time?"

"You've got to figure that out for yourself."

I nodded to him and walked into the nearest corridor, opening three wrong doors when I was out his sight.

#

I eventually found the lift and got back to my room. Locking the door behind me, I got changed into my pyjamas, sat by the window and cried. A tooth I hadn't taken care of was poking painfully through my gums.

I looked out at Loki T. Layers of pipes ran across its surface; halogen on every level kept the details of its structure a blurry, light-blazed haze. Matchstick-like struts below propped it above the water so precariously it didn't look enough to support the mass of metal above. Those pipes that drew gas from the ground collected a constant foam of bubbles around them; a flare stack towered above, such that its base disappeared into the sky of darkness and rain and reappeared again at the tip, where a blustering fire burned.

Stupid Olav and his insecurities had me too tense to get in bed yet, had me thinking I should do something practical. From my offshore bag, I took out my book, a study guide for a dense novel I hadn't understood or enjoyed, then flung it back.

Boooommm...

I woke up as a shockwave propagated across the waters in a flash, shaking my room so hard I thought the window would burst.

I got out of bed and looked to the window. Off in the distance, where Olav had pointed out Loki B, a platform far away but connected to ours, I saw spiralling green flames, as tall as the platform itself, burning through a black mist.

Green flames? No alarm? What was I to do?

I hopped from one foot to another and stared at the flames that turned progressively whiter, burned with greater ferocity.

Well, that was it. Gas would burn back through the pipes beneath the sea and I'd be dead in no time, surely.

Wailing, moaning. I pressed my face to the window and tried to look down at its source.

"Uhhhh!" It sounded so loud and sudden that I withdrew my face from the window and fell back. Something was out there, below my window, and now it was scrabbling against the metal outside. Rake, rake, rake. I'd looked at the living quarters from outside and seen no walkway or railing. Was something, someone, on the other side of the building?

More moaning, rising and falling like the waves, all outside the window. I placed my hands on the edge of the desk by the window and looked above it. Nothing but a black square of night sky. I crept up further until Loki T came back into view. As I saw it again, the wailing ceased instantly. Worse, all noise did. No night-time compressing, no blowing of gas through those pipes, no churning into separators or billowing roar of the nearby flare tip.

Now, fifty years of degradation seemed to befall Loki T in as many seconds, its grids and sheets and valves and machinery and housings stripping of their paint and pitting with erosion and rust, like fruit rotting at high speed, making a lightless, soundless, shadowy husk.

I stared at it with a weird, melancholy horror, and then they appeared. Waifs. Wraiths. Figures skittering around the thing like aimless lice, black rags failing behind them as they screamed with the rage of instant grief, extras in some purgatorial opera. I wailed with them now, their loss mine, and for a second, fifty years of production were over and we were dead, all of us dead in the water, flames snuffed out.

A knock at the door.

"Ahh!"

The handle turned and Olav appeared in the light, in jeans and t-shirt.

The background churn of machinery returned.

"Are you okay, dude?" he said. "You look a little freaked out."

"I'm fine," I said, wiping a tear from my cheek with the sleeve of my hoody. I looked back at Loki T; intact, unweathered, whirring. Maybe he slipped something in my water bottle; he knew where my locker was, after all.

"It's awesome, right?" he said, walking in.

"I-It's insane," I said. "If these things didn't exist, there's no way I would believe they could be made. Whoever came up with the idea was mad."

He closed the door behind him, leaning on it. "I bet they were a lot like you," he said, getting closer, walking into my space and breathing deeply. He leaned down and picked up my book, flicking through it, pouting and nodding, impressed. "A genius."

I sighed slowly.

He looked now beyond me, out the window. I was afraid to turn and look in the same direction again in case Loki T had reverted to decay. He went now to sit at the foot of my bed. I sat cross-legged at the top. He took out a pack of cards and dealt them, though I wasn't sure what game he wanted to play.

"Can't believe it's up and running again like nothing happened," he said.

"What do you mean?"

He gasped. "You honestly didn't know? Can't believe you didn't know. Loki T? Loki T!"

"Don't tell me, then."

"There was a gas and condensate leak from a two-inch line leaving the first-stage separator. It found an ignition source and started a metal fire. A metal fire, man. Can you imagine? Loki T's typically unmanned during the day, but still; five people died."

He'd gotten closer, the pile of cards collapsing into the dent created by the weight of his legs, directing almost deliberately towards the clear bulge in his pants.

"I need to confess something," he said.

What the hell had I gotten myself into?

"I didn't talk to anyone tonight. I just went back to my room and jerked off."

It probably wasn't true. The "art" of suggestion. I looked at his hands. Had he washed them?

"I just felt like I had to impress you," he said. "Because you're so fucking intelligent."

Five people died for this foreplay. It was so unsexy it was a miracle I managed to interpret it as such. Well, why else?

"Thanks," I said. "For dropping by. You'll be wanting to go now so you get enough sleep. I'd hate to keep you."

"Yes, well…" he said, looking like he was about to cry, and he left without saying anything.

Before getting in bed, I turned to the window and saw that all was still normal. I should've said something, asked to see a medic, but I couldn't do that when I was effectively tied to Olav's side this trip. I'd lose face if there was something wrong with me, if I couldn't hack it out here. I'd cause an embarrassing fuss if I was fine.

I laid down and thought I heard a stray moan, but put on my ear protectors before I became too disturbed to sleep. No good. Olav's apparent seduction had me lying there furious. How was I supposed to stay by his side for the next two days?

#

We spent the next morning on Loki A, with Olav's misbehaving freshwater package. He tore a piece of paper from his set of diagrams and placed it over the opening of a drain line. When he removed his hand, the piece of paper stayed there, probably held, he explained, by overpressure from the HVAC system. He was far too pleased with this and segued into a weird speech about what "we as engineers need to do," using plenty more "you need to" than I allow even my closest friends and family prior to disowning them.

I interrupted him, "Loki T."

"H-Huh?" He scratched his arm. "I thought we would at least have lunch first."

We made our way up to the bridge to Loki T, both of us staring down it, hesitant to take a step towards it.

"It's not gonna bite, you know," he said. Once he saw I was uncomfortable too, he was at ease.

I walked ahead, across the bridge, and tried to open the first door I found on Loki T. It was large and looked like it would slide to one side, if only it had a handle. I tried to push it open to no avail.

Hiss…

"Jesus!" I said.

Olav stood behind me, nodding to a handle that he had tugged to operate the door's pneumatic mechanism.

"After you," he said.

He had a solemn expression as I traipsed him around the platform. When we approached a knock-out drum's liquid line, which was causing some unsavoury results in our depressurisation calculations, I pointed at a section that was so cold vapour from the air had condensed and solidified on its exterior in layers of slippery, opaque ice. Olav took off his glove and pressed his hand into it, a reactionary red propagating over his skin, a misting imprint of his hand appearing in the ice. He was still silent.

I tried to animate him by taking out my 3D sketches and piping diagrams and pretending I was having trouble locating this level's tie-in point.

He said, "Look: I don't have any projects associated with this platform anymore so you have to—"

"Figure it out myself. Got it. Thanks."

#

Later, I went back to my bedroom, which was filled with the projected rays of Loki T's many night-time lights, so I figured it was safe to go to the window and give it a two-finger salute. I noticed something at the very edge of the uppermost deck, the flare stack looming behind—a man, naked, shivering, looking to the depths of dark and crashing water below.

I hopped about, trying to shake the panic out my hands.

Damned if I was going to let my shyness get in the way of saving a life. I got my jeans and survival suit on and sped out of the room with the intent of banging on every door until I had a whole bunch of people to assist me, but when my bedroom door swung back, I skidded into the corridor and slammed my head on the floor, gradually sliding away from my room. There was ice everywhere, the same gradual deposition of vapour from the air in smooth layers of slippery crystals that I'd seen on the knock-out drum's piping. It coated every door but mine, softening the corners of the corridor's cuboid into a rounded cylinder, and now I was slipping, with no grip, into a dark and narrowing tunnel which slung me down around the staircase until there was no more ice and I was tumbling down the hard edges of the steel grids of external stairs, pratfalling onto a landing, looking through the grid at nothing, at darkness.

Laughter blew with the wind. I got to my feet and held the railing, creeping down, but soon it was too hot to touch. I looked below and saw that the outer boots of my survival suit were melting into the white-hot grid below me. I pulled my feet up, unsticking them, and bolted along the nearest walkway, lit in a strange, chemical purple by a string of lights above me. As I followed them, they snuffed out behind me, and the laughter grew. I navigated using the dim silhouette of the walkway against the backdrop of deepest blue night.

Once I was round the corner of Loki A, Loki T came back into view, and I found myself standing near its bridge, beside an external closet of spare survival suits. I took one and slung it over my shoulder: provided I could get to the naked man in time, he would need it.

I stepped out onto the bridge, one foot kept on Loki A in case it was some hallucination about to collapse with this simple test. It held. I took another step forward. With dramatic clanks, the bridge split into segments which tilted, one after the other, such that the straight path in front of me curved upwards and inverted, leading to the underside of the walkway above on Loki T, and all the pipes in the rack above me now split and spilled their fluids at enormous pressure, so even if a contiguous path led out in front of me, now it was filled with spills and mists of—shit, piss, blood.

I allowed myself a moment to fall to my knees and retch, and then I took out the survival suit's rebreather and plugged it into my mouth, attaching the clip to my nose and shielding my eyes, running forwards, breathing frantically into the bag on my chest, which quickly heated up and depleted of oxygen as I ran through the crashing fluids in front of me on a path which to my feet felt straight, until the fluids ceased, and I knew I was through. I looked ahead of me: nothing but a wall of corrugated metal lit in pale sodium. I had made it. I turned back and there was the bridge, completely intact again. Except, looking above me, I saw the sea. The bridge had deposited me, upside down, on the ceiling.

I fell and landed hard on my head, body following at a strange angle that strained my neck. Laughter again, deeper this time, curled around the concrete jacket below. I stood and crept towards the staircase on the side of Loki T, which would take me up to the naked man. As I turned the corner and saw it, I heard the hissing of one of those pneumatic doors. Someone had opened it. I slowed my steps.

"Ahhh!" Some figure screamed, coated in fire, flinging itself over the railing and into the water below. I crouched in reflex and watched as its flame resisted the evening's winds and lit a circle of rising black waves for just a moment before, snuff, it disappeared without a splash. Now the staircase was in flames, as if coated with some fuel. I doubted its reality, but reaching a hand out towards it, I could feel the heat. I knew something wanted me to enter the equipment rooms instead of going up the stairs.

I crept into a partially lit room, in the centre of which was the towering, rounded cylinder of a silent separator. Lights above gave it centre stage, every path around it disappearing into darkness. Whatever was to follow was yet another unpleasant part of this performance, of the—

Clang.

The separator buckled with a deafening crumple, collapsing on itself as if under immense external pressure. I rose to my feet again, took my hands off my ears and ventured forward, and there was another CLANG as the separator returned to its former shape, flecks of rust-resistant paint flicking me in the face. Again, I recovered from my flinch and was only a few yards from it as it buckled again, a little gentler, without much noise, and recovered again. Buckle, recover, buckle. It was a breathing metal lung. I reached out a hand to touch it and heard an ominous click, like I'd triggered some tripwire, and a pipe tore itself from the separator's inlet and reared back like a cobra before spewing liquid fire directly at me. I dove to one side. With the separator out of the way and fire behind me, I could see a clear route to an internal set of stairs. I bolted in their direction, feeling the heat at my back, the roar of the liquid flames. I heard a hiss, and what I'd thought was an open doorway had a pneumatic door that was closing in on me now, and I ran, and ran, and—

It slammed shut behind me. The stairs were currently flameless, but who could say for how long? I had to move. I ran up the first flight and slowed as I heard the infernal noise of some other enormous piece of equipment performing some hideous, unforeseen malfunction. Sure enough, doors blasted off a room on the deck beside me and I watched as a gas compressor surged, its whirring internals slipping into the wrong position and using their momentum to eat through the thick metal walls of their housing. The large wheels inside freed themselves from the compressor and barrelled towards me, and I ran up higher and watched as they ate through the stairs beneath. I ran up further and heard all manner of measurement devices shearing off their tanks, relief valves chattering, tanks blowing, fire spewing, firewater streaming. Below me, the stairs dissolved in a way they never could in a non-industrial world—the temperatures, pressures, and flowrates we designed for were so wholly unnatural—collapsing in a way I'd never forget and, should I live, would always fear.

I was on the roof now. The rain battered down upon me as I ran in the direction where I'd seen the figure, tripping over greasy planks of wood, keeping myself steady by gripping onto the leg of a crane.

I saw the man, how his cold, bare skin glistened in the horizontal rain which so easily unbalanced him.

"Olav!"

"Huh?" He turned to look at me. At first, I thought it was the crossbars of the crane casting shadows across his face but then I gasped as he staggered nearer and I saw that some cross-stitched piece of leather kept his lips sewn shut, fresh blood still oozing from the new orifices, his eyes sealed and seeping alike.

"Get away from the edge!"

"Yeah," he tried to mumble. His empty sockets looked through me.

"Can you understand me?" I said.

"Yeah?" he attempted again. I'd heard this type of response before. It was the sleep-talk of someone answering a figure in their dream while thinking they were awake.

He staggered in my direction and, when he was close enough, I grabbed him by the shoulders and shook him. He gasped, and now he was awake, his stitches dissolving, eyes re-emerging from the ooze.

"Luke!" he said.

"You're okay," I said. "You're okay."

He screamed, his arms shaking. While he took in his surroundings, possibly having landed in what seemed to me a worse reality than any nightmare could conjure. I helped him into the survival suit and zipped it up.

"We're gonna go back to the living quarters, okay? We have to get off this platform."

"Are we on Loki T?" he said.

I nodded.

"Oh Jesus! We're fucked!"

"No, we're not," I said, as if I knew. I took his hand and led him back towards the stairwell, climbing over the same planks. Though it was dark, I knew the railing was—

It wasn't there. The stairwell had disappeared.

"O-Okay, um…" I began. "Okay. We need to get to the edge and swing to one of the decks below, alright?"

"No!" he said, gripping his head. "We're done!"

"Not yet. You watch me, and then you're gonna follow and I'll be there to catch you, alright?"

I had no idea if this was going to work, if whatever put us here would let me get away with it.

It was an easy route to the decks immediately below, which expanded out wider than the roof. We had to navigate a nest of pipes to find a way down, but Olav followed without any problem or interruption. It seemed the pipes were propagating, and as we reached one of the mid-level decks, they grew along the walkways in front of us, blocking our path. We ran the other way and, out of the darkness in front, I saw more pipes reaching out into the night to block us once again.

"They won't let us leave," Olav said.

"There is one way off," I said. I looked over the edge of the railing, and directly below us was the bridge. I vaguely remembered some fall-height statistic from a safety course, and we seemed close to serious injury, but there was no other choice.

"Please, no," Olav said, and he was weeping. "Oh, God."

"I know," I said, and I was crying too. "Just like before, just follow me. We'll be okay."

I looked over the railing, took a deep breath, and climbed over, lowering myself down the railing to minimise the drop as much as possible. Olav followed, climbing over, and soon he dangled beside me, offering me his body to climb down further. He clung to the railing and I climbed onto his back, sliding down the material of his suit until I was gripping onto his ankles with my hands. It was then that I looked down and saw no bridge, and then that Olav released his hands and sent us both into the sea.

#

We fell towards the black water and I knew then that it was over. I took one last look up at the night sky, against which Olav's flailing, screaming body moved as if in slow motion. He reached out to me below, to grip onto something familiar before the crash. But we never met the water. Instead, all around us streamed a well-lit tube, coated in repeated sections of pipes, as far as I could tell, since they were speeding past us, and we fell along its centre, veering towards one of its sides, and as we touched it, we rolled along, slowly skidding to a halt and sticking to it.

I opened my eyes and saw raised diamonds poking from the surface's steel sheets and realised it wasn't the side of a tunnel but a floor, and we were horizontal again. I stood up and helped Olav up too. Looking ahead, I saw Loki T, on the other side of the bridge.

#

"It was me," Olav said. "I okayed the routing that caused the leak, the explosion."

We were back in the living quarters, the corridors of which had cleared of ice, leaving us a path to Olav's room. I looked out. Loki T was operating normally again.

"When?" was the first thing I thought to ask him.

"Aksel Future," he said. "My first project. I selected the wrong level valve. It vibrated too much and eventually the piping shattered."

"I don't buy that," I said. "When you just started? You must have been supervised, all of your decisions— if any—vetted several times, in document reviews and studies and all of that! Jesus, you can't really think it was your fault, can you?"

"Then why do I feel like this?"

"Does this have anything to do with why you asked for me to join you here?"

"Will you stay here with me tonight?"

I looked behind me. I'd been too distracted to notice if there was another empty bed, as there sometimes was in these rooms. There wasn't.

When I turned back, he'd taken off his suit and was shuffling in bed to make space for me beside him.

I sighed. "Why do you only want me in this capacity?"

He laughed a deep laugh that wasn't his. Then it was just an extension of the platform's mockery. All the same, it didn't seem right to leave him alone. I sat by the desk and looked out at Loki T.

Since university, I'd suspected he was after me. Thinking about it now, in all likelihood, I profoundly— sure, maybe even willfully—misunderstand the mysterious platonic bonding rituals of straight dudes. Anyway, years had passed and neither of us had learned much about the other. Here we were and, once again, some part of him was reaching out to me for help while something else kept me at bay. I didn't know what to do.

#

I woke up to Olav tapping my arm and looking at me sheepishly. I gave him the same expression back until he said, "Turn around while I get dressed!"

All I knew was that it was the last day, and we were getting off these platforms for good, and I was never coming back.

"I'll wait outside for you," I said, but when I opened the door I turned back and said "Olav!"

"What?!" He held the bedsheets around himself, chest jiggling with the fright.

"I think you should put the survival suit back on."

He put on a t-shirt, jeans and socks and got back in his suit, then followed me to the door to look out.

As far as I could tell, outside was an enormous, dark cathedral, designed for beings at least ten times the size of a human. A long stone step, almost the height of the former corridor's ceiling, loomed in front of us. Light beamed in from a round, stained glass window high above, revealing the top of each step and glancing off the monolithic columns that bounded the cathedral's walls. Looking back to the window, we saw that Loki T had once again returned to rust, the diluted blood colour of the sky reflecting its melancholy apocalypse.

"What do we do?" I said.

Olav's expression had more resolve to it than the night before. "We've gotta climb it, I guess."

We helped one another up each step, seeing that the height of them decayed as we climbed, until they were longer than they were high, and we could stand. Looking down, we saw those ragged creatures I'd seen the first night, and they were ambling up the stairs and moaning, making some sorrowful religious pilgrimage, passing us by as if we weren't there.

A doorway appeared beneath the stained glass, and looking out I saw what might as well have been the cavernous, cracked surface of Mars.

We stepped out onto a high, burning cliff face, looking down below into a hollow, empty canyon of scorched earth and burnt trees, a warm breeze blowing, thin clouds drifting across that same weak sky. Away off in the distance was what at first appeared to be a shimmering heat haze, but I gazed at its surface and saw white bubbles burst from its roiling surface. And were those—people, witches, worshipers, some type of congregation bowing towards the boiling sea? Through the heat I saw figures in black bending towards the light, and beyond the light was a drop-off of darkness from which I heard the mournful crash of dropped hammers clattering their echoes across the canyon walls.

"Do you hear something?" Olav said, looking back towards the cathedral's entrance.

I did. From within came a slow, whistling tone, which was speeding up, getting louder, and we watched over the edge of the cliff face as the cracks in the drought-wracked soil glowed with red flames that turned white and then green, and the ground seemed to soak with water as it saturated with black, and the sky darkened to the dim blue of night, and I felt a railing in front of me, and it was raining, and we could hear the beep beep beep of the platform's emergency alarm. The moaning of the wraiths behind us turned to shouts and thunderous steps and we could feel people pushing us around and the saturated earth begat a sea which rose and crashed through the walls of the canyon. Then our original setting had returned. We were back on the platform at night, during an emergency evacuation, and Loki T's flare stack blew out its flames at beyond its maximum capacity, unable to handle the rate of burning gas ejecting from its tip. So it began to melt, and we felt a great heat rush across our faces, even through the night's icy wind.

Emergency shut-down.

We ran in a flow of orange suits towards the lifeboats, to evacuate, drop into the water, any other scenario all the more fearsome. We ran in near darkness, and then, boom, an explosion on Loki T lit up a circle of path in front of us and the boats came into view. I grabbed Olav's hand and we ran towards our boat. Once inside, we climbed up the black rubber seats and sat together, the rest of the seats soon filling with Loki's crew.

"Is everyone okay?" the safety responsible asked.

We were silent. He shouted something.

The sensation of the drop, while looking at stationary surroundings, was far more sickening than I had imagined. We crashed deep into the water and I saw an external level of black sea take over the orange plastic's glow up to a frightening height and I thought we would just continue on into the depths, an unbearable pressure in my tailbone as it took on the energy of the fall, but we rebounded, lay flat on the sea, floating gently to a safe distance from the disaster behind us. It was too early for cheering, since we still needed to be recovered, but we were almost certainly safe now.

"I'm gonna be okay, right?" Olav said.

The whole time he'd gripped my hand, and only now did I register the painful pressure running through my knuckles.

I used my other hand to wrench myself free of him and said "Mate, I think you gotta figure that out for yourself."

The Missionaries
Edward Ahern

Evenings were the hardest. The dim lighting left us little to do, and my father spewed his hatred of villagers and his disappointment in me. One of those after-dark evenings, about four months ago, someone knocked at our front door.

My father jumped up with a worried look and loped toward the door carrying a candle. I dropped my book and followed him. "Stay back!" he growled.

Father set the candle on a table, grabbed the shotgun leaning up against the hallway wall and called out through the door. "Who is it?"

"John Carstairs?"

"Yes?"

"We believe you have a room available."

"Who are you?"

"Two women travelers, unarmed."

He leaned forward and stared through the peephole in the door, then waved me over.

"Naomi, try and get this right. Unlock the door and open it, but stand behind it so you don't block my shot."

"Yes, father."

"Now."

Moonlight draped two women.

"Come in, quickly. Stop in the hall… Naomi, shut the door and lock it. Hurry up!"

Once I'd locked the door, I turned to look at them. They were distinctive rather than pretty; solidly built, without makeup, hair unbrushed. They wore tattered slacks and baggy sweaters, but so did we. There were no new clothes. My father held the shotgun pointed just to their left.

The shorter woman spoke."John Carstairs, I am Miriam, this is Esther. We wish to lodge with you."

The worried look on my father's face had rewrinkled into a scowl as he studied them "Out after dark in times like this, are you…"

"Yes, we are. Disciples of the Lucent One. We are come to reveal her gospel to those of you still living in this village."

"You'll have to leave. They say it's your kind that destroyed things. The God-fearing residents will put you on spits and roast you."

Esther moved closer to him. "But you have no love for these villagers."

"Nor they for me, once I'd left their puckered-ass church. But there's only one bedroom, with one bed."

Esther spoke again. Her paleness was bordered by India ink hair, and I saw thin scars running across the backs of her hands.

"We two are bonded, day and night. One bed will do. And before you turn us away, hear us out. The collapse and wars are manmade and not caused by the Lucent One. We are simple preachers of her words, teaching the path to fulfillment. We come only to illuminate. And we will pay amply for our lodging."

"Paper money is worthless."

"We pay in coin, or can provide food if preferred."

"You carry nothing."

Miriam's smile didn't reach her eyes. "As instructed by our One. We go out as lambs to slaughter. But we have access to many things. Our Lady is generous, unlike the Semitic god."

She reached under her sweater and pulled out an ivory-colored pouch. I glimpsed what looked like a nipple on the bottom of the pouch before Miriam's hand covered it. "Is that…?" I stopped myself with a head shake.

"Yes, child," Miriam said softly. "A breast of a departed sister. Death is not the end of our service." She turned to John. "Would fifteen silver quarters allow us to stay?"

Father glanced back and forth between Miriam and the pouch. "If the villagers find you, they're apt to kill you. But you already know this." He fell silent, then said. "What would you do here?"

Esther replied. "We're not the demons, John, the powers we have are…instructional. We're simply messengers for the Lucent One."

Father remained dubious. "Where are your men?"

"We are the mirror image, John, the reversal of roles. There are no men. It's been a long walk. May we sit?"

When father agreed, I knew he would take the silver. The villagers refused to share their food with us unless we paid in coin, and we had no coin to give. Fifteen pieces would let us eat for weeks, even feeding these two.

We had two sofas in the living room, both still facing the television, although there had been no electricity for years. My father and Esther sat together on one. Miriam patted the space next to her. "Sit here, child."

I stared at my father, who scowled at me, then shrugged. When I sat down, Miriam reached over and touched my face with her fingertips. The feeling was soothing, like a cat stroke. She looked at me with, not affection, understanding perhaps.

"You're not a child anymore, are you? Fifteen? And still a virgin."

I blushed, and father's face reddened. "That's enough of that," he growled, then held the candle toward Esther for a closer look. "You look young to be part of the original Thirteen."

Esther smiled. "We age well, John, but you're right. The thirteen messengers all were desecrated with religious symbols and martyred. We are the next generation of disciple, in the hundreds. As we convert other women we will become legion, and march toward Millennium."

"Using my house? Putting us at risk?"

"Only with your permission, and for ample pay. Peacedale is a village, John, and our presence will eventually be revealed. But the villagers that shun you don't fear you. If a mob forms, it will be for our benefit, not yours. Here, please, take this silver as token of our agreement."

She poured the coins into father's hands. He counted them and nodded. "Excellent," Esther said. "In a few minutes, there will be another knock at your door. A woman will be bringing us all food and drink. Do not ask her name or look under her hood at her face. Miriam and I are the visible faces, but many, many more work in shadows."

Father scowled, then clutched the coins more tightly. "Naomi can handle your cooking and cleaning, but you're responsible for your own room..." He was half through his listing of house rules when the knock came. I went with him to the door, leaving the two women alone. After all, there was nothing left in the house worth stealing.

He pulled open the door. "Yes?"

The hooded woman turned sideways from the candle light, wordlessly handed him a full plastic trash bag, and turned away. Father stepped through the doorway as if to brace her, but then shrugged and came back in. He hefted the bundle, then thrust it at me. "Shut the door, Naomi, and bar it. Then put the food on the kitchen table. Be quick."

As I walked toward the kitchen, my father yelled.

"You can't burn anything in here!"

The smell of burning herbs drifted into the kitchen. Miriam responded. "This is our temporary temple, John, and we must cleanse it of godly corruption. And the little flame is already dying down. Let us eat."

The food I set out was plain but ample, preserved meat and fish, dried fruit, slightly stale bread, and a jug of fruit wine. The two women consecrated the meal with words I didn't understand and we sipped the wine. It wasn't grape, something sourer and more biting. Once I'd launched into eating, my stomach hurt; it was unused to so much food.

At one point, flushed with the wine, father reached out to tap Esther's shoulder.

She pulled back. "Don't touch me. You're a god-leper, and must be cleansed. In time, perhaps."

Once we'd eaten, I began clearing the table. Esther turned to my father. "Leave us now so we can prepare the kitchen for our use. You will hear chanting, but will not understand the words, so listen all you like."

My father's face bloated into anger, but he couldn't take it out on me or them. "Naomi, take a candle, we're going upstairs."

I turned to go, but stared back at Miriam. "They say you're evil, that you summon demons and curse people."

Miriam stepped over and put her hands on my shoulders.

"You're touching me, but I'm not purified either."

Her eyes crinkled. "There is no need with you. And the answer to your question is yes. After all, if the followers of the Nazarene could cast out spirits, why should we not be able to invite them in?"

"But…"

Miriam leaned toward me and whispered, "There is another life for you, child."

"Naomi, bed!"

"Yes, father."

Once upstairs, the only barrier between the two women and us was one-inch planking, and their chants rose through the gaps. The sounds were high pitched raspings, phrased together tightly.

As I listened, my arteries drummed. My existence was cleaning and cooking and vegetable growing, but these women rode their lives like cavalry. I briefly felt sorry for myself, but the trained hate took over. As I fell asleep I thought that the chanting and my pulse seemed to be in rhythm.

In the morning, I was sent into the village with one of the quarters. Father rehearsed me curtly- how much to pay, how we had found such riches, and most importantly, how to explain buying so much food when there were only two of us.

I was taught to haggle, and the lying came easily. I returned with a silver dime, four copper cents, and a trash bag filled with food. Father, meanwhile, had shuttered the downstairs windows so that the women wouldn't be seen during the day. Once I was inside, Esther nodded at me approvingly, as if she'd been with me at the market.

Father pressed his lips together when I handed him the bag and coins. "You've done surprisingly well."

I shrugged. "It would have been better, but I had to give Donnie the butcher a penny interest that we owed before he would sell us more meat."

During the midday meal, Esther leaned over to my father. "You have seen the nourishment we bring, the coin. For this to continue, we must ask you for two simple things."

"What things?"

"Nothing important or difficult. To remain in our presence, you must be purified. It's a ceremony of a few minutes."

"Like a baptism—"

35

"Just the reverse, John. It's a de-sanctification to remove your baptismal curse. You'll recite some words in the One's tongue."

"What do the words mean?"

"It doesn't matter. The words have power without your understanding them. Secondly, we ask that you remain upstairs after each dinner so that we may have women visit after dark. Women that you should not see."

Father paused. "What about Naomi?"

Miriam answered. "We need Naomi to assist us. We will pay you an additional coin for her help."

"What if I just told you to leave now?"

"We would do so. We must be invited in. But when we shake off the dust of your home, other things may visit. Like your not-friendly villagers."

"You would tell them, Miriam?"

"Never. But without protection, things have a way of going wrong."

"And that's all you'll ask?"

"Oh yes. Everything else would be what you want to do."

My father nodded.

"You must say the words."

"Oh, very well, I agree. You may use Naomi."

Esther smiled. "Excellent, now strip off your shirt."

"What?"

"I must anoint your skin, not your clothes."

My father cursed, but unbuttoned and took off his shirt. Esther gave him a sheet of paper with foreign words on it, and had him repeat them one at a time until he got the pronunciations right. Then she mixed up an ointment, saying more things over it.

She had my father sit in a kitchen chair, and as he recited the words she applied the ointment with a charred bone to his forehead, mouth, hands, chest and back. The rank smelling unguent was applied right to left crossing and bottom to top, a reverse signing of the cross.

Esther's actions were matter-of-fact, and as she worked, Miriam explained to me what was happening.

"We're scouring off your father's contamination. The bone is a relic from the same martyr as the money pouch, one of the thirteen. The salve contains Lucent wine and bread consecrated during our Sabbath. It's a spiritual antibiotic, killing off religious disease."

My father twitched at each application. "Is it hurting him?" I asked.

"Not in the way you mean."

Esther set down the ointment and bone. "There, John, we're almost done. I need to rub the potion into your skin. It's a mild aphrodisiac, so you should enjoy the process. And don't wipe it off when you put your shirt back on."

Miriam touched me on the shoulder. "Come, child, I have things to explain to you."

She and I went into the living room and sat on the same sofa as we had the night before.

"After dinner this evening, ten women will come to the house. Some you will know, but show no sign of recognition, it's considered impolite."

She explained my duties, mostly just serving and clearing things away. "And most importantly, whatever happens, you must not leave. And don't scream."

"What can happen at a women's tea?"

Miriam raised her hand as if to slap me, then lowered it. Her voice took on the piping lilt I'd heard the night before. "The false god of good teaches women to breed and feed. We are the alternative. We lead legions of powerful women who relish adventure and welcome death."

"Death?"

"We all die, Naomi. What difference if a little earlier and with more satisfaction? And before we go we gorge on sensation."

"Is that what you meant by another life?"

"The way of the wicked is at your feet, child."

***

That evening at dinner, my father's expression was vacant. He didn't yell at me, and looked toward Esther as if taking cues.

Miriam glanced at him. "John, are you still willing to stay upstairs this evening?"

My father glared at her, but then glanced at Esther and subsided." Um, if I have to. Naomi, you do as you're told."

"Yes, father."

Miriam stood up. "Naomi, please clear the dishes and set my bag on the kitchen table. John, time for you to go upstairs. If you're still awake after we're done, Esther will explain a few more things to you."

Father left without another word, and I cleared and set Miriam's knapsack on the Formica-topped table. Miriam took out a capped glass jar and artist's brush. "Can you paint, child?"

"Only badly."

"Bad is what's required. Let's start." She opened the jar and took a small obsidian knife from her belt. "Give me your left hand."

I wondered about refusing, about telling them that I wasn't their slave, but I wondered more about what the women could do. While holding my wrist she picked up the knife and slit the back of my hand. I half screamed, but she waved me into silence. She pulled my hand over until it hovered above the jar, letting my blood drip into it. Then she wrapped the hand in a clean rag and let it drop.

"The blood is the solvent, child. Pick up the brush and stir the paint."

My lips half puckered into why, but her expression told me not to ask. I began to swirl the dark blue, almost black paint, and my blood blended into it without a trace.

"Put the bristles of the brush into your mouth and suck the paint off."

"Ugh, Why!"

"Almost sister, you do not know enough to ask questions, just do as I bid. It will not make you sick."

The paint tasted of blood-rust and oil, and herbs and overripe things. "It's foul tasting."

"So are many medicines." She handed me a rectangular piece of paper with symbols drawn in each of the four corners, and a larger symbol in the center. "This symbol," she said, pointing, "goes on the table in the left corner closest to you, then upper left, upper right, lower right and center. Paint them exactly as you see them."

"How big?"

"It doesn't matter, but big enough to see easily. During the day, we'll cover them over with a table cloth."

The symbols were shaped like stretched circles, with odd lines and arcs inside. They were uncomplicated and painting them took only a few minutes. "What now," I asked.

"Gather up thirteen glasses or cups."

"We had to sell our china, I'm not sure we have that many."

Miriam shrugged. "Glasses, mason jars, anything that will hold liquid is fine. Set them on the side table, you'll be serving us from there."

My expression must have been worried, for she stroked my cheek again. Her fingers were rough, but the touch was soft. "Little woman, you won't be injured, and you'll learn many things. Just remember to not call our visitors by name, even if you know them, to never lean over the table top, and not to scream no matter what you see. I'll refer to you only as 'Child.' You will refer to me only as 'Mistress.'"

The women arrived in twos and threes shortly after sunset, all wearing hooded pullovers and jackets. When the hoods came down I saw Donnie's wife Betsy, a prostitute named, I think, Helga, and Shelly, the mayor's wife. Another woman I thought I'd seen two years ago at Christmas services, but I couldn't be sure. I kept my gaze down at waist level and noticed several scars on the backs of their hands.

Miriam and Esther kissed each of them on the lips, muttered something, and assigned them places in a tight circle around the table. Miriam then turned to me. "Child, take this jug, portion out the liquid into thirteen goblets, and hand them out."

"Yes, Mistress." But I smirked. We had four water glasses, three coffee cups, four beer mugs and two soup bowls. I took the jug and carefully poured out portions, a dollop for each of us. I handed out the containers and stood in the circle with the others.

Miriam chanted in high, harsh tones for a few minutes, paused and said," Drink now to the arrival of his servant, to the honor of the Lucent One."

We drank and stood in silence, waiting. It'd tasted like alcohol and over ripe fruit and spoiled meat and I wanted more.

The candle light flickered across the faces of the other women. Their expressions varied from Miriam's serenity to Donnie-wife's fear to the rictus-grin of the Mayor's wife. Miriam handed me her obsidian knife.

"Child, cut the back of your left hand as I showed you, and let your blood drip onto the icon in the middle of the table. Then hand the knife to your right. When we have all participated, grasp the hands of the women next to you."

Once we'd all been bled, Miriam spoke again, but her voice was hoarse as a puma's cough. "What I will say I will say first in the language of the One and then in your words. But know that your words have no power, only the One's words."

She chanted something, then in a flat voice. "Magnificent woman, we your slaves implore your mercy and beseech you for eternity of service." More words, then, "Our infernal lady, this virgin blood signifies our devotion. Send us we pray your slave, who will intercede for us against the godly and the nonbelievers."

Miriam continued chanting in the unknown tongue without bothering to further translate. The women began to sway, and I with them. Our movements caused the candles to flicker and the light to become erratic. I felt aching pleasure and dizziness. The candles sputtered almost to extinction, and when they flared back up there was writhing smoke on the table.

I choked back a scream. The black shape shifted with the candle flames. Rank odors of stale urine, blood, and sweat filled the room. I knew without seeing its organ that it was male. It seemed to leer at me just before it spoke.

"I will service it." The voice was wrong, like stretched audio tape. It didn't belong here. Miriam waved the knife.

"Your services are not yet needed. We are gathered for the One."

"She occupies herself with more important things."

Miriam sliced the knife through the smoke and the shape winced. "Listen to what we require and obey." Miriam shifted into the rasping tongue. She paused once to address us. "He is noting down your presence and vows of service. To back away now means a visit to you will not be pleasant."

Miriam resumed the One's language. The male thing cringed and glowered, but nodded.

"So shall it be done," he said. "Which of you shall I visit tonight in your sleep?"

Miriam nodded toward the mayor's wife, who smirked at being picked.

The demon also nodded, and withdrew within itself, leaving behind fine ash that drifted down onto the pooled blood in the middle of the table. The women released each other's hands and began talking.

"Silence!" Miriam's tone cut across them like a straight razor. "Child, scrape the blood and ash off the table top and into the jar I give you. Be very careful not to taste it."

I wanted to ask why, but only gave her a quizzical glance.

"Because," she said, "Demon ash is used in curses."

***

As my lingering fear dissipated, I felt the sweet/sour taste of having gotten away with something, of having displayed my own arbitrary power. The expressions of the assembled women looked smug and satiated. They said little more before they left, bowing as they exited. Esther and Miriam exchanged glances.

Miriam took my left hand. The blood from my cut had dried during the ceremony. "You are changed more than you know, Naomi. If you go to the village tomorrow, be modest and quiet, the change won't be noticed as much."

"Why did you involve me with this?"

Miriam laughed. "We could not proceed without you. And you appear to be what we had hoped. But you have a choice, your last one. You have seen what we do, what we are. Is it your wish to continue, to learn from us, if worthy to become one of us? Be careful with your answer, for it is a vow."

"Do I have time to think about it?"

"No. If you decline we will leave, and your life will be as it was before, probably worse, for that is the commonplace. If you agree you will know discipline and pain, and pleasure, such as you don't yet imagine. And a memorable death. You will know secrets that no man knows."

"But my father—"

"He will release you."

"How can you be sure?"

"Because he will think he wants it."

Miriam released my hand and stared at me. "You must decide. Which path, child?"

I felt dizzy, as if the potion hadn't worn off. "But I don't really know anything about your religion."

"You know enough. We are not love and charity, and certainly not chastity. We are strong, vindictive, and pleasure seeking, most often sacrificed by mobs for not forsaking our One. And we spread our message and increase our sisterhood. Decide."

My left hand throbbed. All the men and boys that I knew, despised our family and would only want to use me. I wanted more, even if the more was laced with poison. "All right," I said, almost with relief.

Miriam smiled and took my hand again. "Let us sit. You must begin to learn the pleasures of terror."

"Child," Esther said, "I will look in on your father and ensure that he was not disturbed by the evening's events. I may also work with him on a ritual, so you could hear occasional noises from his room."

I said nothing, unsure how my father would react to a late evening visit. Since the death of my mother during the first riots, his moods were usually foul. Esther sensed my hesitation.

"I'm quite sure he will welcome me."

"Bring him something to drink, it will help."

"Of course," Esther said, and left.

Miriam talked and I listened for several hours. When I eventually climbed the stairs toward my bedroom, false dawn was leeching black from the sky. Sounds came from my father's room, the rhythmic squealing of springs on his bed, sounds I had not heard since before my mother took sick. He and Esther were mating, and I sensed relief. He would be focused on Esther, and not belittling me.

***

Breakfast the next morning was quiet. Father and I were thinking through our new roles, and Miriam and Esther were still tired from their varied duties. Once I'd cleared the dishes, Miriam waved me over.

"Leave them, child. Time for you to learn the value of hate."

"That's a contradiction."

"No, that's a guiding principle. Of the villagers who hate you and your father, who do you hate the most?"

"I don't hate—"

"No! Naomi, you're beyond hypocrisy. Which hate burns most fiercely?"

I needed only a second's thought. "Donnie the butcher. He tried to rape me. But his wife is one of you..."

"One of us. Know child, that once beyond postulance, men are conveniences and not companions. Do you hate him enough to hurt him?"

"Yes." I nodded. "I think so."

"I will make arrangements. You will lead tonight's invocation. Can you read?"

"Yes, my mother taught me."

Miriam smiled. "Good. Read this, it's a sounding out of the words you will need to say tonight. Memorize it."

As the women filed in that night, Donnie-wife handed Miriam a clump of gray hair. "From his brush," she said.

At the invocation, the demon smoke reappeared, roiling into and out of itself in sentient ebony.

Miriam prepared the creature in her high tones, then said, "Recite the words, child."

I did, but nothing seemed to happen after I'd finished. Miriam looked pleased however, and dismissed the demon.

The next morning, I went into the village for food. My last stop was the butcher shop, where Donnie was chopping through pig meat held down by his left hand. He glanced at me and said, "you'll have to wait, bitch."

As I waited on the other side of the counter, Donnie's left hand jerked forward as if his elbow had been pushed. It happened as the cleaver was swinging down, and Donnie chopped off the front half of three fingers.

Blood began spurting, and he grabbed his greasy apron and wrapped it around the finger stumps to try and slow the bleeding. "Go get Murphy!" he yelled at me.

I had an urge to make him say please, but turned without saying anything and went to fetch the closest thing we had to a doctor.

Miriam was waiting for me when I got back to the house. "How did it feel?"

I thought to say 'Terrible.' But I said what I felt. "It wasn't enough, but it felt good."

"Oh, I think you'll do."

***

For the next three months, my days were spent with Miriam and Esther, my evenings with ever changing coven members. Each woman spent three evenings with the coven and went back to their lives to serve the shining One in secrecy. Almost three hundred women from the surrounding villages swore allegiance. After the first month, Miriam had trained me to invoke the demon.

I questioned Miriam about my role. "Why am I receiving special treatment? Why was I not dispatched after three gatherings?"

"More is demanded of you. Continue studying the Grimoire. You must be able to recite these incantations from memory."

My father's expression often flared into anger, and his lips constricted as if to speak, but he held silent for all but routine questions, as if his shrunken role was normal. But I knew the man prone to belt whippings must be seething. We spoke only of small things, and then briefly. I still washed his clothes and cooked his meals, but we both knew that would end.

The villagers were increasingly nasty to me, trying to up their prices, and cursing me as I left their shops. When I mentioned this to Miriam she didn't seem surprised.

"We encourage hatred of all kinds, child, and that includes hatred of you. But we must move more quickly. One of our sisters will eventually let slip that we're here, and we should not be martyred just yet."

She had me sit at the Formica table, the symbols covered over with a bed sheet. "Child, it is time for you to become a missionary like Esther and me."

"What does that mean?"

"You will sacrifice family and mate with Her prince consort. You will be a descendent of the thirteen, preaching revolution and invoking demons."

I sat in silence, but knew I could not go back to who I was. "I want to be like you. Do I have to kill him?"

"In a way."

"Will it hurt?"

"Yes, but the pleasure overwhelms and binds the pain to produce an ecstasy."

"And I can join you?"

"Not Esther and me, but a partner who will help your flower to grow. The mob is already clotting together, and we must act now. Would you do anything to join us?"

I couldn't imagine not being with them. "Yes," I said.

"Very well. You will perform the sacrifice and receive the consort this evening, while in coven."

That afternoon my thoughts were so jumbled I could barely do chores. Just before dusk, Miriam brought me a potion to drink.

"What is it?" I asked.

"A love potion that will enhance what you will be feeling. And something that will give you courage."

I drank and prepared the room for the coven. The women arrived after dark and circled the table. I noticed that Esther wasn't there.

"Miriam, where's Esther? We need our thirteenth."

"She's coming. Ah, here she is."

Esther walked into the room leading my father, who was blindfolded. She backed him up against the table and leaned his torso onto it, face up, his legs dangling toward the floor. Miriam handed me her knife.

"Miriam, I can't do this!"

"The sacrificial lamb is willing, child. Ask him."

"F-father?" I stuttered.

His voice was harsh but slurred, he'd drunk something. "Naomi, do as you're told. Esther has explained things to me. Don't cross me!"

I held the knife in two hands, staring at the expressionless faces around the table, trying to control myself. And then I felt the pure burn of hate, and began to chant.

***

The next morning, I was staggering from pain; the potion I'd drunk made my forehead feel as if it were cleaved, and my vagina and anus were torn. But twined into the pain was pride, and remembered pleasure and clouded memory of dark majesty.

Miriam and Esther left that afternoon. I hugged Miriam before she left. "Take me with you."

"We go two by two. When your partner comes, begin your mission. If you are martyred, your remains will be gathered, consecrated, and used. You will always be of service to the One. Goodbye, child."

For two days, I lived off the remaining food, but on the third day I knew I would have to go into the village for provisions and face people who might want to kill me. As I was gathering up coins, there was a rap at the front door.

The peephole revealed a teenaged girl, skinny, with frizzy red hair. When I opened the door, I noticed her eyes. They were old, ageless, like Miriam's had been. And I knew mine looked the same. "Yes?" I asked.

"I am for you. I am Rachel, your partner."

"Yes," I said. "I have what I can carry."

I turned and looked back into the house. "Goodbye, father."

He shuffled toward the door, back bent, eyes cloudy. "That's nice, dear. Goodbye."

There was nothing more to say. I had given his essence as sacrifice for Her, and the husk in the doorway held neither love nor hate.

Red on White
Darren Todd

The snowflakes fattened, coming steady now. Farmer paced the dayroom, staring out the row of windows. Tinsel adorned the upper pains, fluttering in the air from the heater vents. The facility manager had decorated the drab walls with a cardboard Santa, snowmen, and elves. Classic Christmas music poured over the loudspeaker. It's a Wonderful Life played on the television.

All of these things failed to edify Farmer. He thought only of the pending dull ring of the missileer comm line inside the dispatcher's office. His first Christmas away from home, and he'd spend it plodding around a missile site in the snow, looking for bogeymen. Even expecting the call, he jumped when the muted sound interrupted his thoughts five minutes later.

Like a Pavlovian dog, the sound sent chills through him despite the warmth of the dayroom. Not only would he miss the commander and the first sergeant coming around to serve Christmas dinner, he'd be freezing his ass off for nothing.

The dispatcher's voice came muffled from behind the steel door to his office. Conley bounded out of the computer room at a jog. He approached the dispatcher's door and peered in through the tiny window. Farmer joined him.

The dispatcher had stripped off his camouflage top, now wearing only a paper-thin cotton t-shirt. A cheap Santa cap sat askew on his head, worn seemingly with neither shame nor levity. He leaned back in his chair, phone held in place by a shoulder. Eventually, he looked at them, gave a thumbs-up, and a quick nod of his head.

"Suit up, Farmer," Conley said and dove into a drab green duffel bag by the door.

Farmer's stomach sank. "We got an alarm?"

"Well, yeah, it seems that way."

They hustled, though everyone knew the culprit was the soft flakes collecting on top of an already substantial foundation of snow.

After Conley and Farmer donned their thermals, shirts, jackets, and headgear, they paused in the foyer between the station's lounge and the outside. The facility manager had plowed the day before, leaving huge piles of snow surrounding the buildings. Still, fresh powder already covered the blacktop. Conley hopped from foot to foot, staring at Farmer from underneath the hood of his Gore-Tex parka.

"We're gonna miss the dinner," Farmer said.

"Yep. Why don't you bring the truck around?" Conley said.

"I'm not supposed to drive."

Conley rolled his eyes. "I'll still drive, ya fool. Just bring it around."

Farmer sighed. "To warm it up, you mean."

"Well. You are the trainee, and I am the leader."

Farmer took the Bronco keys, zipped his parka to the top, and pulled the rim of the hood over his eyes, leaving only a couple of inches exposed.

Outside, the air felt dry and frigid. No wind yet, for which Farmer felt immeasurably grateful. The Montana climate proved challenging enough, but frequent high winds made adapting harder still. Even in the momentary calm, he was shivering by the time he reached the truck and threw his gear into the back. Already, numbness sank into his exposed flesh. His lungs replaced the hot, recycled air of the station with air so cold it burned.

Farmer unplugged the truck from the engine block heater, hopped in, and turned the ignition. He engaged the heat and defrost at their highest settings, which sent tiny ice particles into the cab, up the windshield, and over his head. They hit the roof and fell in imitation of the flakes outside.

The radio crackled, startling him. He lowered the volume, then keyed the mic to check the level.

"Get to movin'," came the dispatcher's voice over the radio. Farmer looked out the windshield to find him watching through a giant window.

Farmer pulled alongside the building. Conley had cracked the door and was puffing a cigarette inside the foyer, exhaling through the crack.

Farmer exited and circled around to the passenger side. Conley opened the back and loaded his duffel. He shouted around his cigarette. "You got your weapon?"

For a moment, Farmer thought he'd forgotten it, and panic seized him. But when he looked down into the plastic, U-shaped storage racks on the bed of the truck, he saw his M-16 resting there. "Yeah, I got it."

Conley deposited his butt into the fire engine red can outside the station and then pulled himself up into the driver's seat. The cab immediately filled with the smell of musty tobacco smoke.

Conley placed his own rifle into the rack, and they headed through the gate.

The sky shone a pale off-white. As they drove, flakes rushed at the windshield, reflecting the headlights and obscuring visibility. The ubiquitous triple-stranded barbed wire fences on both sides of the gravel roads acted as guideposts. Each road they took to the site lay covered with virgin snow.

When they neared the site, Farmer put on his flak vest, gas mask, and helmet, expecting he would be the one to perform the sector checks. They pulled up to the gate, and Farmer jumped out of the vehicle and moved around to the driver's side.

Conley threw him the handheld radio through the window, but Farmer missed it. The radio disappeared into the snow, leaving behind a light gray ghost in the snow bank. "Jesus, Farmer," Conley said.

"Nice throw."

Once he found the radio and keyed the mic to check that it still worked, Farmer approached the site. A high fence topped with razor wire surrounded the area. The only entrance was through a gate secured by thick chains and a Schlage lock.

Inside, Farmer called in his sectors, running from one part of the site to another in a tightening spiral pattern, checking the fresh powder for tracks. The wind kicked up as he cleared the last sector. The falling snow became less a nuisance than the loose powder already on the ground, which flew in Farmer's face.

Nearing the gate, he threw one more glance over his shoulder — nothing but miles of pale plains beyond the westward fence. Then he spotted something in the stark white. He blinked back the stinging wind, even kept his eyes shut for a few seconds, and looked again. For a while, nothing. Then it came once more — a red glow, like a tiny ball of crimson hovering somewhere in the alabaster. Bolstered by certainty now, he lifted the radio and engaged the button, the tonal beep overriding the whistle of the wind.

The glow disappeared. He saw movement, maybe, but could report nothing more specific. He released the button and the radio chirped. Jogging back to the entrance, he imagined the glow pursuing him, and kept turning to look. He circled the heavy chain around the gate and engaged the lock. He peered back toward the west but saw only the snow now. He shook his head. With the wind kicking up gusts of snow, the motion sensors would never reset, and he wanted away from there.

Farmer approached the vehicle and slung his rifle, winded and freezing. He locked eyes with Conley but said nothing. Customarily, whoever didn't sweep the sectors performed the required perimeter check along the outside of the fence. The site's north side faced a steep grade, which would make the walk-around bearish. Then there was that glow.

"Yeah, I'll do it," Conley said, soured. "Consider it your Christmas present." He shouldered his weapon, barrel down, and held out his gloved hand for the portable radio.

Ten minutes later, Conley returned.

"Anything?" Farmer asked.

Conley stared back him, shrugging finally. "Like what?"

They took turns hauling their gear to the back of the truck and stowing it in their duffels. Conley turned the truck around to face the access road, leaving whatever Farmer had seen at his back. He dropped his visor and checked the mirror, but the wind-whipped flakes obscured even the site gate twenty feet away.

While they waited for the sensors to reset, they listened to holiday tunes on the radio. Conley brought out a Ziploc of some dried meat and gnawed on it. Farmer flipped through a magazine, but grew restless. He turned around to look behind them every few minutes.

"Staring at it ain't gonna make it reset, Farmer."

"Sorry."

Conley sighed. "You got family 'round here? This part of the country, I mean."

Farmer shook his head. "They're all back east. How about you?"

"Same. God knows why. My daddy's a hunter and a fisher, like me, like my brothers. I don't know how they can be satisfied with those little whitetail deer back home when they got mulies twice that size out here."

Farmer swallowed, turning toward the frigid glass of his window. "Seen anything else out here?"

Conley humphed. "What do you mean? Any action?"

Farmer shrugged. "Anything weird. In the snow. I mean, we're a hundred miles from civilization, so who knows?"

"You trying to scare me with some missile field ghost story? A newbie who hasn't even seen a whole year of this shit?"

Farmer shook his head. "Only wondering. You didn't come across anything on the walk-around? Nothing odd?"

Conley pulled out a pack of cigarettes from his sleeve pocket and put one of the sticks between his teeth. "Better luck next time, Farmer." He stepped out into the winter wind and smoked.

As night fell, the snowfall ceased. All hope of leaving darkened with the sky. Farmer worried less and less about the light in the snow. Just his imagination. Instead, his thoughts returned to how meaningless the holiday had become for him. He'd requested leave time to return home, but not only was he low man on the totem pole, his sergeant found it in bad form.

"A lot of these guys got wives at home. Kids, too. You'd rather they spend Christmas Day in the field so you can go back home to Mommy?"

Conley killed the site floodlights then turned off the Bronco headlights, putting the access road into total darkness. Then — as if the tiniest glow would disturb him — he dimmed the dash lights and even took off his watch-cap and stuffed it into the recess that housed the illuminated dash clock. He put his seat back a few inches and pulled down the hood of his parka.

He turned to Farmer. "Keep watch. I'll let you sleep later."

Farmer's stewing anxiety and disappointment had already exhausted him. There was no chance in hell anyone would come out to check on them, not tonight. They should both sleep, if he could. He shrugged at Conley. "We expecting trouble?"

"Don't get wise, Farmer. Leadership knows we're out here, Christmas or not. You start to nod off, spend a minute or two outside and you'll stay wide awake. Just try not to let all the heat out."

After twenty minutes, Farmer's head grew heavy and began to bob. He peered over at Conley, who either slept or lay so still that not a shadow moved. The only sound was the occasional gust and the subtle creaking of the truck's shocks thereafter.

Farmer opened the door slowly, slid out, and eased it shut. The air sought the tender flesh of his lungs like a parasite seeking a host. He coughed lightly, but grew used to it faster without the wind. He looked up to the stars, usually a canopy so packed with faraway gems that it illuminated the night with their collective glow. Tonight, the cloud cover kept all but a few bright shiners hidden.

Returning his gaze to Earth, he caught sight of a gleam in the distance. At least it seemed distant. He did a double-take, then focused his full gaze upon it.

The same soft red glow he'd seen through the snow hours before now pierced the night air. It shone clearly one moment, hazy the next, without discernible edges or texture. All he knew for sure was that it did not come from a tail light or flashlight. It seemed natural, in fact. The undulating glow swelled to bright red — almost pink — before fading to nonexistence, only to start again a moment later. The waxing and waning was too smooth to be artificial, less turn signal than firefly.

Farmer was unable to reconcile the image, though something about it suggested life. Out of habit, he reached behind him for his weapon, but it was still nestled in the truck's rack. Getting it would mean rousing Conley.

Despite his fear, Farmer began to ease toward the light. Every few feet, he stopped and stared, trying to figure out if the light moved. Perhaps it only seemed to move because the warmth of that glow clung to the back of his eyelids when he blinked.

As he neared, he thought he detected the sound of breathing. It seemed out of time with his own respiration. He stood still for a moment, eyes fixed on the glow, and held his breath.

For a few seconds, nothing. Then his body filled with adrenaline when he heard the distinct sound of an exhale. The glow bobbed up and down in time with the breaths. They grew louder, and the glow expanded.

A shape came into view when the glow peaked every few seconds. Farmer's heart increased its already frantic pace. His breathing came quick and erratic. Fear demanded that he run, but curiosity fixed his feet to the cold earth.

In the glow shone eyes like pools of dark water, reflecting the soft red light. Then a sound like someone walking through the snow, but heavier and yet more surefooted. It was animal. He fought back the fear of being attacked and the urge to scare it away, if he even could.

It was nearly upon him by the time he made any sense of it. The glow continued to throw him. It didn't belong in any logical sense, though it seemed fitting, even if he couldn't say why. The thing had horns of a sort, and a long head ending in nostrils that blew white plumes of vapor in steady rhythm. Brown fur covered the animal from top of head to top of hooves, pocked with clumps of snow. It appeared thick and comfortable, like a favorite blanket.

Farmer knew little of wildlife. Enough to suggest that "deer" didn't quite work. "Elk" felt wrong as well, though both lived in Montana, denser than humans in some parts.

The light swelled and contracted over its face, but not until it took another step did subtler features emerge. Something on its flank glinted in the periodic light — a buckle. An ornate and ancient harness hugged the animal's chest and back, a slightly lighter brown against the fur. Redolent of an Old West gunslinger's belt, the rig held volumes more character than his own tack of plastic and nylon. It spoke of care and time, of precision and purpose. Someone long ago had spent countless hours working intricate detail into the leather, so that now it told a story, even if Farmer could only guess its meaning. It covered the animal's body like a second hide, moving with the rhythm of its breathing as if no more artificial than its broad antlers.

In those mirrored eyes — all but invisible when the glow faded, but bright and beckoning when the light peaked — Farmer found the same veneration. The animal aspect loomed, certainly, but behind that he felt something wiser and knowing. He stared long into those eyes, trying to decide how to feel, wondering if the night and the weather had addled his mind.

But then he began to form a connection. How had it remained subdued for so long? When this fantastical explanation surfaced, his initial reaction was to smile so broadly that his teeth soon grew cold from exposure. His eyes widened like a child's and his jaw slacked.

A name took center in his mind. A title that called up imagination and wonder. He wanted to speak it. The animal seemed to lean in, as if anticipating it.

And yet, Farmer considered the absurdity of it all. There he stood, seeing the incarnation of childhood fantasy not an arm's length away, but the logic and reason of his life intruded and continued to hedge out his wonderment.

The glow, the eyes, the breathing of the animal was communication of a sort, despite Farmer's inability to interpret it. He owed more in return than a listless simper.

He spoke, as much to ground the spectacle in reality as to communicate. "But if I believe in you," he said, his voice weak and dry, "then anything is possible."

The weight of this sank in, and he imagined the implications. Every story he'd ever heard as a child now feasible. Each tall tale now viable enough to have a place in a world working so hard to explain itself and make all things safe. Maybe there were fairies and giants and elves, if there was a...

"Rudolph," he said, finally.

The animal huffed and pawed at the snow. He moved his head down and up, as if satisfied that a formal introduction had been made.

"I'm Farmer," he said. "Well, Patrick, I guess. To you."

The reindeer inched closer, turning sideways, revealing himself to Farmer in full. He picked up the subtle smell of the animal, of earth and musk. The nose let out a soft hum as it went from a wet black to a blazing red.

The reindeer pushed his head closer still, so that Farmer's eyes were dazzled by the light, and he knew he was meant to touch him. Meant to receive this connection as a gift, one more important than any worldly object, or even any human bond he had made since stationed there.

He eased his hand out, though the reindeer showed no signs of distrust, and he gingerly put the pad of his middle finger to the nose when it waned. As it glowed again, Farmer tensed at the prospect of being burned, though he knew it created no heat. He stood so close, he would have felt it.

He ran his hand down the muzzle of the beast, feeling the fur both soft and unyielding. Being so close to the animal made Farmer warm and comfortable. Not like the artificial heat from the cab of the truck, but a truer, deeper warmth. He grew content with the cold, instead of simply existing within it.

In that moment, Farmer didn't want to leave the site at all. If not for their replacement crew coming to relieve them sometime in the wee hours, he would stand there in the cold until daybreak.

And then his eyes slammed shut instinctively. Before the impulse could even register, a crack ripped through the night air. His training and rote muscle memory dropped him to one knee as he pulled a non-existent weapon to port arms. He opened his eyes to a hot spray across his face — slung over his eyes and nose and mouth as if choreographed, followed by a second crack. He blinked frantically, eyes stinging, then they refused to reopen.

He had time to form a single, horrid image: The reindeer's eyes wide and scared. His body, faltering in the snow, kicking up powder, looking for purchase to keep his knees from bucking. Mouth agape, white teeth and pink tongue spewing hot breath, emptying his lungs in a fume of rising vapor.

This image stayed in front of him while he wiped at his eyes with gloved hands cold and damp. The image became the still-frame for the terrible noises permeating the air. The reindeer bellowed over and over, a sound somewhere between a foghorn and a screaming child. In this, Farmer heard pain and fear above all. But there was something else — accusation, even anathema, as if the animal blamed Farmer for what was happening.

Through the pain, Farmer forced his eyes open and looked around.

"Out-fucking-standing!" Conley said. He marched over, rifle resting on his shoulder, the bright white glow of a flashlight coming off his harness.

Without another word, Conley slung his rifle, removed a long folding knife from his gear, and straddled the dying animal.

The reindeer now lay in the snow, gyrating up and down, clinging to life, but slipping nonetheless. Head slightly turned, he kept his eyes on Farmer – wide and sharp, knowing. His nose lit once more, but it was subtle and weak, only enough to seem a trick of the brain.

"Wait," Farmer shouted. "What are you–?"

Ignoring him, Conley pulled the blade across the reindeer's throat, rending the flesh and spraying the snow with crimson, where it steamed. The animal made a final gasping rattle, and his nose retreated to a dark, fleshy color. His eyes rolled skyward, only now void of judgment and disdain.

"Man, this hoss is gonna make fine eatin'," Conley said, preparing the carcass further in practiced motions. The sound was that of plunging a toilet. "What the hell?" Conley barked, his hands on the harness. "Jeez-us. This is a goddamn petting zoo animal or somethin'."

"You don't know what you've done," Farmer told him. He vomited into the snow, the hot liquid melted the pristine white and exposed the frozen ground beneath.

"Christ, Farmer. Get a hold of yourself. It's just a reindeer." He cut away the great harness with some effort, his hacking motion causing the carcass to buck and loll. He inspected the leather in the beam of his flashlight for a moment, then tossed it into the snow. "He was about to attack you, right? I probably saved your life. Some asshole makes a stink about a missing reindeer, you remember that."

Farmer spat and spat, trying to catch his breath. "You don't understand."

"Oh, yeah. Right. Don't worry about the ammo. I keep some rounds in my backpack in case I gotta replace a few. I ain't sayin' I've shot at anything out here before, but I ain't denyin' it either."

"You killed him," Farmer mumbled.

Conley quit cutting and looked up at Farmer. "Your light's on," he said, pointing with the bloodied and dripping knife, which steamed as if alive.

Farmer reached to his harness, where his angle flashlight shined subtly red through a translucent lens. The beam went on and off in undulating projections of milky light.

"No," Farmer said. "This wasn't on. That's not what happened."

Conley grunted, still looking down. "How do you think I could see to take the shot, Farmer?" He looked up for an answer, received none, and just shook his head, returning to his work.

Meat is Meat
K. C. Campbell

Coy's children were starving, always starving. If he could scrounge animals, he would; alive or dead mattered little. There was also the other meat, people. Meat was meat and only the truly hungry understood. Coy had promised his mother he would never taste man flesh, but her ceaseless demand had only triggered the hunger and now she was long gone, over one hundred years gone at a guess, and Coy had mouths to feed. He absorbed time from those he consumed, why else would he be so long lived? He was a lone parent now, his wife dead too. Seems the women in his life did not have the same stamina to live. What would his wife think of the children's unexpected enjoyment of human meat?

On route to the decrepit church, Coy eyed the woman who had just arrived, alighting from the fancy coach like a spring rain, refreshing all who spied her. She was too thin, would barely feed the children, but since the gold was drying up as fast as the corpses, Coy had to be practical. The town was dying and there was no room for God or morality in this dusty hole.

The children depended on Coy and he could not feed them on his church stipend, nor with the surrounding farm animals. Farmers were more concerned with a missing horse than a missing wife in these parts. Coy was careful, he thought hard about everything he took. If he were caught and strung up, his children would starve, or worse, they would strike out on their own.

The woman's small nose tilted in a way that spoke of entitlement. Coy wondered what had bought someone like her to this place of desperation and despair, of broken promises and back-breaking heartache. What did it matter? As she entered the sheriff's office Coy felt only hope that she might supply more meat to his family. He imagined she would taste expensive. It would all depend on how long she remained in town. Coy had gathered enough supplies for tonight and tomorrow, but there were always other nights to plan for. So many endless nights of worry and hunger, so many mouths to feed.

***

Betha Cooper was not a violent woman, but she craved to slap this fat lawman's face. He had no empathy for what Betha had endured to gain his audience.

"As I was saying, I just need to find my husband."

"You said you lost a body?" Was this soulless man making fun?

Her children needed her right now, and instead, Betha had travelled for days to untie the knots of their father's death. She had endured her husband's desertion to this wasteland, and was now fighting to locate his corpse. Bill was a proud man who wanted to make his own way, away from the confines of Betha's wealthy father, and gold was on everyone's minds. Back in Chicago, rumour was rife – Betha was a shrew and big Bill Cooper had found someone more to his liking in this backwater.

Betha's lips pursed as Sheriff Lee Reeves adjusted his belt, once more touching his man parts. "Sheriff, do you give a damn that my husband is missing?"

"Sure I do. But lots of strange things happen around here. I got more missing body parts than I got whores." He smiled as Betha started at his crude words.

"Do you realise who my father is?"

"I heard of your daddy. A Chicago lawman, I believe. It's a shame Chicago's so damn far away, your fine daddy might know where the fuck all my citizens are going." He smiled again as Betha paled.

"Are you saying you would only help me if my father were here?"

"It's not safe for a woman to poke at things that should be left to men."

"I suggest you find it in your heart to assist me lest I send for my father. He would not take kindly to his daughter's mistreatment."

The Sheriff took an extended moment to carefully pluck tobacco from his tongue, glaring at Betha from beneath bushy red brows. "Mrs. Cooper, I am a man of the law, while your father sits in his fancy new courts with his pretty new rules and preaches. I serve justice and will never be dictated to by suits that can't ride a horse or shoot a gun."

Sheriff Lee Reeves' resentments sat on his craggy face, repulsing Betha. "My father has served this country, Sheriff. My family has suffered…"

"Your family has sure benefited too."

Betha raised her voice, shaking now with embarrassment and outrage. "I don't like the insinuation that a man of learning is somehow less a lawman than you."

Sheriff Reeves gave Betha's chest a derisive once over before hauling his girth from behind the beaten old desk. "Well, this sure has been fun, Mrs. Cooper. But I've got living people to put in jail. Come back and see me when some drunk decides he cares more for your purse or the contents of your drawers than your sharp tongue. Or call in your big shot daddy. I could sure use some help." He ambled past, muttering quietly.

She nipped her nostrils at the stench of filthy clothing and old sweat. How had her husband survived two whole years in this hated man's town? "Sheriff," She called, furious at his dismissal and her own fear. "I didn't catch that last insult and most men have the decency to say it to my face."

Sheriff Reeves turned, like everything he did it was slow and menacing. "A woman should know her place, else she disappears." He stared over Betha's shoulder as if at a happy memory. "Disappear with all those kiddie fiddlers and whore killers."

Betha noted the Sheriff still refused to meet her eye. Something stirred, that feeling she was purposely being misled. "If you have finished insulting me, can we return to my husband's disappearance? I have children that need their father put to rest."

The Sheriff's smile was cold as he adjusted his dirty hat. "What was his name?"

"Bill . . . William Cooper. I've told you this several times now."

"Name don't ring a bell."

"He was prospecting here for almost two years, and this small town appears very interested in strangers."

"We don't get many folk passing through anymore, what with the gold running dry." He shook his head. "How did you discover your husband's death in Chicago?"

"I received a letter from this office. It had your name on it."

"So I saw his body. What else do you want? I'm a busy man. You're so smart, you gonna raise him from the dead?" The snarl said something was getting to this man.

Betha was furious with offence. "Such talk is a blasphemy against our Lord."

He boomed with laughter, "Plenty of blasphemy happens in this town, plenty of other big fancy words too, but fact is, sometimes looking away from one evil can stop a dozen more. And that's why justice should start and end at my door in my town."

"Where is my husband?" Betha wanted rid of this angry man and his small-town mentality. He was ignorant of the legal system that was changing rapidly to make people safe, make justice fair for everyone, man, woman, and child.

"Your husband's earthly remains were packed on a train bound for Chicago."

"So you remember him after all?"

"Sure, this is my town. I know everyone, even nosy women that judge my ways."

"I am not judging. I simply want my husband. Is that so hard to understand?"

"I don't run the train, Mrs Cooper. Go talk to the railways…"

"I have." She interrupted, exhausted from the stress of Bill's death and now being unable to locate his body. "There was an empty box when it reached Chicago."

"Well, ain't that something?" The Sheriff chuckled, "Perhaps your man ain't dead. Perhaps he found one of my pretty girls from the saloon."

Betha imagined purchasing a weapon and forcing this disgraceful mule to admit what he was hiding. "You sent me a letter, Sheriff. So, is Bill alive with one of your women, or is he dead, his body lost by your office?"

The Sheriff's smug smile was getting to her. Was Bill still here? Living without the frustration of a dominant father-in-law. She missed her husband, had taken her vows seriously, and not gifting Bill back to the earth felt like a sin.

Bill had been thirty, sandy-haired, big, and hardworking. He had wanted to make his own way, live in a home without Betha's father as landlord. Yet Bill's final letter had been despondent, the gold had dried up and he was deciding to move on or come home.

What Betha failed to tell the Sheriff was that Bill's luggage, the sale certificate for his claim and a tiny bag of gold had arrived in Chicago, even his saddle bags and guns had all been packed neatly into two wooden crates. Everything had returned home except Bill's body. Betha would return to her father, she had no money for freedom and she would live with that, was grateful she had more options than some women she knew. But she would not give her father the satisfaction of Bill's body being discarded from the family gravesite. It would be her final act of marital devotion, her children deserved their father back. And this shifty-eyed lawman was purposely keeping that from happening.

"There's nothing I can do for you, Mrs. Cooper." The Sheriff said. "I only deal with the living. The dead are beyond my jurisdiction."

"Who has jurisdiction over the dead then, Sheriff?"

"I send 'em to the next of kin."

Now she was certain that Sheriff Reeves was hiding something. "And if next of kin are not around, do you pack the crates yourself?" Betha knew she sounded like her father, snooty and superior, but she needed this explained plain and simple.

"I got a man does the manual labour."

"And when you don't know next of kin?"

"They go to the church, the bone yard." The Sheriff didn't seem pleased to admit this and Betha relaxed. "I try to ship 'em out, couldn't cope with all what end up dead around here, the coyotes already have enough fun…"

"Where is the churchyard?" Betha interrupted, unable to call it a bone yard. In this arid heat, it conjured up images of rotting meat and brittle chalky bones.

"This is a small town, I suggest you go figure it out on your own." Sheriff Reeves snarled, proof of something sinister, and Betha meant to find out what.

She was her father's daughter, after all. "Suppose you'll be safe on your own. Just don't hang around at night, you never know what devils hide in the shadows out here."

Betha nodded once, happy she had upset him. "I thank you for all your help, Sheriff. I'll remember to mention you to my father on my return to Chicago."

But she was talking to Reeve's back as he stalked from the tiny building. Betha followed him into the dusty street, wondering if he would head straight for the churchyard to contain his secret. But instead the Sheriff's wide back disappeared into the saloon, the swing doors, askew on their rusty hinges, snapping shut behind him.

Did her husband's disappearance have him on edge or was he like her father, an eternally surly man? He knew she would go to the graveyard, so would the Sheriff knowingly lead her into danger? She stared at the saloon doors for a long moment, wishing she had the right to slip inside for a drink. Instead, she entered the hardware store.

"I'm looking for the churchyard."

She was quickly pointed in the right direction with the offer of a good gun at a decent price for protection. She declined the gun, hopeful she would not regret it.

***

At least the Sheriff had been honest about the dimensions of the church's sacred ground. It was tiny, open holes bursting into the surrounding scrubland through broken, knee-high fences. But why were so many of the graves open? Could coyotes really dig so efficiently into graves?

Her confused gaze roamed the mounds of sandy dirt until a strange little man ambled from behind the church with a huge shovel in an oversized hand. He was small and gnarled, frightening to look at, close to inhuman and Betha gulped back a yelp, certain the devil himself had climbed from an open grave. As he hobbled closer, Betha tried to relax, she had been raised to be charitable to all forms of retardation, and this man's strange body was to be pitied not feared. He didn't see Betha until she cleared her throat, only then did he raise his shovel as if to strike in fright.

"I didn't mean to startle you," Betha soothed, hands out to show she was unarmed. "I am searching for my husband, nothing more."

"Who dat, den?" The man replied, lopsided eyes flicking in every direction, those oversized hands still clutching the shaft of the shovel tight enough to show white knuckles, his arm muscles and heavy veins bulging from long years of hard labour. Betha noted that his eyes were beautiful, mesmerising, clear blue like the sky on a perfect summer's day.

"William Cooper. Everyone called him Bill." Betha was certain she had wasted her time after all, this simpleton would struggle with his own name let alone an outsider's.

But the little man's features shifted into a smile. It was another startling event to witness and Betha shook her head to clear her vision.

"Sure, I remember Bill. Nice boy, big son of a gun. Were a damn shame he fell off dat horse, done got hisself killed like dat."

"You know?" Betha touched her forehead, the heat overwhelming as she tried to sort out her feelings of relief.

"I sure am sorry for your loss, ma'am."

A tear slipped down Betha's face and she touched it away with a gloved finger. "That means so much, thank you for being so kind. The dreadful Sheriff…"

"You got you any young'uns?"

"Yes, two boys. They miss their daddy something awful."

The little man nodded and peered into the distance. "I gots me a pile of young'uns so I know what it's like to have 'em. You got someone to help feed 'em, now what Bill gone and got hisself dead?"

"My daddy will look after us."

"Dat's nice. Daddies gots to look out for their babies anyway they can. I'd do anything for my little ones."

Betha smiled, some of the stress of the last few weeks sliding away. "How many children... I'm sorry, where are my manners, what was your name, sir?"

The strange little man with the oddly muscled body seemed delighted to be called sir and grinned, showing that most of his teeth were gone. It made Betha wonder at his age. She had taken him for around her father's age, but now she was not so sure, his face was weathered and lined, probably from endless sun, but those eyes were so peculiar.

"My name's Coy Wendigo."

"Wendigo?" Betha giggled, even though the name had given her the chills. "I thought Wendigos were monsters that ate human flesh? My daddy put a man to death who ate his family up like they were chickens on his farm."

The little man only blinked at her, his lips still slightly parted showing those swollen gums and pitiful teeth. "I'm Betha, and it is so nice to meet a friendly... man."

"Why thank you, Missus," He glanced at the ring on her left finger.

"Betha, please, just call me Betha."

"Alright," Coy's face burst into that lopsided smile again, this time it turned Betha's stomach and she berated herself for being cruel. This odd little man might hold the answer to Bill's whereabouts, and for that she would be grateful.

"How many little ones do you have, Coy?"

"I got me fourteen mouths to feed."

"Goodness, how old is your youngest?" Betha was still trying to fathom the man's age. Fourteen children was not uncommon, but Betha could not stop wondering on the type of woman to have so many with a man like Coy.

"My baby looks about four now. His sisters look out for him while I'm working."

"Not your wife?" Betha was intruding, but her fascination had taken over. And what did he mean, looks about four?

"My wife gone died giving birth to the baby."

"I am so sorry to hear that."

"We seem to have some in common." Coy shuffled his huge shovel from one calloused hand to the other, looking toward town as if embarrassed someone might see him admitting anything to the fancy new lady.

Inside, Betha coiled away from having anything in common with this strange little goblin. "So, what do you know about my husband?"

Eyes rolling everywhere but at Betha, Coy mumbled, "Just that he was a good man, always polite to me when others run off like I's some sort of monster. I can see he got his good manners from his pretty wife."

"Thank you, but there has been a problem with Bill's body. It's gone missing."

The grip on Coy's shovel tightened enough that the wood groaned and Betha took a step backward. "Coy?"

Dropping the shovel Coy ran his hands through his stringy, greasy, grey hair.

"Sorry, Missus. It's just that, well, I'm not sure if you were told but this town is haunted or something. Bodies go missing all the time."

"Dear Lord." Betha hissed. "Sheriff Reeves…"

"He don't want his town's name smeared. But it ain't his town, some folks been here long-time more."

"You mean he's covering it up?"

"How else do you explain it, bodies disappearing," He shoved a thumb over his shoulder, "holes in my yard overnight?"

Betha held her throat, gorge rising, "You mean someone's stealing bodies, digging them up? Why would anyone do that?" Her stomach was full of hot coals and she prayed she was not becoming ill. Illness in this place could end it all.

Eyes wide, Coy beseeched, "I dig holes, put folks in, nice and snug. Next morning, the holes' opened up and they gone."

"Do you tell the Sheriff?"

"He don't like to leave that saloon and 'em whores. I'd sure hate to cause a fuss."

"But this is bodies being stolen. These are real people with families . . ."

"Don't know what else I can tell you, Missus. I'm just the poor fool that's got to plant these folks."

"You're right, I'm sorry. Thank you for being so honest with me, Coy. I really appreciate it."

"If it helps any, Big Bill definite went into dat box, I did it myself. If he came out after that, then it was an act of God."

"He never got to the other end." Betha said sadly.

"I'm sure wherever he ended up, his soul is at peace." Coy's hands pressed together and his eyes clamped shut as he tilted his head to the sky.

Betha nodded and turned to go. Coy called, "Will you head on home now?"

"What else can I can do?" Betha asked, "My husband is gone, I'll never get him back. All I wanted was somewhere to take my children, somewhere to grieve."

"Sheriff tole me…" He became silent.

Betha looked down at an open plot, "Was a body dug out of here?"

"To tell the truth, not many is full." Coy seemed embarrassed, but it actually made Betha feel better. "So, Bill would have gone missing anyway?"

"I guess." Coy shrugged.

"The Sheriff needs to find out where these bodies are going. I might talk to my daddy, see if he could send some men down here to work this out."

"Good luck with that. Personally, I think it's something spooky."

"Like ghosts?" Betha thought of her Bill wandering the world, his soul lost and seeking his family. It was ridiculous. Good people did not haunt the world.

Coy smiled, his wonky eyes twinkling. "Why don't you come on home? My girl's had some meat on the boil all day. I gots to have it slow boiled since my teeth are gone. There ain't much food but we are happy to share."

Betha could think of nothing worse than an evening with Coy, her charity fading with the afternoon. She also felt envious, he had so many children to look after him while Betha had only the two boys who would one day move away, leaving her alone.

"I'm going back to Chicago as soon as I can find a driver."

"But it's almost night."

"I know, but… this town has something wrong with it. No offense, Coy."

"None taken. It sure was nice to meet you, and to know your husband."

Coy collected his shovel and ambled away with only a lingering glance at a mound of dirt. He disappeared behind the tiny church, presumably to put the shovel away, and Betha was relieved to be free of his presence, again guilty at her unchristian thoughts.

On a tired sigh, she decided to pay her respects in the tiny church. Afterward, she felt better for making peace with Jesus. It always gave her hope, that her life had some greater purpose. It was dusk now and, standing on the small step, Betha enjoyed the final rays of sun, eyes closed and face tilted up.

A noise to her left bought her attention back with a snap. It took a moment to realise that the strange little man, Coy, hadn't gone at all but was in the growing dark, digging. Betha's first thought was that he was closing up some of the opened holes but as her eyes adjusted from the candles within the church she realised with a lurch that he was in fact digging a grave open.

Betha was frozen with confused fright. Within half an hour of frantic digging, Coy had a body slung over his shoulder and was ambling from the church yard as though his load weighed nothing.

Finally triggered into action, Betha followed like a cat stalking a rat. It was dark now, she could make out a fire in the distance and slowed, watching with fascination as Coy arrived home.

She snuck closer, her chest hammering hard as she stood behind a huge pile of wood and sticks, the thud of an axe cutting the night, overshadowed only by the sounds of children laughing and playing strangely out of sight. By the light of the cooking fire Betha could make out a small shanty house. It was impossible to imagine where everyone slept in such a tiny place. With a sinking stomach, she forced her exhausted eyes to focus on Coy, who had the body draped over a huge slab of wood. Such a mammoth piece of timber must have been sourced at great expense from a very long distance, it was certainly not from around here. Even from this distance, she could see how dark and stained the chopping block was. Betha clutched her throat, trying to hold the bile down as she finally admitted that Coy was hacking the body into chunks. He made short work of it, those oversized muscles bunching and flexing with ease as each body piece was dropped into a huge pot, its twin dangling above the fire.

A girl's voice called out, "Food should be soft enough for you, daddy."

"Thanks, Darla. You go get all dem kids to sleep while I eat and tidy up."

As if a door had slammed, the noise of children ceased. Coy set his axe aside and hauled the pot from above the fire, using his bare hands. Betha imagined she could hear his skin sizzling but he made no indication of pain as he began scooping food straight from the pot and into his mouth, eating like a starving man. Betha was entranced, scared to breathe, horror holding her in place. Only when the pot was empty did Coy tip it up, bones falling into the fire with a muffled hiss. It was then that Betha heard the yips and howls of wolves or coyotes closing in. When the bones were burnt and cooled enough, the dogs would come for them. There would be next to nothing left of the stolen bodies.

Betha had found what she was searching for. Her husband was here, spread across this barren, hated land. Was it evil or wrong? Yes, but Betha could not yet comprehend it. So, instead of confronting Coy, she backed away, wanting only to leave this town and these soulless people as nightmares for another time. She wanted her boys, to hold them close and explain that their father had been lost in the West while he made his fortune.

She froze as behind her Coy called, "Man's got to feed his family, and meat's just meat. We ain't none of us better than that. I set 'em free to roam, to watch over us, and they are sure happy and grateful about that."

Betha ran then, hard and fast, crying, certain she would die with each step. Coy's voice had been so changed she could only imagine he had somehow grown teeth.

***

The next morning, as Betha stepped into the carriage, the Sheriff stopped her.

"I figured you wouldn't give up so easy."

She peered down her nose at him, hating him as much as she marvelled at his determination to remain in a place with such a monster overseeing them all. "And I figured you for a lawman with some understanding of God."

This seemed to amuse the Sheriff and he laughed long and loud while nervous towns folk scurried away. "God don't live out here, Mrs. Cooper. He might live in your Chicago but I assure you, he don't even pass this way from time to time."

"You know what Coy's doing, don't you?" She asked, uncaring who may hear.

"I know there's a man what lost his wife and all his money in the gold rush and now he feeds them kids as best he can. I don't see no harm in him finding creative ways and means. Only a starving man can decide what's beyond his capabilities."

"It is beyond natural law. You people disgust me."

"That's harsh, Mrs. Cooper. After all, you got what you came for, you now know where your husband is. He's scattered all over this land we're killing ourselves to break in with our bare hands. This land is polluted with ghosts but ain't none of them sad."

"I hope you all go to Hell." Betha said, her throat closing over, tears just a small gasp away.

"We're already there, ma'am. You visit anytime, ya hear." The carriage pulled away and Betha had never been happier to leave a place behind. As she passed out of the town, she felt a prickle of recognition. Bill was here, just out of sight, and Betha craned her neck to see around each corner. Of course, she saw nothing and sitting back as the town fell behind her, Betha tried to relax into her seat, dreading the road ahead.

As she passed the town's final marker, Coy stood, watching her pass, his axe dangling from one hand, his overly long, muscled arms giving him a primitive aspect that was terrifying. Betha averted her gaze as he waved.

Over the next few days, she had many dreams of her husband and when she opened her eyes, she caught glimpses of him. She felt she was showing him the way home. As she opened the front door to her father's house, relieved and at peace with her husband's loss, Betha wondered if that strange little town had infected her with its lunacy for a time. Or did ghosts of the eaten dead really roam the unbroken West?

In one insane moment of weakness, she admitted all to her father.

There was no going back from such a confession and the hammer would soon fall upon that town, Betha's search for her husband the catalyst for change.

***

Back at the graveyard, the Sheriff pulled up on his big, hungry horse and informed Coy that a young man had died in a drunken brawl and that Coy was to collect the body for burial. Coy smiled brightly and scurried off to collect his shovel and his axe.

***

The Wendigo watched his son, always scurrying, always working hard to feed his family. The boy had tried hard to be human, like his mother. That delusion was almost at an end, the Wendigo was bored of watching and waiting. The lawmen were coming, and righteous meat was always the sweetest. The Wendigo was ready to school his grandchildren in the old arts.

The beginning was coming and the Wendigo intended to be head of the feast.

My First Time
Cody D Grady

It is fascinating what the human eye can interpret from a single moment. One minor glimpse takes me hours to process, as sight paints subtle pictures of the memory across my subconscious. Like an instantly developing Polaroid, the snapshot slowly fades into existence, cementing every detail in the mind for analysis and scrutiny. With just a glance I find myself able to extrapolate fantastical stories, see someone's entire life laid out before me. I often wonder if others can do this, or if it's my own special super power. Daddy always said I had great big, beautiful eyes.

"For seeing the world better," he would say with a grin from ear to ear, throwing in some rib tickling for good measure. He always loved my eyes.

I first noticed the taillights from a mile or two off. It is impossible to gauge accurate distances when traversing the hilly landscape of back country roads, but the two distant pinpricks of red light couldn't be mistaken for anything else in this wilderness. The skies had poured earlier today in a futile last struggle... a dying summer's attempt to maintain climate control. The air had been cool when the raindrops fell upon piles of auburn, wilting leaves. But as the clear, moon-filled night descended upon the landscape, the evening had turned frigid. Autumn would be a harsh one this year, I could tell. Winter's cold bite already nipped at its heels. Shivering inside the cab, I adjusted the knob on the dashboard to the right, the vehicle filling with warmth in response.

After some rising and falling of the natural slopes, it became obvious that the red eyes in the distance weren't moving. Instead, they dilated before me as the land flattened out near Jacob's field. I frowned to my reflection in the mirror, bright eyes betraying the sudden wave of nervousness I felt. No one should be out here in the dead of night, not in this neck of the woods. I was traveling well off the main throughways, and even passing local traffic at this hour would have been a surprise. Clearly, it's someone dumping a body, I thought before rejecting the idea. No one had been murdered in this area for decades. There were plenty of other suitable places much closer to the highway for dropping corpses if someone was traveling through the countryside. Fields, small copses of woods, shallow ditches filled by the recent rain… anywhere. Yet my heart still raced as I grew closer to the red eyed monster that took shape as a four door sedan, part of me certain that a hockey mask-wearing psycho brandishing a machete would be crouched behind the trunk waiting for me to slow down.

"It's probably two teens screwing," I said to the empty cab around me, though this more amusing thought dissolved faster than the psycho killer one. For starters, the location was terrible for sex. While the golden and soon to be plowed under fields gave a picturesque view of the clear, autumn sky and nearby trees were rattling their dry leaves pleasantly in the gusty wind, a strong stench of hog shit permeated the air. The Ellis farm wasn't far off, and a blowing crosswind pushed the distinct fecal smell across the landscape. Only the most horny and desperate of high schoolers would be boning in this area. I considered this idea a step further. None of the nearby farms had children of that awkward, experimenting age. A few were probably just starting the process of sexual discovery and spent their time engaged in solo carnal acts, secluded in the privacy of their own homes. The older couples had long since watched their children grow up to have families of their own. Oh god, no. The thought of catching an elderly pairing mid-coitus in an attempted revival of their good old days made me gag.

In this moment, it was impossible to ignore the utter remoteness of this back country road. Though I had traveled down this stretch of cracked and poorly patched asphalt for many years, it was only in this single, surreal instant that it became obvious how distant I was from other human beings. A stubborn farming community had gentrified this part of the county in order to keep out any potential land development deals. There wasn't a lamp post or parking lot for ten miles or more, which was just the way the people who lived in this area liked it. They felt safe nestled between the summer corn stalks and golden wheat; fenced in by hay bales and the soft movements of livestock in the distance, without another dwelling or person in sight. Some called it paradise. But, on a cool autumn night like this, the country made me feel small and alone. All the freedom and independence the land provided by sunlight twisted into isolation and paranoia in the dead of night. Out here, no one would hear me scream, whether in pleasure or pain. An excellent place for an exhibitionist act. A perfect spot to dump a body.

My subconscious whirling with thoughts of sex and death, I barely registered how close I had gotten to the stranded vehicle. My truck was now on top of the two decades old car, high beams illuminating its predominantly rusty discoloration. An attempt to get the faltering sedan into the ditch had failed, leaving half of the junker in the right hand lane. Realizing the possibility of an imminent crash, I smoothly rolled the steering wheel to the left, swinging the truck around the road hazard. It was that exact second that I looked at him. Divine providence I did so, or perhaps a simple attempt to assure myself that I hadn't clipped my side view mirror. Glancing out the passenger window, I caught his eye for just an instant. The mental Polaroid clicked.

He was a heavyset man in his late twenties or early thirties. Attired in a faded metal t-shirt from a band who was popular decades ago, his hair was poorly coiffed; too shaggy and unkempt for the social norm. The bespectacled eyes had been downcast as he bent over the engine compartment, ducking his blubbery frame beneath the open hood to inspect the damage inside. Yet the roar of my diesel engine had caught his attention, and he glanced up at the same instant I looked across the bench seat. His face was a mess of curled wisps of hair that had been attempted to be styled into a passable goatee, yet only served as a further social faux pas. The glass inside the dark frames was thick, giving his brown eyes a disjointed, distant look. In public I would have never given him a second glance, perhaps even avoided this stereotypical basement dweller, but he reeled me in with his wide eyes.

They were full of pain. He was tortured, as if warped by years of suffering. Almond colored orbs radiated a deep sorrow that wounded me by the sheer depths of hurt he had suffered. This man-boy, this lost puppy, was all alone in the world. Scared, vulnerable, even paralyzed by the situation. A sudden nurturing warmth grew deep within my breast, and before I knew I had made the decision I felt my right foot moving over to the brake.

...

Life sucks, then you die, my father always liked to say. I hated how even now, hundreds of miles away and years in the past, that his deep booming voice made raspy from decades of cigarettes could flood my mind and drown out my own thoughts. He never trusted nor believed in me for one second of his short, depressed life. He believed there were no solutions; no way out of this intrinsic existential hell we all find ourselves living. Dad found solace in the idea that you pulled your boots up tight and waded through the shit until something inside of you finally gave out... at which point you fell face first in the muck to rot there for eternity. He had been an even more worthless human being than the trite quips, but sometimes I couldn't help but find myself repeating them. Believing them.

I continued to stare under the hood as these dark thoughts swirled in my brain; not unlike the smell of shit that the wind whipped past me. It must be some private joke between observing gods. Somewhere, someone was laughing at the meta-theatrical comedy that was my life. Things aren't so funny when your role is the sad clown.

The engine was too hot, that much I could tell. The dim bulb mounted on the underside of the hood illuminated waves of heat from every metal surface. It seemed that liquid had sprayed everywhere; judging by the chemical smell mixed with the hissing sound like crackling bacon, it was an important fluid. Perhaps I should have paid more attention to him, I thought, then instantly discarded the notion. Focus on the situation. Attempting to cool my rising anger, I looked again at the engine compartment, attempting to suss out the problem with what feeble knowledge I had. I was fucked, that much was certain.

My father had always been good with his hands. He would tinker away at rusty cars, broken vacuums, old lawn mowers; anything he could get his hands on. I used to watch him tear apart these broken machines, scrutinizing over each worn part with care as a limp cigarette dangled from his mouth. They always seemed half smoked but barely lit, the dull cherry's glow softly illuminating his face. As a child I would sit on the workbench and watch him piddle wordlessly, except for the occasional swear or racial slur about the inadequacy of foreign made machines, until I became green at the gills from the smoke and had to leave the garage. Those were the only peaceful moments I can ever recall sharing with my father.

Realizing the uselessness of inspecting the motor, I kicked the front fender several times instead. The sudden outburst of violence did no damage, but I was immediately embarrassed for doing so. It's a childish act to destroy a thing that is already broken. I'm acting just like the old bastard. The anger quelled instantly, realization dousing me like a cold shower. I hated nothing more in the world than being compared to my father. My family loved to mention the similarities between us during any awkward pause in conversation, usually doing so right before rendering their condolences for my loss... like he was a valiant soldier lost in battle. Again I seethed but forced myself to breathe deeply. I hoped to calm down, yet I had to admit I was also breathless from the physical action. Fat bastard, I heard him say.

Looking around, it became obvious I was stranded here. There were no lights in sight, and I could not recall seeing any indicating signs on the road for a number of miles. My mind had been too preoccupied on the family reunion that awaited me, along with the irritating small talk and painful comparisons that would accompany the event. I had been plotting how to avoid my sure to be drunken uncle when the gauges pulled me from my dark daydream as they all lit up at once, followed shortly thereafter by a loud banging from the engine. Then the car had coasted to a stop, and here I was. I had gotten lost on this cross-country road trip, and it seemed there was no one near to help me out.

Then the headlights caught my attention. Twin shafts of light that promised hope, accompanied by a massive, roaring engine. The monstrous truck was upon me. I couldn't understand why I hadn't heard it coming, the deep thrum of its diesel heart echoed across the landscape. There was no time to shout or wave. I just glanced to the side as the beastly vehicle roared past, crossing the median to avoid my immobilized one. You stupid fucking idiot, I cursed myself, horrified that I had let my one chance of help fly by because I was too preoccupied with my own internal monologue of woe. I turned to watch it go, hoping against hope the driver had seen me and would stop. As if by divine intervention the tail lights began to glow red in answer to my prayer. The beat up old Dodge slowed to a crawl, inched forward slowly, and came to a complete stop.

The truck sat there for a heartbeat or two at most, but those few seconds felt like an eternity. Then the tail lights lit up white atop the red, and the vehicle began to slowly back towards me. That took too long, I thought. Whoever that is, they debated. This isn't an act of goodwill... it's something else. I watched with dread as the pickup creeped backwards towards me at an unnatural pace; the sudden softness of the truck's motion akin to a predator's slight movements, to avoid spooking any unsuspecting prey. Rooted to the spot, my brain screamed at me to act. It had seen horror movies before, assured me of what would happen next. An obese, backwoods dullard would waddle towards me, force me bodily into the truck, then take me back to his inbred family where they would feast on my insides. My body refused to answer, choosing instead to succumb to inevitability. I simply watched as the driver's door eased open and a small, slender form descended from the cab.

...

Up close, he seemed even more lost and confused than I had noted in passing. There was something else in his visage, too, some emotion that I wasn't able to read clearly. Fear? Was he afraid of me? Perhaps it's this, I wondered, hand tightening around the cold, roughened metallic grip. Moving with caution in his direction, I extended my palms outward, up, and open, displaying the Mag-lite in the brilliant white beams that shot across the road from the front of his car. I paused there for a long moment, continuing this universal signal that I intended no harm. His look changed to one of bewilderment. Maybe the fat boy just wasn't used to being around women.

I continued my approach, forcing a smile that I hoped would reassure the massive man-child. He remained silent and unmoving, looking upward at me from downcast eyes. Beads of sweat ran down his face, his lip trembled. The man had a strong odor about him, the muskiness overpowering the animal stench and acrid metallic burning that wafted between us. The smell wasn't awful; it reminded me of farmhands coming in from the heat of the day for lunch. Unpleasant perhaps, but…

Moving closer, I cocked my head to the side, placing one hand on my hip; an open invitation for conversation. His breathing, more accurately described as wheezing, intensified. After several moments of this it became clear as I reached the front of his smoking vehicle that he had no intention of breaking the ice, so to speak. To business, then. Stepping past him, I turned my gaze to the vehicle. With a quick glance under the hood, I confirmed my suspicions.

"Your radiator is busted."

"What?" He said softly, passively. Perhaps he hadn't heard me.

"I said your radiator is busted. I can smell it. Can't you?" My eyes locked with his as the silence stretched between us. The tension hung around us in thick clouds, rivaled only by his strong body odor. I watched as his lower lip twitched unconsciously, his eyes dilating. I told myself that I shouldn't embarrass him further. He clearly had no clue what was going on.

"See that fluid there?" I asked, indicating with the flashlight's beam a large puddle that had formed on top of the engine block. "You can tell its coolant cause it's kinda yellow and smells like bad chemicals." I flashed the light around, showing him the trail stretching back down the country asphalt. "Prolly burst a half mile back or so, and then it just gave out on you. Pistons might be welded shut by now." I turned to face him, hoping to entice further conversation on his part.

"Do you have water?" He asked slowly, in halting tones. "I remember my Dad using water once on summer vacation to get us to the repair shop." A brief smile crossed his face, the first sign of hope he had had in some time, I supposed. He truly had no clue; my heart hurt for him. I did my best to let the fat fool down easy.

"Sorry, it's toast. Look down here." I pointed the beam on the radiator itself, indicating several large gashes in the lines. Fluid still gurgled from numerous holes as the tangled mess of tubing emptied its steaming contents upon the ground. "It's not going to hold any fluid." The face opposite mine pinched with frustration, the lower lip drawn into his mouth as he bit down upon it. I could see my effort hadn't been soft enough, the man was crestfallen. "No worries, my friend. I'll get you over to Al at the service station. He might be able to help you out, and he's a lot closer than anyone out on the interstate." I extended my right hand. "My name is Nevaeh."

"Lloyd," he replied softly, his doughy, sweaty hand engulfing my own. As we touched, I felt a tingle run down my spine, causing me to shiver. I'd only ever been intimate with one man, yet I felt deeply aroused by the simple act of shaking hands with this stranger. Electric, primal, sexual energy radiating from skin to skin contact with a member of the opposite sex. It was thrilling, yet terrifying. We pulled away from each other, shocked. I wondered if he had felt the same.

"Come on, Lloyd, " I said, a slight tremolo my words. Perhaps he didn't notice I was short of breath. Turning quickly from the bewildered man so he didn't see my flushing face, I started back towards my truck.

...

She's beautiful, I thought, and way better looking than a fat, incestuous hillbilly. Nevaeh had shocked me when she dropped herself out of the pickup on the side of the road, her lithe frame unable to reach the ground from the truck's high bench seat. The woman had approached through the dark night in halting steps, and I had been unsure at first of the sex of my benefactor. It was only when she stepped fully into the car's headlights that I had realized a woman had stopped to aid me. She had stunned me into silence, not that I had ever had much courage when it came to speaking with women. Now that we sat side by side in the cab, I took the time to look over her more closely.

She was too thin in a malnourished, supermodel way. Her hair was cropped short but in a fashionable style, all blonde locks swooping to one side. Tits were nonexistent, her body straight and narrow. Nevaeh was a stick person come to life; one solid line from head to groin broken up only by appendages. Though my fantasies and subsequent masturbaory material had been

89

comprised of the more socially acceptable images of tanned, big breasted women, I found her oddly appealing.

It was the vulnerability in her, I think, that made her so attractive. Like a rare and delicate flower, it seemed like a stiff breeze could blow her across the cornfields, her limbs falling from each other like plucked petals. As I watched Nevaeh drive, it was impossible not to notice blossoming bruises up and down her arms, their telltale pinprick centers screaming drug habit. An extensive one. She looked like someone who needed protecting, and the thought of smothering her in a bear hug was as comforting as it was erotic.

The delicate nature I detected while gazing upon her did not apply to the way she operated the truck, however. Nevaeh seemed at ease flying down the dark and twisting road at top speed, her attitude at barreling through the darkness at a breakneck pace both carefree and familiar. We jostled about in the cab together, sliding back and forth across the bench seat in sync with the rural curves. I did my best not to crowd her... I've had more than enough experience with others being terrified at my bulk. Most women turned up their noses, a few would smile, barely concealing their distaste at my appearance. But she seemed not to mind. Was she enjoying my company?

One large hill launched me in Nevaeh's direction, and though I grabbed desperately at the door, my momentum was too strong to halt. As I bumped into her right hand I expected her to pull away as if burned; to shriek, or worse. Instead, the tiny woman reached out and braced my hulking body with her dainty arm, preventing me from sliding further. Horrified she was pushing me away, I tried to pivot to my right, only to find her grip relaxing but not removing itself from my body. Looking down I watched as her delicate hand rested upon my rotund thigh for several seconds, moving back only to change gears. I felt my face flush, a smile accompanied the color.

"How far off is Al's?" I stammered.

"Not far," she replied, turning to flash me a brilliant white grin before returning her eyes to the road. "He's got a wrecker and can sort you out in a jiffy."

"That's good." I was relieved. Hopefully the car wasn't a total loss. Visions of insurance claim papers danced in my mind together with red-inked bank statements, and the struggle to pay for this unexpected accident occupied my thoughts. I brooded for too long, I realized with alarm. She was waiting for me to speak again, but my voice choked deep in my throat. Silence dominated for several moments, the tension mounting. I needed to keep the conversation going.

"You sure do drive this truck well." What a stupid fucking thing to say.

"Thanks," she said with another smile. "My Daddy taught me how. Always said it was good that every woman know how to really handle a stick." I winced at the sexual innuendo of the joke, hoping the twelve year old thoughts within didn't register on my face, much less the sudden vision I had of her hands wrapped around... I shook the pornographic images from my mind, instead trying to read her face. Nevaeh never batted an eye. The awkwardness of her statement seemed lost on her.

"I wish my Dad had taught me a few more things," I said under my breath, the words surprising me.

"I'm sorry he's gone," she said, tone softening as she picked up the subtext of the conversation. "Mine too. Was always there to teach me the important things in life. Hard to keep going without a strong man there to guide you."

I grunted noncommittally. There would be several days of conversation like this when I got home. As much as I wanted to continue the small talk, I didn't need to broach the subject now. Staring ahead, the faint glow of lights became visible on the right. The first sign of civilization... outside of Nevaeh of course.

"Am I making you nervous?" She asked out of the blue.

Yes. "No, of course not." Real smooth, you idiot. I turned to see her smile again, though her eyes never left the winding country road.

"It's okay if you do. I feel a little nervous myself," she confessed, before turning from me suddenly. It seemed her words had slipped out unintended...

I know the feeling.

She flushed, perhaps, though it was hard to see in the poorly illuminated cab. "Daddy always said being nervous was good. It means they like you." I felt heat upon my face at her words, and I turned to look out the window rather than provoking another chance meeting with her eyes.

The old truck was coming up on the station quickly. What had once seemed like a beacon of hope from a great distance turned out to be a shady looking service station. The interior of the main building was dark, its structure casting long shadows in the moonlight. Three out of four pumps were nominally lit by soft glowing fluorescent lights, illuminating the equipment under the awning in a dingy yellow glow. A garage was attached to the side, a single point of illumination visible through small windows in the rolling steel doors. It looked abandoned.

The Chevy never slowed, and station was gone in the blink of an eye. But not before I caught a glimpse of someone moving inside the garage. A face looked out through one of the small garage door windows, the person attracted by the headlights and roar of an oncoming engine. I noticed the visage look curiously at the truck as it rumbled by. Then that small piece of human existence was gone, replaced by quickly moving trees and farmland.

"Hey, wasn't that Al's?"

"Yeah." The silence stretched as I waited for her to continue. She didn't.

"Why didn't you stop?"

"I didn't realize how late it was," Nevaeh replied with a quick glance at the green digital clock display upon the dashboard. "Al's long gone by now."

"But I saw someone." The words tumbled from my mouth unbidden. I hesitated to disagree with Nevaeh, my anxiety levels rising once more.

"There's another station out where the highway meets the interstate," she continued, ignoring me. "It's open twenty-four hours. Just a bit farther." I relaxed back into the seat, confused. I had seen someone, I was positive. And didn't she say the main route to the interstate was in the other direction? I replayed the scene in my mind, trying to decide if it had been a person's face or just a stress induced imagination.

"Do you like sex?" The question took me by surprise.

I found myself mumbling with no clear answer. "What?"

"I said," she began, turning to stare at me. "Do you like sex?"

"Why are you asking me this?" Was I being propositioned? Or was this some poor, self-indulgent attempt at small talk?

"Everyone likes having sex." Her head tilted slightly, blonde bangs falling across her eyes, casting lined shadows upon her face. "I know I want it so bad all the time." Nevaeh began to squirm slightly in the driver's seat, her body writhing in response to her own words. "And it's been so long. Why wouldn't you?"

"I mean... I..."

"You've never done It before, have you?" She paused, emphasizing the object of the phrase. Her tone became one of schoolyard mocking. I recoiled at this thought; maybe she wasn't a delicate flower, but instead more like a venus fly trap. Nevaeh had lured me in with beautiful colors, but now her jaws would snap shut as she drank me dry.

"I'll teach you. It's not hard." She tittered, as if just realizing the unintentional double entendre. "You just need to lay back." Her right hand roved from the stick shift and began caressing my thigh, then moving inward, towards my groin. Part of me wanted her, and I felt my body respond to the stimulation. Then I looked up to her face as Nevaeh turned from the road towards me. Her eyes sparkled, pupils dilated. She stared through my body, and I could see the hunger in her eyes. Lust and desire in extremis. She wanted to eat me alive.

"No!" I exclaimed, pushing away her advancing hand. Without warning, I jerked forward as she slammed on the brakes in reply, my throat catching on the belt which caused me to gag. I turned to see Nevaeh staring at me, her face contorted by rage.

"You don't get to say no," she threatened. "They can't say no."

In a blind panic, I released the buckle and began grabbing at the door handle. Before I could pull the door open, something bit my thigh. An insect sting. Turning back, I saw the hypodermic, it's plunger already depressed, sticking out of my thigh. I felt woozy, and the world began to spin.

"I never got to say no," Nevaeh whispered softly to no one as my whole world rippled and went black.

...

The cool wind swept across the bare ground then over me, causing me to shiver. It explored my body with vigor, like an excited and over eager lover. My nude form responded; I felt goose flesh ripple up my arms and down my legs. Nipples became fully erect, partially excited by the frigid sensation yet also by the anticipation of the pending act. My sex, too, responded to both stimuli. It felt euphoric where the chill outside collided with the internal heat I produced. But not too much, I thought. Part of me wanted to succumb to the uniqueness of the moment, yet I knew doing so would be a waste. There were things to do, greater sensations to come than the cold, roving hands of night. Slowly, I pulled the barn door closed, locking out the autumnal breeze. Latching it, I turned back to the body sprawled across the table.

Lloyd was nude too, because it was necessary. Fat spilled all around and off of the table, but I didn't necessarily find the view unpleasant. Indeed, he added a softness to the harsh metal table upon which he lay; like a plush adipose duvet spread upon an uncomfortable bed. The cold affected him as well, muscles trembled slightly under shriveled skin, and his pretty pink nipples were taut atop large fleshy breasts. His almond colored orbs were still hidden behind eyelids, however, the drug keeping Lloyd asleep. Slowly, I sauntered over to him, quivering in excitement more so than the cold that had creeped in. I took pleasure in the strut, swaying in the most appealing way though I had no audience other than myself. I became more aroused with each silky, hip swaying step. It is finally my turn, I thought. This time I would be in control.

I climbed atop the bulk, straddling his bloated middle. Our skin touched, and where we connected I felt fire dance across my body. The longing became deeper, the urges harder to resist. Slowly I started rocking against him, into him. The power, the need, caused everything to burn. It had been so long since I had sated this lustful human urge, felt the tantalizing taste of flesh on flesh. But I was not reaching the higher levels of ecstasy. There was a roadblock, something wrong with the situation.

Lloyd has to be awake, I realized. That is the way this is done. It's not fair to me if he sleeps through it. We must experience these sensations together, otherwise the act is cheap... it becomes something other than proper lovemaking. Bending at the waist, I pressed my tingling body against his cool chest and started nibbling and sucking his hairless, pert nipples in succession, never ceasing the grinding of our one flesh. The warmth, the arousal, the pain... one of these would wake Lloyd up. It had always worked on me. I worked harder, gyrated faster as I saw his eyes flutter. My insides hummed in response, eagerly anticipating him waking.

No time for sleeping, I heard my father say inside my head. Time for all good girls to wake up.

...

The world was foggy, shrouded in patches of darkness... I felt cold yet also warm. Wet. Sticky. A voice screamed deep within my mind, but I couldn't understand the words. It was impossible to heed the frantic warning. That must be what it was trying to communicate. The voice was loud, its intention clear but the message unintelligible. Something dangerous, deadly even. I struggled for clarity, to find something to focus upon. Slowly my eyes opened to discover a world of color and noise invading my senses... too loud, too bright, too much. I cringed as the sensations overpowered me. As the pain caused by them lessened, I took stock of my surroundings.

The air was cold, the room drafty. Everything smelled of damp hay and sweat. I could see old wooden rafters above me, hanging like the desiccated bones of a creature that had been ravaged by time. They creaked in the strong wind, rattling in defiance to the elements that gradually rotted them away. I must be laid out on my back then, to have this view. My muscles felt softer, more useless than normal. With trepidation I tried to wiggle, flex, twitch a toe or finger. Nothing responded to my commands. I was helpless, unable to move. I tried to speak but the words wouldn't form correctly, my tongue feeling thick and heavy inside a cotton mouth. Then a blur of movement caught my eye.

Nevaeh straddled me, her hips grinding against my pelvis. She seemed eager in her arousal, the rapid and shallow breathing causing her diminutive breasts to bounce in time with her serpentine movements. She whipped her head side to side, eyes closed by the intense thrill of the moment. I couldn't help but gaze upon the nude and writhing body, partially from arousal but also at the state of her torn flesh. Scars covered her body; long shallow blade marks streaked across her torso, lumps had formed around broken and badly healed ribs, and there was a large Caesarean scar that had healed into a long, angry red line. These wounds crackled across her like lightning strikes of pain, dividing her naked form in organic patterns. Track marks and fresh brushing from needles provided aesthetic highlights. Nevaeh was a poorly repaired China doll, more glue than porcelain. Living Kintsugi. My heart ached at the sight.

Her eyes opened, brilliant blue flames alight with sexual passion. She wanted me, hungered for me. Again that voice yelled about dangers, but I paid it no mind. This moment was all that mattered, this searching to satisfy a primal hunger. I hadn't been in this situation before, the stakes felt too high. This was better than any fantasy had ever been. Though mostly numb I began to succumb to the moment. No woman had ever desired me like she did now. The sensation was too good, to be overcome by passion. I felt myself begin to swell, grow hard in response to the desire in her eyes.

Nevaeh screamed. I saw her staring down at our combined sexes, unable to see their pleasurable joining over my own girth. She screamed a second time, and my sluggish mind registered that the cries were not ones of passion, but instead of horror and anger. Her left hand groped for an object out of my line of sight, and my head wouldn't turn to look no matter how hard I tried. Her arm became blur of motion that was impossible to track. I felt a pinch, then a pouring of warmth between and around my thighs. She then held up two objects before me in grotesque display. In one hand a bloody knife, and in the other she held valuable flesh. Nevaeh's face burned with hatred, holding them before me in accusation.

"This isn't your first time!" She screamed, spittle flying from her rouged and engorged lips. She shook my still hard member in anger, blood from it running freely across my prone body. It seemed to soften in her tight grip, hardened muscles deflating like an adult themed party balloon losing air. "It's my turn now. Mine!" Without a care, she tossed that part of me aside; a voice within screamed in agony and horror but I couldn't feel those emotions. I didn't need to be a part of that pain. The knife went back down out of view, blade downward. I felt something enter inside me as she thrust her hips with great force, moaning lustily as she did so. Nevaeh's face relaxed in an instant, eyes closing as the euphoria returned. I felt tearing deep inside, a rumbling and flowing of innards. She shoved herself inside me again and again as my body convulsed in a pain I did not feel.

"Don't worry about the blood," she reassured me, her voice tranquil now, husky with lust and desire. "That always happens at first. Relax. The pain will end. Soon it will feel oh so good." Her pace increased as she rammed harder and deeper, breathing quickened once more. Nevaeh began to writhe again, crying out in ecstasy as she bucked between my legs. The world felt cold, as everything grew dark.

I'm sorry, I thought, though I wasn't sure why. I'm so sorry. Deep inside, I wanted to tell this woman before me that she was indeed beautiful, that Nevaeh didn't need to feel the way she did about herself. No woman did. But the words wouldn't form, and it seemed there was no time.

The voice inside whimpered, spoke of dying. I didn't care so much, not really. But the horror before me, the death mask behind which so much pain was buried... it terrified me. Nevaeh's body began to quake in preparation of the oncoming orgasm, but it was la petite morte I wasn't destined to see. She screamed but no sound came out as the whole world went dark.

...

I felt my body shudder over and over as sticky-hot wetness poured across my hands. This is why he had done this to me all those years. The feeling of being on top, being in control. It was a high so intoxicating I never wanted to come down. I came again, then a third time, quaking as I continued to thrust deep within that warm, serene place. I never wanted to leave; it felt so damn good.

After an eternity, my quivering thighs finally rested, and I felt myself gasping for air, on the edge of losing consciousness. It took every ounce of effort not to pass out from the exertion. Was he alright? Looking up, I saw Lloyd's glossy eyes staring back at me. He was exhausted from the fucking; I knew just how he felt. He had done well for his first time and should be proud of what a good girl he had been. With delicate care, I pulled myself out of him. Both our thighs were covered in blood and excretions; signs of an enjoyable evening, I was always told. I looked down on the knife that was coated in sticky fluids, our orgasms combined with his bloodletting. A lot of blood. Such a sweet little lady. I climbed further upon his hairless, motionless chest, bringing the dripping, sticky thing to his lips.

"Good girls always kiss it after, Daddy used to say." I rubbed my member across his mouth, feeling the smile grow on my own face. The experience was different from this angle; again the power surged through me, holding myself over his exhausted face. His lips were wet… they had been painted bright red. He must have done it for me, to impress me for our first time together. How beautiful.

"What a big girl you are. Give Daddy a kiss." Our lips touched, and I slid my tongue between his teeth, ever so slightly. Need to give them something to remember you by, he used to say. The lipstick was warm and tasted coppery. Finished with the ritual, I climbed off of the table and began to get dressed. As I turned the light out and pulled the barn door closed, I couldn't help but daydream about next time. It would happen soon, of that I was sure.

Peckerwood
S. Bendix

"Jump, Peckerwood! JUMP!"

Now, typically I don't just off and do what anyone tells me, but those assholes sitting at the bottom of the quarry were in need of a good shutting up. So I jumped. As I rocketed down the 40 or so foot drop, I tucked my knees into my chest, forming a cannonball, so's when I hit the water, they'd feel it. They felt it, alright. Old Spag the Fag was just about soaked through to the bone. Spag didn't like that much, but it was worth it to see the stupid look on his face.

"Nice one, Peckerwood," Dickie laughed. But Dickie was laughing at me, not with me, though I highly doubt Dickie could explain to you why it was funny. Dickie was dumb as the day was long and he didn't like me. None of those assholes liked me. The only person who liked me was Zeph, and he was standing at the top of the quarry right where I left him. I bet Zeph was wishing we had never come out here to hunt squirrels right about now.

I got out of the water and Spag reared back to hit me but Amber stepped between us. I guess what I said about none of those assholes liking me wasn't entirely accurate – Amber liked me. Though, honestly, that girl gave me such mixed signals that to say I understood her mind would have been a gross exaggeration.

"Billy, don't," Amber pleaded Spag. Billy was Spag's real name – Billy Spagnuolo. But everyone called him Spag. I called him Spag the Fag but never to his face. I'm smarter than that, as a general rule. As to the subject of nicknames, the assholes at school gave me the nickname Peckerwood on account of my dick being all knotted up like the root of a tree, or some of that ginseng stuff that comes in a jar. This unfortunate detail was revealed back in Junior High when we started having to take showers after P.E. The name stuck, but it had stopped bothering me a while back. There were worse things in life than cruel nicknames.

I kinda had a thing for Amber – she was extremely fine and you'd be dumb not to – but she was currently taking up space as Spag's cum dumpster, so I lost a little respect for her. A lot, actually. But she was still nice to me in the school halls, at least on the days I bothered to show up. Showing up for high school's not a big draw when everyone calls you by the name of Peckerwood and not the name you were born with, Jed Reilly being mine. But, like I said, it didn't bother me so much anymore.

Aw hell, who am I kidding, it bugged the shit out of me.

Spag backed off on account of Amber and I climbed back up the rocks in my wet clothes. The sneakers were the worst. By the time I reached the top of the quarry I had blisters on both feet, squishing and rubbing up against the rotten insides of my Chuck Taylors. But if I wanted any sympathy, I wasn't gonna get it from my old pal Zeph.

"That was really stupid, Jed."

Zeph was right so I didn't argue with him. That's one of my better qualities – I know when I'm being a dumbass. So, I shut the fuck up and we finished out our squirrel hunt. We didn't catch any squirrels. When we got to the fork in the path that would lead Zeph home, I said he should take it because I was gonna stop at the 7-11 and get a Monster Energy. Zeph offered to come with me and I said "naw, go on home, I'll catch up with you later."

Zeph nodded and went on home, and I went to the 7-11 to get the shit kicked out of me.

I knew Spag and those guys would be waiting in the parking lot for me when I arrived and I wanted to spare Zeph from getting beat by association. Amber was suspiciously absent from the passenger seat of Spag's junky pick-up as he had likely dropped her off at home so he'd be free to beat me down without her getting in the way. Didn't matter to me – I was just happy to get it over with.

When I got home to the trailer, Pop was finishing up his third beer and his first joint. He saw my beat-up face and asked me where I got it, and I gave him the shortened version of the story without naming names. I left out the names 'cuz I didn't want Pop and his biker buddies fighting my fights for me. And 'cuz I knew that, secretly, Pop respected me for not squealing. He'd been inside a few times – petty theft, drugs, nothing major – and he had a little bit of the convict code about him. It never bothered me that my Pop had been to prison. He was tough and fair and had always been good to me. I figured I'd probably go to prison one day myself.

He rolled a fresh joint saying it would help with my pain, but in truth I think he just wanted someone to get high with. I cracked a Miller Genuine Draft and sat down in the couch next to his recliner and he passed me the joint.

"Hear from Mom?" I asked after taking a hit.

"Nope." He held out a hand and I passed him the joint, finger to finger. "I don't reckon we ever will, son."

"I know." We'd been down this road – it was just something we did – but I had to ask. My mom left over a year ago and there hadn't been a peep from her since. She had gotten into hard drugs – meth and crack mostly – and that was the sort of shit Pop didn't fuck around with. He'd seen too many of his buddies backslide into that shit and Pop had a better head on his shoulders than they did. In the grand scheme of things, he may not have had his shit together, but in that way he did. But my mom was another matter. "Free spirit," Pop called her.

He called her a lot of other things, mostly when drunk – "goddamn witch," for one. She had run off with one of her dealers, so he was entitled to that opinion, I figured. My feelings were a little more complicated.

Didn't matter. God only knew where she was. Probably in prison. Or dead.

We watched some shitty TV – shows where people hoarded junk and tried to get off drugs. Pop fell asleep in his recliner and I listened to him snore for a while. I rolled another joint from his stash and took it with me to bed and got high listening to my iPod. Then I crashed.

A few days later Zeph and I were in the old Langford Mall site throwing rocks at pieces of glass when he elbowed me in the ribs. I looked across the lot and saw Amber walking over through the crumbled cement piles and rusted barrels. Her hair was wavy and wet, like she had just gotten out of the shower.

"Watcha doing?" she asked. Jesus, Amber, what'd it look like?

"Nothin'," Zeph answered. I threw another rock, wishing I'd come alone.

Amber came over and sat on a big chunk of concrete that had a stick of rebar jutting out of it. It sat between her dangling bare legs like a rusty, corrugated cock. I found myself jealous of that rebar. "Hey, Jed, I'm real sorry about what happened the other day. With Billy."

"No biggie," I said and threw another rock. But the goose egg over my eye told another story. "Your boyfriend don't scare me."

"Yeah, well, maybe he should." She kicked at some stones with her boots. "He can be a real psycho. One day he might really hurt you if you keep fucking with him."

"If he's such a psycho, why you with him?" Zeph asked. He had a knack for asking the questions I wouldn't. It might be why people liked Zeph more than me as a general rule. He had a way of making people feel that he cared about them.

"I dunno," Amber answered, eyes on the ground. "I'm a girl. We like bad boys."

"Billy Spagnuolo's not a 'bad boy', he's a moron," I said, landing a rock with a smash. "Christ, Amber, there's a difference."

"Yeah, well, I ain't gettin' any other offers, so..."

I'm not gonna lie – I had the hots for Amber real bad right then. Yeah, she was a skank and, yeah, that made me not respect her. But, man, she was fine. Tanned legs, full lips, just the right amount of freckles. I jerked off with her in my head nearly every day, sometimes more than once. But I was not gonna let her know that I liked her because... well, I don't really know why. Because if I did, then she'd have power over me. I think that was the reason.

I think Zeph might've had a thing for Amber too, but he was too chickenshit to do anything about it. If he did, she might have gone for it, 'cuz Zeph was a pretty decent looking dude, all the girls thought so. I was okay looking too, but I kinda dressed shitty and looked like a creep. It was part of my "mystique," I liked to say. It was also 'cuz I had jackshit for money; but mystique sounded cooler, as if looking like a loser hoodlum was some kind of act. You gotta get your coolness points where you can in this world.

Amber left and we didn't see her around for the rest of the day. Zeph and I stole some forties from 7-11 and got drunk in the woods out by Old Tub Ryerson's lot. After Zeph stumbled off home, I hung around the woods a while. Thinking of Amber and those tanned legs got me all worked up and horny. Fuck it, there was no one out here. I decided to jerk off.

The good thing about having a weird knotty cock is that you can really get a grip on it. Not that I would know what other dudes' cocks feel like. Though the subject of school yard ridicule, my cock is a decent size and I imagine there are plenty of women who would enjoy riding it. Amber, maybe, or one of her other skanky friends. Lot of pleasure to be had on that twisted root for a pussy willing to give it a go. I thought of Amber taking my cock into her pink, pillowy lips, pushing its knottiness deep into her throat. I thought of fucking her, first from the front then from behind. I could feel hot wetness as I sunk my cock deep into her, feel the tight flesh of her ass hugging me as I pounded her. In my mind, my cock grew in her body, branching out like a tree, filling her like no cock ever could, making her scream, "Oh Jed, oh Jed, baby, fuck me harder Jed, fuck me hard oh yes Jed fuck me, cum inside me Jed, cum inside…"

Shooting jizz is just about the best feeling in the world, but I'm hardly the first dude to make note of that. I really let it rip, spraying seed all over, careless as to where it went. Once the itch was scratched I stood there a moment and let the cool air ease my knotty root back into a state of softness. I had just tucked the gnarly thing back into my jeans when something rustling in the sperm-frosted brush made me jump.

Down on the ground, tangled in the brush was a dead bird. I know the bird was dead because I could see the bones in its body sticking out and its stomach was half gone, probably eaten by a stray cat. But the thing was, this dead bird was moving, flapping around like it was gonna fly away to dead bird heaven or something. Somehow, it struggled to its little birdy feet and looked up at me, and I could see that a big wad of jizz had gotten shot right into the bird's chewed-out eye socket. It tried to chirp but all that came out was this sad little gasp, like the last of the Dust-off when you get done huffing the can.

The thing jumped up and started flapping, its ragged wings catching some air, and it tried to peck at my eyes. I smacked it back down with the flat of my palm, and when it hit the ground scrabbling I pinned one of its rotten wings down with my bare foot. Nearby was a nice rock the size of a baseball, so without taking my foot off the bird I got the rock and crushed the zombie-thing's skull with it. It crunched like a mouthful of stale popcorn. Then I slammed the rock down again several times, making sure the dead stayed dead.

Needless to say, I didn't mention it to Pops when I got home that night. But the bird haunted my dreams, all ratty and flapping, and when I woke my dick was hard and stiff as a steak knife. I jerked off again just to relieve myself, careful not to get cum on any dead things, then went to the kitchen to see if there was any food. There wasn't, and Pops was gone for the day, leaving me broke. It dawned on me that I might weasel a free meal at school from one of the soft-hearted lunch ladies. I didn't like going to school, and it wasn't like Pop gave a shit if I went or not. But maybe I'd run into Amber or something, see if she wanted to hang out. Crazier things had happened.

I skirted the parking lot to avoid Spag and another beating, coming up to the entrance by the gym. When I got there, my eyes nearly dropped outta my skull. There in the grubby doorway, a couple of kids were making out, the guy with his hand all the way up the girl's jean-skirt. After my brain processed the shock, I realized it was Zeph and Amber, going at it like a pair of pigs in heat. Guess he had grown some balls after all. If I waited around much longer, I might see Amber popping them into her mouth.

If they saw me or not, I couldn't say. I turned tail and hoofed it out of there, free meal be damned. I wasn't hungry anymore anyway. What I was was mad, even if I had no right to be. I felt betrayed by Zeph, even though I never admitted that I liked Amber. But a guy should know when his best friend is hung up on a chick and can't admit it to himself.

When I walked in the door of the trailer, Pop was there at the kitchenette table, pulling on a Genuine Draft.

"What's going on, Jed?" he asked, reading my face. "Something the matter?"

"No more than usual," I lied.

I grabbed a beer from the fridge and sat down at the kitchen table, so small that our feet practically touched. We sat there a moment, not talking, and I tried to push my angry thoughts about Zeph and Amber out of my mind. But when I did, the image of that crazy bird came flapping in to fill the void, all dead and crusty from my jizz. If there was something about me, some power I was born with, there was only one person around who might know what is was. And he was sitting right there across from me.

"Look," I said. "You gotta be straight with me, as crazy as it all might sound."

Pop reached into the pocket of his flannel shirt, pulled out a pack of smokes. He tapped out two and offered me one. I took it, and he lit up. "Shoot."

I lit too and dragged deep. "Was Mom a witch? Like a real, honest-to-god witch?"

Pop looked at me, and for a moment I swore I saw fear hiding behind the redness of his eyes. He swigged his beer, followed with a drag from his smoke and tapped out the ash. "Son, the truth is that I never fully understood what your mom was... is, I mean.

"Some people have a greater connection to this world. It's like they can talk to the earth, the trees. Your mother had this gift. Her father had it. You might have it for all I know. You come from a long line of freaky wiccan-types and I have never totally understood it. But I'd be lying if I said it didn't attract me to your mother in the first place. In the beginning, it was almost as if it drew me to her.

"But over the years, it got sour. The magic." He took another drag of his cig, and the air hung as thick with regret as it did with smoke. "She was frustrated with the world and her place in it. Wanted more. I didn't help much, I'm afraid. Never had much use for money or stuff. Or the kind of things that tend to make a woman happy. When you find yourself the right girl, you do everything you can to make her happy. Promise me that."

I was not in the mood to go making promises. "Pop, where's this going?"

He gave me a smirk and went on. "The point is that with people who have the sort of power your mom had, when they go bad, it goes right to the roots. Everything is poisoned by it. And the truth of the matter is that she became dangerous. Not just to me, but to you too. And I couldn't have that."

"Are you telling me you did something to her?"

Pop blanched, shocked that I would even ask him that. "What? No. Of course not. But it was me who sent her away. And I told her never to contact me again. Or you. And so far, she's been true to her word."

We sat there a while as I gave this some thought. Truth was, something about it didn't sit right with me. Now, my mom was selfish, don't get me wrong. But she did love me and I didn't believe for a second that she would ever intentionally hurt me. She was a trainwreck, no doubt about it, but I couldn't believe she'd go this long without even once trying to contact me. Hell, she knew all of my hangouts – if she wanted to avoid Pop, she could find me real easy without running into him. There was something about this that just didn't wash.

But, whatever the truth, Pop was sticking to his story. I didn't see the point of pressing him any further, so I thanked him for sharing and made up some excuse to leave. Pop could tell that I was troubled by the whole deal but he was always good about giving me my space. If there was one thing we were solid on, it was giving each other space.

Not wanting to show my face around town, I hoofed it to the woods out behind the trailer park. It was a place I had played a lot in as a kid, but since I had grown up my hangouts had moved elsewhere – parking lots, rundown buildings, rock quarries and, on the very rare occasion, school. Mostly in the pursuit of pussy, and there wasn't a whole lot of pussy hanging out in the creepy old woods.

My memory of the place came flooding back as I walked along the scrubby trails. The area was smaller than I recalled, really only a mile or two in total, but back when I was a kid it seemed like a kingdom. Now it just seemed like a sad patch of forest well suited for meth-heads and maybe the random serial killer. When I was a kid, the scary part was imagining a ghost or a monster somewhere out here, lurking among the trees, ready to pop out. Now the only thing I worried about popping out was some junkie with a switchblade.

I came to a clearing and was immediately struck by something odd. First of all, there were rocks bordering it in a circle, and it was clear that they had been placed that way by hand rather than occurring in a natural formation. The ground itself was mostly hard dirt but, in the center, it seemed that the dirt had been disturbed, dug up, then redistributed and packed down as neatly as the digger could manage. The area of disturbed ground was just the right size to conceal a body underneath.

Odder still than all of this, in the center of the re-packed area, a small root had sprung up from the ground, sprouting a few scant leaves. As if someone had planted it there.

I walked over to the root and bent down on my haunches, touching it with an outstretched hand. I felt a tingle, like a live electrical wire, and pulled my hand back, fearing it was toxic – poison oak or some shit. But something about it called to me, willing me to touch it again. So I did. This time the electricity traveled all the way from my finger to my groin.

A heat rose deep within me, blotting out the logic center of my brain. I was being willed to act by something greater than myself, and I was powerless to do anything against it. I was also really, really horny.

I stood, my cock already so stiff in my jeans that I had trouble standing upright. Reaching for it, I felt it throbbing with heat, like it was full of fire. So I unzipped my fly and started to pull. At first the usual imagery came to me – Amber, looking at me, legs spread, her finger rubbing exposed panties, making them wet. But as I got close to cumming Amber's face changed into someone older, more familiar but gone these long months. I tried to push the image away but it was too late, so I pushed my cock downward and came in a hot spasm.

I looked down at the ground, to the strange jutting root. Jizz dripped from the tiny leaves, glistening like diamonds in a wad of snot. I tucked my dick back into my jeans and went home.

When I got there, Zeph was sitting in one of the lawn chairs we kept in front of the trailer. Pop had given him a beer and then taken off in his tow truck. I wasn't in the mood to see Zeph, but he had seen me, so there was no point in trying to sneak off. I went over to the lawn chair next to him and sat down.

"What up?"

"Heard you actually went to school the other day."

"Yeah," I answered. "That was a mistake."

Zeph took a swig of his beer. "Is this about me and Amber?"

Man, I wished I had a beer too, but getting one would just be inviting Zeph to stay longer. "I got bigger problems at school than you and Amber."

"Good, because I really like her, you know."

"That's great Zeph. I'm real happy for you."

You didn't have to know me as well as Zeph to read the sarcasm in my voice. "C'mon man, don't be that way."

Truth was, I was mad as hell at Zeph – I was mad at everyone. Zeph. My pop. Amber. Spag. But most of all I was mad at my mom for leaving me. Being mad at things wasn't exactly a new thing for me, but what was really boiling my blood was that there wasn't anything I could do about any of it. All I could do was sit here and eat all the shit that was shoveled into my mouth.

I felt so goddamn... impotent. That was the word, wasn't it?

Then it hit me like a drunk driver. I could do something about it. If what my pop said about my mom was true, then she was some sort of witch. And it would seem that, as her son, I had inherited some weird version of her power. My demon seed could possibly be used to my advantage – provided the things I brought back from the dead could be bent to my will. Some dark place inside of me told me that they could. All it would take is a little practice.

"Well, look," Zeph said, finishing his beer. "Some of us are heading out to the fire spot tonight to hang out and do a little drinking. I'd really love it if you'd come hang, man. Amber would too. And who knows, maybe there'll be some chicks who are DTF."

Any chick that was Down To Fuck me better not have had an abortion recently. Who knew how dead baby parts would react to my devil jizz. Not that it mattered. I wouldn't be fucking anyone tonight. No one alive, anyway. "Is Spag going to be there?" I asked.

Zeph shrugged. "He usually is."

It dawned on me that this really could be a good time – just not in the way Zeph was hoping it would be. This could be a good time to show these dirtbag fuckers that I wasn't some piece of shit redneck they could kick around at their leisure. That I was a force to be reckoned with and to fuck with me meant one thing and one thing only – death.

"Sure man, I'll be there."

Zeph smiled.

After he left, I went back in the woods to do a little practicing. It wasn't hard to find a dead field mouse, and even less difficult to muster up a hard-on. Just knowing what I was about to attempt made me horny, as if my rage could summon up the demon seed at will. In my head, I pictured Zeph and Amber fucking, and less than a minute later I was raining hot sperm down on the half-rotten animal. A few seconds later, it started twitching.

Despite my natural revulsion, I crouched and held out my hand to the zombie mouse, willing it into my palm. It looked at me with its white, rotted-out eyes and scampered right into my hand. Then it stood there, motionless, awaiting my command.

"Bite me," I said. It occurred to me that asking a zombified creature to bite me might be inviting zombification upon myself – that would be the way it played out in a movie, at least. But this wasn't a movie, and these things, whatever they were, were not zombies. At least not in the Walking Dead, 28 Days Later sense of the word. These things were agents of my will, not mindless, shambling monsters. They were the instruments of my hatred and rage.

The mouse stared up at me, as if questioning my intent. "Bite me!" I shouted. The mouse bit. It hurt way more than I expected. I yelped and shook the thing off of me. It scampered off into some brush and I was damned if I was gonna go look for it.

My palm bled but the pain felt good. It worked. I could re-animate dead animal matter and control it with the power of my command. It was going to be one hell of a night down at the old fire spot.

The quarry was surrounded by a mile of shitty woods so I went there good and early to search for the necessary "materials." And did I ever hit the jackpot. There were all sorts of dead things in those woods – it seemed like the go-to place for animals to die. The one that would be my masterpiece I found near a small cluster of caves. I'd save that bad boy for the big finish.

I stayed hidden in the scrubby trees outside the fire spot, waiting for the party to start. As soon as the sun went down, kids started to show up. The spot itself was little more than an ashy pit dug into the ground beyond the quarry pool, sheltered by an overhang of rock. A mainstay teenager hangout for as long as I could remember, a place to drink and smoke away the unmemorable hours. But tonight would be memorable – I'd make shit sure of that. Tonight would live in fucking infamy.

There were only a handful of kids at first, none of whom I knew, and I started to worry that my real targets wouldn't show. But then Dickie arrived, bringing with him a keg, nodoubt bought for him by his older brother. Spag followed soon after, some pizza-faced skank hanging on his arm. Guess he wasn't too broken up about Amber ditching him for Zeph. Or maybe this was all some set-up to lure Zeph here and kick the crap out of him. Didn't matter. Zeph was gonna be the least of Spag's worries tonight.

The sun had gone down and the fire was up when Zeph and Amber arrived. They were greeted loudly by an overly-friendly Spag, who immediately started feeding Zeph cups from the keg. Softening him up for the kill, I figured. There was a part of me that wanted to see my best bud get what was coming to him, but I knew in my heart that was a shitty thing to think. I never really had any claim on Amber, and Zeph liked her just as much as I did and had been a good friend to me when no one else would. But there was something burning in me, a fire that went straight from my brain to my balls, and it cried out for bloody revenge. I didn't want to target Zeph outright, but if he ended up caught in the crossfire, I don't think I'd be able to save him.

Once the party was in full swing I got my first "soldier" ready – a half crushed raccoon I had found on the side of route 91. As luck would have it, Dickie wandered into the woods to take a piss, choosing a spot mere yards away from where I was spanking my meat. He was just about finished when the raccoon twitched and rose, snapping with its tire-mangled jaw.

"Go," I said, pointing at Dickie. The thing scampered off to do as I ordered, and I crept along behind it, wanting to get a good view of the action.

Dickie must have already been real loaded, because he stumbled around in a circle, trying to find his way back to the fire which was blazing bright enough for any idiot to see. My raccoon zombie scurried in the brush, dragging its crushed hindquarters up on to a fallen log that Dickie was about to trip over. When Dickie finally saw the thing, he did a double-take.

"What the fuck," I heard him mutter. The raccoon hissed at him the way raccoons do, and Dickie picked up a loose stick and swatted at it. The raccoon hissed again and clawed at the stick, but didn't seem the slightest bit intimidated. Guess when you've been dead once already, a drunk human swatting at you with a stick is no big deal.

"Jesus," Dickie slurred. "You are one fucked up little dude."

Tired of foreplay, I sent a mental kill-order to the raccoon, like I was playing it in a video game – Sonic the Zombie Hedgehog or some shit. True to my command, the undead creature leapt at Dickie, landing right on his pimply face. How the thing managed it with those fucked-up legs I'll never know, but the raccoon tore out one of Dickie's eyes and bit into it, popping it like a green grape. Dickie screamed and tried to pull the nasty little beast off of him, but the fucker dug in and hung on, taking a big chomp right out of Dickie's nose. Blood spurted everywhere, and I wished that I was closer so as to catch the full color of the red.

Dickie stumbled to the ground and the raccoon bit into his throat, needle-teeth puncturing right into the jugular. It was like a faucet had been opened on the side of his neck, and when Dickie tried to scream again, all that came out was a thick, wet gurgle. A few seconds later, his limbs stopped moving, and he lay there staring stupidly up at tree branches.

"Hey, Dickie!" Spag was calling from the fire spot. "What the fuck are you doing, pulling your pud?"

I smiled from the shadows. Dickie's pud-pulling days were over, but I was just getting started. I left the body there to be munched on by my furry, undead pal.

The next stage of my plan was pretty tasteless, even by my twisted standards. You see, there's no shortage of unwanted animals in a town this shitty, and the quarry with its many pools is a good place to dump, say, a trash bag full of kittens. The one I happened to find hadn't been out here more than a day or so, and the poor little kitties inside managed to claw out their own throats trying to get air into their lungs. Reanimating them was a miserable task on so many levels, but my lust for revenge overrode my queasiness at the sight of those rotting kittens lying in the bottom of a Hefty CinchSak. When I was done, the wormy cluster of fur within started to wriggle and mew.

From behind a large rock, I watched. Most of the girls had already gotten giggly-drunk, except for Amber who seemed to be keeping her wits about her. Spag's skank wouldn't stop laughing, each time ending with a snort like a zit-covered horse braying for its own amusement. I didn't know this chick from Adam, but that laugh alone was enough to warrant her death.

The first of the kittens came crawling out of the brush and immediately drew attention due to its weird, strangled mewing. Horse-skank immediately went into Hello Kitty mode. "Aww," I heard her coo. "Look at the kitties!"

More kittens emerged and other girls moved in, cooing and awwing along with Horse-skank. Amber went to join them, but to her credit picked up on the fact that something was wrong and backed away before getting too close. Horse-skank crouched down.

"Here, kitty kitty." The kitten nearest to her meowed in a tortured rasp, and Horse-skank's eyes widened suddenly as she got a good look at the animal's shredded throat. The cat slashed its claws across the girl's zit-caked nose, sending her stumbling back with a scream.

Taking their lead from the alpha, the other kittens leapt at the girls, clinging to legs and latching on to short-shorts. The place erupted into screaming and the boys sat there watching, all of them wearing stupefied, slack-jawed looks. One or two of them stepped in to help, guys I didn't really know, and the kittens took to them as viciously as they had to the girls. Soon the whole fire spot was an echo chamber of screaming and shouting and it killed me that I had to slink off and see to the glorious final act.

The cave was just a quarter of a mile away, on the other side of a hill that shouldered the quarry. The monstrosity I had stumbled upon earlier was still there waiting for me, rotting among the rocks. Not wanting to waste a second, I whipped out my dick and got to work, but I needn't have worried. I was so high on bloodlust that I shot off quick, a real two-pump chump.

It was a nice big wad. This was gonna be sick.

On my way back to the fire spot, I was so pleased with myself that I didn't notice Spag coming at me out of the woods. He clotheslined me, and I hit the ground hard on my back.

"What the fuck are you doing out here, Peckerwood?!"

Looking up, I could see that Spag's pupils were dilated and crazed. He was on something, acid probably – he was known to score some pretty decent shit from his older brother's friends. Damn, they were all tripping this whole time while my little helpers were attacking. Somehow that made it even better.

"You look a little freaked out, Spag." I said. "Pussy got you down?"

It was a dumb line but I couldn't resist. Anyway, it was better than 'cat got your tongue?'. Spag didn't think it was funny. He hauled me up hard by the lapels of my jean jacket. "You can see them?!" he asked, voice shaking. "I didn't think they were real!"

"Oh, they're real alright. They're real and I made them." I smiled and widened my eyes all crazy and Spag got so freaked out he pushed me away. "And I'm not done yet."

"You!" Spag stumbled back, pupils huge with acid-laced terror. "You're the Devil!"

"Not the Devil, but I've got a little in me." I moved toward him and he started to back away. That was a first. "And you're about to see what Peckerwood can really do."

Peckerwood. That's right, I said it. Owned it. And it felt good.

Spag turned to run but I knew he wouldn't get far. I'd been watching the woods behind him, watching the big black shape coming up fast like a furry freight train. It popped up from behind a fallen tree, rising to its full height of maybe eight feet or more. Black worms wriggled from its rotted-out eye sockets, and when it opened its mouth a grey tongue lolled over a row of gleaming, jagged teeth. Spag screamed as the zombie bear bellowed, its once proud roar a dry, hollow wind.

"This is Boo Boo," I said, my voice cracking with glee. "He eats asshole rednecks."

Boo Boo swatted, taking Spag's head clean off with his claws. It bounced off a tree and tumbled off, lost in the woods. Blood jetted from the stump, flailing arms grasped at nothing, and Spag's headless body fell over. It was over so quick, I was kinda disappointed, truth be told. But then Boo Boo tore Spag's corpse apart, feasting on his intestines, so I took some satisfaction in the carnage. I just wish the dickhead had been alive to feel it, is all.

I could've left things there. I should've left things there, probably. But the rage inside me just wouldn't go away. I wanted more. I wanted them all to pay.

I wanted Zeph and Amber to pay.

At least part of me did. The other part of me, the part of me that was still a decent person, hoped that they'd be gone by the time I reached the fire spot. But Zeph and Amber were still there, cowering together on a rocky ledge as zombie kittens hissed and spat at them from below. It was really quite comical. All of the others were gone, run off into the woods, but I didn't care about them. In my blackened little heart, it was Zeph and Amber that I really wanted.

Amber saw me first. "Jed!" she yelled, full of concern. "Get out of here! Go get help!"

That was sweet – she was looking out for me. Boy, was she in for a surprise. Wanting to be dramatic, I waved my hand like a wizard and the kittens scattered off into the scrub. It was fun seeing both of their jaws dropping at the same time.

Zeph jumped down from the ledge, then helped Amber down. He turned to me and I could tell by his normal, un-dilated pupils that he wasn't tripping, just scared. Too bad. "Jed, what the hell is going on here?"

"It's a party, my friend," I said. "And that makes me the master of ceremonies."

Some wide-eyed ginger – Ricky, I think his name was – came running and screaming out of the woods. I really didn't care about him but I wanted to prove a point so I gestured with my hand and Boo Boo charged out of the darkness, pulverizing Ricky into pulp. It looked as if the dumb-struck ginger had been hit by a Mack Truck doing ninety. A Mack Truck with buzz-saw teeth and jackknife claws.

"There's nowhere in these woods you can run that I can't get you," I warned Zeph and Amber. There was a wet smacking sound as Boo Boo ate his fill of Ricky. I just stood there and smiled like a proud papa.

Zeph stepped toward me but I wagged a finger. "Not too close, stud."

"Jesus, Jed, what is this about?"

"This is about betrayal, Zeph. This is about not being pushed around. Treated like shit."

"I never treated you like shit!" He glanced back to Amber. "She never treated you like shit. We're your friends!"

"Some friends." I glared at Amber coldly. "You stole my girl."

"She was never your girl!"

Shell-shocked, Amber stumbled towards me. "Jed, I'm so sorry, I had no idea." Jed tried to hold her back by the arm but she pulled away, keeping her eyes on me. "Had I known... I mean, I'm with Zeph now, but if you had just asked me –"

"Shut up," I said. "You're just saying that to save your ass."

"No, it's true," Zeph cut in. "This is all on me. I cock-blocked you, big time. And I'm sorry. Just let her go. This is between you and me."

"That's why before I kill you," I said, "you're going to watch her die."

Apparently, that was all Boo Boo needed to hear, because he came into the clearing and barreled straight at Amber. Now, I've never known Zeph to be super courageous or anything, but he stepped right in front of that charging bear, tackling it around its mushy, rotten mid-section. The thing was so decomposed that Zeph's arms sunk into it right up to the elbows. But that didn't stop old Boo Boo from coming down on him, hard.

The bear clawed and tore at Zeph's back, ripping away long strips of flesh. Somehow, Zeph stayed standing, dug in his heels, and pushed the massive beast back; like a linebacker pushing through a defensive end or whatever it was football players did. The bear howled and tore, stripping big bloody chunks off of my old buddy's shoulders. But Zeph kept on pushing, a steam-shovel plowing through a giant, furry pile of death. What was he trying to prove?

Too late, I realized what Zeph was doing – he was pushing the bear, and himself, into the bonfire. "Shit," I said, and picked up a sharp rock. I spent too much good seed on that bear to see Zeph turn it into barbecue. I came up behind him, cradling the rock, ready to smash in his skull...

"Jed, please!"

I don't know why, but I stopped and turned around to Amber, who was full-on crying and begging. A part of me wanted to bash her head in with that rock instead of Zeph, but I couldn't do it. The truth was that the rage inside of me was starting to burn out, and in its place was this empty feeling, a mixture of regret and embarrassment. The same feeling you got when you spent the better part of the day jerking off.

"Please stop this," Amber begged again. "Please, I'll do anything you want. I'll be anything you want. I'll be your girl."

At that moment, I might've been the evilest sonofabitch on the planet, but I was not going to be happy getting Amber under that set of terms. Truth was, I don't even think I cared about Amber anymore. Or about being mad at Zeph, for that matter. I was a person of true power, a god among ants – why did I give a shit about two pieces of white trash in love? I ough to go off somewhere and be a real rock star, an evil wizard like Aleister Crowley or a cult leader like Charles Manson or something. Why was I wasting my time on this bullshit?

"Fine," I sighed, turning back to Zeph and my murder-bear. "Boo Boo... down!"

But Boo Boo didn't go down. Guess I didn't have as much control over these zombies as I thought. I yelled the order again but the bear just shook Zeph's head in its mouth and clamped its paws over his ears, boxing them. I expected Zeph's head to pop right off, but the kid got a final burst of energy and pushed himself and the bear the last few feet into the fire. Unfortunately for Zeph, the bear held on, taking him with it into the flames.

Boo Boo loosened its jaws from Zeph's head and howled as the flames lit up its fur like dry tinder. Zeph tried to escape but the bear wouldn't let him go, and I was struck with a sudden desire to help my friend. I ran over to the fire, and with everything I could, smashed the rock into the thrashing bear's head. Its skull split open like a rotted jack-o-lantern. Then it sunk into the fire, reeking of scorched fur and death.

Freed, Zeph stumbled from the fire, dropping to his knees and rolling. The dirt and gravel extinguished the flames, and Amber ran over to him crying. From where I stood, old Zeph wasn't looking too good – I'd be surprised if he lived through to morning. And, if he did live, it'd be in agonizing pain and crisped like a burnt piece of bacon.

Someone must have called the cops, 'cuz I heard sirens coming. Not that anyone would be able to prove this was on me, but still, I didn't see much point in sticking around. In fact, soon as I got home, I'd be packing up and leaving this shithole for good. Had to be some place out there where a man of my talents could make use of himself.

So I left, leaving Zeph and Amber to the rest of their lives, whatever that amounted to. As I passed the dead dog I was saving in case of emergency, I felt a slight twinge of sadness.

When I got to the trailer I could tell right away something was wrong. As lax as he was, dad never left the door open, yet here it was, swinging by the hinges. Had someone gotten the drop on me, the cops or one of Spag's chickenshit cronies? Now I was regretting letting anyone leave the fire spot alive.

Well, if someone was here, they would be sorry they fucked with Peckerwood. I stepped into the trailer.

She was sitting at the kitchenette table. It dimly occurred to me that she was dead, murdered all this time, and that I resurrected her when I jerked off on that strange root growing out of her grave. But none of that

123

mattered now. It didn't even matter that Pop was sitting dead in his chair, a chunk bitten out of his head. All that mattered was that she was back.

"Hi, son," Mom said. She stood, smiling with a face that had mostly fallen free of her skull. But that didn't matter either. She was my mom and I loved her. She opened her arms, drawing me into a hug, and as my head pressed against her rotting breasts I smelled the sweet scent of perfume and the grave.

It smelled like home.

Covered in Snakeskin
Alejandro Torres

"And here's the best of 1987!" the radio DJ said before music started playing.

"I don't know why you listen to this stuff," Catherine McDonald said as she crossed her arms. She didn't care what her boyfriend played in the car just as long as it was contemporary. Her parents listened to this music.

"C'mon, Cat, it's great," Vince Williams said. He rolled the dial to turn up the volume. He then put one arm around his girlfriend while leaving the other on the steering wheel of his Toyota.

The road snaked through the country of western Pennsylvania. It was what photographers called the golden hour, that golden gleam of sunlight about an hour before dark. Cat pulled her sunglasses out of the console and put them on. They were one of those huge designer pairs that no guy could tell apart from the other ones on the rack in the store.

Cat pulled her smartphone out of her pocket. That was actually an understatement, because the phone was so large that it didn't fit in the tiny pockets of her short shorts. Her eyes went directly to where the screen showed her how much cell service she had, which at the current moment was none.

"Where are we, Vince? I have no service! What do I do if someone texts me?" Cat asked, shaking her phone as if that would make it get more bars.

She hadn't had any service since they left her cousin's graduation party. Jonathan Wellings, her cousin, had just graduated high school. Everyone invited, even the estranged family members that Cat did not know, as well as the drunks from the town bar. It was easy for the new couple to fit in.

In his head, Vince was thinking she should start by not whining, but he bit his tongue before saying that. Who was supposed to be texting her when he was with her, anyway? Regardless, he had no idea where they were. He had missed his turn miles back but, just like any other man out there, he would figure out the way by himself.

"Just be patient, we'll have some service down the road," Vince ended up saying. It was the best thing he could think of. He really wanted to tell her to stop whining, though.

The fields around them were overflowing with golden wheat. Vince felt they were somewhere in the mid-west instead of driving through Pennsylvania. Vince had never driven on these roads and was waiting for a savior road sign to appear. He'd suffered enough at Cat's cousin's graduation party, and now he was going to have to suffer just a little longer until he could figure out where they were.

No electric lines ran alongside the road. It gave the area an old timey feel, almost Amish. No cell service and no electric. Where on earth were they?

Vince squinted his eyes to tame the glaring sun. Music was blaring through the radio when Cat first saw the Ford pickup swerving down the road ahead of them. It was the first car they had seen since they got off the highway an hour and a half ago, and it was in their lane driving towards them.

"Vince," Cat said her voice wavering. Her cell service was the least of her worries now.

"I can see it," Vince said sitting up in his seat to block out the sun. Truth was he couldn't see anything, but he lied to put Cat at ease.

The pickup kept swerving back and forth as it drew closer. Cat was bracing herself on the dashboard, ready for impact. Vince put his hand on the windshield to blot out the sun, but that was still not enough. He wrenched the steering wheel to the left as he caught his first glimpse of the beat up Ford. Vince was lucky his first glimpse was also not his last as the drunk swerved even further across the yellow line.

They ended up in the ditch in seconds. The front end plowed over the weeds that lined the side of the road. The roadside dipped down a small bank and the car went airborne. Metal smashed upon the crash landing.

Both of their faces went into airbags that deployed when the Toyota nosedived. The windshield cracked all the way from top to bottom but did not shatter. The radio went quiet as the airbags returned to their deflated forms.

"Ah, shit," Vince said, coming to. He took a few hard breaths. He looked around him and the wreckage sunk in. It was real. He didn't imagine it. Then he began to raise his voice as he hit the steering wheel. "Shit, shit, shit!"

Cat blinked a few times before unbuckling her seat belt. Thank goodness she had worn that. If not, Vince's girlfriend may be lying motionless out ahead of the car somewhere. Cat's phone left a dent in the window beside her.

Before she could control herself, tears began to stream out of her eyes. Vince rolled his at the sight. They both opened their doors and fell out of the car. Vince could feel the symptoms of shock settling in and, from the way Cat was acting, he knew she already succumbed.

Vince wrapped his arms around Cat and embraced her. It was the longest hug they had since they began dating two months ago. This was by far the most traumatic event they had experienced together, and it would lead to even more trauma.

They looked at the wreck and Vince pulled his cell phone out of his pocket. The screen was black and reflected the golden glare of the sun. On top of no service, the only surviving phone was dead. Vince looked at Cat and she wore the same expression he felt. Defeat.

"You alright?" Vince asked once he could get his voice back. He wanted to double check that Cat was swaying back and forth, and it wasn't just his eyes making her move.

"Yeah, I think," Cat said holding her arm. It really didn't hurt, but she needed to hold on to something, something to help anchor her.

Vince took her by her hand and led her up to the road. "Let's see if we can thumb a ride."

"Thumb?" Cat said, almost taking her hand from his. "That was the first car we saw! We might not see another one!"

That was true, but at least it was something to do. Vince had no other options. They had no cell phone or service. His car was reduced to a shadow of its former self. Their only hope was that someone, anyone, would drive by. And the only way they could get that passerby's attention was to be by the roadside.

They walked hand in hand up to the side of the road. There were no tire marks on the road, but Vince could trace the lines as they moved off the road and into the ditch. The road was as empty as it was before that devilish pickup drove by.

"See? No one," Cat said as she sat down on the side of the road. Vince looked back as his car, his baby.

"We're going to have walk up the road," Vince said as he watched the sun sink lower in the sky. "Unless you want to spend the night by my pile of junk?"

Cat thought the proposition over in her head. Her answer was obvious. "Let's get walking."

The two of them began walking up the road. Vince felt completely alone. Nothing but fields around him, not even the occasional groundhog or bird. The sky went through a kaleidoscope of colors as they walked along. It went from a charged blue to bright orange before settling on a light pink/purple.

Vince thought he was hearing things when he could hear the rumbling of a car engine behind him. Twilight had set in fully when he turned around to see an old white Ford Escort coming down the road. Vince could feel his heart leap in his chest and Cat grabbed his hand. She looked at him and smiled.

As the Escort got closer, Vince held out his thumb, and the car began to slow down. Cat was so excited she was close to giggling. The Escort slowed down and stopped beside the couple. Vince looked into the window and saw just a single person inside.

The driver side door opened and the driver stepped out. "Hello there, I'm Todd Rowelings."

"I'm Vince and this is my girlfriend Cat." Vince looked at Todd and saw he looked like an old man of at least seventy years, but he had the skin of a twenty year old. None of it drooped or sagged but instead was taught and firm, yet the man was clearly very old. The odd appearance threw Vince for a loop, but he redirected his attention to his wrecked car. "We ran off the road and need a ride."

Vince pointed over to the remains of his Toyota and Todd could see the couple was indeed in a jam. He then walked around the Escort and opened the passenger side door. Vince hoped there was not an ax or a shotgun in there. In his mind, countless nightmares unfolded.

"I can give you two a ride," Todd said as he walked back around the car.

Vince looked into Todd's green eyes. There was something there he did not like, a sort of personality trait that he was lacking...or possessed. Was it rage, anger, or even evil? The thought entered his mind but he dismissed it as fallout of his wreck.

The old man waited patiently for the couple to decide. Vince looked at Cat and tried to transfer his concern mentally, but that almost never worked between them. He was lucky to think the same thought, let alone be on the same wavelength.

Vince thought about his options again and weighed whether it was worth getting into the car or spending the night outside by his wreckage. He knew what Cat's answer would be, that much was certain, but he did not know whether he could trust Todd or not. He was a stranger, but he had to. Thumbing was his idea. Cat would never let him live it down if he backed out now.

"Thanks, Todd," Vince said, accepting the offer. Cat hugged Vince and they got into the two-door Escort. Vince opted to sit in the back with Cat; after all, it was a stranger's vehicle.

The interior lights lit up the area and they could see how dark it had become. The sun was safely tucked beneath the horizon for the night and the last remnants of light were fading fast. As they began down the road, the night stayed blackening. The ride had an eerie silence to it. Todd did not turn on the radio.

Vince peered around to see if Todd had turned on the headlights, but the old goat's (even though he did not look like an old goat Vince knew he was, he had a feeling in his gut) shoulder was in the way.

The further they went down the road, the darker the night got. How far were they from Vince's car now? He hoped not too far. One day, he would have to get it towed. The moon was now out in full and the road blended into the fields around them.

"Why don't you turn on the headlights?" Cat asked Todd. Vince gave a sigh of relief. He was going to ask himself but he did not want to. Something was off about Todd.

"They are burnt out, dear," Todd said chuckling. Todd could not see Cat's eyes, but they almost fell out of her head.

The rest of the ride was quiet, a scary quiet that enlarged the shadows in the back of their minds. The backseat wished that the ride would end soon. This ride was far worse than the one back from Cat's cousin's graduation party. The Escort rumbled along until they could make out the black shape of a house along the road.

Vince could see the white paint peeling off the sides of the two-story house. A dirt driveway led up to the porch. Most of the boards looked like they needed replaced on the porch. All of the windows were dark, and Vince understood when he saw no electric cables running up to the house.

Todd pulled the Escort up to the porch and killed the engine. He then got out of the car and opened the passenger side door. Vince and Cat filed out of the Escort and could hear crickets in the fields around the house.

"This is my humble home, Vince, Cat," Todd said as he walked up the stairs of the porch.

The couple followed him onto the porch. Cat was hesitant. Vince led her up the stairs. As they walked up the stairs, a snake slithered past their feet. Cat jumped down the stairs and came close to a scream, but it got caught in her throat. Vince kicked the reptile away and pulled Cat up the stairs.

The front door opened with a creak and Todd entered his home. The old man held the door for Vince and he in turn held the door open for Cat. The inside of the house was dark, and had the smell of burnt wax.

Todd led the couple into the kitchen and lit a match from the table to light the candle in the center. The little candle let a loose glow on the room. The cupboard doors lay open and empty. A shadow slithered out of the room and further into the house.

"This is the kitchen," Todd said into the silence. "We will meet here tomorrow morning. Follow me upstairs to your room."

Cat watched as the old man moved to the stairs that were in the hallway. Vince disappeared into the darkness behind him. She could hear the stairs creaking beneath their feet. She felt uneasy about the kitchen, let alone the whole house, so she followed the men up to the second story.

There were two rooms upstairs, the master bedroom and the guest room. Vince noticed the walls were poorly kept and cracked. He imagined the floor bowing under their combined weights. The next image was of them falling and being crushed by the debris of the house.

Todd waited for Cat to get up the stairs to show them the guest room. As he opened the door Vince got the first look at the bedroom. Cat walked in after the door opened and she kicked up the layer of dust on the floor. There was a dresser and a bed in the room, but that was it. Vince did not expect much for a guest room and he was content.

Vince walked in and sat down on the bed. He was thankful dust did not plume up. Todd smiled and said goodnight as he shut the door. The door however did not shut completely and stayed opened just a crack.

Cat pulled the covers back on the bed to reveal the mattress. She gave Vince the look.

"So, this is how it's going to be?" Cat said as she slipped under the covers.

"I guess so," Vince said as he took her in his arms. This was not how he pictured their first night sleeping together, but he would take it. He would have to with all the twists and turns of the day.

They lay under the covers and murmured to themselves so that Todd could not hear them. Most of their murmurs were about the noises. The noises came from the walls and the floor, everywhere. It sounded like someone was pushing a noodle through a pipe, Vince thought, or more likely something moving around under the floorboards or in-between the walls.

Vince held Cat tightly and tried to ward off the noises. As they closed their eyes they failed to notice their door was open just a crack…

…just open enough for an old man's eye to watch them all night long.

***

The night went by fast. Vince had no recollection of any dream he may have had and Cat did not mention any either. The window on the wall had a film of dirt on it but the sunrise shone through. The room looked smaller in the light. Even though they both had a good night's sleep, they could feel a layer of dirtiness covering them.

Vince enjoyed waking up to Cat being right there by him. It saved him from getting his phone and texting her good morning. This morning he just had to tell her himself.

"We're to meet Todd in the kitchen," Cat said rolling out of bed. As her feet hit the cold floor she could feel her scream from last night escape her throat.

A legless reptile slithered underneath the bed. Cat ran to the door and down the stairs while Vince stayed in the bed waiting for the serpent to reappear. He did not know what he was going to do, but he was going to do something, even if that something was running away.

Vince jumped off the bed and dashed to the door. While he was running away, not just one, but two snakes poked their heads out of the underworld beneath the bed. How many dust bunnies could be left down there with two snakes preying on them?

Vince made his presence known to the home owner and his girlfriend in the kitchen. They were sitting eating from a bowl of fruit. He looked at the fruit bowl and knew that it was not there the night before. Vince wore an expression of surprise and terror.

"There's two snakes in the guest room," Vince said to Todd. All Todd did was grin.

"Have an apple," the old man said as he handed Vince an apple.

Vince took the apple and bit into it without taking his eyes off the old man. Cat looked just as frightened as Vince felt by the old timer's non-reaction to the snakes. Instead, Todd peeled an orange and ate it joyfully.

"Is there something to kill the snakes with?" Vince asked after he bit out a portion of the apple. He could not remember the last time he had fruit for breakfast. The old man whipped around and was close to a fit of violence.

"You will not kill the innocent," Todd said.

"You mean the snakes?" Cat asked as she killed an apple herself.

"They are my friends," Todd said as he picked up the fruit bowl and put it in one of the cupboards. "You are forbidden to harm them." He then went into the sitting room at the back of the house. Todd left Cat and Vince alone in the kitchen.

They looked at each other like a married couple whose dream vacation just plummeted into the disaster realm. First was the graduation party, then the car wreck followed by the creepy old man picking them up, and finishing with spending the night at his house. On top of all that they now had to operate with the knowledge of at least two snakes in the house.

He just would not go back upstairs, Vince decided. He knew Cat would not object and, since they had not brought anything with them into the room, they had no need of returning to it. Vince thought keeping the bed messy and unmade would teach the geezer a thing or two about being a good host.

Since Todd was in the back of the house and the snakes were hopefully in the upstairs somewhere, Cat and Vince sat in the front room. There were two chairs for guests to sit in and a small coffee table that gave the room a quaint feel.

"I don't like Mr. Todd," Cat said as she sat down in the chair. "He's a bizarre old man."

"Well, we'll just have to get back on the road," Vince said looking at the front door. "We can walk up the road until we find someone else, I guess."

Cat had not heard the last part because she heard singing coming from the back of the house. She crept out of her chair and peered around the corner. Her eyes fell on Todd with a snake wrapping itself around his arm to the music of his voice. Another snake was slithering across the floor to the old man.

Vince pulled Cat back into the front room. She was breathing heavily as he sat her down in the chair. The morning light bathed the bookcase in the room. Vince picked a book off the shelf to calm Cat down. He wished that she did not overreact to everything.

The title was Snakes in the Grass, and Vince put back where it was. He picked a second book off the shelf and it was titled Reptiles in North America. It appeared none of the books were going to help the situation. The only thing the books accomplished was cementing Todd's obsession of serpents.

The singing from the back of the house died down into a whisper. Todd was talking to the snakes now. Vince could her him calling the snakes by name. Asking them how they had been and where they had gone off to the night before.

Vince could feel his face fall and Cat's did the same. The couple quieted down so they could hear the old man's ramblings with the snakes.

"Ah, Gerald," they could hear Todd say. "I can't wait for everyone to get back either. I hope everyone does make it back…my guests are not friendly, you better watch out, Wanda…." That was all they could make out through the walls.

Vince had heard enough. He got up and walked to the front door that he had entered the night before. The night before he knew Todd Rowelings was crazy. Cat sat up but then sat down again silently. Vince opened the door and yet another snake poked its head through. The temptation of smashing the door shut and decapitating the serpent coursed through Vince. As he wrapped his fingers tightly around the door, Vince felt an equally tight hand grab his shoulder.

"Where are you going Vince?" Todd asked as he turned the young man around. Vince saw the skin stretched across his face grew tighter. It was like he got an after breakfast face lift. "There is a storm coming, best to wait it out."

Vince looked at the old man and then to the overcast clouds outside. Vince stepped back into the house. "Thanks for the heads up, but we really should get going. Thank you for everything."

"No problem, wouldn't want Ruth here to get drenched," Todd chuckled walking back to the back room.

"What?" Cat said confused. Why could he not let them leave?

Cat scrunched her face together trying to register what he just said. Vince joined her in looking around the room to see if there was someone new there. Thankfully not even a snake had slithered into the room. Did that mean that Todd had called Cat Ruth?

Cat and Vince sat down it the front room. Vince picked up a book and opened it up to a random page. The illustration of the rat snake in the book was outlined in red pen. In the margins were notes scribbled in illegible handwriting. Vince could see letters spilling out of the mess of chicken scratch that read Ruth a few times as well as mentioning a Tah.

Some pages were blank while others held lines of writing. Only a small section on page 6 was legible. It read, Oh Tah, the snakes have come. Yes, they are here, but Ruth is still dead. Why have you not raised her like you promised?

"This guy is nuts." Vince said closing the book. "He's scribbled stuff about this Ruth in his book. Maybe she was like his girl?"

"Regardless, let's go back upstairs," Cat said standing up. "I feel like Mr. Todd is watching us and listening to us. It's more private up there."

The couple walked back up the stairs while Todd sat in the back room. Vince stole a quick glance and saw that he had more serpentine friends among him. He could hear Todd laughing and chuckling to his good old buddies all the way upstairs in the hallway.

There was another room upstairs beside the one they had slept in and that was the room Cat entered. Vince thought it was because she knew there had been snakes in the other room, but knowing Cat it could be because she wanted to snoop around. Vince had no way of knowing.

This room was nowhere near as dusty as the other room. It was well kept and showed signs of actual use, but a different kind of use. There was a small bookcase that had candles burnt down to little wicks while the wax ran down the sides of the bookcase. All the books were covered in black leather.

"What the heck?" Cat said as she pulled a book out of the bookcase. Wax had fallen onto it and created a seal that she broke easy enough.

Vince looked around the room more as his girlfriend delved into the book. The bed had the appearance of an old motel room bed, the kind that one would not actually sleep under the covers, but rather on the covers. Vince could see a snakeskin lying neatly placed on the bed crossing a yellow rose.

Vince walked over to the bed and could see a word written on the bed's coverings. It was scrawled with a sort of dust, or at least he hoped it was a dust and not crack or something like that. The dust formed the word Ruth.

As if the setup of the bed made enough sense, there was a black and white picture on the pillow. It was of a young couple standing at the altar. Vince figured the Reverend had just said you may kiss the bride right before the photo was shot.

"Vince," Cat said. She turned around holding a book out in her hand. Vince went over to her and looked down at the pages.

He could feel the hair on the back of his neck stand up as his eyes ran across the pages. There was a drawing of a snake coming out of the mouth of a woman. The scales of the reptile were being peeled off by the teeth of the depicted woman.

Vince flipped the page. This page had more words than the last one but there was still an ominous illustration of a serpent. Cat's face dropped as Vince's did. All the blood stayed away from their faces. They could not hear the noises from the first floor anymore and these books were not something they wanted to get involved with.

Vince looked at the wardrobe in the corner and opened its maw to throw the devilish book in when he instead dropped the book. As he opened the door to the wardrobe he saw several skins, human skins, hanging up on coat racks. The empty eye sockets peered out at Vince as he shut the door.

"We are going," Vince said as he turned to Cat. She had been beside the bookshelf and not seen what was in the wardrobe. "I mean it this time." At that moment, he turned to face the doorway. Todd Rowelings was standing in the hallway.

The old man did not look a day over twenty now, the skin on his elbows covering his bones tight. The man smiled at them and entered the room. As he shut the door, a bizarre symbol was drawn on the back of the door that reminded Vince of the occult.

"I see you have discovered my reading material and extras," Todd said as he cornered the couple across the bed.

Todd then bent over and reached below the bed. Vince imagined him pulling a tangle of snakes from beneath the mattress, but instead a long thin knife was in the old man's hand. Todd stretched his hand out to Cat and motioned for her to crawl across the bed.

"Don't go," Vince whispered in her ear, but she had to go. Something pulled her to the strange senior citizen. Something of another world.

Vince watched as Todd handed the knife over to Cat. His girlfriend's eyes were veiled and she opened her mouth, from which no sound escaped.

Todd took off his shirt to reveal, to Vince's surprise, the body of a teenage swimmer. His skin was as taught across his chest and stomach as it was on his face.

Nothing hung or dangled but instead was in better shape than Vince's body.

Cat pushed the blade closer to Todd until it touched the bare skin on his back. Then she pushed further and punctured the skin. Todd did not scream or make a noise as Cat created a long thin cut down the old timer's back. She then grabbed ahold of the separate pieces of skin and ripped them apart.

Blood squirted all over the room and across the bed. If Vince had been two feet closer he would have been drenched in the man's blood. Vince watched as Cat finished opening the wound and as she collapsed onto the blood-soaked bed.

"Cat!" Vince said looking down at her. His first thought went to the knife. He ran across the bed and saw that she had dropped it on the floor. One crisis avoided. Vince then checked his girlfriend's pulse, he did not know why but he did, and she was great.

"Hhuhh…Vince…"Cat murmured as she came to on the bed. Vince looked down at her while she opened her eyes and looked about the room. As Cat's eyes met the blood on the walls and now on herself, she about went into shock. "What, what the hell?!" Cat screamed as she jumped out of the bed and into Vince's arms. Her screaming went down the road and stopped at sobbing before getting to its final destination of crying.

"You did that, Cat," Vince said, holding her by her shoulders. "All of it. You took that knife and sliced the psycho down the back and then ripped him open."

Cat looked around the room at the recollection of her acts. She then looked down at the body of Todd Rowelings. Vince had forgotten about the homeowner, and rightly so, but now their attention was turned to the real problem.

"Vince," Cat said, stepping past Todd and into the hallway. "We need to leave. I'll explain later."

"What?" Vince thought. How could they leave a dead man in his house? They were as good as gone, with their fingerprints all over the house, books...and the knife. "Seriously? Now you choose to leave?"

"Because I didn't do it! Something made me do it! You have to believe me, Vince! He's-" Cat was cut off as her worst-case scenario unfolded.

Todd's body trembled, rumbled on the floor. The meat inside of him began to turn upward and emerge from the opening in his back. The flesh began to mount up when a thick piece, most likely an arm, spilled out from the side. It was followed shortly by three other meaty appendages and a cephalothorax.

The man of raw meat then stood up on trembling legs. Vince could feel his breakfast, even though it consisted of mere fruit, coming up his throat. Cat stood in the hallway with her tears streaming down her face. Typical Cat.

Although the being appeared to be made of raw flesh, Vince could see a thin lining, a new skin, coating the being. Eyes opened up and looked around the room and a familiar voice spoke.

"Thank you, my dear," Todd said as he picked slime off of himself.

"Your...welcome..." Cat said as she peered through her tear stained eyes. Even in the worst situations, her manners could come out.

"Thank you for releasing me from my old skin," Todd said, slowly stretching his arms out. "I am cursed to outgrow my casings much like the snake. I have Tah to thank for that."

The couple locked eyes and Cat nodded. Somehow, Vince could feel the scream in Cat's throat across the room, and before it could come out, Todd began to speak again.

"I was married once," the newly redone man said. Vince stopped everything he had been doing and directed his attention to the being in the room. "But then Tah took her away from me, with a promise he never kept."

Vince looked at Cat through the air. They needed to leave, but were caught with this madman in between them. The Todd creature continued to ramble on and on. Vince thought there very well could be some invisible entity about them but the creature's next words affirmed his assumption.

"You thought you got the best of me, did you? Did you!" the Todd creature said to the air around them. "When you took Ruth, I believed you could bring her back tenfold. But alas, you spat in my face and cursed me to shed my skin like the animal you hold dear to your heart!"

Vince looked at the creature as pieces began falling into place. From the crazy snake obsession to his occult book collection, Todd Rowelings began to make sense. Vince began to slide across the floor towards his girlfriend in the hallway; all the while, the creature's mouth kept spilling out words.

"You thought your ambiguity could protect you, hide you," the creature said as Vince passed within feet of it. "You thought you could best us! We have gotten the best of you, dear friend!"

When the creature closed its mouth a gust of wind blew open the windows across the house. The yellow rose and dust blew off the bed. Over the smashing of the glass, Vince could hear Cat's scream finally come around. The creature turned to Vince, who was now in the doorway, and held out its meaty palm.

"Help me vanquish him," the creature said.

"Hell no!" Vince said as he grabbed Cat's hand and flew down the stairs. The wet sounds of feet sliding across the floor chased them as far as the stairs before dying off.

Vince ran through the kitchen and front room, kicking a snake out of his way and before Cat could see it. Was it Wanda or Gerald? Better yet, did it matter? Not at all to Vince. He actually felt good about it. That Todd Rowelings was a terrible host.

Vince led Cat outside and dragged her through the driveway and towards the main road. The clouds had gathered above them and a storm was coming for sure. The wind blew Cat's hair all over her face and into Vince's as well. It was not until they had gone halfway down the driveway that the cursed Todd came out of the front door. Vince could not tell if it was the distance, but the old man looked almost normal.

They began to cut across the fields to get back to the road. The grass and weeds were at least knee high but they pressed forward. Nothing in the tall grass could be worse than what was in the house.

After minutes of jogging, Vince could see the blacktop ahead. The road was just as vacant as when they left it. Vince had never been so happy to see a stretch of road. He could feel Cat squeeze his hand and he took her and hugged her tight.

They jumped through the remaining grass and onto the asphalt. The hard, unforgiving road felt good beneath their feet. The lack of sunshine today had left the road cool. Vince went all the way across the road and to the other side before looking back at the house off in the distance behind him.

"We should get far away from there," Vince said as he began walking down the road.

"We don't even know where we're going," Cat said to remind her boyfriend that they were still lost.

Vince looked up to the sky. He knew they were still lost, but safely away from whatever Todd Rowelings was . Right now Vince's only plan is to walk down the road and hope they got to a little town. He was done thumbing for rides.

"So, about what happened back there," Cat said. She broke Vince's train of thought. "I think that thing Mr. Rowelings was talking to took control of me."

"Seriously?" Vince said, but even as he said it, he knew it made sense. He knew his girlfriend would not intentionally knife a man. Cat nodded her head.

"Seriously, because I knew that ghost's, or whatever it was, name before Mr. Rowelings said it," Cat said. She lowered her eyes and grabbed her elbow. Vince gave her a quick hug as they walked along. "Tah really does like snakes a lot. That's why he took Ruth from Mr. Rowelings. She killed every snake she found and, when she died, Todd made a pact with him to bring her back. Tah just cursed him instead, though."

"Well, that's all behind us now," Vince said. It was true, figuratively and literally. "Let's just get home now."

The wind was picking up its speed and rain began to fall from the sky. The weather would not stop Vince, but Cat was another tale. Vince knew he had to think of something to do and fast before she began to whine about being wet and cold. Neither could tell how much sunlight was left, the day had been a hazy gray, but it had to be at least midafternoon.

The couple kept walking on as the rain kept falling down. It was a steady rain, light but never ending. Vince could feel his shirt become heavy and stick to him. He could feel his eyes drawn over Cat more and more to see if her clothes were experiencing the weather the same way, and boy were they.

Vince looked over his shoulder and could not see Todd's house behind him anymore. That was his only landmark in this desolate plain of farmland. They were now worse off without it chasing them down.

"Hey, Vince," Cat said as she swayed her stride into his. "Are you going to try and hitchhike again?"

NO! Vince thought but bit his tongue. "What do you think?" he asked instead, but could feel regret seeping in. He knew what his girlfriend would say. Why did he always put himself in these situations?

"I think it's worth a try," Cat said as Vince sighed.

"Really?" Vince said. After everything, she still wanted to give it a try?

"Yes. Unless you can think of something else to do?" Cat said crossing her arms. Vince must have looked unmoved because she said next, "Tell me what else we should do, then?"

"I don't know," Vince said, giving in. "I guess I'll throw out my thumb when I hear an engine coming up the road."

The couple kept walking along, now hand in hand. Vince thought Cat's fingers were frozen and was thankful she had grabbed his hand because his fingers were getting chilly as well. The rain ran down his face and onto his chest as they walked down the road. Cat's hair was a mess now and Vince kept himself entertained by messing it up even more every now and then.

Vince found himself thinking back to Todd Rowelings and what happened in the upstairs room. That old man wanted him to help him defeat some supernatural entity that he pissed off? How was he to do that? Vince could only imagine what witchcraft that man had in mind when he made the offer, probably something from one of those books on the shelf. He didn't want to bring it up to Cat again after her talk earlier about it.

The rain began to pick up and soak the young couple further. Through the falling water and brisk breeze

Vince could hear a humming. He paused on the side of the road to listen.

"What are you doing?" Cat asked as he raised his hand to his ear.

"Shh, do you hear that?" Vince asked as he felt a smile crawl across his face. The couple looked down the road behind them and could hear the humming. It sounded rhythmical, mechanical, like a car.

"Is that what I think it is?!" Cat asked, squeezing Vince's hand.

"I think it is," Vince said as he took her under his arm. Their rain soaked clothes stuck together like glue.

As the rumbling of the engine drew closer, the couple could see the vehicle coming up the road through the rain. Vince readied his thumb for when the car would be close enough to see him, and watched as the car drove closer and closer until he could make out a few more details. The smile that had crawled so effortlessly on Vince's face ran away just as fast. Vince kept Cat under arm as he turned them around and ran off the blacktop.

Cat looked back over her shoulder as Vince directed her through the untended field. She saw a white Ford Escort pull up to the side of road and stop. Its headlights were out. As the driver opened the door Cat could see a meaty palm grasping the door.

The Clean Room
Mike Mayak

Participants must stand erect during sessions. Bracing against a wall is permissible. Participants must remain within one (1) foot of the wall at all times. Moving to another location is not permitted during the session.
----from Handbook for Participants

Shit! The first ones were the hardest to take. DeShawn clenched his fists behind him and held tight to his wrist. He gritted his teeth until the grinding filled his ears and the pressure made his jaw ache. The next razor blades, he guessed they were razor blades, slipped smoothly into his shoulders. He squeezed his eyes tight, and grabbed his right wrist with his left hand. Tears started rolling down his cheeks to his chest. They tickled.

No yelling, the rules said. No reaction, no talking. But it had been DeShawn's experience, he could get away with the occasional grunt or moan. He let out a moan right then through his clenched teeth. A blade had gone into his bicep. That made six so far. He opened his eyes; he caught a glint of something in the dark. The nite-sight goggles the customer was wearing. He could see DeShawn but DeShawn couldn't see him.

Sessions will last from 45 minutes to one hour. Customers will be issued one (1) set of Nite-Sight Goggles. Customers will be issued one (1) set of razor blades. Length and number of blades determined by which session package the customer has purchased.
----from Handbook for Customers

Participants will be issued one (1) pair of regulation shorts which must be worn at all times. Participants will be issued one (1) pair of canvas shoes. Participants are reminded that no talking is allowed, even if addressed by the customer. This will result in a reduction in pay.

----from Handbook for Participants

DeShawn heard a strangled grunt from a few feet away. He wasn't sure if that was another of the participants or from a customer pushing a blade in as far as he could. That was the good thing; a lot of the customers really didn't have the strength or the nerve to use the blades to the extreme.

Not this guy. Fuck! DeShawn shuddered as the man dragged the corner of the blade in a circle around his belly. DeShawn was shaking, his body dripping sweat. He realized the glint in the darkness was more than likely from the customer's teeth as he grinned, using his supply of blades to inflict pain on DeShawn. Probably wondering how much more DeShawn could take.

Not much more, DeShawn realized, steadying himself against the wall, maintaining the acceptable position.

Areas covered by participant's shorts are off-limits to customers. Areas above participant's neck are off-limits to customers. Verbally taunting participants is allowed, but not recommended. Customers are responsible for cleaning blood, vomit, etc. off their own clothes.

Once inserted in a participant, blades may not be removed to use again. Doing so will result in forfeiture of customer's remaining time, regardless of amount purchased.

----from Handbook for Customers

A blade went into DeShawn's thigh. He grunted and heard the customer chuckle. He heard the blades click as the customer sorted through the blades he'd been issued. DeShawn strained to see the man's face as he stuck a blade in his belly. He closed his eyes and imagined he was reading a game program with his profile in it:

DeShawn Scott
Power Forward.
6' 8"
240 lbs.

Shit! Two more blades. DeShawn had lost count of how many blades he had in him. He could hear someone in the darkened hall whimper.

Individual sessions will end when time expires or the participant collapses. Payment is determined by how long the participant remains standing in place. End of the entire session will be signaled by the reactivation of the lights. ABSOLUTELY NO REFUNDS.
----from Handbook for Customers

DeShawn could feel the man's breathing as he went back over and pressed or wiggled the blades left in DeShawn's body. DeShawn let out a yelp; that would cost him some pay. What would happen if he hauled off and belted this guy in the mouth? DeShawn smiled grimly. The handbook had warned they would be monitored at all times.

DeShawn heard the customer's footsteps as he walked away, he must have gotten tired of him or lost interest. DeShawn was shaking. He felt cold. The longer you stand, the more they pay, he kept saying to himself.

When DeShawn toppled over he made sure to twist and land on his back. There were no blades in his back. He was sprawled on the cold floor. In his mind, he saw himself grabbing the ball, running down the court, jumping, shooting, the crowd roaring.

The light had been shining in DeShawn's face for quite a while by the time he forced himself to open his eyes. The Clean Room. He wasn't sure how long he'd been out. He didn't even remember passing out. He was groggy and weak. He knew from experience not to try and raise his head but he glanced down at what he could see of his naked body. Bloody scars on his chest, belly, and arms. He could see some of the scars were closed up; they must have had him under the machine for a while. They usually did it in stages.

Cost of post-session restoration will be deducted from payment to participants.
----from Handbook for Participants

DeShawn tried to shift his position. Mistake. He hurt all over. He clenched his right fist and flexed his arm. He winced at the pain but it felt good to move. He closed his eyes tightly.

"Hey! Hey, guy! You all right?" came a male voice.

DeShawn opened his eyes; the light hurt them so he shut them again. It was like a hangover, but less fun.

"Yeah, I'm okay," DeShawn said. "How about you?"

"I'm all right," the voice said. "I was here when they brought you in. You were out cold."

"Yeah, being a pincushion wears you out!" DeShawn said with a laugh.

"I heard that! Hey, I'm Anthony."

"DeShawn. DeShawn Scott. 'Scuse me for not shaking hands."

"Hey, you were All City about ten years ago!"

"Yeah," DeShawn said. "When I was a kid, before I blew out my knee." DeShawn opened an eye and tilted his head in the direction of the voice. The guy was lying on a table a few feet away. Redhead. As muscular as DeShawn and about as big. A bunch of scars in various stages of healing on his arms.

"Any idea how long this takes?"

"They give us another treatment after a bit," DeShawn said. "There's another session tonight, but they don't recommend our doing two of them a day."

"You sound like you've done this before," Anthony said.

"The money's good. This your first time?"

"Yeah," Anthony said. "I needed the cash."

"Me too, man." DeShawn laughed and then grimaced. There wasn't anything in the Handbook about not laughing with a bunch of cuts healing in your chest.

It was just a little bit later when one of the attendants rolled the bed DeShawn was on into the adjoining room and put him under the machine with the purple lights.

"Just hold still and keep your eyes closed," the attendant said.

DeShawn could hear a clicking and then a low hum. There was a prickling sensation on his open cuts as they began to slowly come together and heal. Then his entire body began to feel warm, like he was in a warm bath and there was another sensation that spread over him like a cool breeze. A feeling of completeness, of infinite bliss. Pleasure making every nerve tingle.

"Yeah," DeShawn whispered. "Yeah."

It was just like the first time. Just like all the other times. He felt like he had fallen backwards into the starry sky. He let out a moan. There was tightness in his crotch, his cock was rock-hard. This was why they recommended the participants shoot their wad before a session. But this was better than anything any girl or guy had done with DeShawn. Better than any fantasy.

It was why he kept coming back.

It was why he would keep coming back.

Demons
Elizabeth Zemlicka

You haven't seen pure evil until you have looked directly into the eyes of a person so disturbed but so calm and rational they could actually convince you they are justified in their actions, no matter how insane or gut wrenching those actions may be.

Every week for a year, I stared into those mesmerizing black eyes, into absolute nothingness. There was no soul, no conscience nothing. Just dead eyes that saw things that would leave you or I a babbling, drooling fool.

In the beginning, I felt sorry for him. This poor man with his horrible childhood and crippling mental illness; he just needed someone that could help him.

Turns out, he just needed someone he could brag to, someone who would be unable to report him to anyone. Someone he could show his nightmares to.

I am a psychiatrist, I am trained to listen and not let any of it affect me. What they don't train you for is the ones that give you nightmares without saying a word, the ones that can show you what they see and take a twisted sort of pleasure in it.

I was naive, I thought I was so smart, that I could fix anyone. I would piece together my hour-long sessions with patients and make a diagnosis in a purely cold and clinical way. I never spent enough time thinking about what they said to me. Oh, how I wish I could go back.

I can't disclose his name, even now, after he is no longer my patient. I can tell my story, as a warning to you.

There is evil in this world, it lurks around every corner and hides behind sad eyes. The kind that make you feel actual human emotions, like compassion, that lure you in, only to be swallowed whole by this inhuman monster.

He talked of his childhood, of bouncing from foster home to foster home. He spoke of extreme physical abuse in these homes, of taking his anger out on animals and of detaching himself from feeling anything. I had offered medications, he politely refused and convinced me he had coping mechanisms that actually worked for him. I believed him.

One day, he came in and said "Doc, I need something to take the nightmares away. The nightmares you see when you're awake."

This startled me. "What do you mean by that? Are you having visual hallucinations?" I asked.

"No, I don't think so. I just see the things that you normal people don't see," he stated matter-of-factly.

I studied his face for a few moments, trying to decide if he was messing with me, trying to get a reaction. His face remained serious, his eyes were blank, like black holes I felt I would get sucked into if I stared too long.

"What...what kind of...of...things?" I was hesitant on asking. I'm unsure if it was because I didn't want to know, or if I was expecting him to crack into gales of childish laughter.

"Nightmarish things, creatures. Monsters. Whatever you want to call them. They lurk in dark corners and creep up on you when you're not paying attention. You know that feeling that starts in the back of your neck and pulses down your spine, making the hair stand up, then you want to run but have no idea why? That's them."

I sat there, silently listening, making every effort to slow my steadily climbing pulse.

"I don't want to see them anymore, doc. Is there a magic pill you can give me for that?" A slow grin was curling on his lips and there was a brief glimmer in his black eyes.

I cleared my throat. "Uh, well, we can try a few things. It's really just trial and error until we find the right...what are you doing?" I jumped, alarmed, as he reached for my arm, catching my forearm in his strong grasp. My vision went dark, I couldn't see anything and I couldn't speak.

I felt like I would suffocate as panic settled into my chest.

Then I saw flashes of light, just quick glimpses, like splashes of color. Pretty soon, the world swam back into focus. His face was inches from mine, that curl of a grin still on his lips, those tar black eyes staring directly into mine. But now they were swirling, like hypnotized cartoon eyes.

Then he was back in his chair. I didn't see him move; he was just sitting there like he had been there the entire session. He looked at his watch

"Times up, doc, you've been a great help today. I'll see you next week" he said cheerfully and walked out my door.

I called the front desk as soon as I got my bearings back. My receptionist, Annie, answered on the second ring.

"Yes, Miss Baker?"

"Annie, do I have any more appointments today?" I asked

"No ma'am, he was your last. Good thing, too. He gives me the creeps," she said, keeping her voice low like he would hear her.

"Thank you, Annie. And please stop calling me ma'am."

"Sorry about that ma...uh, Ella," she stammered sheepishly.

I laughed. "Have a good night, hun," I added cheerfully.

"Good night, Ella!"

I hung up the phone and sat at my desk, trying to retrace the events of that session. Did I black out? Did he actually hypnotize me? I was so lost in thought I didn't realize how late it was getting. The shadows were getting long in my office. I flipped on my desk lamp and began to organize my paperwork to go home when I heard a scuffling sound by the door.

"Annie, you don't have to wait for me, I'm fine," I called out.

Nothing.

I walked to my door and opened it to a dark, empty hallway.

"Ann..." the words died on my lips.

"Now I'm hearing things," I said to the empty hallway.

I was beginning to get uneasy, I hurriedly stuffed my paperwork into my briefcase and grabbed my coat when I heard it again.

This time it sounded more like a mouse in the walls, I relaxed and laughed at myself.

Still uneasy, I hurried out the door to my car. Deciding to make a strong drink and cancel my appointments for tomorrow on my way there.

That is the last thing I remember. When I try to bring a memory out of the darkness, it comes in flashes like photographs and what I see in those photographs is so terrifying that I pass out.

When the world swam back into view, I was in my apartment, although I have no recollection of getting there. Once I got my bearings, I realized he was sitting in the shadows in the corner of my living room, like he was waiting patiently. I jumped.

"What are you doing in my living room?" I asked, getting angry.

He threw his head back and laughed, his face shrouded by shadows, but I knew it well. Sharp, chiseled features, smooth olive skin with a well-groomed mustache and goatee, he was normal looking, attractive even. But those eyes, those haunted charcoal eyes. He suddenly leaned forward but his face looked different than I remembered, more sunken and pale, there was silver highlighting his dark goatee. He noticed me looking.

"Now you see the real me, and you will see my demons, lurking in the shadows. Not just the flashes of them that seem to short circuit your brain, which I must admit, is just *fascinating*. No, you will soon get the whole picture, you will see what I see, those horrible creatures that no one else sees." His eyes never left my face, he seemed to be studying every line, his face was calm, almost bored as he sat back again, a grin slowly forming on his thin lips.

"Demons?" I asked stupidly, this made him laugh, his booming voice seeming to come from all corners of the room. I snapped my head around to follow the sounds, shadows scurried from the corners of my living room.

"What was that?" I was panicking again.

"You need to relax, doc. You will pass out again." His voice softened in exaggerated concern.

"What are you?" I asked, deciding he couldn't be human.

He just grinned and stood up, stretching.

"I'm very much human, just like you." With that, he winked and strode out the door.

"Wait!" I called after him, but he was gone.

I ran to the window, my car was in my parking spot, no strange cars were anywhere near it and no one was leaving.

Am I hallucinating? He drugged me; that has to be what happened, I thought, trying to relax.

I flipped on the light in the kitchen, deciding against a strong drink just in case he really did drug me with something. I grabbed a bottle of water from the fridge. I kept replaying the day's events in my head, trying to make sense of it and trying to piece together the missing time between leaving my office and waking up in my living room.

I stood in the doorway between my kitchen and living room, sipping my water, lost in thought, when I heard the scurrying again, snapping me back to reality.

I started flipping lights on in every room, looking in every corner. Nothing.

Shaking my head, "he drugged me," I said to the empty room. Leaving all the lights on, I settled into the couch and turned on the TV.

Nightmares plagued my sleep; creatures with claws and teeth surrounded me, whispering things I couldn't understand. Some had two legs and looked human with small nubs on the top of their heads like small horns. Their noses were sharp, as were their teeth. Some had hooves, some normal human features. They surrounded my couch and chattered in their hushed voices.

I wasn't scared; they seemed more curious than threatening. I watched them for what seemed like hours, until the room was suddenly silent, I looked around and they were all gone. Confused, I got up to look for them and that's when I saw it. It was tall, impossibly tall, its head brushed up against the ceiling. Its face looked like a Neanderthal man, with the protruding forehead, sunken beady eyes that were fixed on me. I could hear it breathe in snorts as it moved out of the shadows, revealing fur-covered arms and hands with fingers that were long and thin, ending in sharp points. Claws, maybe?

It began to walk towards me. My breath caught in my throat and I couldn't move. It slowly ambled towards me, I panicked but still couldn't move. It was like someone was sitting on my chest, holding me down; all I could do was watch this thing get closer and closer, until it reached out its long, clawed fingers to my face. Suddenly, I'm sitting straight up on the couch, sunlight is pouring in through the windows. I jumped up and threw my arms up in defense, but there was nothing there.

I decided to go to work the next morning, as I was feeling better. Convinced he had somehow drugged me, I spent my downtime googling hallucinogenic drugs that can be transferred through skin contact. At the end of the day, I decided to go to the hospital and get checked out.

All drug tests came back negative and the doctor sent a psychologist into my room to set up an appointment. I looked at this young twenty-something girl, clearly fresh out of college, and I laughed.

"I have been a psychiatrist since you were in diapers, I am not crazy. I just need to clear my schedule and take a vacation, I'm clearly overstressed," I told her and was instantly embarrassed.

"Look, I'm sorry. I shouldn't talk to you like that," I apologized.

She smiled.

"No worries, Dr. Baker, I know who you are." Her cheeks flushed.

"I figured you wouldn't make an appointment for therapy, I told them that. I would love to pick your brain sometime, though. I start medical school in the fall, and I know I have no right asking, but I could really use an internship. You don't have to pay me or anything," she added sheepishly.

I smiled at that.

"Call my cell number on this card, it's my personal number, we can set up an interview over coffee next week," I handed her my card.

She beamed. "Thank you, doctor! And yes, I would definitely take a vacation if I were you," she added.

"Good advice, uh..." I reached out to shake her hand.

"Oh, gosh, I'm Emily, uh, Brown. I'm so sorry," she gushed, holding out her hand.

"Thank you for blowing off my rude comments, it's been a long week," I apologized again.

"Oh, I read your file, I didn't take it personally. You're human, you're allowed to get stressed too." She shook my hand and turned for the door.

Feeling better, I packed up my things and went home to work on clearing my schedule for next week.

By 8pm, I was officially on vacation and feeling better already. I changed into sweats, poured myself that drink I skipped the night before, and settled in in front of my bedroom TV, about to start scrolling through Netflix. My phone chimed telling me I had email.

Realizing I had forgotten to set my auto reply on work emails, I picked up the phone and saw my patient's name highlighted in bold with the subject line:

Do you see them yet?

Knowing I should ignore it, but unable to help myself, I opened it....

They say, after a while, a psychiatrist needs to talk to another psychiatrist on a regular basis; to keep all that information from tearing a hole in our minds. I didn't "go crazy" like they say I did. I am more sane, more lucid, and more terrifyingly here than I ever have been before.

I woke up in a hospital, a state run psychiatric hospital, it was two weeks after I opened that email. That is two weeks that I don't have any recollection of. They say I had a manic episode and I seemed to be speaking an unknown language when I was found.

I do see them now, everyone has them, we collect them over the years. Sometimes they go away when new ones show up. But the really bad ones, those demons are with you for life.

That patient gave me this curse, I intend to give it back to him somehow. I called in a favor from the few people who will talk to me now, I asked them to look into the background of the patient and now I could see the orderly hurrying down the hall with an envelope. Finally, some answers.

He was out of breath when he got to me and handed the sealed envelope over and hurried away again. I excitedly tore it open to a piece of lined notebook paper that said:

"John Christian Roberts DOB: 3/14/76 - DOES NOT EXIST"

What? I started flipping through the pages that were included that showed my empty block of time on Thursday afternoons. How could this be possible? My receptionist, Annie, she saw him; she knows he's real.

Then I flipped to the last page which was a copy of an ad that I posted over a month ago, searching for a receptionist, after my last one, Annie, mysteriously disappeared along with a 21-year-old intern named Emily Brown.

What have I done?

Whore's Moon
Stanley Webb

Shirrel's cunt perspired in the night's heat, sweat flowing down her thighs at a thermometer's pace while she walked her block.

A sedan turned onto her block. Shirrel stepped into his headlights, and stuck out her thumb. He stopped beside her. She leaned into his open window, adjusting her neckline to display her tits.

Shirrel smiled. "Hi, I'm Mary, are you dating tonight?"

"Yes."

"What's your name?"

"John."

"I have to ask you, John, if you're looking to hurt someone tonight?"

"No."

"Are you a police officer?"

"No."

"Can I get in your car with you?"

"Sure."

Shirrel circled to the sedan's passenger door. The car's interior smelled of industrial grime, John had probably just ended his shift at the factory. Shirrel watched him closely, measuring the truth of his reassurances.

John also seemed nervous. He asked, "Are you a police officer?"

"No. A police woman won't get in your car. She'll just send you around the corner to where her friends are waiting to ambush you." Shirrel grinned. "And, she'll never do this."

She grabbed his crotch. His cock already felt hard, cramped inside his jeans.

She chuckled. "Let's go somewhere so I can take care of this for you." John pulled away from the curb. "Drive through that intersection... turn right here... left there... park between those dumpsters."

He turned the car off.

Shirrel massaged his erection. "What do you want, John?"

"How about a blowjob?"

"Yum. Can you give me fifty for that?"

"I've got thirty."

"Don't make me beg for it, John."

"Honest, that's all I have."

"Okay." Shirrel pocketed the cash, then licked her lips. "Take your dick out."

John unzipped. His throbbing meat popped through his fly. She closed her fingers around him, and pumped slowly. John's cock twitched in her grip, his big cum-vein swelling full. John groaned.

"If you keep that up, I'll come in your hand."

"We don't want that!"

Shirrel opened a condom, fitted it on his cock-head, then used her mouth to roll the latex sleeve down onto his shaft.

"Jesus!" He slipped his hand into her shorts, cupping her ass.

Shirrel raised her head. "No fingers in my pussy."

She resumed the job, pounding her fist and mouth up and down on his meat. John grunted, thrusting his hips at her. Shirrel made eager, wet sounds. She worked hard for a minute and a half, then his fingers clenched on her ass.

"I'm coming!"

Shirrel moaned while John got off. She held him in her mouth for a moment, then sat up. The condom's receptacle tip fell limp across her knuckles.

"Did you have a good time?"

"God, yes."

"Good. Would you mind driving me back to my block?"

\#

John drove off.

Shirrel spit the condom's lubricant onto the sidewalk, then strolled to the next block. Her friend Britty hung out there, near a vacant lot. A small, yellow blossom adorned her dark hair.

Britty toked on a joint. "Hey, want a hit?"

"Thanks." Shirrel drew sweet smoke down her throat.

"How you doing?"

"I made two-fifty."

"It's a slow night."

Shirrel took the flower from Britty's hair. "This is a buttercup?"

Britty shrugged.

Shirrel held the flower under Britty's chin. "If it glows on your skin, that means you like butter." But, in the shadows, nothing showed.

Britty said, "Maybe it tastes like butter." She bit the flower off its stem, and chewed. Shirrel laughed at her friend's antics, until Britty spit violently.

"It's burning!"

Britty gagged. Shirrel pounded her friend's back. Britty leaned over her knees, and vomited thin bile.

"Are you okay?"

"No," said Britty. "Let's go home."

"It's too early, Vic will be mad."

"Vic's always mad."

Shirrel put her arm around Britty as they walked home, concerned for her friend's well-being. Britty's skin had turned pasty, and she shivered in the heat.

"That flower is poison," Elsa said. "You should go to the hospital."

"No, I'll be okay."

They walked in darkness, most of the streetlights in the neighborhood broken. From far away came the noise of Friday night traffic. Neon lights reflected on the scattered clouds, and snatches of bar music intruded on the deserted blocks. Shirrel felt as if an alien world bordered on theirs.

Their communal home was a one-bedroom apartment in a condemned building. Two mattresses occupied the living room's floor. Elsa, Victor's third girl, lounged on one. Make-up, underwear, and a jar of petroleum jelly littered the surrounding carpet. Victor sat on a tattered recliner before a plasma-screen television. A music video's soundtrack rattled the walls.

"Britty!" Victor cried. "Come here, my favorite girl."

Elsa scowled.

Britty curled herself onto Victor's lap. He groped her tits.

"What have you got for me?" Victor asked.

"Three-fifty."

His smile faded. "That's not much."

"You know I like saving my pussy for you."

His mood recovered. "Don't let pleasure come before business." He turned to Shirrel. "What do you have, my second favorite?"

Elsa's scowl darkened.

Shirrel offered her wad. He counted it, then frowned. "This isn't good. What did you do?"

"Two fucks, and four BJs."

"Shit, that should be four hundred, at least! How much did you charge?"

"I ask fifty for a BJ."

"That's what you ask, but what do you get?"

"As much as I can."

"How much?"

"The last guy only had thirty."

Victor shifted Britty off his lap, stood, and crossed the room to Shirrel. He slapped her. Shirrel reeled against the wall.

Britty said, "It's not her fault—"

Victor turned on Britty. "You keep out of this!"

Elsa smirked.

He returned to Shirrel. "You're holding out on me."

"I'm not, that's my whole night's wad. I'll do better tomorrow, I promise!"

Victor crossed the room to a safe with a digital lock. Hiding the keypad with his body, he punched in the combination, deposited Shirrel's income, then returned to stand before his second-favorite girl.

"You'd better improve, Shirrel, because I don't need any cheap whores around. I'm trying to save enough cash so I can get-so I can take you girls out of this hell-hole. You've made me feel like a bad provider."

"I'm sorry, Vic."

"Maybe you're just not good enough." Victor pushed her to her knees, and opened his fly. His cock thrust out in her face. "Show me how you blow a man."

Shirrel produced a condom.

"Put that damn thing away, I'm not a trick!"

He twisted her hair in his fist, and pushed his blunt cock at her lips. Shirrel opened her mouth. Victor's cock thrust in deep, crowding her tongue, and nudging her uvula. Shirrel controlled her gag reflex. He drew his cock out, she gasped a breath, then he pushed himself deeper, into her throat. Victor employed both hands, forcing her nose against his belly. Her lungs strained. She grabbed his ass, urging him to get it over with.

"Yeah, you like it now!"

His balls quivered against her chin. His cock seemed to reach halfway to her stomach. Shirrel's esophagus lurched, seeking to eject the obstruction. Victor groaned, his cock pulsating in her stretched jaws. He clenched his fingers in her hair, then sighed, and let her go. His softening member slid out of her mouth. Shirrel tried to gasp in breath, but his ejaculate blocked her throat. Victor watched her sternly. Shirrel swallowed, and felt the warm mass slip all the way down. His semen floated in her gut. Shirrel's stomach heaved. She forced her reaction back down, and put on a smile.

"Did I do it good?"

Victor stroked her chin. "Really good. Don't make me mad anymore, okay?"

"I won't, I'm sorry."

Victor zipped up, and left the apartment.

Shirrel fled into the bathroom, throwing herself headfirst at the toilet, but the nauseous reflex had passed. She stuck her finger down her throat, to no avail. She had already digested his emission, made it a part of herself.

Britty entered, closing the door. She knelt beside Shirrel, and lifted her top, offering her erect nipple.

"This will help."

"You're unwell."

"No, I feel better."

Shirrel gratefully took the stiff teat into her mouth. Britty sighed, her heart racing between Shirrel's lips. Shirrel sucked, holding Britty tightly. She caressed Britty's shoulders, then slid her hands downward, pushing Britty's shorts out of the way, and massaging Britty's ass. Britty's cunt-scent rose. Still nursing, Shirrel reached further down, and caressed her friend's wet, hairy slit. Britty moaned, stroking her other tit against Shirrel's cheek.

"This one's getting jealous."

Shirrel obliged, and also slipped a finger into Britty's hole. Britty's cunt tightened.

"Put it all inside me."

Shirrel inserted a second finger, then a third, then a fourth. Britty's cunt gushed lubricant. She gasped, clawing at Shirrel's back.

"More!"

Shirrel slowly inched her knuckles inside, while Britty whimpered, rotating her hips. Britty's cunt stretched to receive Shirrel's hand, then snugged tight around her wrist. Shirrel closed her fist.

"Are you ready?"

"Do it!"

With a slow, steady rhythm, Shirrel fucked Britty. Britty's cunt slurped, dripping thick juice to Shirrel's elbow.

"No man can fill me like you do!"

Shirrel leaned down, and pressed her nose into Britty's pubic hair. She stretched out her tongue, and flicked Britty's clit.

"Oh God yes!"

Britty rammed herself up and down Shirrel's fist. Her clit stiffened against Shirrel's tongue. Britty groaned. Her body trembled. Her cunt tightened spasmodically. Britty grasped Shirrel's shoulders, pushing her friend closer. Shirrel licked faster. Britty came, her nails biting through Shirrel's halter top, then she leaned, shaking, on Shirrel. Shirrel waited until her friend's contractions eased, then slipped her fist out.

"I guess you liked it."

"That was incredible! What do you want, Shirrel baby?"

"Lay on your back."

Shirrel dropped her shorts, and straddled Britty's face. Britty licked up and down her moist folds, then pushed her tongue deep into Shirrel's cunt. Shirrel stroked herself against Britty's face, then shifted her position.

"Eat my ass!"

Britty licked around the tight hole, then thrust her tongue inside. Shirrel moaned, and rode harder. Britty slipped two fingers inside Shirrel's cunt. When the fingers were slick with juice, she slipped one up the asshole. Britty returned her focus to Shirrel's cunt, sucking Shirrel's clit in and out between her lips. Shirrel played with her own tits, riding her friend on growing waves of pleasure, until her holes clenched, orgasmic contractions spurting vaginal fluid into Britty's mouth.

The door opened. Elsa said, "Vic told you two to stop doing this."

Shirrel rolled off Britty. "Don't tell him."

Elsa smirked. "I'll tell him, for sure, then I'll be his favorite girl."

Britty rose, and said, "No, you won't." She lunged.

Elsa dodged out of the bathroom. Shirrel scrambled after Elsa, and caught her by the ankle. Elsa fell with a curse. Britty grabbed Elsa's other leg.

"Get her arms."

Shirrel caught Elsa by the wrist. Elsa slapped with her free hand, but Shirrel caught it, as well, and pinioned Elsa face down. Britty yanked Elsa's shorts off. Elsa kicked at her. Britty evaded the clumsy attack, and lowered her face toward Elsa's crotch. Elsa clamped her thighs together.

"Stop that, I'm no lezzie!"

Britty caught up the stray jar of petroleum jelly, scooped out a handful, and smeared the grease on Elsa's ass and thighs. She lubricated her hand and forearm, then slipped her fingers between Elsa's clenched legs.

"Hey, no means no!"

Britty grinned. "Your cunt is wet." She stroked Elsa's crack.

"Shit," Elsa gasped.

Britty continued, her hidden fingers making sloppy noises. Elsa shivered, and her legs slowly parted. Britty lay prone between them, and nuzzled Elsa's cunt. Elsa cursed, but her hips began to move, thrusting at Britty's tongue.

"You filthy dykes!"

Elsa's thighs opened wider. Britty pressed her nose deeper, slurping. Shirrel watched, her own cunt heating. She moved her crotch near to Elsa's head, letting the captive sniff her juices. Britty massaged Elsa's ass cheeks, licking faster, moaning into Elsa's cunt. Elsa pumped her hips, panting, her belly slapping the floor. Her groan rose into a scream. Her body went tense, then fell limp.

Britty withdrew and sat up, her face shining slick. "Now, you are a lezzie, and if you tell on us, we'll tell on you."

"Fuck you, that was rape!"

"You liked it."

"I'll get you bitches for this!"

Elsa stood up. She wiped her crotch with Britty's shorts, then recovered her own, and left.

"We probably shouldn't have done that," said Shirrel. "She'll tell Vic for sure."

"So what? I'm his favorite girl. Anyway, Vic's gone until morning, and Elsa won't be back. We can sleep together."

Britty led Shirrel down the hall to the Victor's bed, and lay atop her. They kissed languorously, Shirrel caressing her lover's backside.

"Someday we'll get out of here," Britty said sleepily. "We'll sleep like this every night, forever."

"Forever," Shirrel replied wistfully.

Soon, Britty's gentle snoring tickled her ear. Shirrel drifted to sleep under her friend's comfortable weight.

Britty whispered, "Was that the door?"

"…I didn't hear nothing…"

The lovers shared the night's dream.

#

Shirrel awoke, and met the full moon's gaze through the bedroom's open window.

She heard Victor unlock the apartment's door. Shirrel slithered out from under Britty, and fled the bedroom as he entered.

Victor paused at the end of the hall, scowling at her. "Where did you come from?"

"The bathroom."

He glanced around the two empty mattresses in the living room. "Where's Elsa?"

At that moment, Elsa appeared behind Vic. "I've been out working."

"This early?"

"All night!" She offered him a wad of cash. "Someone has to take up the slack around here." Elsa sneered at Shirrel.

Victor counted the wad, his smile growing. "Thanks, Baby!"

"Maybe you need a new favorite girl, Vic."

Victor crossed to his safe, keyed in the combination, and opened the door. He stiffened.

"What in fuck?"

Elsa asked, "What is it, Baby?"

Victor stood and whirled, his eyes wide with rage. "Where's my money?"

"I don't know, Baby. I've been out all night."

Victor charged across the room towards Shirrel, and seized her by the neck. Over his shoulder, she saw the empty safe.

"Where is it?"

Elsa smirked, and Shirrel realized that Victor's third favorite girl had engineered a coup. Elsa had robbed Victor's safe, and returned him his own cash as fresh earnings. Victor's hands crushed the truth in Shirrel's throat. She pried ineffectually at his fingers. Shirrel's visions speckled.

"Baby," said Elsa. "I think you should ask Britty where your money is."

Victor released Shirrel, and whirled on Elsa. "What are you saying?"

Elsa shrugged. "I'm just saying, ask Britty."

Victor stormed down the to the bedroom.

Shirrel staggered after him. She tried to protest Elsa's accusation, but her larynx snapped painfully.

Victor awoke his favorite girl with a slap. Britty sat upright, her eyes wide. "Where is it, bitch?"

"What?"

"Where's my money?"

"Elsa," Shirrel gasped, but her voice was unintelligible. She grasped her neck in pain.

Victor ignored Shirrel, and pounced atop Britty. He clenched his fingers around her throat.

"Give it back!"

Britty's eyes bulged.

Elsa turned away, laughing silently.

Shirrel screamed, feeling as if her throat ripped asunder, and attacked Victor. Shirrel clawed at his eyes.

"Get the fuck off me!" Victor twisted, throwing an elbow into Shirrel's chin. The blow knocked her back across the room, where she lay dazed.

Victor resumed choking Britty. Her feet drummed on the bed.

Shirrel mouthed, "Please don't kill her."

Victor bared his teeth. His finger's pressed into Britty's skin. Her eyes rolled back, her legs went still, and her body shuddered.

"Please, don't."

Britty's tongue protruded. Her sphincter relaxed.

Victor leaped away with a cry of disgust. "What the fuck did you shit for?"

Britty lay dead.

Victor did not notice. "I asked you a question!"

He slapped Britty, whose head rolled limply.

Victor backed away. "Shit!" He wiped his hands on his pants. "Shit, shit, shit! Look what you made me do! Shit, what am I going to do? I don't want to go to prison over some whore." He turned to the corner, his back trembling.

Elsa said, "Don't worry, Vic. We'll throw her in the lake, where your DNA will wash off."

"They'll still come for me, they know she's mine."

"Then, we'll remove her identifying features.

Victor turned to Elsa with hope in his eyes. "Identifying features?"

"Her teeth, and fingerprints."

Victor nodded, then clicked his switchblade knife.

Elsa said, "Let me do it!"

Elsa skinned Britty's dead fingers, then hurried out with the scraps. The toilet flushed. Elsa returned a moment later with a pair of vise-grip pliers. She adjusted the steel jaws, and thrust them into Britty's mouth.

"Eat this, bitch!"

The full moon witnessed.

#

Shirrel had never considered the weight of death.

They hauled Britty's corpse through the city's beaten neighborhoods, avoiding the rare pools of streetlight. Shirrel carried one dead arm, and Elsa the other, while Victor took the legs. The corpse slipped through their hands, forcing them to pause often to renew their grips.

The head lolled back, glassy eyes staring up, toothless mouth agape.

Shirrel felt too numb to scream.

They crossed the deserted lakeshore park, and hauled their burden to the end of the wooden pier.

Victor said, "Get her swinging, and let go on three. One… two… three!"

Britty splashed two yards from the pier, and floated face-down.

Shirrel turned, and walked back down the pier to the shore.

Victor said, "Shit, she's drifting back."

Shirrel wandered away along the water's edge.

Victor hoisted and threw an overflowing trash can. Britty's corpse rolled over. Gas bubbled from her mouth, and she sank.

Moments later, the ripples struck the shoreline at Shirrel's feet.

Victor gave a satisfied sigh. "Let's go home."

"Not yet," said Elsa. "We have to take care of her."

A moment of silence followed.

"Where is she?" said Elsa.

"Shit," said Victor. "She went for the cops!"

Their footsteps slapped along the pier to shore, then faded across the park toward the streets.

Shirrel had no thought of going to the police. She wandered the streets like a zombie, feeling a hollow where her soul had been. Shirrel ended up on Britty's working block. As the eastern sky brightened, Shirrel's soul filled with grief. She collapsed behind the venomous, flowering weeds in the vacant lot, screaming and weeping. Morning people ignored her cries, hurrying on their ways.

I have nothing to live for now.

She harvested the buttercups, and stuffed her mouth full. The flavor was acrid. Her mouth blistered. She forced herself to swallow, but then regurgitated. Shirrel forced the bile back down. Her guts burned. She gathered more flowers, eating until convulsions took her. The poison burned into every cell. Her limbs stuttered on the earth, then went still. Numbness spread from her belly, crawling up and down her limbs. Her colon spontaneously purged. She lay paralyzed, staring at the brightening sky. Soon, flies gathered, buzzing around her waste. The sun rose into sight. She could not close her lids, or breathe. No pulse thrummed in her ears.

When do I die?

The sun climbed past its zenith, burning into her open eyes. Rats investigated her. More flies came, gathering all over her.

Is this death?

The sun set.

This is Hell!

She could not scream.

Hours later, two figures appeared above her.

"She's here," said Elsa. "She's dead, too."

Victor said, "Thank God! We'll do her like we did Britty."

He offered Elsa the pliers.

Shirrel tasted the oily steel. The plier's jaws crunched into one of her incisors. Elsa pulled, grunted, then pulled harder. Slowly, the tooth slid out by its roots. Shirrel felt everything. Elsa continued, her perspiration dripping on her victim's face, until she had extracted Shirrel's last tooth. Then, Elsa traded the pliers for Victor's knife. One by one she peeled Shirrel's fingers.

Victor said, "Bury the stuff, then help me carry her."

Shirrel swung between them, her ass brushing the ground. Her head hung back, forcing her to stare up at Victor. He averted his eyes. Elsa dropped her legs, and her tailbone cracked on the pavement. Later, Victor dropped her arms. Shirrel's skull split. Eternity seemed to pass before they dragged her down the pier. The weathered planks shoved splinters up her ass.

"One... two... three!"

For a moment, she felt weightless.

Then, the cold, watery impact drove her under, but she floated back up, her face submerged. Water filled her sinuses and her ears, flowing down her throat. Wavelets danced across her back. Her limbs hung in the deep, black water. Fishes came to nibble at her.

Shirrel heard Victor, his voice muffled oddly by the water. "Good, the wind's blowing her out."

Victor and Elsa's wooden footsteps echoed into the distance, and she was alone.

But then, gradually, the water brightened, until a dim ray penetrated the depths. Britty lay below her, on a bed of water weeds. Their dead eyes met, then Shirrel drifted on. The lake's floor dropped away. She hung in a world of strange, fluid light.

A ghostly sensation caressed her back, intensifying, seeming to penetrate her skin. Her fear and pain diminished, for she sensed something profound above her. Energy tingled in her spine. Shirrel's heart gave a sudden, agonized beat, then went still again, but the pulsation left a spot of warmth inside her. Her heart throbbed again. The warmth grew, filling her core, and spreading through her veins. Her limbs convulsed, rolling her supine in the water.

The full moon hung above the lake's eastern shore, as large as a god, shining brighter than the sun. The light stabbed into her eyes, filled her brain, and charged her nerves.

Her mouth gaped. Cramps twisted her gut, purging her channels of water. Shirrel's chest expanded, sucking in a new breath.

A series of vicious contractions took her, the muscles seizing until her bones snapped. Her skin writhed. Razorblades erupted through her gums. Her pelvis and shoulders folded into unfamiliar shapes, then her fractured skeleton knit itself back together. Her face seemed to burst. Shirrel had never imagined that she could live through such agony. She screamed, but howling echoed from the lake's shoreline.

Blessedly, the pain abated, turning into a dull, and somehow pleasant, throbbing. Shirrel felt herself capsizing, and struggled. Her limbs obeyed her once more. She paddled to the shallows, then crawled on all fours. Her hands had transformed into black-furred paws. Her eyes, white and glowing, reflected in the lake.

I've changed into a wolf!

Shirrel felt no fear. Instead, she felt joyous vindication of all her life's misery. She raised her voice to her benefactor, the moon. The city's dogs barked in response, and she recognized the terror in their cries, terror of her. She could even smell the thousands of pets, and the tens of thousands of city residents, including Victor and Elsa.

Shirrel had never felt so confident and strong. She hungered for vengeance, and flesh.

Shirrel crossed the city in moments.

She broke down Victor's door.

Victor lay on the recliner, his pants down, Elsa blowing him. They both leaped to their feet, screaming terrified obscenities. Victor tripped on his pants, kicked them off, and rose with his knife.

Shirrel said, "You shouldn't have killed Britty."

Victor turned pale. "Jesus Christ!"

"His name lacks power in your mouth." Shirrel bared her fangs.

He grabbed Elsa as a shield. Elsa screamed, fighting to escape, clawing at his eyes. Victor stabbed her belly, then threw her down before himself.

"Take this bitch, not me!"

Elsa lay at his feet, her hands over her gushing wound. Her eyes and mouth gaped round.

Shirrel stepped over the dying woman.

"Get away from me!" Victor brandished his knife.

Shirrel coiled on her haunches.

"No!"

Shirrel leaped. The impact threw Victor against the wall. She lunged for his throat. He shoved his arm into her jaws, and stuck the knife between her ribs. The steel blade found her heart, but without effect. Shirrel laughed with her new voice, then bit through his arm. Victor shrieked. Shirrel spat the broken limb aside, and bit his neck, crushing his trachea. Shirrel held her grip, watching his eyes. Victor struggled, unable to breathe, stabbing her repeatedly. Then, his eyes lost focus. The knife slipped from his hand. His bowels had released, but he smelled delicious.

She licked his cock, which strangely remained erect. She took it whole into her mouth, tore it off, and swallowed it. Shirrel then set her teeth into his belly, ripping away the fat and muscle layers. She gobbled his liver, then uncoiled his entrails, gulping their length unbroken. Then, she pried his ribs open, and tore out his heart. It slid down her throat, lubricated with dark blood.

Elsa lay gasping in a congealed pool. Shirrel licked the floor clean, then broke Elsa's neck with a bite.

Feeling sated, Shirrel went to sit by the window. She licked the blood from her mouth, then cleaned her feet, while the moon descended in the east. She paused, regarding her paw, which soon would become a hand again. The scent of gore still allured her senses, but as a woman the stench would seem repulsive. She could not remain in Victor's condemned apartment, but she had nowhere else to go. Her satiation turned hollow in her stomach.

A miracle had returned her from death, but she still had no reason to live. Shirrel howled in distress.

Someone howled in reply.

Shirrel recognized the voice. She sat straighter, whimpering with excitement, anticipation thrilling her nerves.

Another she-wolf raced under the moon, lake water still draining from her fur. Shirrel greeted her friend with a howl of joy.

Sigma Hell
Shelby Thomas

His high had way past worn off, and after dealing with idiots all day at work, Eric just needed to unwind; a night off with a few friends was exactly what he needed. Eric stood as he heard the car horn out front in his driveway. Picking his backpack up off of the bed, he made his way out past his mother, who was currently screaming at him. After almost 26 years of living with the woman, he had grown used to her daily rants. It was always the same: *the world is a miserable speck and it should burn, I pray every night to die! you're a worthless fuck-up and a drug addict, go kill yourself or get yourself killed!* None of that even fazed Eric anymore. In fact, he often loved to tell people that there was nothing anyone could say to him that his own mother hadn't already said.

As Eric slipped into the back seat of his friends' car, he handed a ten-dollar bill to his buddy, Matt, over the driver's seat. "You have no idea how much I needed to get out of there, man".

"Not a problem," Matt spoke up as he looked back at Eric in the rearview mirror. He put the car in drive and hit the road.

Eric sighed as he threw the empty medicine bottle into the trash can. This habit was becoming more consuming as time passed. He had been told countless times that this was an addiction and that he needed help, but as stupid as getting high on over-the-counter cold medicine might be in reality, it helped him get through his fucked up, day to day life.

Eric Ripley really didn't have a lot going for himself; he was a 26-year-old addict who still lived at home with his parents, and whose existence consisted of playing video games in a dark, cave-like bedroom and doing odd jobs to fuel his addictions - both to gaming and drugs. He looked up as he heard his friend's voice break the silence as she hung up her cell phone.

"Alright, so we have to get mom to Chrissy's".

"Kylie!" Matt complained, "you do this shit to me all the time! You make plans and never tell me until I can't say no. Your sister lives almost two fucking hours from here and that's only one way!" Kylie simply rolled her eyes, ignoring him as he ranted.

Eric chuckled softly as he listened to the couple's argument. He had never though that he would be okay with seeing Kylie with someone else, even after their terrible break-up, but after seeing how she lit up around Matt, he couldn't even bring himself to attempt to cause problems between the two of them. He loved her still, even more than he cared to admit to himself, which is why he couldn't bring himself to hurt her like that again.

"She wants mom to stay with her for a few days. Don't you want the house to ourselves for a bit?" As the couple bickered back and forth, getting ready for their journey, Eric's high began to kick in. Emptying his pockets, he found two more bottles as well as an empty box and a couple of loose blister packets. This wasn't good. He had taken way… way more than he intended to and his high was going south quickly. "Eric, you okay, man?" Kylie looked up at him, concern darkening her features. He simply nodded silently. "Too much again?" she quizzed, glancing down at the trash before them and he nodded once more.

"I'll be fine, I promise," Eric spoke, patting her on the head as they walked out the door towards the couple's car.

After about fifteen minutes or so of decrepit buildings, fields, and pastures filled with farm animals, things began to take an even more unusual turn. It seemed to Eric that the car was no longer driving on the roads, but was floating just above it. A quick look out the window told him that not only had the car grown wings, but that the roads themselves had changed and had begun to rearrange themselves before them and then twist away and become engulfed in flames behind them. Terrified, Eric turned his head to the front of the car to alert the others of the chaos that now surrounded them, when he saw that his traveling companions were also changing. Matt had grown quite a curious set of horns, one being straight and the other being broken off and pointed downward. Even as Eric looked at him, his skin began to turn blue. The blue-skinned demon that now sat in the driver's seat still retained some of Matt's visage, but now wore a leather jacket and a newsboy cap with a small, metal pitchfork emblem on it. "What's wrong man?" the demon queried, leering back at Eric with a devilish grin on his face.

Only the cackling sound of Kylie's laughter pulled Eric's attention from the driver, but the form that housed it was unfamiliar to him as well, though it was both terrifying and arousing. A purple forked tongue with three small gold piercings was visible as her mouth was ajar with laughter. Her skin was a dark crimson color, and her sharply pointed ears came up to gold piercings through both. Her under-bust corset did nothing to ensure even a shred of modesty, not that the creature before him minded in the least. Her razor-sharp teeth glistened in the moonlight as she smiled back at him. "What's wrong, handsome?" the succubus asked in her sing-songish lullaby tone. Her breasts bounced as she giggled softly, and strange as it seemed, Eric couldn't take his eyes off of her.

Kylie's mother, or at least what had once been her mother, was now a dull, gray screeching harpy. It was unclear to Eric whether or not it was continuously flapping it's wings on purpose or not, but by this point he was sure that he could take anything that was thrown at him. He just stared blankly out the back window of the car, watching as the ruins surrounding them rearranged themselves constantly. Music from the radio seem to creep eerily behind the car instead of being in the car with them. This was it, he decided. He had overdosed and killed himself, and now this was his personal hell. His mother always told him that he would end up here. At least the company is good and somewhat entertaining, Eric thought to himself as he listened to all the noise from the harpy's screech and the bickering demons in the front seat.

Everywhere he looked there was debris. This place was familiar and terrifying all at the same time. It looked as though there had been a nuclear war; barren, scorched earth as far as he could see. A huge building, Eric assumed it to be a hospital, sat in the distance, what remained of it in flames.

How long had they been riding? Time seemed to have no meaning to Eric anymore at this point. The more miles that went by, things around them had slowly faded back into reality as he knew it and by the time they arrived at Kylie's sister's home, Eric had come down off his high completely and was thankful to be back with his friends. On the drive back to the couple's house Eric had begun to recount to Kylie and Matt his experience on their drive. "A red-skinned succubus, you say?" Kylie mused as she turned in her seat to face him as they pulled to a stop at a red light, "I knew that there was something different about me." She chuckled.

"I'm so done with that shit," Eric said repeatedly "That was more than I ever wanted to experience, man." He stretched out on the back seat, continuing to ramble on about his trip.

"Eric, shut up for like, five seconds… please?" Kylie requested playfully. He sighed, looking up at the night sky through the back windshield of the couple's car. A sigh escaped him as he closed his eyes and drifted off into a much-needed sleep following what he had just gone through.

Once they finally made it back to their house and Matt got the door unlocked, Eric breathed a sigh of relief as they walked into the house. He plopped down onto the sofa with a smile on his face and whistled for the couple's dog, but his smile faded quickly. It wasn't the couple's playful bulldog that stepped out of the hall, but a large three-headed black dog with red eyes. As Matt's hysterical laughter filled the room, a chill went straight down Eric's spine. As he slowly turned he saw the demons standing once more in the door. "Say," the blue-skinned demon spoke up smiling, "Wanna go for a ride?"

Deranged
Thomas S. Gunther

"Are there any side effects I should know about?" Jim asked. "I won't end up foaming at the mouth or acting deranged or anything will I?" He felt conspicuous in the sterilized silence of the examination room, erratic keyboard noises the only interruption. His doctor peered up at him over the rim of glasses too large for her face. Her deep brown eyes twinkled with a merry glow that reminded him of an old Christmas issue of *Playboy*. She momentarily looked back at the monitor, then gave Jim Bum her full attention.

"It's virtually the same as the Wellbutrix, just a little stronger." She smiled. "All drugs come with potential side effects, of course. I doubt you'll experience anything worse than occasional diarrhea, though. But it may take some time to get used to it. Just let me know if you start feeling weird."

Jim loved his doctor. She wasn't like most of the doctors he had encountered in his fifty years. Dr. Julie Love--short, brunette, and bubbly--actually listened to him, and made him feel as if he were an equal. He liked to believe that she maybe even saw some promise in him, and even found him charming, if only with a condescending sense of humor. He was very comfortable around her. She was warm, friendly, and didn't do anything to remind him that he was a loser. She finished typing up his prescription, grabbed her clipboard, and patted him on the arm as she headed out, saying, "We've got to get you to quit smoking before you end up on oxygen."

"I'm trying, doc," Jim insisted. He looked down at the floor from his perch on the examination table and sucked air, then exhaled audibly. She was right, he knew, but he still wanted a cigarette. His exasperation didn't stem from her gentle reminder of his guilt, though. Rather, it was lingering energy from an earlier aggravation, a source of stress which repeatedly thwarted his smoking cessation goal. Dr. Love had a naturally soothing vibe Jim could swim in all day, but he had nearly drowned at the hands of a contractee. His impromptu meeting with Alexis that morning had not gone well, and the joy of picking up his check was blackened when she berated him for ten minutes for leaving a can of disinfectant on top of the water cooler. He wondered if she'd noticed that he had eaten two of her chocolates out of the jar on her desk, as well, and how she felt about that. Don't hold back, he thought.

Alexis Cruise, whom he had quickly learned to loathe, was the director of a local library Jim had recently counted among his cleaning contracts. From day one he had decided that she was rather imperious, always looking down a nose too thin for her face, and always overdressed. She dressed more like a bank teller than a librarian, wearing bursting-at-the-seems sweaters and stuffing roomy hips into pencil skirts sized for younger, slimmer women. He knew it was a stratagem, conscious or unconscious, something she had probably done her whole life out of some repressed fear of rejection. It bothered him, though, how she used this wintry sex appeal to intimidate other women and reduce men to boot-licking sycophants, making sure the groveling monkeys knew she was the ringmaster.

Everyone cringed whenever they heard the approaching clackety-clack-clack of her heels, and her uncanny ability to walk across an icy parking lot in them assured them all she was, in fact, the Devil. Jim knew she was Satan because she had reminded him once a week for the last month, being sure to point out his trespass if he left any of his cleaning supplies out, missed a paper clip or minuscule piece of paper on the floor. Or, God forbid, vacuumed in the wrong direction. Why such a beautiful woman resorted to Machiavellian torture techniques, keeping her circus chimps on edge and locked in their cages, was beyond him.

Jim prided himself on doing an impeccable job, so he didn't understand why she picked at him relentlessly. While his other contractees praised him, his work never seemed to impress Alexis. He reasoned that maybe it was because he refused to kiss her ass anytime she wanted to reprimand him, or that she was just naturally an opportunistic predator. But, lately, she was beginning to convince him that his work was less than satisfactory, and this thought gnawed at him with growing hunger. Especially at the forefront of his paranoia were the glass entrance doors. No matter what he did, Jim could never seem to keep them clean of prints, smudges, or smears.

A pet peeve for Alexis, the glass was Jim's bane. He knew there was a logical explanation for it. Glass was tricky. The library was hotter indoors, keeping the inside of the glass warm while the outside remained cold. It had to be something scientific like that, anyway. It always streaked, and it seemed that no matter how thorough he thought he was, he always missed a spot. There was always one more grubby little handprint he had missed, usually toward the bottom of the door. He could not explain why it proved so difficult, he only knew that it caused him a great deal of vexation. He didn't experience this phenomenon at his other jobs, and this knowledge led to his musing about the place being haunted, and that these phantom handprints belonged to the ghosts of lost, murdered children, captive in Alexis Cruise's Library of Purgatory. Were they trying to escape, or were the smudges created when the children pressed their ghostly faces to the glass in anticipation of his weekly visit? Did they like him, or did they serve

Alexis, working toward dragging the poor man the rest of the way into Hell? Smudges, smears, and streaking, he knew, would be even worse that summer, particularly on a humid, rainy day. He wished it was summer. Spring, anyway. But it was February, and cold, drab, and dreary.

Jim was sick of winter. He was sick of trying to give up smoking, even if he knew it would probably lead to cancer. He was sick of Alexis Cruise. More than the smoking, she was the biggest reason Dr. Love had put him on the Wellbutrix—and now the new stuff—in the first place. His nerves were shot. Jim truly wanted to quit smoking, but that vile woman... She was just a miserable, frosty bitch, he supposed. Pulling on his coat while he waited for the nurse to return with his new prescription, Jim again recounted the morning's debacle, angrily fantasizing about bending the snooty director over her own desk, pulling her perfect platinum hair with one hand while eating her damned chocolates with the other. It was terribly violent, he knew, and he would never have the guts to do such a thing; but he could dream.

The idea burned in his mind, keeping him warm in an unforeseen and ruthless wind as he left the health center. Feigning alarm to his own morbidity, he lit up a square as soon as he got in his van. Intense shivering caused him to choke on the smoke, evoking breathless laughter.

The new medicine, and a break in the weather, ushered in brighter days.

He felt better about himself, his future, and was encouraged to try harder. He had smoked far less, probably smelled better, and with some careful maneuvering his relationship with Alexis had improved. She had even complimented him on his haircut and overall appearance. But, after about a week, the new pills had revealed their darker side. He had been watching television, and was deeply relaxed, when the quirky side effect hit him. At first, it was nothing more than a random thought, but it had taken hold of him, and intensified into something that terrified him. Looking back on it, he couldn't recall just what he had been watching, some show about travel, men's fashion, or the environment's demise, maybe. But he had thought, what was the point? It was hopeless. It all was. Everything. He remembered being so calm, so complacent, and the irrelevance of it all had cracked the shell of his squirming mind. It had been beyond a feeling of hopelessness, of utter defeat and insignificance. It had overwhelmed him, enveloping him in a shroud so dark he could no longer explain nor justify his own existence. For an instant, he had believed he understood the peace death offered. Then he had searched about his cramped and messy apartment until he had found a cigarette, telling himself that he should call Dr. Love. But he had downplayed the experience instead, secretly relishing the mildly orgasmic elation that had followed the spell.

The following Sunday, Jim had what he could only call a chance encounter with Alexis. He had started work about an hour late that day, having slept in, and was unable to finish before the director made one of her unexpected visits. Since her desk was barren of anything resembling work, so unlike the other desks that were folding under the weight of mountainous stacks of files, folders, and books, he figured she must have come just to hassle him, having found some reason. But Alexis actually walked in smiling, and the click of her heels even sounded less ominous than usual. She seemed curiously kind, of late.

"I'm sorry to intrude while you're working, Jim," she said in a voice that was almost pleasant. "I went to take my medicine this morning, but I couldn't find it, and I'm feeling a tad woozy." Jim smiled and nodded, frozen in place, knowing she would probably bite his head off when she realized he had carelessly left a roll of trash bags on her desk. It was possible he'd done it unconsciously out of spite, but it was just a convenient place to set them. As she removed her long gloves one finger at a time, she followed his eyes, spying the offending trash bags. The almost honest smile fled from her lips, pulling them downward in disdain.

"Sorry," he mumbled, jumping to remove them. But Alexis was a sleek cat, and reached her desk first, making Jim so nervous he dropped the roll on the floor. As he stood back up, he recognized the label on the bottle of pills Alexis had fished from the top drawer while he had fumbled with the trash bags; she had high blood pressure. It was the same medicine his father had taken, so long ago. Having moved in such a hurry, the two suddenly found themselves very close to one another, and their eyes met. What happened next was both disconcerting and exciting for Jim Bum. As her eyes fluttered, and her knees quit, Alexis put a hand to her head and collapsed backwards into his arms. Time stopped. Her hair tickled his face, her breasts found their way into his hands, and her perfume beckoned him. Fearing she may have had a stroke, Jim was just contemplating dialing 911 when the woman came to, gently removed herself from his arms, and slid into her chair.

"Would you bring me some water, Jim?" she asked. Her voice was shaky, but had resumed the familiar tone of superiority. He was vaguely reminded of Katherine Hepburn's character in *The African Queen,* his favorite movie, though he doubted Alexis had ever been that prudent or pure. Nonetheless, he decided that she rather looked like Hepburn, albeit a younger and witchier woman. This all went through his mind at lightspeed as he fetched the water. "Thank you," she said. He trembled imperceptibly at the touch of her slender fingers against his rough hands. She took her pill, and rested an elbow on her desk with her forehead in her hand.

"Are you gonna be okay?" Jim asked.

"Yes, I think so. This isn't the first time this has happened."

"Have you told your doctor?"

"Yes, of course," she snapped, rolling her eyes. Jim nodded and said, half stuttering, "Okay. I'm gonna finish up. Uhm… Just holler if you need anything."

"Thank you, Jim."

He went back to vacuuming, though his attention was fixed on Alexis. This was mostly out of concern, but he found it difficult not to soak in the odd combination of her weakened state and her sexual magnetism. It was bewitching. She caught him staring. He turned the vacuum back off. "Just, uh… I just wanted to make sure you're all right."

"I'm fine, Jim. Excuse me." She gave him a catty look as she headed for the restroom. Jim's eyes narrowed at her icy rebuttal, though he doggedly lapped up her stockinged legs when her back was to him. He was winding up the extra long cord of the vacuum cleaner when she returned, quickly donning her coat and fancy gloves. "Do me a favor, Jim," she said. "See what you can do about the toilet in the employee restroom. It's not flushing right." He started to ask how it was flushing wrongly, but she was out the door, leaving him with a cold blast of air and her lingering fragrance.

The experience stuck with him for the rest of the day. It was as close as he had been to a woman in years, and it was more than enough to stir a reoccurring and extremely uncomfortable erection, something he hadn't had any time of late he could recall. It was odd, though, her behavior. Had she really had a spell? How had she turned just so, to fall into his arms like that? She had to have faked it, he determined, the timing was just too coincidental. But, why, he wondered. Had she felt like she had to prove her medical condition to him? She couldn't possibly like him, could she? That wouldn't make sense, as she always treated him like a trained pet. There were no obvious answers, but neither was there any denying that what had transpired had made a significant impression. He could still smell her perfume. He could still smell her, almost tasting her essence. So taken was he with the experience that he hardly gave any thought to smoking, and when he realized he'd gone all day without lighting up, he decided the new medicine was a godsend.

That night, he had the strangest dream. He dreamed he was in the library, and Alexis was yelling at him. She was actually yelling, and loudly, but her mouth never moved. She stood like a statue, all alabaster with thin, pouting lips that beckoned his need. He didn't understand. How was it she was so hauntingly alluring while simultaneously giving him the what-for with toxic viciousness? Still, he wanted her, and moved to take her, but something was wrong. Everything was growing dark, ominous, and forbidding. His attempt to love Alexis was denied, and he found himself instead fighting for his life, swimming in gallons of rushing water that was flooding the library from nowhere and everywhere. He was drowning, choking on mouthfuls of cold water as he called out for help. A small lizard, green like a gecko, swam with him, darting through the water, but in slow motion as if it was fighting its way through jello. And then another, and another, and soon the water was teeming with thrashing, drowning lizards. They were latching onto him, as if he could save them. But they were heavy, like cinder blocks, pulling him down, down into the darkness. Jim Bum woke up screaming for his mother and coughing as if he had actually swallowed water down the wrong pipe.

He smoked a few cigarettes that morning, without guilt, having retrieved an emergency pack from the kitchen drawer. He put a pan on his tiny stove, cracked a couple of eggs in it, and put some bread in the toaster for an egg sandwich. He knew the dream was a warning, but why so vivid? The lizards distressed him. They resembled the toy Alexis had recently posted as a guardian atop her coveted jar of chocolates. He had not had a bad dream, nor a nightmare in which he awoke crying out for his mother, in many years. The memory of his mother's gentle voice soothed him while he scraped at his burning eggs. It was during troubling times such as these that he missed his parents the most. He didn't know what it was. Their memory, or guilt, maybe, or perhaps the loneliness for a woman, but for some reason he was reminded of the employee restroom toilet when his sandwich dripped mayonnaise on the floor. It reminded him that he was alone, and weary, that his life sucked, and that he was a loser. There was no point in wasting his time that morning watching Hepburn and Bogart in *The African Queen* as he had planned, even though he had all day, as it was his day off. There was no point in quitting smoking, there was no sense in living out his days hogging air, when he should save it for the more worthy, and there was no sense in eating a burnt egg sandwich. He threw his breakfast in the trash, inadvertently stepping on the forgotten glob of mayonnaise as he, shaking, lit another cigarette.

He was sitting at the end of his Murphy bed, blankly staring at his old television and VCR, absently wondering where he had stashed the ashtray when Mr. Lizard appeared to him. He stood in the archway that separated the room from the miniature kitchenette, somewhat in a shadow. "Hey, Spanky, what's up?" he asked. Drool slowly seeped from Jim's agape mouth. Mr. Lizard was anthropomorphically humanoid, except for his oversized gecko head. He was pleasingly green, and wore a sharp suit and tie. "Your shoe, man. Look at the bottom of your shoe!" He was chuckling like some prime-time cartoon character. "You know that'll make you go blind," he said.

Stupefied, Jim examined the bottom of his shoe. He didn't see anything. Why was there a talking lizard in his apartment?

"No," Mr. Lizard laughed, "the other one."

Jim obeyed, and discovered the mayonnaise he had stepped in. He looked up at the creature with the face of a bewildered child. "Oh, forget it," Mr. Lizard said, putting up his hands and waving them in dismissal. "Bad joke. It's me, not you. May I?" he asked, pointing at the pack of cigarettes Jim was fairly crushing in a clenched hand. He found one that wasn't broken, gave it to Mr. Lizard, and pulled the filter off another, sticking it in his mouth. He lit it, then handed the lighter to the reptile. Mr. Lizard politely thanked him, lit his smoke with the cheap lighter, and winked mischievously.

That was Jim's first encounter with Mr. Lizard. Mr. Lizard had a British accent, and admirable taste in clothing. But he was a bit narcissistic, Jim decided. Mr. Lizard was quite affable, though—he was polite, anyway, always observing a gentleman's code, of sorts—but he was sneaky, as well as charming. He seemed to be, and indeed turned out to be, one of those guys who claimed to be your friend, but had ulterior motives. At least Jim kept that suspicion in the back of his mind. Nobody else seemed to be able to see him, but Mr. Lizard liked hanging about, and commenting on whatever Jim was doing or thinking. He incessantly nagged him about his smoking, even though he was constantly bumming cigarettes. Meanwhile, Jim functioned in a sort of daze. He went through the motions day by day, counting on his medicine to keep him calm and sane. But he had completely given up on quitting smoking.

The weird thing was that while Mr. Lizard increasingly harassed him, Alexis Cruise had been abundantly praising him. He had finally fixed the toilet. It hadn't been flushing right at all, and was always threatening to overflow. But, other than that Jim didn't know that he was doing anything different, and decided she had, perhaps, finally recognized his dogged efforts, rewarding him with occasional pats on the head. She was even giving him treats. "Jim," she would call from her desk, "you can take the rest of that cake home with you, if you like." She had begun showing up regularly on Sundays, staying just long enough to execute some minor task and briefly converse with Jim, asking him how he was doing that day. She was always pleasant and quick with a compliment. Jim would just nod and smile, though he never remembered saying much of anything. He would only ever recall her alluring smile, and how Mr. Lizard would stand behind her and make absurd faces or sexual innuendos, determined to ruin things for him.

"Why do you keep doing this to me, Mr. Lizard?" he finally demanded one particular Sunday after Alexis had left the building. He absently ran a hand through his thinning hair. "It's not funny anymore. You're going to get me in trouble. If she finds out about you, she'll never speak to me again."

Mr. Lizard snorted. A little fire flamed from his nostrils. "You've got to be kidding me."

His face twisted in disgust. "Are you really going all dozy? You really are a bum, aren't you? You know that's English for your back door, don't you?"

Jim's face felt hot.

"Bullocks. I don't believe you. What happened to all that anger, all that business about bending her over her desk? You like her now, or something? What? Are you going around imagining you're Humphrey Bogart, piloting your toy boat down the Congo as you work your way into her heart? What a sap. She's not into you. You're just another one of her pet monkeys." Mr. Lizard lit a smoke with fire from his nose. He loosened his silk tie.

"I doubt she would like you," Jim retorted, looking away. He needed a cigarette but didn't have any.

"Here, you need a smoke?" asked Mr. Lizard, reading his mind. "It's the least I can do. You're gonna need it, anyway."

Jim flinched at Mr. Lizard's cryptic tone. "Why?" he dared. "What did you do?"

"Oh, I didn't do anything, not yet anyway. I just thought I'd save you the trouble of embarrassing yourself."

"How do you mean?" Jim's eyes were practically slits.

"Well, I asked her, you know, how she felt bout jumping in the sack. You know what she said?"

Jim didn't know. He didn't want to know.

"She said the only way I was ever gonna have her was if she were dead," Mr. Lizard said, chuckling. "Can you believe that?"

Jim didn't know what to believe. When did Mr. Lizard ever talk to Alexis? How could she even see him? And, more importantly, why hadn't she mentioned it. He was all at once very jealous of his spectral associate, his mind filling with unbidden visions of the reptile pawing her with all the charm of a sophomoric baboon. And he was very worried that he had misjudged and misunderstood the signals Alexis had been giving him. He walked away until he could no longer hear Mr. Lizard's inane laughter.

The days that followed were a foggy blur. Jim continued his work at his other jobs as usual, waiting patiently for Sunday to arrive, and hoping Alexis would be there. He wanted to remain vigilant, hopeful, and somehow apologize for Mr. Lizard's caveman behavior. He prayed that, somehow, he could tell her how he felt. That he was going to have words with the rude cretin, and that he was ready to take their relationship to the next level, if she would have him. Thankfully, Mr. Lizard left him alone, and by Friday he was starting to feel human again. Around six o'clock that evening, Jim's archaic cell phone buzzed like an angry bumblebee. Squinting to decipher the numbers, he realized the call was from the library.

"Yes," he answered, his voice wavering. He wanted to sound professional, jubilant, but with a touch of suave apathy. Instead, he just sounded excited and nervous.

"Hello, Jim," the smooth, feline voice said. "It's Alexis. Listen, I hate to be a bother, but that toilet overflowed again. Is there any chance I could get you to come in and mop it up? Do be a dear, won't you? I'll get a plumber to fix it as soon as I can."

Jim promised he would be right there to clean up the mess, and that he would look at the toilet.

"You may want to wear an old pair of shoes. But, don't bother with the toilet, just mop it up. We just won't use it until we get it fixed, okay? Oh, and before I forget, I gave the new accountant a key. I doubt you'll ever see her, but if you do, her name is Mrs. Kravitz, and she'll know who you are."

Jim again pledged his servitude, and thanked the library goddess when she said he could have the leftover donuts in the break room. He rushed to the library, hoping to glimpse her, to swoon her before she left, but Alexis had already gone. He cleaned up the restroom, made it spotless, and wondered at the toilet that worked just fine when he flushed it repeatedly. It was dark, but oddly warm, when he locked up. A light breeze swept myriad scents, previously trapped in the cold ground, into his flaring nostrils. He shook, scrunching his shoulders as he scrambled to get in the van and get it started before ghoulish ghost children sprang from the moonless ink to claim his soul.

Sunday saw him waking up feeling better than ever, though, and he showered and shaved quickly, skipping a fifth cup of coffee and any kind of breakfast so he could get to work early. As he headed out to clean the library, he realized that he hadn't had a cigarette for several days. Encouraged, he fought the craving, and drove to work whistling contentedly to the tune on the radio. His happy mood skyrocketed when he pulled into the parking lot and spotted Alexis's Buick.

She was nowhere to be seen, though, and the library was eerily quiet as he looked around for her. He decided she wasn't there at all, and perhaps had only parked there as a meeting place with the new accountant, and that the two had most likely gone out to get breakfast. So he went to work, dragging out the vacuum and extra cord, and getting hot water and oil soap ready to clean the wooden tables. He listened to his favorite station on the little radio, be-bopping to the music as he worked. But he kept the volume down in anticipation of Alexis and the accountant's return.

Today is gonna be a great day, he thought. He just knew Alexis was going to give him that obvious, undeniable sign that she liked him, and wanted more from their relationship. This filled his mind and, before he knew it, an hour had passed. He looked out the window in earnest, like some loyal mutt awaiting his master's return, but the lot remained empty and quiet, save for the silvery Buick.

Gotta use the can, he thought, and headed for the public restroom. An impish temptation gave him pause. Why not use the employee restroom? He was practically an employee, anyhow, and no one would ever know. Just remember to put the seat down. Mr. Lizard would do it, he figured, regretting the gecko's absence. He had never dared to use the employee restroom before. Why it should make any difference, he didn't know, but some misplaced sense of loyalty had always stopped him. But Jim felt good, confident, even manly. Imagining he was Mr. Lizard, or that he was as slick, he opened the door wide with animated gusto, then quickly closed it, blushing.

"Whoa! I'm so sorry," Jim blurted out, wringing his hands. How embarrassing to walk in on her like that. But Alexis never responded. He tried to pretend that it hadn't happened, and hoped terribly that she wouldn't speak of his faux pas when she finally did exit the restroom. Nervously doing his own business, he listened for her from the adjacent restroom where he hid, hoping to regain his composure. But he never heard the sounds of the other toilet flushing, or her washing her hands, or any indication that Alexis was moving at all. When she still hadn't made a peep after several more minutes, he went outside to fish through the van's ashtray for a good butt he might smoke. When he returned inside, and saw that she had not come out of the restroom, it dawned on him that something must be wrong.

"Alexis?" he dared to call through the closed door. "Are you all right?" His question went unanswered, and he just knew he was going to have to open that door again. Maybe he was just seeing things, he thought. Maybe hallucinating was another side effect of the medication. Grimacing, he opened the door.

He had seen her, after all, and she was sitting on the toilet, looking right at him, but she never flinched. "Miss Cruise?" She did not respond. She did not move. She did not call him a masher and hurriedly move to pull up her nylons from around her knees, nor smooth her skirt to hide her treasures. Jim realized the queen was dead. Then Mr. Lizard showed up.

He stood by the sink, crowding the woman's dignity, a savage humor in his big eyes. "Looks like old girl's had a stroke," he said, matter-of-factly, as if he were about to light a pipe, and tell everyone that Colonel Mustard had killed her with a candlestick in the library, then hid her body in the restroom. Case closed, Watson.

Jim could only marvel that the woman was still sitting upright. He thought of gently shaking her by the shoulder, just to make sure she wasn't sleeping or something, but quickly withdrew his hand. He thought he detected heat emanating from her body, but could see plainly that she was not breathing.

"She's quite dead, old boy. No need to be so timid with her."

It took Jim a moment to process what Mr. Lizard had really said and connect it with something he'd said before. He felt a twinge, his heart skipped a beat, but then he clenched his fists, shaking his head as if he were having a seizure. "Don't even think about it," he spat fiercely.

"What? She won't feel a thing. Look, she's already stiff as a board." Mr. Lizard poked the lifeless body with a clawed finger and it fell over on its knees, legs slowly sliding on the tile, spreading apart as gravity pulled the dead woman downward. He smacked his hands together. "Now we can finally have some fun."

Jim's outrage metamorphosed into awe of Mr. Lizard's cool bestiality. The reptile whistled a strangely familiar tune, stepping over the body to relieve himself. Too much coffee or too much excitement. He flushed the toilet, washed his hands, and then crouched behind the woman's still form, positioning the body just where he wanted it.

You can't let this happen, Jim, he told himself as he watched numbly. You've got to stop him. This is sick and ungodly.

Mr. Lizard ignored him, unzipping his trousers to free his green willy and mount Alexis's hapless carcass. At last finding some courage, Jim attacked him, bent upon preserving the woman's honor. But Mr. Lizard was too quick, too powerful, and without breaking his rhythm he knocked Jim out cold.

The blackness was without time, and Jim floated in it like so much driftwood, aimlessly spinning around in the void, just dodging being sucked down into the whirlpool. His eyes were open, but he couldn't see. He thought he heard something, though. It was annoying, whatever it was. He wanted the noise to stop, but it grew louder, more intense, and higher in pitch, like an unrelenting alarm clock robbing him of sleep. Why did his sock feel wet? He knew then that he had to get up. He had to stop spinning. He had to wake up and stop Mr. Lizard! He forced himself awake and dumbly recognized the disturbing noise.

Stopping abruptly, he stupidly looked up into the contorted face of a woman, most likely Mrs. Kravitz the new accountant, standing in the restroom doorway. She was screaming bloody murder at the sight of the sick man—dressed in the suit and tie—unspeakably defiling the corpse of Alexis Cruise.

Jim insisted on his innocence, crying out, "No, no! I tried to stop him! I tried to stop Mr. Lizard." He staggered to his feet, pulling up pants that were soaking wet with toilet water. He slipped, and fell over his dead lover. Mrs. Kravitz screamed again, running for her life, believing the heinous pervert was chasing her, tripping madly over his wet pants, and yelling something obscene about lizards.

About a week later, Jim Bum made friends with the fact that it would be some time before they let him out of the funny farm. It was a sterile place, but not half as clean as Jim had kept the library. The doctors there were nice, but nothing at all like Dr. Love. They had changed his medicine, and he would often find himself staring off into space and drooling a great deal. He had given up the suit. His new outfit was white and ill fitting, and he missed his silk tie. But he was allowed to wear a bandanna about his neck like Bogart in *The African Queen,* his new mental masque, maintaining some shred of dignity. Mr. Lizard had returned, and had apologized profusely for his wickedness, and all the confusion and what not—they were chums again.

In the courtyard, they would share a smoke, admire the roses, and dream of Dr. Love. They would go see her as soon as they got out. "We could break out of here fairly easy, you know," Mr. Lizard proposed. Jim agreed, and the two whiled away the hours of the long days planning their escape, and mulling over various scenarios. Best of pals, they agreed on just about everything except for one minor detail that left them in a quandary. Which would feel better, they wanted to know, to take Dr. Julie Love alive, or kill her first?

Going Home
Stephen Clements

Leaving my research assistant behind, safe and asleep in her bed, I took off into the Pyrenees, to climb alone their high peaks. I didn't come to this patch of French nowhere after the culmination of ten years of research to share my glory with someone else, to bring someone else to steal my credit. From the moment my head hit the pillow at the cabin, my mind was alive with a fire, a fire that wouldn't be quenched until I found the ritual site, if indeed it still existed.

All this time, I had purposefully given my assistant directions that were slightly off, so she could not leak that information to anyone else, like that bastard Crabgrass at Princeton. At the twilight of the second day of my trek through the mountains, here it was: a tumble of rocks, partly covered in moss and snow, but clearly the still-standing altar of Rex Mundi, the wicked demon god of the physical world as described by the heretical Cathars.

There could be no doubt that I was the first person in over 800 years to lay eyes on it. I so excitedly set about taking notes and pictures that I jumped when a dark shadow blotted out the dying sunlight behind me. When I looked back, I was astonished to see a man dressed in a clean, pressed, and immaculately tailored black suit. My nerves frayed, as I expected no guest.

The man's appearance from nowhere disturbed me, but something about him made my mind and body panic, with bile rising in my stomach and my chest tightening with fear. There was no reason for anyone else to be here, so far from anything the modern world desired. My subconscious screamed up at my racing mind, "This is no man!"

"You are right; I am not a man. I believe you came in search of me," the thing in the perfect suit with perfectly coiffed hair said. "But I see you did not expect company. Calm down, you have nothing to fear," he said, his tone reassuring and measured.

As he spoke, it confirmed my heart's innermost desire, the fruition of a lifetime studying not merely anthropology, but the occult. Even as my body quieted itself at the stranger's command, my mind still raced with the details of my guest that may also be true. Was he really a god? A demon? Something else?

Still wide-eyed with alarm, I asked, "You will do me no harm?"

"No."

"How can I trust you?"

"I promise, but you know you don't have a way out if I choose to," the stranger said matter-of-factly. "I'm glad you came, though, because I need your help," he said beseechingly.

"Me? You need my help? Aren't you eternal, all-knowing, and supernaturally powerful?"

"You are correct. I have existed since all this began, I am still capable of wonders and marvels, but I am limited in certain knowledge."

"What could I possibly teach you?"

Looking longingly at the sky, he said, "How to go home. I have been locked on this rock for longer than you can comprehend. Not simply here crafting mountains or managing the elements for the Creator, because then I could always go home. Indeed, I always had it with me. But when we, I…fell…"

"You are a demon, then?" I asked.

My mind raced with the possibility of finding out what had really happened. The answers to so many fundamental mysteries faced by mankind lay inside the head of this demon standing right here! Why had the fallen angels rebelled? Was this part of God's plan?

"I am not a demon, I am a fallen angel. Demons are things that existed from before Creation was made and still seek to undo it all. Fallen angels are just that, angels no longer in the graces of the Creator. We are often, um, rowdy, it is true, but we are part of this Creation as you are, and we once personally knew the Creator. The Jews simply got us and demons confused, thinking we were the same thing. Yes, we are both terribly powerful, but at least you and I are made in a likeness. They exist in a form of madness."

"Sorry, I did not know. Thank you for telling me. Please continue."

"When I was cut off from the Light, I raged. I destroyed. I did awful things to your ancestors and those who came before them. I taught them to do awful things to each other. I want to be sorry for that."

"You mean you feel sorry for that and want to apologize?"

"No. I want to know how to feel sorry. You and I are so different that what is natural to you, like feeling sorry, having that emotion, I do not have. I was purpose-made to do specific tasks, so I was not made with your heart. I can look at you and describe to you every molecule and atom of which you are made, what ties them together and to the fabric of Creation, and how to bind and unbind them. If you will hear me out, I need your help and am willing to tell you everything I know in return."

He'll tell me *everything*. "Of course, I will help you. On one condition."

"Yes?"

"All access to you goes through me. I help you in your quest, you help me to know everything. You tell your secrets only to me."

"Be careful when you ask to know everything. Not all knowledge is good to have. But if you ask it of me, I will tell you."

I went straight for it. "What is the meaning of life?!"

"Not yet. Free me first, free me from the occult bindings trapping me to this mountain. Then I can go with you and learn what it is to be…like you. As you teach me what it is to be like you, to be redeemable, I will tell you the secrets of Creation."

"Why do you want to be like me? Why do you want to feel sorry?"

"When the Cathars had found this place and began worshipping me as their mad god, in their rantings, they mentioned redemption from sin was possible and needed before you can go to Heaven. While they killed themselves off in their fanaticism before I could learn more, it seemed as though you need to feel sorry for what you have done before you can repent of it and be redeemed for it. Maybe redemption is only for men, but maybe it can work for a fallen angel, too. I have to try."

"They worshipped you," I stated. "So you are Rex Mundi, King of the World, creator of this physical world?"

He shook his head. "No. People often see me as what they want me to be, and this band of Cathars thought I, a fallen and incredibly powerful being, had to be their evil god. Having found what they thought was proof that their Devil existed, but still having no proof that their God existed, they threw their lot in with me. They worshipped at this altar left by another foul civilization, made pacts, and sacrificed themselves and their children to me, in the hopes of a…reward."

I had to ask, "What is your angelic name then?"

"I have been worshipped by many names, though you may call me…Cyril. That is a safe name to use. I was the spirit of the second life to those that worshipped me. I was once free to roam, but then anchored to this place by a people who were stargazers and worshipped the second life I could give. But they were so wicked and cruel that the Celts slaughtered every one of them and destroyed my massive temple, long before the Romans came here. I could describe it all for you. While the other mysteries may wait, you did come here to study my temple, and I wish to deal with you fairly.

"I want to go home. If you break this rock, I can go out into the world and find out if there is any salvation for one such as me."

I looked at the stone towards which Cyril gestured, and it stood in the center of the site, a plinth with faded, but intact carvings on it. As I looked closer, the lines carved into the stone were filled with an unsullied metal, which should be impossible for something so old. In places it was covered in moss, but as I brushed the growth away, I saw it glow in almost a luminous silver light, and it was completely intact in its interlacing design. It was a marvel to behold.

Possibly more fascinating, the design was not one detailed by my books on summoning or binding demons. The only symbol I recognized was centered in the four sides of the plinth, obviously a type of cross. But the symbol in the center at the top was intriguing, perhaps indicating Cyril's true name.

"What does this symbol mean?" I asked.

Cyril hesitated. "You have my promise of good will. Please do not ask for that. It is my true name, and every man who has learned it has destroyed himself with the power it granted him."

Disappointed for now, I asked, "Very well. Then how do I free you from it? I can't break this rock with the tools I have."

"Use your chisel to break the metal lining the carvings. The seal just has to be broken, and then we can leave this dreadful place."

I hurried to do as instructed, as I frantically grabbed for my tiny tools meant for the careful removal of dust and debris, not the destruction of the precious historical site I was investigating. It was a small price to pay.

With much sweating, blistering, and a little bleeding, I did it, tearing out a piece of the silver lining.

I looked around, expecting a dramatic change to occur, for the fallen angel to cackle with glee and swell to some terrifying form and rain fire down from the sky. All I saw was Cyril looking relieved.

Cyril flashed a quick smile and said, "Let's get out of here. I can tell you all about this forlorn place on the way."

I found my strength complete and weariness to be only a distant companion, as Cyril and I sped toward the rental car, which I had taken as far as I could toward the site. Admittedly, that had stranded my research assistant, but she was even less of a concern now than she had been before. She always talked about being an empowered woman, she'd figure it out.

Cyril was perplexed to hear me describe what a car was at first, but as I turned it on for our drive to Paris, he grew intrigued. As an artificer, he was amazed by what mankind had created and wanted to learn everything about it. For now, though, I drove.

"I warn you, we will have to go through Paris and the airport to get to my home in America."

"America? What's that?"

"It's a big continent to the west of here."

"Oh, that place! It's still there? I'm amazed they didn't destroy that whole place ages ago."

Surprised, I asked, "Who would have destroyed it?"

"All in due time," was all Cyril said, frustratingly.

"Do you have a problem with crowds of people? There are millions of people in Paris. Lots of Christian churches, although few people go to them."

Cyril explained, "I appear this way, because something in you sees me this way. I will appear differently to others, depending on how their spirit sees me. I have no material form, as I am a spirit of the air and light. I can interact with the physical world, but I have no body. Most people will not even notice me, and I can sense people who might…react poorly. I can avoid them. I do not want to start any fights."

Intriguing. I wondered how any of that worked.

"So I've been thinking about how to best teach you to feel regret," I said.

"Yes?"

"I think you should meet my family."

"They are that bad?"

"No!" I could not contain a laugh. "I have deep, long-lasting relationships with these people. They mean the most to me of anyone in the world, and it would seem the root of your problem is that you no longer have a relationship with the person, entity, er, place with which you want to reconnect. So I propose that you meet them and watch us interact. I trust you are an observant person, er, being, so pay attention to how we interact, and pick up on the obvious affections we have for each other.

"I will steer the conversation toward things we wished we hadn't done to each other. The transgressions will be light at first, memories we can laugh at now, and then get more serious. We get along well, so have no fear of harming our relationships. This may enable you to learn of our remorse for having harmed each other, the pain they felt, and how we found a way to forgive one another. Perhaps that will stir something in you upon which to build."

Cyril nodded. "This sounds like an excellent plan. Start at the roots and build up from there. Are any of you particularly religious?"

I didn't have to think long. "Not really. I teach at a Catholic University, but it's religious only on paper and for the couple of priests that work there. The Catholic Student Union is the smallest student group we have on campus."

"Why are you not?"

"I'm a good enough person, I give to charity. If there is a God," I paused, looking at the fallen angel sitting in the passenger seat to my right. "I figure that sitting in a church pew on Sunday isn't enough to get one to Heaven, and that surely deeds count for more. And frankly, if you look around the world, there is slaughter and death, famine, disease, child rapists, adult rapists, everywhere. Where is God for those people?"

Cyril responded, "You're more right than you know."

I looked over at Cyril excitedly, my eyes asking for the answer.

Cyril smirked back, "Not yet. Greedy human."

"Sometime soon you will tell me, and then I can quit studying books! I can just ask you! What better source than the being that made the mountains and the air about climate change? Who better to ask about how to cure disease than the being who helped make these bodies? Who better to ask about how to travel through space than –"

"You do not want to do that," Cyril swiftly and firmly interjected.

My eyebrows furrowed in puzzlement. The intensity of Cyril's tone told me not to press for why.

Cyril changed the subject. "Tell me about this airport. You said we're going to fly to America. How?"

"Yes, well, in the last century, the people living in America discovered the technology to fly ourselves around in tubes, with wings to guide us, and propellers to move us."

"But how do you monkeys, er, people know how to fly?"

"Lots of practice! We rarely crash anymore," I said proudly.

Cyril's tone of interest waned, replaced by sorrow. "I remember what it was like to fly. When I had wings."

AHA! He gave something away, angels DO have wings, which also means that when they fall from grace, they somehow lose them. I must remember to ask more about that.

At that point, my cell phone rang for the fifth time now that it had service. It was my damned research assistant. The anger of her crushing the call button came across in the otherwise neutral ringtone, but I did not dare answer.

"What is that?"

"Oh, this. It's a cellular phone."

"A what?"

"Almost every person in the world has one of these, and with each one you get a special numerical code assigned to you. If I want to call my mother, I can dial her code, and wherever she is, no matter how far away, she can answer and talk to me. The technology has even advanced to where we can look at each other as we talk."

Cyril's eyebrows rose in wonder. "You monkeys, er, people are amazing. Being able to talk to anyone in the world instantly, AND being able to shut it off when you do not want to speak with them. That second part was a luxury I did not have until I was cast down."

My curiosity could bear it no longer, so I asked, "What is it like to be you? I find it amazing that you, an eternal being that has witnessed the entirety of history, are impressed by a cell phone."

"I like knowing how things work. Remember, I'm a builder, but I haven't been able to create anything in a very long time."

"But even your imprisonment was a drop in the bucket in years for you."

"It didn't feel like it."

"Do you ever just turn off your mind and rest?"

"No. I was aware the entire time. We do not sleep."

"How did you not go mad?!"

"As I said, I'm built differently than you. I will share this: you get bored and frustrated when things do not happen quickly enough, because you know that you have a finite amount of time to do everything you want before you die. I do not. I am eternal. I do not have a rush to have children, I do not have a need to impress the other mon-, er, people with my prowess to allow me to move up the pecking order. None of that. I can abide."

"Ha! Like the Dude?"

"The what?"

"The Dude is a character from a movie, er, a play that has been recorded and can be watched at any time, and his tagline is, 'The Dude abides.'"

"Hm. He must be a well-adjusted person, at peace with the world."

"Mostly." That bit of jest aside, I did not mean to waste a captive fallen angel on Coen brothers' trivia. "You stated you created the mountains and the sky. What else did you create, and how much of it did you individually do?"

"I was of an order of angels that could create anything non-living, so the materials used in making this car, the things I already mentioned, anything. I was not made to create animals, and unfortunately, the Creator was jealous on the details of how mankind came to be. Only the favorites created the things that breathe, and only three knew what went into making mankind.

"After I fell, I experimented with creating life, because I wanted to see if I could make men better than the Creator, since the Creator made such flawed creatures so subject to death and pain. All I could make, though, were automatons with no spark of life or free will. Apparently, only the Creator had the ability to put that special something into your kind. I also cannot resurrect the dead, but I heard that Jesus could. Having tried that before, it bewilders my mind that he could do such a thing. The Creator never did that."

How interesting.

"You keep saying the Creator. Is that a he or a she?"

"I would not use either, which speaks to my point about perspective: mankind cannot move themselves and how they think about themselves out of the picture long enough to accurately describe much of anything. When I start laying out the unified principle of Creation, it may become clear as to why I say that.

"To answer your question of what it is like to be me, I promise to let you reveal everything you want to the world after the dinner party. I will tell you everything I know, from my perspective, so you can see how a being such as I sees reality. That in and of itself will transform how you and your philosophers and scientists see the world. You can tell your guests, you can write papers, you can tell the world everything. All I want is to know if there is any chance at freedom for me."

At that moment, I wondered if I would share my discovery, my fallen angel, with the world. Most people would be horrified or unsettlingly pleased to find out that a fallen angel existed, and was available for questions, no less. It may be better to keep him hidden, perhaps bound someplace safe, to ensure nobody else would steal my greatest discovery. Cyril just finished stating he had no interest in self-aggrandizement, so why not use his revelations to build up my own glory? I would teach Cyril what he desired most and be greatly rewarded in the process.

"So how did you come to rest in the Pyrenees?"

"I did promise you an explanation of that site, but let me think. How do I reckon where I am from? From Heaven, from the place I fell, from the cult site of my greatest power? The earliest culture that worshipped me that you would know of was the Phrygians of deep western Anatolia. From the look in your eye, I can see that you don't know much about them. Then Astarches' plan worked. Once the rulers of that necromantic oligarchy had sacrificed the last living child of their nation, torn from Astarches' helpless arms by the crazed mob, he slew them all. He didn't stop with the rulers, as he realized the common people were as wholly corrupt as their wicked masters. He spilled their blood wherever he could find his countrymen, and find them he did. Not one of them survived his blade, and neither did he. I did nothing to stop him."

My eyes widened in alarmed. "Did you...corrupt them?"

"They were broken vessels when they found me. A poisoned well kills no one until they drink of it."

"But some people do not know the well is poisoned."

"Not water that reeks of brimstone."

"What about the people that didn't deal with you? They were innocent and subjected to...what role did you play in their society? I've gotten ahead of myself."

"It began with Mirah the Sorcerer. He discovered me and when he learned what I could do and teach him, he made me an offer and turned that power against his people's gatekeeper. When I undid the gatekeeper, he showed the people signs and wonders to cow them into submission. At first –"

"Wait, 'gatekeeper'? You undid their gatekeeper? What does that mean?"

"You don't have them anymore. Long before Abram spoke of the Creator, the gatekeepers were entities that defended their chosen people from monsters, demons, great beasts, and other horrors the likes of which you have never known. However, gatekeepers were created entities, so I could break them. Any other fallen angel would have had a titanic struggle on their hands, and I cannot imagine it would be worth the trouble. But Mirah betrayed the Conqueror of Leviathan and Queller of Pyriel. I know I done awful things. The Creator could not have been pleased with that.

"But at first, I was hidden as Mirah came to power. He astonished his people with power not his own, so they followed him out of fear and awe. Fear because the people knew the terrors the gatekeeper had held at bay, and now they were defenseless. To prove his worthiness, I staged a battle where Mirah proved himself as a worthy champion against the untold horrors, and they reluctantly accepted him as their leader. They had no choice, because they faced certain devouring otherwise.

"As time went on, though, he drank too deeply of the knowledge I possess and abused it. The people again came to fear him, as his madness flourished and his cruelty grew. The judges of Phrygia slew him in his sleep and then managed to destroy his raging corpse in a vicious magical battle."

I shook my head in disbelief. "Magic? Sorcerers? You don't mean to say that claptrap is true?"

Cyril was silent for too long. Looking over at him, I saw a dead stare coming from his eyes.

I swallowed hard. "Continue."

"The surviving judges discovered the source of his power and swore to themselves that they could use me for good. They were not the first to make such a claim. When Astarches bled out their throats after the centuries of atrocity they inflicted on their nation, I could not blame him for it. I have not always delighted in carnage, which makes me think I may be able to someday know remorse for it."

He smiled weakly at me. "I have to try. I will make myself try."

He next said, "When the next wave of settlers came to Phrygia, they brought a cult worshipping what they thought was a fertility goddess name Cybele with them, and based on what little they could recover of the previous inhabitants, they eventually named me her consort, Attis. By then, though, I had little interest in them, and I roamed free for a time, wreaking havoc, er, interacting with people around the world.

"However, millennia ago, and I will be more precise later, the demon-worshipping stargazers learned from their masters how to bind me. They summoned and bound me against my will, using secrets it took me years to understand. I feared their demon masters sought to destroy me for my crimes against the darkness, but they used me to reward and guide their followers. They were even more cruel than the Phrygians, and there is good reason you will find no trace of the horrid wonders they made. Whatever evils the Celts and Romans committed, it was as nothing compared to the stargazers."

Cyril stopped talking and looked at me. "But you look tired."

I suddenly realized the exertions of the past days had caught up with me.

"Indeed. Perhaps we should find the next hotel and stay there."

"I'm not tired," Cyril offered. "I've been watching how you operate this machination, and I never tire. Let me drive."

I awoke as Cyril suddenly stopped in front of the airport.

"Here we are. Sleep well?"

I felt great. "Yes, I did. I never sleep that well on car rides."

"Your luck is turning around. Now come, I have a thousand questions for you," Cyril said, as he turned off the car.

As we made our way through the airport and over the course of the flight, I was amazed to simply watch Cyril, as he examined and questioned everything. As I explained what I could of aircraft and the technology he saw around himself, he spouted out principles of aerodynamics that would revolutionize the airline industry (or even make it obsolete) as simply as if I were telling him how to make a cup of tea. His clear pleasure at being in and then above the clouds, looking down at the Creation he helped build, made me beam with pride. Here I went to look at some mossy rocks, and I set free a prisoner of the centuries, who seemed to be looking at the world with new eyes.

Upon landing, I called my mother Betty, my brother Adam, my cousin Chris, and my closest colleagues and collaborators on this project, Nyumbu (from the Anthropology Department) and Diego-Baares (from the French Department). They were pleased to hear from me, but mystified by my insistence on them coming over for dinner this very evening. I told them, honestly, that I had the most exciting news of my life to share with them and could not wait. All that mattered was that they agreed to come.

When the bags were all packed into the car and I finished making the phone calls, Cyril asked to drive the car to the house. I was too busy to remember that I had not told him the way, but when we pulled into my circle drive, I could see that he found his way just fine.

"How did you know where to go?" I had to ask.

"I see you, I see your energy, and I sensed the location where your energy is strongest, to put it simply. You know when you get the feeling that you should do something or not do something, but cannot say exactly why you feel so?"

"Yes."

"What I did was an outgrowth of that feeling inside of you. I can teach you to develop yours further, although it will take time. You will be amazed by what untapped potential you will find inside mankind."

Knowing that was all Cyril would say for the time being, I changed the subject, thinking my home worthy of explanation to this freed angel. "So this is my home. I'm very proud of it, as it is one of the few remaining antebellum homes left in this city. I painstakingly restored it," I began bragging. As the words left my mouth, I immediately felt embarrassed for bragging over the age of this pile of wood and plaster to an eternal being who had built the very bones of the Earth.

No doubt sensing my sudden hesitance, Cyril said, "It is lovely and grand. Someone was certainly inspired to create such a thing."

I took that as a graceful excuse to stop talking, and I showed him into the house, explaining the different rooms and their functions, briefly touching on some of the modern marvels of technology incorporated into them. Cyril was most interested in the air conditioner, and I left him to examine how it worked, while I took my leave to prepare what dinner I could cobble together for my guests.

I had selected each guest carefully, as while I had many friends and acquaintances, frankly, not all people are equally valuable, especially in trying to demonstrate the principles at hand. My mother Betty, dear sweet Betty, she had dealt with so many disappointments out of me, but still loved me, despite her personal objections to my lifestyle. She would be useful in showing the unconditional love so many people ascribe to God, which, if true, may jog Cyril's memory of having felt that before. The desire to feel that again may motivate him to be thoroughly sincere in his pursuit of forgiveness.

My brother Adam and cousin Chris were also family, and they liked me well enough, as I did them. They could show the voluntary ties we place on each other, the more typical varieties of transgressions and insults people give each other, and the ensuing repair process of relationships. And I truly did pick my favorite kin, as if all of my siblings and cousins were drowning and I could only save two of them, it would be Adam and Chris.

As for Professors Nyumbu and Diego-Barres, while we have dealt no real injuries or harm to one another nor had to make up for such things, I could not wait to show off my new prize to them! I had consulted with them extensively about elements of my public research into ancient ritual sites, even as I had kept them in the dark about the simultaneous occult research going into the project. They were uninitiated in any way to the hidden truths behind our reality, but now I felt that they deserved to be the first witnesses of my triumph.

I scrounged for something edible and wine sufficient to please my guests, but could not truly bring myself to care about nibbles and drinks. Instead, my mind ran through the words that had sparked my sense of wonderment with an otherwise bland reality and so led me to this very moment, those spoken by Hamlet, "There are more things in heaven and earth, Horatio, than are dreamt of in your philosophy." When I was younger, I could not explain why those words touched me as they did. But as time and my intellect grew, I vowed to never settle for being Horatio, or that bastard Crabgrass, to only exist to fiddle with scientific-sounding words and meaningless papers in the attempt to impress my peers, who were all trying to vainly do the same.

Indeed, it was Aleister Crowley that did more to interest me in Anthropology than Desmond Morris' exploration of our animal nature could. I found a copy of Crowley's *Book 4* at an antique shop I visited with my mother, and something within me made me steal it, which may be part of that undeveloped sense of which Cyril spoke. Even then, it was guiding me toward hidden truths, truths soon to be revealed in their entirety, by the being that wrote them!

Interrupting my spinning thoughts, Cyril entered the kitchen. "May I assist?"

In preparing to leave for France, I had left virtually nothing perishable behind. The research trip was anticipated to last weeks, but here I was with a bare larder and guests coming over. They would not care, once I confessed to them my true purpose…

My desperate eyes caught Cyril's, and he understood that I had nothing to offer my guests, or myself.

"Stand aside," he said simply. "Turning water into wine is a feat more than one being can do. Same with bread   and   fish."

In a series of what can only be termed miracles, Cyril finished making the last can of tuna in soybean oil into a copious plate of immaculate bluefin tuna sashimi and set it next to the jug of freshly made wine on the table when the doorbell rang. One after another, my guests arrived only to be instantly charmed by Cyril. I shushed requests to know what this big secret was that I invited them over to find out, and the incomparable quality of the dinner set out quickly quieted them.

Dinner was joined, and I gloated over all the details I discovered about the ritual site itself: what made it peculiar and what the implications of those details meant for the culture that made it. In one of the rare instances of explaining the significance of an artifact, I was overjoyed to be absolutely certain that my assumption was right, as Cyril had told me everything about the place during the car ride to Paris. Unlike other researchers of the humanities, I did not have to guess based on a few pottery shards who these people were and what they did; I had an eye-witness account with complete reliability and ability to recall! This small taste of the gift that was Cyril I found very sweet.

My guests found it all incredibly interesting, but it was time to earn my keep with my benefactor, and I did not want them to leave or beg off remaining here before I kept my word. I switched the conversation by working in a bon mot about a childhood incident with mother, she took the bait, and the conversation about past wrongs got underway. As we talked, I could not help but glance at Cyril, to see that he was paying attention.

As the evening wore on, my relatives exchanged meaningful glances, suggesting to me that they suspected I had another "special announcement" to make regarding my life choices. Which was fine, as it kept them here and sympathetic. Cyril needed to see what sympathy looked like. My academic colleagues were too awkward in personal interactions to ever be so bold as to leave on their own accord, so we had time yet.

Just when Chris was about to tell a joke, Cyril rose from the table, looking uncomfortable. "Pardon me. I must excuse myself for a moment."

I had not expected this, so I asked a bit worriedly, "Is everything alright?"

"Wine comes in, but it also has to go out!" he jested. "Sorry, I have a small bladder and low tolerance. I find it saves money."

My company giggled, themselves heavy with the sublime port he had turned my tap water into. Cyril left the dining room, and I could not help but watch as he went.

DING-DONG.

The doorbell? I had not invited anyone else. Who could that be?

"Excuse me," I said, rising from my seat to check.

The sight of a short, pudgy, white-haired man in black vestment greeted me at the door, and by the rosy cheeks, I knew it had to be Father Denham. I didn't care for his rough manner, but he was one of the Deans of the college, so I had to deal with it. But not at my house.

"Father, why are you here?" I asked brusquely. I had plenty of stout wine in me and he wasn't invited, so it was his fault if he was dealt with rudely.

"Professor Armitage, so glad to see you! I heard you had returned, and I could not wait to see what you found on your expedition! I got some strange voicemails from your research assistant, and then Professor Diego-Barres told me you were here, so I wanted to drop by. I had a function to attend earlier, so sorry I'm late. I hope I didn't miss too much."

"I had already gone over what I found, and…"

He brushed off my rebuttal swiftly. "I don't mind waiting around for the second telling! But let me go out back for a smoke first, be right back," he said, pushing past me, cigarette already in mouth, fiddling in his pocket for a lighter.

I sat back down and stalled the conversation, as both Cyril and Father Denham took an impossibly long time in getting back to the dinner table. It may have only been a minute, but it felt like forever. Shockingly, my colleagues made a weak attempt to leave, but I kept them in place. Did Cyril know how to use a toilet? Did he even have a use for a toilet?

To my chagrin, the first to return was Father Denham. From the look in his eyes, that was no tobacco cigarette he had smoked outside. Having a pot-smoker in the holy orders would be a surprise.

Father Denham silently turned to face the lit fireplace, so I began a recap of what I had told the group about the ritual site. My description was violently cut short by Father Denham burying the hook of the fireplace poker into my mother's neck!

She screamed, as did we all, as we jumped up in shock.

The priest pulled back hard on the poker, pulling her out of the chair onto the ground. Adam and Chris charged the completely silent Father Denham, with the old priest sending Adam sailing across the room behind him, and Chris tackling him.

The smell of burning hair proved that Chris had knocked the Father back into the fireplace, but his black coat began burning as well. I watched in horror as the still-quiet old man wrestled with Chris on the ground, oblivious to the fire.

Behind me, I heard Professor Diego-Barres cursing her cellphone. "This damn thing! I'm calling 911, but it says 'no service' available! What the Hell?!"

Professor Nymbu was nowhere to be seen, but just then I heard the front door slam shut. Something told me those two things were connected.

The fight continued on between a now flame-engulfed Father Denham and cousin Chris, and I noted that Adam had not gotten back up off the floor after he had struck headfirst into the wall. My mind raced with the awful, inexplicable fight going on in front of me, but I had to do something!

I picked up a chair and used it to try to push Father Denham off Chris, but he was impossibly strong. With my help, Chris found the opportunity to squeeze out from under the Dean of the Liberal Arts Department and scurry away, hacking for air. My offensive completely stalled, however, and the Father calmly, silently stood up, even as I pushed with all my might.

Too late, I heard a womanish grunt and saw a glass jar flying through the air, burst on Father Denham, and the flames on him explode with renewed fury.

"Did you throw the wine at him?" I screamed.

"YES! I DIDN'T KNOW WHAT ELSE TO DO!"

"ALCOHOL IS FLAMMABLE!"

"AHH!" was her response, as she turned and ran away, towards the front door.

As I feebly held the wooden chair up, holding the flaming Dean arm's length away from me, I could see that neither Adam nor mother had stirred. Mother lay in a growing pool of blood, silent.

Father Denham continued advancing on me, pinning me against the wall, but safe for a few seconds longer.

I could hear the door being wrestled. "I CAN'T GET THE DOOR OPEN!" Diego-Barres screamed.

"I CAN'T HELP YOU!" I very honestly said.

Just then, Chris swung the fireplace poker at Father Denham, hitting him hard, hard enough to drive him back. There was no way Father Denham would do this, I thought, no way this was really happening. Maybe it was something in the wine, making us see things.

Father Denham stumbled back against the window, setting the curtains on fire, which was sure to take the rest of the house with it.

Remembering the fire extinguisher, I ran into the kitchen and shrieked when something caught me. It was Cyril. He was distraught.

"Cyril, help us!" I screamed at him.

He held me still, and then he spoke. "I, I am so sorry. I did this."

"What?" I asked, things falling into place.

"I..." he spoke haltingly. "I...sensed the priest approaching the house, so I excused myself to prevent a fight in front of your family. I waited for him to leave, but then he said he would stay, and he went outside alone. I thought, 'Here is my chance. I can ask this priest if I can be saved.' But when he saw me, he..."

I could not even ask what came next, so exasperated by what I was hearing.

"He immediately started trying to banish me, to exorcise me, to hurt me. I did not even have time to think it through or talk him down, I just...killed him. And then I panicked, thinking, 'What have I done?' His cross dropped when I separated his soul from his body, barring my way into the door, but his body kept moving with the second life, because it still lives. I found a way around the cross, but I had to warp the rest of the house to get in."

"Cyril," I said, as clear and directly as I could. "I need you to fix this. Can you do that?"

He looked like he was going to cry. "No. Your mother is dead, so is the priest, Adam, and so will be you, your cousin, and your friend."

"WHY?!"

"Did you not hear me a minute ago? I said, 'I am sorry.' You did it! You and your family taught me what it is to feel sorry for something I have done! You showed me what these people meant to you, how you related to each other, and this sense of loss you feel over them dying, which is entirely different than the groveling victims and power-hungry bloodletters I met before. Their deaths meant nothing to me, but these do," he finished, excitedly.

"CYRIL! We are going to die here! Get us out!"

He shook his head. "I cannot do that. You taught me the first of many lessons I have to learn before I can finish my journey to redemption, and if word gets out that all this happened because of me, nobody will help me finish it. I thank you so much! You taught me something the Creator never meant for me to know!"

I heard screaming and spreading flames behind me in the dining room, and I knew they would devour the rest of the house. And me.

"But, I…" was all I could muster.

"Shhhh," he said to me. "You do not have much time left, and I made you a promise: I will answer every question you have before you die. First, you wanted to know what it is like to be me. Well, you are living it right now. The upside for you is that it will end soon. That despair, that trapped feeling, the pain of the flames; that is what it is like to be me. Until you! Now I have a sliver of hope for something better!"

"Now what is your next question? Quickly now, you do not have much time."

Coney Island, Here I Come!
D. Norfolk

Pure skies of rich unbroken azure set a backdrop for the intricate iron work that stretched up to the heavens like the spires of a gothic church, that loomed on the horizon, on that sweltering summer's day. The Dreamland sign obscured by the hot afternoon sun as Jake made his way through the bustling crowds thrumming in and out of the spectacle.

He'd promised himself this trip for a long time, so many times in his own heart, changing his mind and opting to block his access to these high and colourful gates. Always something to do, somewhere to go, somebody to see, procrastination on its most epic scale.

But now he was here, wasn't he, amongst the Sunday gawkers and ghoulish onlookers. Ten more steps and he'd be through. The sweat was already soaking his navy shirt. One he had specifically picked for this trip, the one that wouldn't show the perspiration darts that epitaph his fear. That was a strong word, wasn't it? He wasn't per se afraid of the freaks in the show, just nervous that's all. Yes, mindful was the best way to describe it.

The massive signboards played it all out as he shuffled mechanically toward his objective. The ten foot high painted boards, their depictions clear, graphic and grotesque. The Tattooed Lady, The Wolf Boy, The Four Legged Girl all picked out in bright oils to extenuate their deformities. Jake gulped and looked toward his feet in quiet meditation, a slow tickling bead of sweat made its way from the nape of his neck, snaking its way between his shoulder blades, spider like in its movement. He could feel his breathing quicken and made a conscious effort to wrestle it under control, as he promised himself he would.

There was no turning back now, he thought as he gripped the rough, thick paper of the ticket he'd just purchased. The fleshy pink colour melded with his own hand, the thick black ink of 'admit one only', felt like no return from the dread he felt.

Next to him, a fat woman, hot and flustered in a canary yellow dress with petite black arrows, dripped with exertion as she ushered a twirling tornado of a child through the gathering thrum. He was fatter than she was, his chubby pink legs exploding from shorts quite possibly indecent for a boy of his proportions. She struggled and swayed, she elbowed him in the ribs, hard, didn't even turn round to apologise. He was reminded why he'd put this trip off for so long.

Sooner than he expected, he was outside the tent, its devil's candy stripes of black and blood red loomed around him, stitched by Lucifer himself. On a small stage outside, a barker bellowed loudly as he clutched a fat, smouldering cigar in one massive hand. There was no need for a bull horn here, his voice carrying not just above but through the crowd.

"Ladies and gentlemen, step right up and see the wonders science can't explain. Look if you dare at the unnnnnnnnnnbelievable sights we have to show you. The girl with four legs who scuttles like a crab. Captured in the forests of Europe, the vicious Wolf boy, watch as he tears meat with his terrrrrrrrible claws. You won't believe your eyes, come on now, step right up!!" he finished, ushering people through in the entrance, a gleeful knowing smile on his face.

Jake stepped forward reluctantly, the carnie watching him as he approached. Those dark, happy eyes lost behind a grey pungent haze of smoke from his stogie that seemed to rise from the bowels of hell itself.

"That's right, son, come right in, come right in. Show the ladies you aren't afraid," he laughed, turning and winking at a bunch of girls, no older than fifteen, leering at every petite curve. Jake glared at him, trying to meet the man's eye line, but the moment for outrage was gone.

Inside the tent, there was a brief respite from the heat outside, the dark interior cool and sheltering. The noise was tremendous, though, as in the distant rooms he heard gasps and screams, frittered conversations conducted at hypertensive volume. He smoothed the sweat patches in his shirt and focused on the gangway ahead. He was in now, no turning back.

First room, the tattooed lady sat in skimpy garments displaying her full body covering, leaving little to the imagination. She wore heavy make up to detail the only part of her body that wasn't covered with the green and blue ink. Jake felt easy here, she wasn't a freak in his mind, not like what he imagined was to come. Next a strong man lifted mighty barbells on which hung a number of grotesque dwarves, who tumbled and flipped when he finished his reps. The man was intimidating with his barrel chest and waxed moustache. Jake moved on, feeling the man's eyes looking over his meagre frame. Still not really freaks, he thought as he passed through into the lair of the Wolf Boy.

A small crowd had gathered by the rail, watching the diminutive form tear apart a massive flaccid bloody steak, as the liquids oozed from the meat and mingled with the glossy black fur that covered the boy's body. He noted that not much of the meat was consumed just hurled about for dramatic effect. Pieces flew into the audience causing screams and terror in the onlookers gathered. He moved along behind cautiously, now his apprehension was growing. Before he could hit the next room, the Wolf Boy leaped at the rail seeing his terror, growling and screaming savagely. Jake bit down hard and backed into the next room quickly.

Turning slowly to face the nearly empty room, he tried to focus in the dark red light at what sat on the stool, before he could form a clear picture, something clattered forward, unnaturally, legs slapping in a chaotic gate. Jake backed up against the tents rough canvas as the four legged girl leered at him with red rimmed eyes.

Tracing the bar behind him, he shifted sideways away from the horror, but the girl moved with him, taunting him, her eyes never losing contact 'til he left the room.

He was spooked now, maybe this hadn't been such a great idea. The next room bathed in blue light was more comforting initially. That was 'til he saw the cast iron tank in its centre, the rusty port holes windows into the object, to view the spectacle. But Jake had had enough, needing in every fibre to dash from the attraction. Just then, the water erupted from the tank's glassy still surface, droplets landing on his skin causing him to flinch. A scaled man burst from below the shimmering waters. His lips twisted to a massive deformed grin, he gripped the rim and went to leap from his tank.

Before he could, Jake was gone. Eyes half closed, he bolted, passing through glimpses of rooms, things lurking there from his nightmares. Limps at awkward angles, cat calls from the things that waited there, flesh perverted by cruel tricks of nature.

Out through the exit, smashing people aside through the gates and along the boardwalk. His legs did not stop 'til he reached home, 'til he reached sanctuary. By now he was panicked, sweat poured from him and he had to strip away the sodden clothing immediately, with shaking hands. Off they went, even bandages that bound him beneath, ripped away until he stood naked in his kitchen, panting. Now, seeing the limb again made him sick, the deformed hand that now awoke and began to flex. The achy, gnarled knuckles that cracked with terrible popping, as it stretched out from his sternum, making him feel sick. Around its base, a hundred tiny hesitation cuts smiled bloodily back at him, a band of failure, taunting his cowardice.

He would not be one of those creatures. He shall not be ogled and pitied, he thought as he reached toward the kitchen drawer, tears now running from his eyes and splattering noisily on the chess board floor, as his hands trembled around the hilt of a long butcher's knife.

Emasculation
Spinster Eskie

I fell in love with Gina when I was eleven years old. She was my next-door neighbor, with huge tits and long yellow hair. She babysat me and my little brother when my folks were visiting with their rich friends, which they often did. Gina was perky and enthusiastic. She excelled in school and was popular. She was sweet and soft spoken. She wasn't very good at discipline or being authoritative, and was way over her head with me and my brother, John. We made sure she knew she was on our turf.

Like most teenagers she watched a lot of TV and talked on the phone with her boyfriend, so I'd find ways to demand her attention by making messes in the kitchen and beating on my brother until he was sore and whining. One time, just to be an asshole, I drew naked pictures of Gina all over my white bedroom walls. Gina was mortified and nervously scrubbed the pictures off, crying and yelling at me that I was going to get her in big trouble. But I was proud of my artistic accomplishment and enjoyed watching her panic. Her tits bounced as she feverously washed the walls with soap and water. Her shirt dampened, and her red cheeks and tear-stained eyes showed me that I had an effect on her.

Gina was frustrated with me, I could tell. John was less willful than I was. He usually just did what I told him to do, so Gina paid him more attention. When this happened, I knew only to act out and cause problems that would require her emotional reaction. I challenged her and then she would challenge me, sometimes by grabbing my arm and calling me a little brat. "I'm telling my mom on you!" I would threaten.

"Good!" She'd yell back, "I'd be happy to not come

back again!" But I never did tell my mom, and Gina kept showing up every Thursday through Saturday night, since my parents paid her well and she was saving up for college. But, as a safety net, Gina began inviting her boyfriend over to the house. He was an empty-headed, beefy jock she was obviously too good for. They'd make out while John and I watched from the top of the stairs. Her eyes would be set upon me as the boyfriend kissed her breasts and neck, but she would tell him to stop before he went any further. I hated him. I thought about murdering him. Maybe stab him in the back with a kitchen knife. He was too dumb to ever suspect. John would help me dig the grave. He'd find it thrilling, like a game. It would be so easy.

"Get off of, me Robby!" I heard Gina cry after she had already sent us to bed. I ran downstairs and saw the two on the couch as usual, their clothes wrinkled and unbuttoned.

"Come on, Gina, when are you gonna let me love you?"

"When I trust you, Robby!"

"We've been going together for two months! How much more trust do you need?"

"I'm just not ready, Robby!"

"Well, I'm done with waiting for your trust, Gina!" The boyfriend zipped up his pants and slipped his shirt back on.

"Where are you going?"

"It's over, Gina. I'm tired of the games!"

"You're breaking up with me?"

"I'll see you in class tomorrow," the boyfriend said coldly, and he left, slamming the door behind him.

"Robby!" Gina yelled after him, and she started to whimper solemnly. I approached her quietly and offered my hand on her shoulder. Gina was startled at first, but then held me close and cried softly as I held her back.

We held each other for a while and Gina looked at me once again, examining my expression, the adoration she could feel. She kissed me. Not a gentle kiss, not a babysitter's kiss, not a kiss that would be deemed at all appropriate, but a kiss that was meant for a boyfriend. I kissed back at first, but when I felt her tongue, it shocked me and I pushed away. "What is it?" She asked, "Don't you want me?" I did. But this was wrong. She then took my hand and guided it up her skirt and under her panties and I felt the unkempt, coarse, curly hair between her legs and the wet layered flesh below it. I came at an instant and ran upstairs, embarrassed and overwhelmed. Gina knocked on my door, but I shouted for her to go away. "Leo, it's completely normal! Please, just let me talk to you!" She said in her sweetest tone.

"No!" I yelled, "Leave me alone!"

My mother told me she was hiring a new babysitter since Gina would no longer be available on weekend nights. It didn't take her long to replace the girl. My mother was a busy socialite and to her, partying was a necessity. How else would she get laid? My father certainly was no use to her in that department. The new babysitter was an old religious woman, fat and mean. I did what I was told to do and was well-behaved whenever she came around to watch us.

"Something's wrong with the boy's fingers," the fat old woman informed my parents one evening. I had tried to hide it from everyone. At first, I kept my hands in pockets, then gloves. I tried to bandage my fingers up, but they only got worse, to the point where writing in school was painful, basketball was near impossible, and teachers were gravely concerned. Three of my right-hand fingers had swollen up to twice their normal size and the skin was oozing and crusting as if I had scorched them on a frying pan. That is what the doctor believed, at least, although I told him I had no recollection of ever burning myself.

"He'll be fine," The doctor told my mother. "Some antibiotic ointment and some ice oughtta clear that right up!" I followed the doctor's instructions and, sure enough, my fingers healed within a few weeks and I went right back to doing my school work and playing basketball like any other eleven-year-old boy. But I missed Gina. I obsessed over her. I'd see her next door, casually among her family and cheerleader friends as if nothing ever happened between us. She'd see me too, but rarely said hello. I wrote her letters, but she never wrote back. I'd spy on her through her bedroom window, wondering who she really was, what secrets she possessed, and she'd catch me and would defensively shut her curtains. A few months later, she left for college, and I barely saw her at all. Then, eventually, the house was sold and Gina's parents moved, and Gina had become nothing more than a cherished, but distant memory.

In time, I too went to college and graduated with high honors. From there, I went to law school and became a defense attorney for Christian rights. I became dedicated to my faith and chose to love Jesus over all else. Thus, I was celibate in body and mind. Sex, I discovered, was a superficial desire, a weakness of Adam and a sin of Eve. I was stronger than Adam and I was not much impressed by Eve's temptation. I witnessed it constantly, whores and tramps shoving their hideous twats in the faces of my colleagues. I witnessed infidelity, and the guilt and torment that it always resulted in, and I would thank God I had it in me to resist. Poison, that's what a cunt was made of: Juicy, velvety, pink, hot poison. I wanted no part. I despised the power it had over men. The suffering it caused my father, each time my mother paraded her lovers around in public. Sluts were the enemy and I worked effortlessly to fight legislations that granted easy access to abortions and birth control. These laws, in my mind, made it acceptable for women to be ravenous perverts.

Of course, I was not without moments of desire, like any other man, and I had plenty of obstacles to overcome. In college, my best friend George showed me a way to maintain our celibacy but still get off. He proceeded to blow me and for a while, this was how I stayed off women. However, George's behavior conflicted with my deep religious beliefs and I finally told him to stay the fuck away from me or I'd kill him.

At the firm, my assistant, Fran Anders, worked alongside myself, representing Christian civil rights and standing against anti-Christian values. We became very close in our work together and there was a great respect and appreciation between us. "What you do is so important," Fran spoke to me over dinner, as we celebrated another victory together as a team. "I admire you."

"I admire you too, Fran. You're a rare woman. You understand that you are meant to support men, not compete with them."

"And I support you most of all," she said, calmly and with a charming humility. We tapped our wine glasses and when our meals were finished, I drove her home. We were both drunk at the time and laughing about liberal hypocrisies and office in-jokes. She was pretty. Not as pretty as Gina, but she had dimples that I liked and she smelled nice. She always smelled nice. I walked Fran to her door and we kissed. I enjoyed kissing her. It had been a long time since I had been intimate with a woman and the alcohol in me was overriding my self-control. "I have been enamored with you for years!" She admitted in my ear. "I know you don't make love, but I hope you will make an exception for me." I lowered my head and mentioned that it was late and I had been drinking. "Come upstairs," Fran whispered. I declined. "I am so in love with you," she choked out. I was still feeling the victory adrenalin and my penis was harder than I could recall it ever being. I finally allowed Fran to lead me to her bedroom where she peeled off her clothes and revealed to me her flawless, fit body. I imagined what it'd be like to slip inside her just once. Inside her silk, hollow, nest.

We ended up on the bed, our lips entwined, and our hands all over each other. She unbuckled my belt and I remembered the poison that touched my fingers, burning the skin right off. Girls were the enemy and Fran's tiny, smooth body wasn't going to make me forget that. "Stop," I suddenly breathed.

"What?" She responded, as if she couldn't comprehend the language.

"Get dressed!" I insisted angrily and I handed her back her clothes.

"I'm so sorry." Fran told me as she fastened her bra and covered herself up with the professionally modest outfit she had on before. Then she started to weep.

"Quit it!" I said to her, but that only made her cry and apologize more. "I said quit it! What do you expect me to do, Fran? Feel sorry for you? Comfort you? Let you rest your head on my shoulder so you can try to seduce me into your sick, depraved world? You're evil! You disgust me! You're a degenerate whore!" Fran just kept sobbing rainstorm tears as I continued to abuse and demean her. I was not an unreasonable man, though, and I didn't fire her. We had both been drinking that night and we both acted out of character. But things were never the same between us. From then on, we were boss and assistant, nothing more.

Women were poison. This I knew, because Gina had ripped out my heart and crushed it like a rock to sand. All women did this. None of them deserved my time. I would have rather stuck my dick inside the open jaw of a sharp-toothed lion than stick it in a woman's Hellish tunnel.

Then, out of nowhere, I saw her. The gorgeous, yellow-headed, curvaceous princess I had dreamed about for over twenty-three years. Time had been well to her, but she looked sad and alone, reading the ingredients of each food item before placing it in her cart. I wanted to say something but I just could not. She glanced in my direction and I couldn't tell if she saw me or if she even recognized me. I watched as she purchased her groceries and then followed her to the parking lot and drove two cars behind her to where she lived, only a town away from me. I parked my car far enough down her street so that she wouldn't notice, but I was close enough to view her struggle with bags and then fiddle with her keys. Her place of residence was nearly a shack. She attempted to make it look inviting by placing a welcome mat and a dream catcher on the front deck, but that hardly disguised the run-down condition of the place. It seemed, to my surprise, that Gina lived by herself. It was about two p.m. when she went inside her house and I remained in my car for hours, watching and waiting for her reappearance. Eventually, she opened the door again to call in her cat, but then returned inside her safe, secluded walls. The sun set and finally I gained the courage to ring her doorbell. My beloved Gina answered.

"Yes?"

"Gina."

"Yes?"

"It's me. Leo. We were neighbors. You used to babysit me."

"I'm sorry, who are you?"

"Leo! I lived next door to you in Weston! You were my babysitter! I – Oh god, I've been dreaming of this moment for so long." Gina's face expressed confusion and she denied knowing me. The door closed forcefully on me and I rang the doorbell again, and a third time, and a fourth time, until she had no choice but to speak to me again, although she kept the latch locked.

"My husband will be back any minute now. And if he doesn't take care of you, the police will!"

"I work at Christian Associates, about eight miles from here. Please come see me!" I left, knowing that was all I could do. Each day I imagined her walking through my office door. Each blond that resembled her caused false hope. Yet after weeks of nothing, I gave up the fantasy and figured she had forgotten me and was happily married. However, like the mysterious vision that she was, she had managed to find her way to my apartment as I returned home late from work one night.

"I figured we needed to talk in private," she said to me, and I let her in and offered her some tea. We sat together, quiet at first, but then her sweet, dainty voice continued. "Leo, what happened when we were kids should have never happened. What happened was a mistake. I was a fucked up girl and I did some fucked up things and I'm sorry I hurt you."

"Don't be sorry. You're the only woman I've ever loved. I know you're married now, but-"

"I'm not married. I only said I had a husband to scare you off. My relationships with men have not been good, and I can't have children."

"I'm sorry to hear that."

"I did bring a child to term once, but he died right after I gave birth to him." It had become clear to me then. It wasn't all women. It was just Gina. She was defected.

"I read about you online," Gina went on. "You seem to be very active against the rights of women."

"I'm against anti-Christian values," I corrected her.

"Not women's rights."

"But I read that you're against birth control. I didn't know anyone was against that."

"Reproduction is God's law."

"But what about population control? What about women like me, who miscarry and shouldn't have kids?"

"Well, Gina, not all women are like you."

"What do you mean?" I couldn't tell if she was curious, fascinated, or outraged, but I tried to remain confident as I stumbled over my explanation.

"Your vagina is - how should I put this? Defected." Gina let out a laugh that wasn't much of a laugh, but more the sound of disbelief. However, I continued to defend my views. "When I touched you, when we were young, I experienced an intense allergic reaction that was quite frightening. Until now I thought it might be all women, but I am beginning to realize that perhaps you are different." She briefly stared ahead at nothing, then cracked up, as if suddenly she had gone mad.

"I should go. I'm gonna go." Gina grabbed her purse.

"I didn't mean to offend you."

"Leo, I know what I did to you was wrong. I know I took advantage of you and probably fucked you up for life. I still see a therapist over the horrible shit I've done to people, but you might wanna seek help too. You have a lot of anger and I can't fix that." I blocked her from the door as quickly as my body could move.

"Don't leave. I have waited for you for so long. Please don't disappear from my life again."

"Get some help, Leo!"

"Please don't go! Please!" I fell to my knees and buried my head right in the lower area where her demons lived.

"Leo, stop this!"

"Poison me!" I begged. "I don't care if you fry my

dick off. I want to be inside you!"

"I'm not poisonous, Leo. You're sick!" She pried me off and left me in my desperate misery. I thought to overpower her. Maybe even rape her, but I was too scared and the risks were too great.

I drove aimlessly around the city. Gina's fantastic form carved into my brain, with permanent scarring. I hit the bars and with several glasses of scotch in me, I ended up in front of Fran Anders' place. I knocked and she let me in immediately, as I figured she would.

"Leo? You look awful. What's wrong?"

"You're not poisonous." I managed to say, my words slow and my head fuzzy from the booze.

"No, Leo. I'm not poisonous and I'm not a whore. I'm a woman who loves you." I took her right then and there and when I made my way inside her it felt like the world around me had melted away. So this is what it was like, exhilarating, sticky, blissful magic. No pain, just release. I didn't last long, of course. But my orgasm was so powerful I was barely present and, for a moment, I looked down and saw Gina smirking with her eyes wild. A sudden fear possessed me. That defected bitch had a grasp on my entire psyche and at this point I was convinced she would never let me go. "Leo?" Fran wrapped her arm around my chest, hungry for affection, but I could give her none. "We can go again if you'd like."

"I need to use your bathroom." I said to her and she pointed to where it was. I took a piss, my mind still on Gina and how she provoked me to give up my chastity, my sacred vow to God and to myself. That bitch, that horrible, indecent slut. My dick started to tingle then swell. The puffy skin around my shaft began to ooze and it felt like my whole crotch was on fire. I started to scream. Fran rushed in and also started to scream at the sight of my pulsating, inflamed cock. "Oh my god! Leo,

I'm calling an ambulance!" I tumbled to the floor in violent pain and, as I did, my dick pulsated and exploded like a volcano, splattering blood everywhere. Red covered Fran, who kept screaming even louder than I. She was frozen, unable to move from the place she stood, but all I could focus on was the bloody, grotesque wound where my penis used to be. Suddenly, I saw Gina again. Standing where Fran had been, smiling at me, as if she had passed her dark gift along to Fran in order to destroy me. In my vicious rage and extreme, mind-consuming hatred, I attacked Fran, wrapping my hands around her throat and squeezing until she became purple and jolted and thrashed for her very last breath.

Gina was of the devil and so was Fran and so are all women and all cunts. Don't go near them. Don't touch them. Don't even look at them. No matter how sweet they smell, and how good they look, they are deceptive and we must not let them win. There's a conspiracy out there disguised as "women's rights." They want to rule us, enslave us, emasculate us, and ultimately ruin our very livelihood. Women are venomous snakes and they won't stop. They won't stop until they've annihilated every last one of us.

Lovely Boy
Nathan Robinson

In a universe not too dissimilar from our own, Donny MacLeod opened his eyes as a crunching pressure pushed against the confines of his skull, giving his alcohol soaked brain the feeling that it was stewing away inside a pressure cooker. Aspirin, he thought as he rolled out of the stranger's bed.

The girl next to him groaned as he kicked a bottle of whisky. It spun across the grimy green carpet, clattering against the skirting on the far wall. The noise rattled like a thousand cold needles hammering deep into his brain. The girl mumbled an incoherence, then rolled over before laying as still as a corpse.

Donny looked around the room and at the cluttering of feminine paraphernalia, half of which he didn't understand or care for. There were various pictures pinned haphazardly on a corkboard; she was in most of them, sometimes with other equally fat women with drinks in hand or smiling plainly with various obese family members.

He looked over to the window where bright, horrible daylight streamed in, polluting the cave of a bedroom. They hadn't shut the curtains last night, they just got down to rutting like beasts in the midst of doom. With it being a ground floor apartment, many a passerby must have been looking in at the gruesome scene all morning.

Donny glanced over at her. She hadn't looked too bad in the bar, she'd appeared slimmer, but had a curvy vivaciousness about her. But now, in the hard light of day, she looked like a greasy hippo. The dress she'd had on last night was clearly contoured to shape her body in the most desirable way; with her pasty white skin and tumbled folds she resembled a lump of melting ice-cream with hair.

Hadn't she kept asking him to buy the drinks? Yeah, she insisted that he should because she was on welfare, having spent the last of her money on household bills.

How could he have fucked that?

The rum and cokes, the tequila, the absinthe and milk; a Green Russian, might have all helped her intentions to fuck him blind. He could never say no to the attentions of a woman. It was one of his weaknesses. He saw a beautiful woman and he had to kiss her. Kisses, more often than not, led on to him grabbing sweet pussy.

But what lay before him was no such sweetness; it resembled a mangy alley cat.

Where had he lost Waxy? He remembered being with him at Mulligan's, but after that his memory blurred.

Donny MacLeod stood up from the bed, wincing as it creaked under his shifting weight. His head pounded harder in protest of the exercise. His mind whispering and cajoling that he lie down and be quiet, just rest. But his mind screamed to get out of there you fucking idiot before she wakes up and finishes you off.

He pulled on his chinos, stuffing his yellowing underpants and a single sock into his pockets. Slipping on his shirt he left it unbuttoned, peeling off a half-used condom that had congealed to his sleeve. He had the vague memory of pulling it off of his cock last night when the rubber had started to annoy him, flinging it over the side of the bed before carrying on.

He picked up his cheap Italian shoes

MacLeod crept towards the door, slowly, caution determining his next step. He made it, opened the door, and made his way through to the hallway. Where the floorboards creaked that little bit more.

Don't fucking wake her.

Don't fucking wake her...

"Where are you going, honey?"

Fuck. He'd woken her.

He looked over, she hadn't moved from her previous position.

"Gonna make a coffee," he grumbled, "want one, sweetness?"

"Please. Four sugars."

"No worries, honey tits. Back in a sec. Keep the bed warm for me." MacLeod closed the door and slipped on his shoes.

He headed deeper into the kitchen, blaring adverts sounding from a side room.

The damp patched kitchen was much the same as the bedroom, strewn with glitter and more fucking photos. Donny MacLeod didn't like photos. He looked bad in them when they were developed, often his face was caught at a bad angle, making him appear like a loon.

As Donny filled the kettle and put it on the stove, his stomach gurgled a familiar tune. He needed a shit. Bad.

His guts lurched, jumped, and cart-wheeled as he shuffled with haste to the bathroom; he dropped his chinos in time and evacuated his bowels in one messy splurge into the awaiting porcelain. It sounded like he was turning inside out. He groaned in relief before the smell hit him; a mixture of rancid, eye-watering vinegar and fetid, festering meat.

An empty toilet roll tube laughed at him with its little tissue beard.

He grabbed it and, using the edge of the cardboard, he reached around and scraped off what he could, dropping the soiled tube on top of the beckoning vile mess.

Donny looked round and grabbed a towel from the rail and leant forward and wiped what he could of the remnants from between his flabby white cheeks, then tossed the towel into the bath. He pulled his chinos up and caught his reflection in the mirror, the sight of which always disappointed him.

His sunken piggy eyes, the ring of sagging jowls, the deep-set wrinkles that made him look like the surface of a desolate planet instead of rugged. Something new plagued his face, a bruise on his forehead, half hidden by his receding hair line that he swept forward in effort to maintain the illusion. There was a little blood, the bruise spreading out to the size of a tennis ball in a deep purple that soured his skin. He had fallen at some point, banged his head, and this is what had brought on the headache. It was more than just a hangover.

The kettle began to whistle.

He washed his face, removing the crust of blood then headed back into the kitchen and made himself a black coffee, buttoning up his crumpled, semen stained shirt. The odour from the bowl began to drift and follow him into the kitchen, turning his stomach more.

As he sipped his coffee, he passed a living room strewn with toys. A little boy dressed in dinosaur pyjamas sat alone watching a kids' cartoon. The bright eyed - though strangely thin boy, considering the size of his mother- looked at Donny, his innocent honesty burning deep into MacLeod's soul, warming it a little. He looked as frail as a little bird.

"Are you one of my uncles?" the boy asked.

"Yeah. Tell your mom that Uncle Donny popped out for some milk," MacLeod said, spying a purse on the dresser top. He snatched it and opened the clasp. It was full of notes. The lying bitch. MacLeod snatched the cash up, stuffing the eighty dollars or so in his pocket to replenish what he'd spent last night.

"Okay," the little boy replied.

"What's your name kid?"

"Bernie."

"Huh, Bernie. That's a stupid fucking name for a kid."

"I was named after my gramps, he-"

"Whatever, kid. Little bit of advice for you, Bernie Boy. Never trust women. They're just snakes with tits."

Having imparted some essential knowledge to the endearing child, Donny MacLeod headed for the front door, opened it, and stepped out into the cool, bright Sunday morning, taking his headache and his black coffee with him.

***

Donny's first stop was a gas station where he bought some aspirin which he paid for with one of his stolen, scrunched up twenties. He added two packs of Marlboros and a Baby Ruth to top up the total. Outside the shop, he greedily necked four pills to take the jagged edge off the hangover from hell, scoffed the Baby Ruth for energy and then lit a cigarette. He dropped the chocolate wrapper and downed the coffee in one to jangle his booze addled brain. He tossed the mug into a front yard, then stomped his way home, wishing he'd bought some ice for the bruise.

***

He spent the rest of the day in bed. When he woke in the late afternoon, the headache clung on like a parasite to the inside of his brain, nibbling its mandibles into every thought. It hurt to think, but he contemplated the week ahead anyway. He'd blown off steam like he did every Friday night with the guys from the car lot. Monday would start and he'd get back to the grind, selling shitty fourth-hand cars with clocked mileage to the schmucks of Long Island.

Donny eventually pried himself from bed and filled a glass of water from the kitchen faucet. He downed the whole thing and swallowed four more pills to again take the edge off.

His answering machine said he had seven messages. He knew who it would be, so he sat in front of the TV, where he watched a repeat of Wheel of Fortune, then fell asleep.

***

Donny awoke early Sunday morning to the sound of his phone clattering through the remnants of his hangover. He answered.

"Yeah?"

"Are you coming today?" His mother said curtly with a little edge to her voice.

"I'm ill."

"You're drunk. You used to be such a lovely boy. A good baby."

"I'm ill. Poisoned. I think I had a bad Mexican."

"It's time for your Auntie Rena. Are you coming to pick me up?"

"I told you I'm ill."

"Do I have to get a taxi... again?"

"Don't guilt trip me."

"You're bringing the guilt on yourself. I'm merely asking for your help. If you don't want to come and help your mother, just say."

"I don't want to come, but I will. If it makes you happy."

"It's not about making me happy, Donald. It's about family. We have to remember those we've lost."

"I remember she was a bitch."

"Don't you say that, Donald!" his mother's chide pierced his eardrum. He still had a headache throbbing throughout his entire brain. Usually, his hangovers were concentrated to one spot, common most around the temples. This particular annoyance was special, though he'd had quite a bit to drink; still it didn't justify a full-blown mind spasm. Perhaps the bruise was deeper than he thought.

"Listen mom..."

What he said didn't matter. His mother had already hung up. He checked the time. Ten past six. Donny MacLeod groaned and fell back asleep.

***

The shrill clatter of the phone woke him again.

Donny lurched for it, catching sight of the time. Quarter to ten.

"Shit," he answered groggily.

"I expected as much, you charmless fuck."

"Diane."

"It's your weekend with the boy. Where were you yesterday? I had plans. You fucking screwed them up. I can't have him all the time. You've got to take some responsibility for him. The poor little bastard."

"Don't call him a bastard, Di."

"Well, he is a fucking bastard."

"Di, is he there?"

"Yeah."

"Could you not swear as much in front of him?"

"Fuck you, Donny. Every time I look at him. All I see is your stupid, pudding round face. Now get round here and pick up your cunting son!"

Diane hung up.

The headache that had plagued him since he'd woken up on Saturday morning continued its vengeful hum. With a disgruntled slur of words, Donny peeled himself up and away from the sofa and into bedroom where he changed into a fresh set of clothes. He hadn't time for a shower.

He found some co-codamols in the bathroom cabinet, necking two and washing them down with a slurp of water straight from the faucet.

In the kitchen, he drank some orange juice straight from the carton, grabbed a bag of Cheetos for breakfast, and headed out of the door with a cigarette in between his lips and a war of straining rage between his ears.

***

His mother wasn't happy. When was she nowadays? Dad was long gone, her family were dead, including her twin sister Rena the year before last. She only had him, and he was a terrible, terrible son. He didn't even need to try to be bad. It took no effort at all.

Donny MacLeod flicked the cigarette over the grave three plots down. His mother sighed and shook her little pinhead. The cigarette smouldered in the still dewy grass. His mother's cat-like gaze drilled into him like the day he'd smeared shit over the hall walls when he was five. Like the day he took a dump in her fish tank when he was seven. Whenever he thought of his mother, it was this judging feline face he held in his mind.

"Why do you even want me here?"

"To teach you that we should remember our past, cherish those that we still have in our lives."

"I didn't like Auntie Rena. She didn't like me."

"That's not the point. It's about respect."

"Fuck respect. It's a graveyard."

"Language, Donald! We're in a churchyard."

"They're dead. Whogivsesafuck?" he bleated. A shock of sudden pain flared through the side of his head. He winced, tapping the bruise lightly.

More pills, he thought.

"That may be so. But you're here for me. My sister is dead. I have no one else. You won't even let me see my only grandson."

"His mom is a bitch."

"I know where they live, I should just go round and see him."

"If you do, I'll fucking hate you forever."

"But he's my grandson. If you'd just let me see him."

"No."

"Why not?"

"I haven't got a reason. I'm just being an awkward cunt. I know it'll make you happy. So I forbid it. I have little control over some things in my life, but this I do."

"I've never done you wrong, Donald. I tried to bring you up well. You can't keep putting up these walls."

"Well, you did a shit job, mom. If you'd done better, maybe I'd think different. Maybe if you'd been a little harder with me, I wouldn't be the screw up you see before you now. You were too nice. I don't want you doing the same to my son. I couldn't help being the terror I was as a kid. You could've. Maybe you should've smacked me about a bit, then maybe I wouldn't be such a fuck up. Maybe I could've been a billionaire, or an astronaut, or the fucking president."

Donny eyed his mother with contempt while she chewed over what he'd said. She was aghast. Her eyebrows arched up so high they nearly creased over the back of her head.

"Donald, I… I… I," she shook her head.

"Fuck you too, mom."

Donny started to walk back to his car. Naturally, his mother was pissed off when he turned up an hour late; the sniping and criticisms of every life choice he'd ever made came under fire as usual.

"Why can't you find a nice girl?"

"Are you still looking for a job?"

"Your friends are all deadbeats and weirdos, you should get out more."

He cast his gaze back over the churchyard as he climbed back into his Volvo. His mother's shoulders convulsed as she cried. Donny winced as the headache spasmed through his mind. It felt as if someone was squeezing the fluid from his brain.

He needed some headache tablets.

He needed a drink.

He needed a lot of things he didn't have right now.

Donny gunned the engine, slipping the aging Volvo into first and speeding off down the lane and back towards town, leaving his mother to cry alone. Dots of moisture spoiled his view. It had started to rain.

You shouldn't have done that, said a voice that Donny assumed to be his conscience. He was good at ignoring his conscience. No matter how much it screamed at him.

He'd do well to ignore this voice.

Donny put the wary thought to the back of his mind. It was the headache. He was still hung-over. He must be. He needed some tablets to take the edge off.

***

The pitter-patter of the rain on the roof of the car brought him out of misty fugue. He couldn't remember driving here. The engine was off and his hand was on the door catch as if he was about to step out into the downpour. His other hand rested gently on the centre of the steering wheel.

Donny looked around, a little lost in the moment. He recognised the closest house as Diane's. He had no plans to pick Danny up at all. He loved the boy, but he cramped his style. With it being a Sunday, he would usually meet Waxy and the boys down the bar for a few beers. This Sunday, he just wanted to lay in bed and see off this killer headache.

Though, at this moment in time, he felt fine. Maybe it was gone?

But what of this loss of time? Why would he drive to his ex-wife's place?

A little hand banged on the glass. Donny jumped. He caught his breath and wound the window down. Danny's eyes were wide and full of innocent enthusiasm.

"Hi, Daddy! Where are we going?"

"Oh, hi Danny. I just came to see your mom."

"Are you taking me with you?"

"'Fraid not buddy. Daddy's poorly."

All hope and sense of joy faded from Danny's face, as if he'd been drained by an emotional vampire.

"Okay. I'll go get mommy." Danny loped off back towards the house, trailing his feet through oily puddles. Donny fought the urge to floor it and get the hell out of there. Before Danny had got to the front door, Diane was already storming towards the car. She looked well. He knew that she worked out, ate well. He also knew that she was fucking a plastic surgeon, which wasn't a surprise or a coincidence, considering the shape of her tits. Her face was still angry as ever. Even in mid-orgasm she had always managed to look pissed off. He called it her severe beauty.

"What the fuck are you playing at? If you're taking him then fucking take him. If not, don't fucking bother getting his hopes up!" Her blue eyes shone coolly. Just looking into them made him feel cold and horny at the same time. In a way, he feared her ferociousness; she was like a lioness carved from ice.

"There's something wrong with me, Di."

"No shit, dickhead."

"No, please. I mean, I don't remember driving here. It's weird."

"You're coked off your tits, then?"

"No, no drugs. Just headache tablets."

"Knowing you, you'll be on something."

"I ain't. I'm ill."

"Still hung-over?"

"Di, I'm serious. I don't remember driving here."

Diane's brow furrowed as she feigned concern. "So, what's the last thing you do remember?"

"Uh…leaving my mom and driving home."

"Why here? I assumed you'd be keeping the fuck away."

"I don't know. Maybe I'm still in love with you," Donny grinned, even though he knew it might piss Diane off. Unfortunately, his poor attempt at humour did nothing to alter her stoic grimace.

"Fuck you. Fuck off. Bye."

Diane strutted back to the house. Danny was peeking out from the window; his palm held up in a goodbye, his smile broken, and his bright eyes darkened by disappointment.

The door closed and Donny felt a sense of loss. An urge inside told him to stroll up to the front door, knock on it, and take Danny somewhere. Take him out for ice cream, spoil him rotten, hell he was entitled to. So, why didn't he? A bizarre sense of pride maybe? He'd kept up the routine of a deadbeat dad for so long now, it would be out of character to spoil the illusion.

Huh, what illusion? It was the truth. He was a deadbeat dad and still Danny loved him. Danny made his old man birthday and Father's Day cards from scratch whilst the best effort he could manage was a non-descript card from the gas station. Bewildered and still wary of his own mind, Donny started the engine and headed home through the rain, wondering where exactly he would end up. He couldn't sit outside Diane's, so he headed home. And on cue, like seeing a despised acquaintance; the familiar drone of the headache settled back into his head.

Donny cringed in disgust at his own illness. It was time for more pills.

***

He made it home without any mental diversions, having stopped only at the grocery store of his own accord for supplies, namely cheap whisky and pain pills. It looked like a suicide attempt, but it was anything but. It was a cure, temporary at best.

Donny headed straight into the bathroom, stripped off, and had a shower in effort to free the grime that had settled onto his skin over the past two days. Washing might help his evil hangover. It would refresh and invigorate him, maybe he wouldn't even need the pills afterwards.

His left eye started to ache after he had scrubbed his face with a stagnant flannel.

Even after the shower, his eye kept twitching and the headache remained. He felt refreshed, partly, but no more invigorated. He rubbed his temples in effort to ease the strain forming inside his head. With each stroke, the pressure gave way, returning as he lifted his fingers away.

Donny looked at his naked reflection in the mirror. His gut disgusted him. He should've taken care of himself more. His saggy white moon face was comical, how could anyone fuck a face like that? He'd considered using fake tan to give his cheeks some colour. His eyes looked bloodshot, especially his left. He leant in and pulled down the lower lid. The white of his eye raged pink, the rawness making it look like every blood vessel had exploded with irritation. He blinked a few times and felt a horrible twitch behind his eyeball as if someone was scratching it from inside with a dirty broken nail. He blinked again, flaring the irritation more. His eye started weeping.

Doctor's tomorrow. Ring up first thing and book himself in for an emergency appointment. Feeling this bad wasn't right.

Fuck it. Whisky.

Donny dressed in an old t-shirt and some baggy jogging bottoms stained with a multitude of past sins, then planted his wary body on the beaten-up sofa. He necked five high strength painkillers, washing it down with a healthy glug on the bottle of the finest and cheapest Texas bourbon.

The burn in his throat gave him a brief distraction from the flame in his head. He took another swig and thought about Danny. He took another and thought about how he'd fucked things up with Diane; the cheating, the verbal abuse, the one time he threw a chair at her across the kitchen and knocked out three of her teeth when she caught a leg in her mouth. Thankfully, she'd decided she wouldn't press charges, as Danny needed a father on this side of a high wall. Instead, she took Danny and left him, filing for divorce a week later. He'd gotten off lightly for his actions; it could have easily turned out a lot worse. He'd apologised for his actions but knew Diane would never forgive him. This was one of the reasons he kept a distance from Danny. Shame. Pure, unadulterated shame. He managed to show up on birthdays and a present sometimes at Christmas. He'd never been the father he aspired to be. So why bother? Nothing ventured, nothing lost. He didn't need further reminders that he was no good, reinforcing the evidence that he'd well and truly fucked his life up.

There was no reason to drag Danny down into his mire of a life.

He spun the cap off of the whisky, sinking two mouthfuls for a few seconds of relief from the headache.

"Why not end it? Why not sink this whisky and down all the pills and just end it all?"

"Because you'd probably fuck that up as well."

Startled, Donny looked up to find the source of the voice, but no one was there.

"Who said that?" he asked the room, surly and discombobulated from the booze.

"Why don't we pour the whisky down the sink and flush the pills down the toilet? There's a good boy." It was less a question and more an order. Donny looked around for the voice, waiting for Waxy to jump out with a grin and a case of Bud ready to join the non-party he was having. But it wasn't Waxy's voice.

"Who is that?"

"That is no concern of yours. Now do as I say. It's for the best."

Donny jumped up and tore around the room looking for whoever was hiding. The voice was close, coming from inside the room. He flipped over the sofa, looked behind the TV, and opened the doors on the dust-skinned cupboard. Whoever was hiding was hiding well. They must have a microphone stashed somewhere. This was Waxy's doing. Fuck knows why, he had a shit sense of humour. It wasn't his style. The headache faded, as did the irritation in his eye. He didn't notice.

"Yawn."

"Where the fuck are you?" Donny still had the whisky bottle in his hand. He imbibed a mouthful to settle his fraught nerves.

"Close, but very far away from you," the voice said, toying with Donny.

"What do you want?"

"What do you want?"

"I want you to fuck off or show yourself."

"Go to the bathroom."

Wary but curious, Donny did as he was told, taking the whisky with him, gripped in his tight, white-knuckled fist. He was scared. He was scared that he'd have to fight whilst drunk. He was scared that this was a setup. He'd wronged a few people over the years.

Tony Hayden?

The Clintons?

The Marton Brothers?

Could be any of them.

A fearful sweat spread across his back at what horror he might find in the bathroom. The voice remained silent, which unnerved him. Donny touched the door and pushed it open, eyes wide, his muscles jerking in fright. His upper arms quaked as the adrenalin prepared them to punch their way out of any given situation.

The bathroom was empty, devoid of any being aside from himself.

He expected something horrible in the toilet pan, but all he found was the familiar ring of scum that haunted the bowl.

The bathroom was as he left it. The residue of steam had nearly cleared from the mirror, the wet towel slumped on the floor in a grey, disappointed heap.

He gasped a sigh, embarrassed at getting worked up over the fear of what he'd find.

Nothing was out of place. What was he supposed to be looking for?

He caught his scared, fearful, animal gaze in the mirror. The reflection wasn't his, it was of a man unnerved by his own life, anxious and teetering close to the edge. Beneath his eyes lay smeared bruises of sleepiness. He looked old and worn. Like a tyre, he needed changing before he lost his grip.

"Can you see me?" the voice asked, "Hello, Donald."

But it was Donny's mouth that moved.

The whisky bottle slipped from numb fingers and shattered, wet fragments dancing across the bathroom floor, showering his bare feet with alcohol soaked glass teeth

"What the fuck is going on?" Donny said.

"Let's not get into the details, but I'm here to help you." Donny's mouth moved and it sounded a little like his own voice, but younger, less grizzled by foul experiences and bad decisions.

"Who are you?"

"I'm the voice inside." Donny's mouth remained immobile, the voice echoing inside his mind. He looked left then right, trying to cement his confusion.

"But who are you?"

"I'm here to help." The voice stayed inside his head. In one way, it was considerate – as seeing his mouth move with someone else's will was a terrifying sight. But the voice in his head scared him just as much.

"With what?"

"Your life."

"I don't want help."

"You don't want help. You NEED help."

"Just who the fuck are you?"

"You know I can't answer that."

"Are you my conscience?" Donny asked, still staring at his reflection.

"From what I've seen, I don't think you have much of a conscience, Donny. I'm yet to be convinced of that fact."

"How did you get inside my head?"

"I'm really small and I climbed into your ear when you were asleep. Is that explanation enough?'

"You're being sarcastic. Please tell me what's going on."

"I've being watching you, Donald MacLeod. You disgust me. It's time to live your life right; before it's too late."

Donny leant forward, placing both palms on the mirror and stared into that red eye of his.

"You're in there, aren't you?"

"Maybe. Maybe not." The voice used Donny's mouth again, like he was a puppet to be picked up and made to speak at will. He was a dummy.

"Am I possessed?"

"What do you think?"

"You can control thoughts, can't you? That was you driving this morning. You took me to Diane's. Why?"

"You should spend more time with your son. You won't be around forever."

"I know that. I stay away so I don't disappoint him."

"You already disappoint him. You might as well enjoy it. He's still young. He might forgive you."

"Huh, how would you know?" Donny MacLeod was beginning to feel a little bit ridiculous talking to himself.

"I don't," said the voice, calm and knowing, "but then again, neither do you. The future is yours for the taking. So why not take it?"

Donny pondered. The voice had a point. He had nothing to lose. Apart what self-respect he had left should it go tits up.

"Are you an alien?"

"Are you? I am you after all."

"Am I an alien?"

"I couldn't answer that. You're a bit of a dick, I know that much."

"You're not my conscience, not an alien. Are you like, my subconscious?"

"That would be a little obvious, wouldn't it? A little too easy."

"I don't know how psychology works, for fuck sake!" Donny slammed the flat of his hand onto the bathroom mirror; it rattled but didn't break. His image shook.

"Don't get angry Donald. Anger is like swallowing poison and expecting the other person to die. It leads only to dark roads."

"I just want to know who you are; what you are."

"Don't worry. Just listen to the sound of my voice; I want to help."

"How? You're a figment of my imagination. Unless I'm crazy."

"You're not crazy, Donald. I'm real. Crazy people don't realise they're going crazy, nor would they admit it to themselves. Crazy people believe that they're right, no matter what."

"You want me to listen to you, and then you'll go away?"

"I can't promise that. But what choice do you have?"

"You're not gonna get me to kill the president or anything?"

"Ha ha ha...," the voice chuckled softly, "...not yet."

"Huh?"

"I'm kidding."

"Huh, good."

"Now clean up the glass before you cut yourself."

Donny looked at his feet and the scattered remnants of the whisky bottle. He had a few little cuts on his feet, thin lines of blood seeped out. At least his head didn't hurt; strange, that. But a flicker from his left eye let him know that he had irritations elsewhere.

Donny stepped back over the crowd of glass fangs and headed to the kitchen to fetch a dustpan and brush, then returned to the bathroom and cleaned up the mess.

His efforts swept up more than glass. Deposited in the pan were greasy dust bunnies, ancient fragments of blown tissue from the back of the toilet and a couple of piss-rusted bottle tops from when he drank beer on the toilet; even a used condom that was stuck like a shed snake skin to the bottom of the rug. How did that live there for so long and get away with it? Christ, he was scum. He needed to clean the entire place; the carpets needed replacing, the walls wanted decorating. He needed to clean up his entire life, in fact. Not just his bathroom floor.

Maybe the voice was right. Whoever it was.

Donny dumped the collection of rubbish in the kitchen bin, put the dustpan and brush back, and then returned to the bathroom to face the mirror.

"Okay… what do you want me to do, then?"

"Do you promise to listen to me?" the voice said calmly.

"I'll listen."

"You've got to do as I say if you want to improve your life and others around you."

"I want Danny to be happy."

"That's the spirit."

"Get to the point. You want me to start helping old ladies across the road or something, for me to start being a good citizen?"

"In a way. I want you to kill your friend Bruce Wax." Donny's reflection changed; just for a second, just his eyes, as if he'd caught a momentary glimpse of reality slipping. He saw a monster behind his eyes as they darkened. A monster that was losing control. But it wasn't the voice. It was him.

"Waxy? What the fuck? He's my buddy. I ain't killing him."

"If you want your life to improve, you're going to have to. There isn't any other way."

"What do you mean?"

"If you want the best life for Danny, this is the way. I'm sorry. I can't think of anything else."

"What do you mean you can't think of anything else!? Why would you even think about this?"

"Listen Donald, let's face facts. You're never going to earn it, you're not going to be left it in an inheritance, nor will you win or find it. You've got to steal it."

"What?"

"Money, Donald. It's what makes the world go round. What legacy can you leave Danny? This shithole? It's rented anyway."

"What's Waxy ever done to me?"

"He's subhuman scum. He needs to be eradicated. He sells drugs to kids. He steals and he cheats. More than all this, you follow him like a dutiful little puppy, going on with his evil little schemes."

"He's good company."

"People said that about Hitler."

"But why would I kill Waxy? How would that benefit me, or Danny for that matter?"

"You know where he keeps it, you know his grand plan."

"Waxy's retirement fund?"

"Exactly. What does he intend to do with that money when he's got enough?"

"Thailand." Donny gulped; he already knew the answer.

"And what does he want he want to do in Thailand when he gets there?" the voice asked, dulling its tone to a careful, calculated whisper.

"He wants to drink, smoke, and fuck all day. Because he thinks that he's earned it."

"Who does he want to fuck Donald?" The whisper, whilst hushed, was perfectly audible.

"Girls. He wants to fuck girls."

"Little girls, Donald?"

"I don't know."

"Yes you do. You found those pictures one time at Waxy's place, didn't you? The ones with the two girls tied up. Who else was in the photos?"

"Waxy."

"And why did you hide this little nugget away? Why didn't you tell the police?"

"Because he's my friend."

"He's a dirty paedophile and he needs to be destroyed. It'll make the world a better place to be; for you, Danny, and a lot of little girls around the world."

Donny stopped breathing. His mind wandered in dislocated spirals. Every train of thought was broken, for he came back to the same unanswerable conclusion. How? His left eye twitched, darts of pain bursting in and out of his eye as if he'd somehow caught the socket beneath the hungry needle of a sewing machine.

"How could you know all this? I never told a soul," Donny said, rubbing the pain from his eye without success. His vision watered, blurring his reflection.

"Your mind, Donald, is like a big house. It has many windows. From where I am I can look into any window I want and see what's going on inside. Every thought you've had, everything you've ever done, good-and-bad, are here. It's an amazing place. The windows are a little dirty and there's a lot of trash inside, but it's fascinating nevertheless."

"Are you a demon? Are you the Devil?" Donny said softly.

"Would you like me to be? Would it make this easier?"

He shrugged.

"You've got to do what's best for Danny, even if it is blood money. It'll give him good start in life and his conscience will be clear. He never has to know."

"How do you know this is the way?"

"I don't. It's a risk you're taking. Not me. It's for the greater good. Keep telling yourself that."

"How? How would I go about it?"

"As long as he's dead, it doesn't really matter, does it? And make sure you get the money. You know where he keeps it stashed away?"

"In his bedroom?"

"Correct."

"He has a safe bolted to the floor of his wardrobe."

"You're remembering, you know everything you've ever done, don't you?"

"Yes, it's horrible."

"What's the combination?"

"I don't know."

"Yes you do. It's zero-nine-one-one-six-nine."

"His birthday?"

"Yes, you know this to be true. They're your memories."

"How would I know this?"

"You don't, you're just guessing. But you'll more than likely be right. Bruce Wax is a predictable character. He's not a creature of original habit."

"Yes, but how do you know this? How are you getting in my head?"

"I just do. It's best not to question it. I know all your guilty little secrets. You're not a nice man, Donald MacLeod. You have to redeem yourself."

"It'll be blood money."

"So? Danny needs the best chance in life, doesn't he?" the voice reasoned.

Donny thought for a second, he even looked away from the mirror. "You have a conscience?"

"I do and it's very clean."

"But you're inciting me to murder. How can you call that a clean conscience?"

"There'll be no consequences for me if I get caught, so I'm not worried. I'm just thinking of the boy, of Danny. You have to provide like a good father should."

Donny thought for a second. He didn't trust his reflection. His left eye was far too red. It was a demon's eye, something not to be trusted. But he had no choice. The voice was right.

"I'll do it."

"Of course you will."

"For Danny."

"For Danny, always."

"Always."

"Don't forget to wear gloves."

"I won't."

Donny left the bathroom with the horrible feeling that somehow, by a fluke of reality, his reflection was still standing inside the mirror, grinning manically with that gruesome bloodshot eye.

Outside, an early winter darkness had shrouded the street.

***

An hour later, he was back from Bruce Wax's place. A bag in each hand. One was a battered blue sports bag filled to the brim with used tens and twenties, the pinnacle of Waxy's frugal savings for the past seven years, approximately eighteen grand, a good start for anybody, good or bad. The birthday combination had been a stroke of luck and the safe's door had open with ease on well-oiled hinges, revealing its paper prize inside. Amongst the notes had been Bruce Wax's photo and film collection. Donny left these alone in the safe and closed the door. The horrible secrets would be found by someone else's intruding eyes. In his other hand, Donny held a black refuse bag, inside which was a blood-stained claw hammer that had been used to end Waxy's deviant life.

Waxy had opened the door with a half-stoned smile, a blackening joint hung from his lips

"What you doing here, I thought you were ill?"

"Are we alone? We need to talk."

"Come in, you want a beer?" Waxy asked through a friendly realm of sweet smoke.

"Yeah sure."

As Waxy turned to head back down the corridor, Donny struck out with the hammer, which connected with a meaty crack on the back of his neck.

"Whaychafucka!"

Donny kept hammering until he could see the top of his friend's spine spiking through the broken skin. Waxy lay still on the floor, limbs splayed. A flower of blood bloomed out on the hallway floor while Donny retrieved the money from the bedroom, stashing it in a sports bag he found. He was out the door and driving back through the refreshing rain within five minutes. No one saw him, nobody tried to stop him. He felt that the task was too easy and he expected blue lights at every turn.

It never happened.

Then he was home.

Donny breathed for the first time in what felt like hours. The oxygen was wrong, tainted even. He didn't deserve air. He wanted to choke.

Donny dumped the bag of blood money on the bed and then took the hammer from the bag and into the bathroom to wash off the sinful blood and skin and flecks of bone that decorated the club end, placing the weapon in the sink with a clatter.

His reflection was waiting for him. It had a healthy splattering of blood across his solemn face, his left eye was a red ball with a black dot in the centre. He looked like a mad man.

The voice had kept quiet during Donny's venture to end the life of Bruce Leonard Wax. Donny took this to be strange, he was even tempted to call out as he debrained his friend and ask if he was there. But that would have been crazy, wouldn't it?

He'd had no headaches whilst he'd been out and no pills had passed his lips since that afternoon. It seemed that the voice in his head had some control over the agony he'd been in.

"It's done."

"I know. I was watching. It went well. A little messy, but needs must."

"Will the headaches come back?" Donny queried.

"I'm quite comfortable now, so there shouldn't be any more discomfort. Unless you misbehave."

"My eye hurts. It really fucking hurts."

"I can't help that I'm afraid. I can only turn things on and off. Not off and on. It's beyond my control."

Donny leant forward into the mirror, pulling down his lid. The white of his left eye was swamped by bright pink rawness as irritated blood vessels throbbed. He pulled his eyelid down further, tipping his head to get a better look at the irritation which he was sure was coming from beneath his eye.

"This doesn't look good. I'm going to have a shower, and then I think I'll have to call an ambulance to pick…"

Donny stopped as he saw it. A thin line that poked out of the red ball of his eye, maybe half an inch, if that.

"What the fuck?"

Donny toyed at the end of the line with his finger. It looked like a hair, a thick blonde hair. Not a thin little sweep like a traditional eyelash, but a thick, coarse length of pubic hair. He blinked and the annoyance tripled in intensity as the sharp end jabbed into the interior of his lid.

He shrieked in pain, then held his eye open with his thumb and index finger to prevent further involuntary blinking. It felt like a salted needle was being born from the once white of his eye.

"Son of a bitch!" Donny cursed. He spun round and flung open the bathroom cabinet behind him, his fingers performing a tango as they searched, knocking over old shampoo bottles and out of date meds, scuffing dust bunnies and sliding through a film of grime that had settled on the shelf over the years.

They chanced upon metal; he grabbed whatever it was up and returned to the mirror.

"What the hell is this?" he asked the voice.

The voice didn't answer.

"Where are you?"

A strangely ominous silence in his head.

"What is it?"

"I don't know," the voice replied, "I'm scared."

"You're fucking scared! I've got a hair in my fucking eye that feels like a fucking ice pick."

Donny stretched his eye wide. The hair had poked through a little more.

"I've got you, you little bastard!" he said, moving the tweezers in around the end of the hair, unperturbed by the proximity of the metal to his delicate fleshy orb. The flat ends clamped together, catching the hair in between. Donny smiled, then began to tug.

A few inches came free until Donny was able to drop the tweezers and grasp the thick hair with his pudgy fingers, winding it around the digits to keep tension.

He felt a twinge in his brain, and the hair stopped coming. He gave it a light tug and it felt like cheese wire pressing against his eye.

"Is that you?" the voice asked. Donny a detected a note of fear on his tongue.

"Yes it's me. You made me do a bad thing."

"Be careful, Donald. That hurts."

Donny tugged again, staring at the eye that stared back. The red eye. The bad eye.

"Donald, that hurts."

Each tug sent a searing headache through Donny's head.

It was him.

Donny wrapped the hair around his fist and pulled until it felt like he was pulling a plug out of his mind. Then the intense migraine burned brighter until a white red heat blinded his eyes. Donny collapsed, his fingers palsied, yet he kept pulling.

"Everything you've learnt, I've learnt and more. Whilst you were fucking up your life, I was paying attention," Donny heard the voice talking to him through the explosion of pain.

"What the fuck are you?" Donny shouted into the empty bathroom. He gave another tug on the hair, his other hand gripped to his face to help brace the socket.

Something popped inside his skull, and the hair came free, twisting and curling around his fingers. The voice let loose a shrill, primeval call that shattered the glass of Donny's mind. A full-blown shriek exploded, crippling Donny, sending him to his knees, then onto his side. He began to quake and froth and spit as the voice continued its psychic assault on his mind. Tears of blood fell from his eyes, ears, and nose.

Donny found the strength to lift himself up from the floor, then smashed his forehead into the floor in a fury in order to erase the pain from within. The paralysing scream stopped temporarily. Donny headbutted the floor again, jarring and altering the strength of the voice's power. The voice had been jolted.

He'd fallen. Bashed his head. Awoken something inside. That was it. He'd roused something that had lay dormant in his mind for all these years.

"I know you're in there!"

His entire hand shook as it lifted up and felt around the bowl of the sink. The raging headache blew on, keeping him bound to the floor, his other hand pressing fingers into his pounding temples.

Donny's searching fingers found the hammer handle and raised it up.

"I'm getting you out of there, you dirty, evil, little bastard!"

The voice screamed a vehement protest, the pressure of which nearly popped out Donny's eyes from their sockets. Clearly it saw what he intended in his thoughts.

With a furious strength born of the intense pain that the voice had caused, Donny smashed the hammer down upon his own forehead. A calm blackness replaced the blinding white flush of pain, but this new blackness only brought a temporary reprieve. The voice's pain flashed backed tenfold, an A-bomb going off in a teacup; a pure, undiluted madness that frothed his brain into paste.

Donny's smashed again, seeing his own blood spray up above him in conjunction with a horrible crack louder than anything he had ever heard.

Blood blind, he smashed again.

And again.

And again.

The voice was still screaming his protests long after Donny had ceased his self-smashing.

***

The bell of his phone clattered through his still apartment. But he never answered. The first person to check on him was his mother, three days after he'd

271

killed Bruce Leonard Wax in cold blood. She knocked on his door, after her efforts had failed to rouse an answer, she used her own key and let herself into his dingy, mildewed apartment.

Following her nose, she unknowningly walked past the bag of money in the bedroom and into the bathroom where she found a hoard of flies swarming over her son's black blood-stained corpse. He had a hammer in his hand and a hole in his head. It ran from his forehead to his crown, his mashed grey brain sitting inside like a bruised, browning jelly; broken fragments of skull littered his face, inside and out like scattered eggshell. Mary MacLeod had never seen such a sight before in her life, but she couldn't take her eyes off the gruesome scene. The smell was atrocious. Judging from the aroma, her son had evacuated his bowels sometime during or after his death.

If someone had murdered her son, for some strange reason they had placed the hammer in his hand in effort to make the wound look self-inflicted, which was ridiculous. The other answer would be that her son, Donald, had been out of his mind on drugs of some sort. She'd read in the papers about addicts who'd plucked their own eyes out like plums. She'd seen one report on the news about a man who'd cut off his own penis and thrown it at the pursuing police.

She looked at the wound and the broken china that was his shattered skull beneath. She looked into it. Something looked back at her. It was around the size of a plastic army figure that Donald had used to play war with and dismember when he was a child. A tiny, hairy being with black eyes stared back, its body was green with decomposition, its limbs were thin useless sticks. The majority of its being was its bulbous ball like head, which was plastered with thin strands of blood stained blonde hair.

Mary MacLeod's first thought was the thing lying in her dead son's head was an alien. But then a terrible realisation came to her. But then a terrible suspicion came to her. Her mind flashed back to a day from her youth.

It was the day Donald's father walked out after she told him she was pregnant. He didn't respond, simply packed a bag and left their tiny apartment. That night she cried herself to sleep, when the dark veil of slumber finally took her, she dreamed. She dreamed that she had two children. Twin boys. Both blonde haired and blue eyed. Happy children. She was so sure she was to have twin boys, two strong males to replace the fiancé who'd abandoned her, she was disappointed when only one child was born.

Mary looked down upon her dead sons, everything making terrible sense. She couldn't explain what she saw, but somehow, she understood.

Mary pulled off a few rolls of toilet paper then leant down next to Donald and plucked the little boy from his head. It was a strange sensation, but it felt right. She wrapped him gently in the tissue. She had already planned where to bury and what plant she'd buy to mark his grave. No a tree, an apple tree. She'd call him Adam. The first child.

She left Donald where he lay. She'd call the police anonymously when she was far from here.

Mary shuffled down the corridor with her unborn son snug in her coat pocket. Her head was dipped in reverence when she passed the bedroom, spying a stray twenty dollar note on the bed. Mary Anne MacLeod entered the bedroom. Standing over the bag, she ran a hand through loosely tumbled papers.

She didn't ask, for there was no question. Mary picked up the bag without further consideration and left her son's apartment, smiling as she planned on spoiling her grandson rotten.

Recognition
David Owain Hughes

"There is nothing to writing. All you do is sit down at a typewriter and bleed." — Ernest Hemingway

Julian's fingers glided across his PC's keyboard with frantic yet accurate movement. The clack, clack, clacking sound of the keys acted as a background score to the shifting images, sounds, and voices inside his head.

He braved a glance up at the clock above his computer, but didn't dare stop his enthusiastic typing as he did so.

"Eleven-thirty," he mouthed. "I have until midday, right? That's what the guidelines had said in my editor's e-mail. I'm sure of it. Bloody *deadlines*!"

Julian muttered and cursed to himself as he averted his eyes from the keeper of time to his monitor. His lips moved with rapidity as he read over the last few sentences he'd constructed – his chain of thought had been broken by the clock's distraction.

A smile developed on his face, and he fought the urge to laugh like a schoolgirl. The story he was working on, a noir novel called *Neon Ice*, was coming along better than he'd wished for.

It would be his best creation yet.

The critics will love it!

Not only would it be his unsurpassed work of fiction to date, but his fifth novel – a landmark he'd thought unachievable when he'd first started writing some twenty years ago. This would also be his first crime story.

Horror fiction was all Julian had ever known, had ever created. But, of recent, crime had taken his fancy.

And when an idea for a noir novel had started forming in his head, he knew he'd have to undertake it – to push himself and explore different avenues and genres with his writing.

For the first few years at the beginning of his journey, Julian had practiced his craft by pumping out short stories one after the other. The ideas had moved around inside his brain as though they were on a conveyer belt. All he had to do was write them down. Back then, Julian had thought his mind was incapable of running dry. Thankfully, it hadn't.

Julian put this down to the love of storytelling and the admiration he had for the horror genre itself. When he wasn't writing stories, he was speaking them. He told strangers, family members, and work colleagues various lies and fabrications. Why? To garner reaction. Also, he got a kick out of it.

He lies and tells tales.

It's what he does.

He's a writer, so he spins yarns.

It makes him smile.

Julian also thrived off deadlines and ate them for breakfast.

To this day, he saw submission closing dates and timeframes for work to reach editors as motivators, or drill sergeants, as he liked to refer to them. Julian loved having them lined up on his calendar like little soldiers on parade. When one objective was finished and scrubbed off his schedule, he liked having another two or three jotted down for later in the year to replace the fallen troops.

Like some kind of Greek mythical monster, he thought. *When you cut one head off, six more grow back!*

Deadlines get fingers tapping and creative juices flowing. They leave you with little time to think about anything else. A writer does not take a holiday. They are incapable of having such a luxury. When a writer is away from his desk, they are still working. Committing unsolved murders and dreaming, scheming and plotting sex scenes, monsters (real or otherwise), dark places, creepy hangouts, sex-starved maniacs, real-life situations... The list is inexhaustible.

Their mind *never* shuts off.

When they are with you in a room or on a date, they're not really there. They might be in body and soul, but not in mind and heart. They're in their own little world, cheating on you with a person you will never know.

Ever since his schooldays, Julian had thrived off such organization. He found at the time, and to this day, that being governed by a date and time drilled and dieted his creative mind. It kept him trained, primed, focused and the cogs in his creativity machine turning.

That, and the amount of reading he devoured week in, week out.

"Stories to a writer are important. It doesn't matter if the tales are trash, good or ugly! We need to understand and analyse the use of language and grammar to appreciate and recognize how professional wordsmiths use their tools of trade," one of his creative writing tutors had told him at University during a semester. "As King points out, 'If you don't have time to read, you don't have the time (or the tools) to write. Simple as that.'"

An impressionable Julian had lived by those words upon hearing them. King's quote, along with two from Kurt Vonnegut – "Here is a lesson in creative writing. First rule: Do not use semicolons. They are transvestite hermaphrodites representing absolutely nothing. All they do is show you've been to college" and "We have to continually be jumping off cliffs and developing our wings on the way down" – were pinned to his wall for inspiration.

The first quote by Kurt always made him smile, as it had enraged many people he'd told it to over the years.

Success had soon followed in the wake of Julian's hard work. His short stories found their way into online magazines and physical ones, along with local anthologies and compilations from reputable publishing houses.

Money flowed in dribs and drabs, but what did that matter? Being published and recognised were the only concerns. The house and Ferrari would come in due course, not that he was a materialistic person in the least.

As long as I earn enough to keep me writing, I'll be happy!

Soon after it started coming together for Julian, he gave up his full-time cleaning job and married the girl of his dreams. The blocks of life started falling into place. All he had to do was sit and wait for recognition to register – to push him up the publishing charts and make him a household name among the big guns.

Yeah, but it wasn't all champagne and caviar! he thought, continuing to smash away at his keyboard as though he intended to destroy it. *No, there were a* lot *of... dark days.*

On his path to success, Julian had suffered from depression, confusion, self-doubt, self-loathing, and mental blocks, and had found himself lost on the road to glory. All the aforementioned were crippling. When the infamous 'black dog' showed up, it would shut Julian's creativity down for days, weeks, or months at a time.

The black dog, whom he'd lovingly named Morose, would attack without warning. He'd set on Julian with a snarl of its flashing fang and robust body, enveloping him in a world of misery and inner pain.

The coffee pot got me through most of it!

A smile creased his face.

But it wasn't the caffeine alone that aided him.

At his lowest it was Jack Daniels and his good friend Gordon that got Julian through his black spots and banished Morose to his hellish kennel at the back of his brain. When it wasn't the booze, it was cocaine and pills. It didn't take long for things to fall apart. His wife and house went, followed by his reputation as a stand-up writer and person among his peers. Some of the bigger publishers washed their hands of Julian when his addictions and wife's vilification hit the newspapers.

Luckily, his agent stuck by him and steered him back onto the straight and narrow.

Julian had found the fall from grace hard, but got through it.

Recognition. It was the thing he needed. *Craved.* Without it, he'd seen himself as a failure. A flop. Julian and his agent had tried all the marketing gimmicks to push him into the limelight, which had worked, but not enough for Julian's liking.

The local rags, as much as they spouted about 'supporting local talent', turned a blind eye to Julian and his work.

"We hardly see blood and guts as *intelligent*, Mr. Griffiths," he'd been told by one journalist. "Our paper will not be associated with such drivel."

After years of little appreciation, a meagre fan base and a bunch of hit-and-miss reviews (after decades of hard work), Julian had been driven to the brink of obliteration.

His mind had started to come away at the seams.

"Why don't you leave it there, baby?" his wife had cooed.

His response, after smashing the kitchen up, had been, "How the *fuck* do you expect me to do that? It consumes me, woman. It *is* me!" He'd refrained from slapping her.

A cold shoulder is the worst thing you can give a writer! he thought, flashing the clock another fleeting look. *I should have this book wrapped up and sent off with time to spare. It's not like me to let a deadline get so close. I never did agree with that Adams fella. "I love deadlines. I love the whooshing noise they make as they go by." Such a juvenile way of thinking.*

Once he'd knuckled back down to his work, cleaned himself of drink and drugs, and cleared his name of wife-battery in court, his fortune started to turn for the better.

Sales picked up. His fan base grew.

"Even bad press is good for business!" his agent had said.

His money stack started to grow, along with his dream, and it wasn't long before Julian had it all, and more: dream house by the beach, a horde of readers who gathered outside his home daily, interviews and guest appearances on TV shows.

I have to keep it up. Stay focused, continue to crank the work out – my editors, publishers, and fans expect nothing less! Who knows, maybe I'll get film rights one day?

"Maybe," he muttered, adding the last few sentences to his novel. "I could see this being played out on the silver screen!"

He wrote 'The End' under the last paragraph.

Looking up, Julian noticed it was ten to twelve.

"*Perfect!*"

He opened his e-mail and created a new message. In the address bar, he typed his publisher's address and added his agent's in the 'Cc' section. Once he'd written in the body, Julian attached his novel and hit 'send'.

"*Ah!*" he huffed, collapsing in his chair. He felt spent, drained, but also relieved, as though a huge weight had been lifted off his shoulders. "Good to have the bugger finished."

Now for the waiting game.

It would take Paul, his publicist, a few days to reach the e-mail, what with it being a bank holiday. However, it didn't matter. Not to Julian. Now that his deadline was filled, he could spend the next few weeks relaxing and writing return e-mails to his fans.

Before getting up from his roller-chair, Julian rotated his head, stretched his arms and arched his back – everything seemed to click into place. *I need to see my chiropractor next week,* he thought. *I don't know. Who'd be a bloody writer?!*

He then busied himself by organising his work space and replacing his notebooks, pens, pencils, eraser, Tip-ex and sharpener. If it was one thing Julian hated, it was a messy desk.

Slowly, he stood. The joints in his knees cracked.

"*Ooh*! That's better," he said, turning to look out the window. Sunlight slanted in through the glass. "A room with a view. No. An *office* with a view!"

Julian walked over to it and looked outside, seeing Alejandra tending the flowers. "I have it all, right down to the female Mexican gardener," he uttered, his eyes darting from her arse to her tits. "Mmm, my buxom burrito!" He smiled and waved at her.

She didn't return the greeting.

"She's a moody one, all right! Maybe a pay raise will perk her up? Or possibly a threat to deport her Spanish–speaking arse?" he said, laughing. "No, I kid…"

Julian placed his hands behind his back, stood on tip-toes and cast his gaze across the plush garden. He half expected to see copies of his books littering the lawn and neatly trimmed hedges. Some of his fans had thrown their editions over the wall in hopes he'd sign and toss them back over.

"Madness," he mouthed, his breath fogging the glass before him. Julian glanced over his shoulder and saw it had gone midday. "What about a bite…"

His words slurred and trailed off.

A bout of dizziness washed over him, causing him to stagger to his left, pin-ball off a wall, and stumble to his right. He collapsed to all fours and closed his eyes. His thighs trembled.

"What *the*?!" Julian put a hand to his face. "Jesus!" A fog clouded his brain. "No, I *don't* have it all," he muttered, removing his hand before standing up and turning to the window again. "There is *one* thing in my life I'm missing."

To his amazement, there were now more than a dozen people wandering around the garden.

"Who are these people?!" he yelled, and slammed his fists against the glass. "Get off my lawn! This is private property. Where in the hell is…"

What's the one thing we're missing, Julian? his mind asked, startling him.

"I can't remember! Why are all these people in my garden? Who are they?"

Think, Julian. It's important you remember. Think!

He turned from the window and faced his desk, but there wasn't one. All that remained was a small plastic toy in the shape of a PC. His writing equipment – pens, pencils and the rest – was nothing more than a stack of safety crayons. Their once fat nibs had been shaved down to needle points.

"What's going on?!"

Julian rapped his knuckles against his head as he rocked back and forth. "Whose white gown am I wearing?" Tears rolled down his cheeks.

Information dripped into his drug-addled mind.

Julian had been a writer, but wasn't any longer. He had been tried and convicted for the murder of seven people, two of whom had been his publicist and agent. When he had crashed into his black hole the last time, he had taken on a more sinister personality. He'd killed in the name of recognition.

He had slaughtered people in ways he'd killed characters in his novels in an attempt to garner him a bigger readership. The idea had been meant to look as though he had a crazed fan on the loose, one who had a deranged obsession with Julian's novels and other works of horror fiction. It had worked too, until the police had finally linked the murders to Julian.

"Whacko Wordsmith Slays Seven!" one newspaper article had read. "Writer Wreaks Havoc for Ratings!" said another. A third: "Modest Author Murders Many."

Julian brought his trembling hands to his face. "Who am I?"

Catherine Tramell, a voice inside his head whispered. It was the name Julian had started penning stories under.

"*Who*?!" The name rang a bell. "I got it from a TV show. No, a film! But why?"

Because we thought it was funny, Julian!

Julian shook his head.

He was more scared and confused than he'd ever been in his life. The walls around him were padded, and closing in.

"As long as he thinks he's still a writer and dosed up on his drugs, we shouldn't have a problem with him," he remembered someone important-looking saying.

"We could give him this. When he's up to his eyes on meds, he won't know any different!" another had said, displaying a Fisher Price toy in the shape of a computer.

"I killed my ex-wife!" he blurted. "Oh, God!"

Focus, damn it! What's the one thing we're missing?

Julian's eyes frantically flicked from left to right, right to left. "*Freedom...*" he whispered, his gaze coming to rest on the crayons with the vicious ends. "I sharpened them with my thumbs." He looked at his digits – there were coloured filings underneath his nails. "I remember now! When the drugs wore off the last time and I was free to think in a rational state, I'd planned to kill my nurse and make my escape the next time my medication wore off..."

By pretending he was not a danger to himself or anyone in Castell Hirwaun, home for the criminally insane, Julian had got them to move him to a less secure part of the hospital.

When he heard the turn of a key in his lock, Julian grabbed the crayons and hid them behind his back. As the door edged open, the young nurse greeted him with a "Good morning", to which he calmly replied.

She had with her a tray filled with needles.

You're not making the rational-thinking Julian go night-night this time, bitch!

"I'm telling you, my characters came to life! They're roaming the real world! You have to *do* something!" a bearded man screamed in the hallway as he was dragged off by two male nurses who looked as though they ate bullets for brunch.

"Calm down, Mr. Hughes," a female said soothingly.

Then the door closed.

Julian pounced, raising the crayons high. She dropped her tray. The needles and bottles of serum smashed against the floor.

"Whore!" he bellowed, stabbing the children's playthings into the young woman's neck. When he retracted them, blood sprayed up the pristine walls. As she gargled and held a hand out to him, he stabbed again and again. The crayons ripped out one of her eyes and slashed and tore the flesh from around her mouth, nose, and cheeks.

Gore showered Julian.

"Die, die, die!" he screamed in her face.

Breathless, he stood over her. A pool of blood spread rapidly beneath her.

"My keys now!" He sniggered, plucking them from her pocket and making his way out into the corridor...

The Ascent Made Him Plunge
Todd Sullivan

Francisco stepped through The Doors, and almost stumbled back out when Wabi pounced from around the bar, bright smile splitting his mustached face, wiry arms opened wide in a hug that pulled Francisco into intimate contact with him.

"My man!" The words vibrated in Wabi's chest and, if possible, he pulled Francisco closer, their thin frames pressed flat together threatening to become one. Francisco peered past Wabi's shoulders to the windows at the other end of The Doors, and contemplated breaking the bar owner's hold and pushing, sprinting him through the tinted glass to the ground five stories below.

"My band's been practicing that song you wrote for me last month, and it's going awesome!"

Francisco squashed the image of Wabi lying broken and bleeding on the street below. Physical violence didn't lure the muse from the hidden crevices of his soul. He'd discovered that truth years ago.

"You have to join my band, brother." Wabi took a step back from Francisco, but kept his hands firmly on the other's shoulders. He'd dressed in his performing clothes, a pair of leather pants and a black leather vest hanging open revealing his smooth hairless chest. His eyes sparkled with warmth, and he shook Francisco with excitement as he said, "I've been begging you all month. Just say *yes*, brother!"

"No."

Wabi threw his head back and laughed, his gold fillings dully twinkling in the dim light of the bar. "Am I going to have to start taking music for rent from now on?" He shook Francisco by the shoulders again. "You drive a hard bargain, you crazy mutha', you!"

Four weeks ago, Francisco had spent the rent money his parents deposited monthly into his account on a new Rosewood Body guitar. Wabi, who owned the one-room apartments above The Doors, had looked at him in bemusement when Francisco originally suggested paying last month's rent with a song. That expression shattered when Francisco brought the guitar to life with a savage stroke, his fingers strumming the six strings and sending a frenzied melody to slam against the stained walls of the narrow hallway outside of his tiny apartment. When Francisco opened his mouth to sing, he let loose lyrics stuffed on sex and death heat the air around him. Droplets of sweat sliding down his temple plunged from his chin and sizzled with a release of steam before they could hit the stained floor. Doors to the other seven apartments sprung open, and heads stuck out to listen as the song reached a crescendo of rape and suicide before Wabi covered Francisco's hand with his and exclaimed, "I'll take it, brother!"

Ever since, Wabi had been begging him to join his band, or at least write a new song. Days going into weeks now, he'd catch Francisco on the way up to the floor above The Doors and plead with the young musician, only to get the same, flat *No* in response. Francisco gave no further explanation. Even if he wanted, which he didn't, how could he explain that he couldn't write another song, not with the emptiness stealing away the muse's voice?

Francisco tried to detach himself from Wabi, and the bar owner looked past him to Julia shying away behind them. His girlfriend had released his hand when Wabi had pounced upon Francisco at the entrance into The Doors, but she was in his sights now as he turned his full attention upon her.

"He's been telling me *no* all month," Wabi said to her, slipping past Francisco to take Julia's hand. "You have to help me out. The guy's a genius!"

Julia smiled. She drew a lot of stares in Seoul, her blonde hair tumbling down her head in thick curls, her blue eyes sparkling. "I'll see what I can do," she said, her Italian accent making her English sound like she was singing. "But what are you gonna do to motivate me?"

Wabi snapped his fingers. "I had something already planned." He went around the counter and grabbed a bottle of whiskey from the top shelf. He placed it on a silver platter alongside an aluminum pail, which he filled with ice and four beers. Settling several glass cups in-between the beverages, he directed the two to one of the scarred booths against the wall, and told them to sit.

"All on the house," he said with a deep bow.

Julia, eyes opened wide, said, "That's way more than we can drink. How do we finish it all?"

"Invite a friend. Invite several friends. Tonight, we play and the place is going to be jamming." Wabi checked the time on his smartphone. "Show begins in an hour. Sit back and relax until then." He popped Francisco in the arm. "And you," he said, "you have to say yes."

Before Francisco could respond with another *No*, Wabi was gone. Julia sat down, smartphone already in hand, fingers a blur over the glowing screen as she texted friends. "Alice lives the closest," she said without looking up. "She'll be able to make it fast."

Francisco sat down in the booth across from Julia, popped open a bottle of beer, and filled two glasses. Besides the band members and barkeepers, they were the only other people in The Doors. The main patron area stood wider than the typical cramped Seoul bar, with five round tables in the center, and four long booths settled against the windows overlooking the narrow street below. Behind the serving counter, rows and rows of classic rock albums in immaculate condition ran along the walls, stretching from the roof down to the floor.

While Julia texted friends over the next hour, The Doors filled with students from the three surroundings universities: Yonsei, Sogang, and Ewha. Wabi bounced from the stage, where he helped his bandmates set up the lighting, tape down the black cords, and position the instruments, to behind the bar, where he served drinks alongside his bartenders. The smile he wore never left his face as he chatted amiably with usuals and fans. Minutes before the band was set to play, Alice stepped through The Doors. Her frayed blue shorts hung loosely on her shapely hips, and her shirt was cut low revealing her deep cleavage. Her hair, lightened brown, was pulled back from her tan skin and tied with a pink ribbon.

Julia waved her over, and Alice's eyes opened wide when she saw the bottle of whisky, yet untouched, standing tall on the silver platter.

"You guys are crazy," she said, sliding past Julia into the booth to sit beneath the window overlooking Seoul. "It's just for the three of us?"

"Other people are supposed to come. But come on, let's get it started." Julia gave Francisco the honors, and he uncorked the whiskey and filled three slender glasses, which they toasted before drinking down the fiery liquor.

"And this is a good one," Alice said with a breathy hiss. "How'd you afford it?"

Julia beamed at Francisco. "It's all him. I told you he's a freaking genius. That crazy guy who owns this place is begging him to join his band." She reached over and laid her hand on Francisco's, her palm sweaty in the humid bar.

The bar gradually dimmed as the stage lights brightened. The voices in The Doors dropped to a hush, and several moments passed before the percussionist sat down behind his drum set to loud applause. The keyboardist came next, followed by the violinist, the saxophonist, and then the guitarist. Wabi stepped on the stage last, and bowed deeply. He gave the university students a brilliant grin that made them roar in anticipation. Grabbing the mike, he thanked everyone for showing up, then dropped into his first cover, The Doors' *Break On Through*. He belted out the lyrics to The Rolling Stones' *Symphony for the Devil* next, then Queen's *Bohemian Rhapsody*.

Wabi flawlessly executed the American classics, his accented voice hitting each note in perfect imitation of the original. Over the next hour, Francisco, Julia, and Alice polished off half the bottle of whiskey. Julia's speech became slurred as she spoke to Alice, even as Alice's face colored to a deep red hue because of the alcohol. Alice's glances to Francisco increased in length each time Julia focused on the stage, and when Francisco poured yet another round into their tall glasses, Alice placed her hand on his wrist. He glanced at Julia, who was bobbing her head to The Rolling Stones' *Paint it Black*. She seemed completely unaware of the physical contact between him and her best friend. He said nothing, and allowed several seconds to pass before simply lifting his glass to toast Alice's.

Wabi ended the set with The Doors' *People Are Strange,* then left the spotlight, along with his band members, for a five minute interlude. When he retook the stage to chants of *One more song*, Wabi opened his arms in a warm embrace to the cheering students.

"Shin Chon! I love your energy!"

Shrill whistles and raucous applause met the proclamation. Wabi grinned and held out the microphone to amplify the noise. Then he said, "We do have one more song to perform for you tonight, and it's going to drive you wild. It's an original, and the creator is sitting out there right among you."

Eyes swept the bar, and Francisco pulled back into the shadows of the booth. Julia turned to him and smiled, her eyes half-lidded and glazed from the whisky. Alice rested her hand on Julia's shoulder and turned to Francisco also. She playfully placed her finger to her lips and breathed out a *shush*, her eyes twinkling with amusement. He briefly met her gaze from the darkness, then looked to Julia.

"Nervous?" his girlfriend mouthed at him, and he shook his head.

"I won't tell you where he is," Wabi continued with a laugh. "Not until he's ready to rock with us out here under the lights. Until then, Shin Chon, are you ready for *The Ascent Made Him Plunge*?"

Applause filled The Doors once again. Wabi bowed his head and closed his eyes as the keyboardist struck the first notes. The drummer came in next, the fast beats rising from the taut leather in a rapid-fire tattoo. The guitarists and trumpet player flung themselves in quickly after, the music swelling, pulsating, breathing with life.

Awed silence swept the rapt audience as the first waves of the *Plunge* rose up in high swells from the stage. The opening instrumental, tortured by pent up longing desperate for release, created cords of sound that latched around young limbs in The Doors and set them to dance. Firm bodies paired up in twos, threes, fours, to the wild rhythms of *The Ascent*. Boys shadowed the graceful gyrations of girls, girls snaked between the forceful thrusting of boys. Minarets to the song, they circled each other in tight orbit, the music magnetizing lithe limbs and flinging bodies together. Hands swept beneath clothes damp with sweat trickling down tight flesh and evaporating in the air to create a mysterious mist that rolled across the low ceiling.

Alice's arms wrapped around Julia from behind, and Julia clasped Alice's hands against her breasts as they both moved to the beats bouncing against the dark walls. Wabi's eyes snapped open, a wide grin stretched across his face. He raised the microphone to his parted lips and inhaled, his exposed chest beneath the open vest expanding. Words spilled forth from him, so fast and with such intensity that the music seemed to play him like another instrument. Gravity flung the dancers together, eager mouths meeting eager mouths, wet tongues discovering wet tongues as the tempo of the song mounted and reached a frenzied crescendo of naked longing that finally found a breaking point to explode out with a force that reeled senses.

Alice's hands slid down Julie's body to her bare thighs; Julia inclined her head to her friend, their kisses feverish as the music encircled them. Francisco's gaze swept across the two girls to the students, to the band, to Wabi. His frustration peeled away to anger, his rage simmering right beneath the surface. *This*! He cursed the muse with its massive appetite for sacrifices. *This* was all he wanted, all he ever wanted. The power to freely create music, on his own, without having to hurt others to lure the muse from the yawning darkness inside of him. The power to give raw emotions sound that infected minds and stripped away abandon.

Francisco took out a cigarette, but didn't light it. Instead, he rolled it back in forth between slender fingers that hadn't written lyrics in weeks. The melodies in his head had dried up with this song, the buds of flowering words shriveling beneath the terrible burden of emptiness the singer carried. The notes needed a cruel master to weave them into existence.

His student's death had satisfied the muse a month ago. The autistic boy who committed suicide at the private school Francisco worked part-time at teaching English in the afternoons. The boy had trusted Francisco when he advised him to seek out the girl in class he'd been crushing on all year. Francisco encouraged him to buy cheap convenience store gifts, to stutter out earnest compliments to her impassive stare, to not give up even when he wilted in the face of her obvious derision at his attention. Francisco, the student's favorite extra-curricular teacher, convinced the boy to hold steady with promises of eventual success. He watched the boy's soul wither as the girl's friends teased him. Soon, the other boys in the class joined in in tormenting him at his persistent, awkward efforts.

One afternoon, the student, alone in the classroom in a corner, crying, looked to Francisco for comfort, and Francisco simply shrugged. This is your future, Francisco informed him, the usual warmth dropped from words that chilled his tongue to speak. The autistic boy, plunging to his lowest point, shattered at the revelation as Francisco said, "Your longing will never be satisfied. Loneliness will be your life companion. Get used to it, and suffer knowing no one will ever care about you."

The anguish on the autistic student's face filled Francisco's own emptiness, the desperate emotion twisting his features fueling Francisco's soul and sending it soaring. The boy stepped off the ledge of his apartment building that very evening and dropped twenty stories to the embrace of gray concrete that must have seemed more inviting than a lifetime of rejection. When the school's headmaster informed Francisco the next morning, the muse gifted Francisco with a new song that burst out like a bright star ascending to the heavens from the deep hole it existed in. It gained form as it soared, took a title, discovered a purpose, to finally find existence, and adoration, here in this bar, The Doors.

Watching the reactions of those around him, Francisco knew he needed a new sacrifice, knew he needed to invoke new pain in one who trusted him. Francisco rolled the cigarette back and forth, back and forth between his slender fingers as he stared at the two girls across from him and contemplated the best way to hurt the best friends and make the muse sing again.

The Ascent ended abruptly. Melody fell away to harsh breathing from the exhausted band that'd fought to tame the beast they played. The young audience untangled arms and legs wrapped around each other and shook their heads as if dislodging dreams from the abstract infinities between their ears. What they would remember about the previous several minutes, what they'd be able to separate from reality and illusion, remained in question. Julia and Alice separated, and as others in the audience began to applaud the band, breaking the muted silence, the two girls looked around in dazed confusion.

"Oh my god," Julia managed to say at last, "what the hell just happened?" She looked to Alice, who shrugged, then Francisco, who spread a thin smile across his lips.

"Let's have another drink." He reached for the half empty bottle, but Julia raised her hand.

"I don't think I should," she replied. "I'm already out of it enough, I don't want to lose total control."

Francisco poured her a fresh drink despite her protests, then one for Alice and finally himself. He wouldn't let her refuse, and finally her reluctance fell away to acceptance, and they tapped their glasses and drank. Wabi put on Pearl Jam's *Vitality*, and his band members came to Francisco's table one at a time to buy the group shots.

Towards the end of the second hour, half of The Doors' patrons had left to late night clubs in the Shin Chon neighborhood. Julia, quiet now and breathing unevenly, was slouched down in the wooden booth, her eyes crescent moons going new. Alice, her arm around her friend's shoulder, hadn't looked away from Francisco since he'd come back in after smoking a cigarette outside. He'd ordered three more beers despite his churning stomach. He was unsure if he'd be able to keep down all he'd already consumed, but now wasn't the time to ponder on it too much. He held Alice's gaze, her tan skin glistening in the dim light, her loose shirt clinging to her breasts.

Julia suddenly jerked forward, her lips pressed together. Francisco couldn't move fast enough in his addled state, and if his girlfriend had let it go, she would have vomited over the table hitting him dead in the chest. But she kept it down with a loud snort, and leaned into Alice, who stroked back her blonde hair clinging to her damp forehead.

"I think she's going to be sick," Alice warned, to which Francisco shrugged.

"She'll be alright." Francisco leaned over the table, beer in hand. Julia, eyes vacant, reached for hers.

"Don't," Alice scolded Francisco, but he shrugged again, and tapped his bottle against Julia's, who actually managed to lift it to her lips and take a sip. Her eyes slid closed as Alice reached for her own beer.

"You live right above the bar?" Alice asked.

Francisco nodded.

"How do you sleep at night with all this noise?" Alice frowned. "Doesn't it keep you awake?"

"It's not so bad," Francisco said. Sleep didn't come easily to him anyway. Usually, he sat alone in his apartment listening to the echoes in his head, trying to decipher sounds to spin into songs.

"I like hearing the music coming from downstairs," he continued. "Helps inspire me. Come on up, I'll show you my room."

Alice's breath caught in her throat at his casual invitation, and she stared at Francisco for several moments without blinking. "Are you going to carry Julia up with us?" She nudged her friend, who muttered in Italian. Even now Francisco found her words pleasurable to hear. Julia's voice had first attracted him to her, and whenever she spoke, he longed to strike the right emotional chords to make her voice rise in rage, crackle with grief, descend in despair, moan with anguish.

"She'll be okay." Francisco slid out of the booth, and the room spun so violently that he was forced to take hold of the side of the table to keep from losing his footing and falling. "Don't worry about it," he added, forcing the world around him to settle down. "I'll let Wabi know, he'll look after her."

Wabi was sipping a beer from behind the counter and regaling his bandmates with a story about a wild night he spent last year in Busan. He smiled brightly when Francisco stumbled up to him.

"My man!" He laughed. "You look wasted!"

Francisco shrugged, disinterested in discussing the obvious. "Hey, can you watch over Julia?" he asked, nodding to the table behind him. "I want to show Alice my room." He hadn't turned to see if she'd joined him, but when Alice took his arm, her soft body pressed against his side, he knew she'd made her decision.

Wabi arched his eyebrow, and looked past Francisco to Julia, then back to Francisco again. "You know I'll make sure she'll be cool," he said. "But you don't want to take her up and put her away? She looks out of it, brother."

"I will in a moment," Francisco replied, turning to the door. "Thanks. I'll be right back down."

Without waiting for Wabi's reply, Francisco stumbled out of The Doors to the next floor, Alice in tow behind him. The narrow hall had four apartments on either side, and they went to the second door on the right. When fully open, the door touched the bed, a thin pallet on top of a wooden frame with two drawers at the base. At the foot of the bed, a small chair pushed beneath a short board attached to the wall acted as a desk. Two squat shelves tucked in the corner by the narrow window sat on top of the board. Across from the desk was a cramped, doorless bathroom with a sink, toilet, and showerhead.

Francisco motioned for Alice to sit down on the bed. He grabbed the guitar case, took out the dark brown guitar, then dropped onto the bed beside her. The sudden movement set the room spinning again, but instead of battling the cyclone of chair, door, desk, light, window, he played into it, strumming notes that went round and round until his stomach lurched.

Alice grabbed his hand to stop the playing. "You're going to make me puke," she said, and he looked at her, her lips inches from him. He leaned over and kissed her, and for moments they did nothing else, their bodies bent towards each other, their breathing heavy. All of the alcohol they'd consumed that night created thick, noxious fumes in her mouth, and he could taste the whiskey and cigarettes odors on his own tongue being pushed through his saliva down her throat. But they didn't pull apart, and only the guitar slung around his shoulders kept them from drawing closer to each other.

When they finally separated, Alice said in a breathy whisper, "Maybe I should go home."

Francisco, staring at her, said nothing, his fingers playing lazily over the guitar strings.

"You sure Julia's okay downstairs by herself?"

"With Wabi watching over her, she's fine," Francisco replied, and fetched his phone from his pocket to text him that he'd be back down in a moment. "He's the kind of guy that runs into fires to save little kids and old women. He wouldn't let any creep mess around with her."

"He seems really nice," Alice said. "Why can't you be more like him?"

"He's downstairs if you want him," Francisco said, but when Alice didn't move, he reached over and cupped her chin. He said nothing as she unzipped his pants, and when her head lowered down, he adjusted the guitar to give her space, and played the notes of the beginning of a new song. The muse, only slightly stirred from its profound darkness, hummed a melody of betrayal and jealously that barely made it up from the depths it existed within, deep down inside of him. Francisco was dimly aware of Alice's head bobbing up and down in the periphery of his vision, dimly aware of her lips clasped around him, her saliva dripping down into his pubic hair.

This wasn't enough. He needed more, and so picked up his phone and turned on the camera. He held it high over both of them while he continued to pluck the guitar strings with his free hand. Words swirled up from the muse, and he sung them softly to Alice, who licked lower, her fingers massaging his inner thighs and sending slight convulsions to ripple through his body. He did not touch her, but he directed the musical notes to her and felt her body shaking, her breathing quickening. The apartment's light took on a reddish tint, the heat rising, simmering. Low moans built up in Alice as the music increased the tension within her, and she grabbed hold of his waist, her nails digging into his flesh. She buried her face into his crotch, the breath from her nose tickling his pubic hair, and he grimaced at the tight wetness of the back of her throat. He almost lost the song for a moment, but then it roared back into him, and he tried to desperately hold on to it, desperately tried to make it complete, make it real.

But then he could do nothing for several seconds but inhale and exhale with low, guttural groans as the orgasm caught him off-guard and sent his senses reeling, his back arched, his spine pressed against the wall, his palm flat on the wood panel of the guitar.

"Damnit," he whispered, watching the song dissipate in the hot air filling the tiny apartment. This private betrayal between them wasn't enough, this blowjob too mundane, too ordinary to truly give birth to inspiration. Alice's mouth finally released him, but when she sat up and attempted to wrap her arms around him in an embrace, the guitar stood in the way.

"Come on," he said, and sliding out of the bed, zipped up his pants. "I need to make sure Julia's okay downstairs."

Alice appeared uncertain for a moment, as if she didn't want to leave, and perhaps wouldn't. Francisco turned away from her, put his guitar back in its case, and opened the door. He didn't look at her again, and simply waited in the hallway until he heard her get off the bed and exit the room. They went back down to the next floor, but Alice stopped at the entrance to The Doors and tried to catch his gaze.

"What are you?" she asked, voice low. "Julia's my best friend, and I love her. And she loves you. But..." and she trailed off.

Francisco, sensing a moment of opportunity, now faced her fully and stared deep into her soft green eyes. "I'll call you, and we can talk about it later. Don't worry about what just happened," he said. "Whiskey, beer, shots." He grinned, reached out to grasp the back of her head, and pulled her to him to kiss her. When they parted, he brushed her cheek again before sending her stumbling down the stairs, her shoulders brushing the wall as she made her way to the bottom floor.

Francisco entered The Doors and saw only a handful of patrons left. Wabi and his band mates had taken the table where Julia slept. They sat on all sides of her in a protective circle. Wabi himself had pulled up a chair at the head of the table, and turned to see Francisco approaching from behind.

"She's sleeping like a baby, man," Wabi said proudly. "Had to come over here to scare off wannabe creeps trying to make a move on her in this condition."

"Thanks," Francisco remembered to say as the other band members moved aside so that he could haul a semi-conscious Julia from the booth.

"Need help, brother?" Wabi asked, but Francisco shook his head. He put Julia's arm around his shoulder to prop her up, and whispering encouragement, he marched off with her across the bar. The floor swiveled under his feet at the exertion, and he had to reach out to catch himself on the wall to keep from tumbling over. When he got to his room, he threw open the door, dumped Julia unceremoniously on the pallet, and rushed to the bathroom. Dropping to the knees, he projectile vomited into the toilet, the water splashing back up to sprinkle his face. For several minutes, he hung over the bowl as the alcohol forced its way up out of him in explosive streams. Finally, when he'd emptied himself of the gift of whiskey and the shots of gratitude, he crawled into bed beside Julia and gratefully passed out next to her.

***

Francisco woke to a percussionist banging out a discordant beat behind his eyes, his temples throbbing. Sitting up didn't improve the drummer's playing, and he placed the balls of his hands tightly against the sides of his head with a groan. Francisco opened his eyes to slits to mitigate the light reaching his pupils. He climbed out of bed and went to the bathroom to be greeted by a noxious smell, and barely managed to avoid stepping in vomit. Julia must not have made it to the toilet at some point in the night.

Francisco sighed, unhooked the showerhead, and lifted the sink handle. He washed the mess down the bathroom drain, and then rinsed out his mouth, gurgling and spitting repeatedly until the awful taste in his mouth diminished. Washing off his face, he went back dripping to his bed, plopped down next to Julia, and grabbed his guitar. His phone vibrated next to him. He saw a message from Alice, but didn't read it. Instead, he tried to play the song he'd caught a glimmer of last night. It floated right beyond reach, teasing him with a power that wouldn't be released until a proper sacrifice had been made.

Francisco cursed softly, and looked at his girlfriend again. She woke in stages, stirring increasingly as the morning hours wore on. At one point she yawned, and flipped over onto her back. Francisco kept playing the same notes over and over again, the mounting tension giving him an anxious energy that pulled him out of his hangover. When Julia finally opened her eyes, he offered her a wide smile that felt artificial on his lips.

"Morning, you," he said, and leaned down to kiss her forehead.

She shied away from him with a groan. "Don't get too close to me. I must smell awful."

Francisco shrugged, and snaked in quickly to plant a kiss on her cheek before she could dodge him. "You're always beautiful to me," he replied, and she kicked his leg hanging over the bed.

"I don't remember coming back here." Julia sat up and leaned back against the wall. "You need a better place. This apartment is claustrophobic. Like a freaking cell."

"I was looking at some new spots yesterday," he lied, and grabbed his phone. Unlocking it and opening up a web browser, he quickly found a site advertising apartments in Shin Chon. "Most of them are way more than I can afford, though."

Julia scooted up beside him and placed her chin on his shoulder.

"Here," he said, handing her the phone. "I'm about to take a shower. If you see anything, let me know."

"Hurry up," she said, nudging him as he got out of bed. "I'm starving. We can grab lunch and walk down Han River. It's supposed to be a beautiful day."

Francisco returned the guitar to its case, went into the bathroom, stripped, and turned on the water once more. Normally he showered quickly, but today he let the lukewarm stream from the showerhead flow over him for almost ten full minutes before he soaped up, rinsed, then toweled off. When he stepped back into the room, Julia was staring at him, and he grinned at her. He hummed a bar that came from deep down within himself, his spirits lifting as he pulled on a pair of ripped jeans and a t-shirt.

Once, when he and Julia had lain on the pallet, naked and sweaty, the sheet balled up at their feet, they'd had a late-night conversation about their childhood. She'd told him how, only three short years ago in high school, she won several track and field competitions, played football with the boys, and even got a black belt in taekwondo. Now she lamented the weight she'd gain, the cigarettes she smoked every day, and the late nights she drank away.

Time may have passed since her last kick to an opponent's chest or final sprint around the field, but she seemed to have maintained the jumping off power in her legs because, when she sprang forward off the bed, she surprised Francisco before he could evade her blow and struck him flat in the face. His head snapped back into the wall, and stars briefly crowded his vision.

"Last night, motherfucker?" she yelled at him. "And you bring me up here to sleep on the same bed!"

"Julia," he began, but she slapped him again, and his ears rang. Peals filled his mind, took shape into chords, and a wild song vibrated with hot intensity through him.

"How could you do this to me?" She struck him again and again. Francisco didn't duck, didn't attempt to shield his face even after his lip busted. It was only when heavy knocking sounded on the door that Julia paused, breath ragged, tears streaming down her cheeks, mucus flowing from her nose, her hand raised again to strike but hanging suspended in mid-air.

No!

The knocking distracted the song and became a discordant rhythm in the music. A growl of frustration built up in Francisco, and smothering the scream surging up within him, he turned to the door and flung it open so that it banged against the side of the bed.

"What?" He wanted to yell the word at the intruder, wanted to snatch the question out of his mouth and stuff it down the person's throat so that they choked on it. Instead, he spoke quietly, his voice subdued, and Wabi took one look at him and gasped.

"My man," he said, "what happened in here?"

Francisco strained against the violence desperate to lash out at Wabi for the interruption. Behind him, he heard Julia collecting her things, and when she rushed out of the apartment, bumping him out of the way and sliding past a distressed Wabi, Francisco had relaxed his body so much that he slammed against the doorframe at her passage. He couldn't even raise his hand fast enough to stop her from leaving before she was already down the hall.

Wabi called after her, but her steps on the stairs quickly faded. He turned back to Francisco leaning heavily against the door and said, "You're bleeding, brother."

Shadows writhed at the edges of Francisco's vision and reached out long tendrils towards Wabi's jugular. In a subdued voice, belying all of the anger, the violent intentions he knew wouldn't draw out the muse even if he acted upon them, Francisco said in the same muted voice, "Sorry for the ruckus. Julia thinks something happened between me and that other girl last night."

Wabi nodded. "You have to be sensitive to their needs, brother. She's a good girl." He reached into his back pocket, grabbed a towel tucked into his jeans, and handed it to Francisco. "I usually see you hanging out by yourself, but when you're with her, you look happy, my man. Hold on tight to her and treasure her."

Francisco let loose a low sigh through gritted teeth. "I think you're right," he said. "Right now, I feel awful. Sorry again for the disturbance. Were a lot of people complaining?"

Wabi shrugged. "Brother, don't worry. You got to expect some madness from genius types." He clasped Francisco's shoulder. "Don't stay up here too long by yourself today. I'm with my band right now and we're just about to practice. Come on downstairs and jam with us. You'll feel better."

Francisco laid his hand over Wabi's and refrained from twisting Wabi's fingers at unnatural angles for the pleasure of hearing them break. "When the time is right,

I promise I will," he said. "I'm working on a new song now, and it might be a good release to play it with friends."

Worry fled Wabi's face, and he smiled brightly. "My man!" He pulled Francisco into a sudden embrace and slapped his back as he laughed. "You're awesome, brother. Yeah, when you're ready with the new hit, just slam it on me. I promise you, we're going to be famous!" He stepped back from Francisco, his eyes twinkling with the great joy that he always shined upon the world. "I'll leave it to you then, brother."

Francisco returned the smile, and controlled his impulse to slam the door behind Wabi when he turned to go back downstairs. He snatched up his phone, his thumbs dancing over letters as he texted Julia *sorrys* in his most persuasive language. He sensed the phrases he'd use in the song pouring into his apologies, the surface of the phone warming under his touch. He asked if they could meet later. He begged her to let him explain himself. A small smile settled upon his lips as he delivered a torrent of promises to her if she'd just give him another chance.

Finally, he tossed the phone on the bed, grabbed his guitar, and strung a few notes as minutes passed, then an hour. Before the second hour, his phone chimed, and he looked down at it and saw Julia had sent him a single response.

"Ok."

Another thirty minutes passed before she asked where, and Francisco immediately suggested The Doors. He told her that everyone here was worried about them after the fight, that Wabi had told him that he needed to make this right with her. Julia didn't respond directly to these reasons, but she did issue a single, final message.

"Sure."

With that done, Francisco laid the phone by his side and watched the shadows move across the room as the day died to afternoon, and afternoon fell to evening. He didn't eat. He didn't drink water. When he finally stirred from his room, he stumbled down the stairs to the bar on weak legs. Francisco heard Wabi still practicing with his band, and he sat on the steps outside of The Doors and sent a text to confirm with Julia that they'd meet here in an hour. After she sent another single word response in confirmation, he sent a message to Alice asking her to meet him at New York bar two blocks away at the same time he had scheduled to meet Julia. She didn't reply, but he knew she'd be there as a savage melody sprang into his thoughts.

Francisco sat on the steps for the next half hour, barely aware of the trickle of people squeezing past him. When he finally got up and went downstairs and outside, it was half past 9:00 p.m. Saturday nights in Shin Chon started slower than Friday nights, and the usual busy streets filled with bars, clubs, and restaurants were anemic this early. Couples walked hand in hand, their animated conversations punctuated by carefree laughter. The New York bar was on the 3rd floor of a nearby building, and when he went upstairs, he saw Alice already seated there, a beer on the small round table before her.

"Are you okay?" she asked after he ordered a drink and joined her at the table. She peered at his face. "You're bruised."

"Took a tumble on the stairs," he admitted, and hung his head in embarrassment. "Things like that never used to happen to me."

"We were really wasted last night," Alice replied. "I thought I was going to die this morning. When did you take Julia home? I hope she's okay."

Francisco engulfed Alice's small hands in his larger ones to comfort the worry in her gaze. "She hasn't contacted you today?" he asked, and Alice shook her head.

"Don't worry. She was really out of it when we got back to my place." He smiled. "She was apologizing to me so much this morning. She got sick in my bathroom and missed the toilet."

"Aw, gross!" Alice laughed. "That sounds like Julia. She did the same to me when she stayed over at my *hasuk-jip* one night. I was cleaning up all day afterwards."

Francisco nodded. "That's my girl. Actually, she texted me like an hour ago. Said she's staying in today. Drinking lots of fluids, I guess." He tightened his fingers over Alice's. "I wasn't sure if you would meet me here today."

"I wasn't sure I should come," Alice admitted. She leaned in towards Francisco, her green eyes coy, her red lips slightly parted. "There's something about you, *Kim Seung-Ho*," she said, using his Korean name. "Something bad." But the way she said it sounded like a compliment, and Francisco arched his eyebrows but said nothing.

They sipped their beers together. New York bar was one of several western-styled bars in Shin Chon, with a pool table in the far-right corner, and three dartboards across from it. Closer to the door stood a narrow beer pong table. A group of blonde haired Europeans entered and started up a loud game. Alice grimaced, and Francisco took that as his cue.

"You know, Wabi is playing again tonight. Lot of really good music like yesterday." He drained off the rest of his beer and checked the time. "If we go now, we can just make the beginning of his set."

Alice shrugged, finished her drink, and together they left New York bar and headed to The Doors. Outside of the entrance, a group of Koreans stood smoking, and Francisco and Alice joined them for a quick cigarette before heading upstairs to the fourth floor. It was another crowded night, and they pushed inside and slithered through the people packed tightly together.

"We won't find a seat this time," Alice said into his ear, and Francisco nodded in agreement. He bought two beers, handed one to Alice, and led her near the stage. Whatever happened next, he wanted to make sure he had an audience.

Tonight, as last night, the band members filed onto the stage one at a time. Wabi came last, and when he saw Francisco, a bright grin spread over his face.

"Brother," he said, reaching out to clasp his hand. Before they made contact, Francisco felt someone grab his shoulder and spin him around. Alice stepped back at Julia glaring at him, her anger coloring her face scarlet with rage. Her lips parted, and a stream of Italian exploded from her mouth. She spoke fast, her facial tics animated, her eyes wide. Though he understood none of the words she spewed at him, the hatred behind her emotions impaled him as he stood there, a spectacle in the front of the bar that gradually grew silent.

An unbidden smile slipped onto his busted lips, and Julia decked him in the eye. Wabi hopped off the stage to catch her by the wrist before she could make the next blow she aimed at him connect.

"Don't, sister," he said, holding onto her gently. She struggled in his wiry arms, her gaze narrowed on Francisco, her intent to hurt him as he'd hurt her evident in her every movement. His eye began to swell shut. She'd gotten a good shot in. But he didn't turn away from her, couldn't miss the intensity of emotions he'd birthed inside of her that was now ripping her apart.

Wabi stroked her hair to calm her. He whispered soft words in her ear that Francisco couldn't catch. To his amazement, despite all he'd done to her, Francisco saw the hatred draining from Julia. Wabi gave Francisco a pained look and mouthed to him, *Why, brother?*

Francisco didn't respond. Instead, he took the stage, reached down to Wabi's guitar leaning against the microphone, and slung it around his shoulder. He closed his eyes to fully embrace the darkness, then struck a mournful note that spread up from the guitar strings to engulf those silently watching him. He quickened the tempo, and sent rolling waves in succession across the bar. Steadily the torrent grew, rising to drown the senses in grief. Someone sobbed, and then another person, and another, yet Francisco remained relentless, merciless, not giving them a moment to breathe.

His lips parted, and he spun a tale of lust and betrayal that created heavy stones around limbs and weighed down lovers, sinking them beneath the tides set forth from the guitar. With a deep inhale, he sucked the oxygen out of the air, and heard moans turn into groans that drifted up to him on the stage. When he finally opened his eyes again, he saw the students caught up in the song, enraptured by the music even as it tortured them with the angst it unleashed inside of them. Every heartbreak, every broken relationship ever experienced by them became a shared experience. Through the music, he connected them, assuring them that they were not alone in their pain.

After some time, Francisco wound it down, slowly, allowing the heavy waters to drain back into the guitar so that the university students packed close before him could breathe once more. When his fingers finally lay to rest on the strings, when the muse no longer sang through him, minutes passed before the audience collected itself enough to erupt into applause.

Francisco turned to the band members behind him, their expressions awed at the power he wielded through his art.

"Stay with me, and I'll make you all famous," he promised them, and they bent their knees in supplication and bowed their heads in worship.

Then he turned to Wabi, looking up at him, a brilliant smile splitting the bar owner's face making him glow with that unique light he wielded. "Finally, brother," he breathed out, "you're ready to take the stage with us."

Francisco nodded. "But I only need one vocalist in my band," he said. "And that will be me." He paused, before adding, "Sorry, but you're out."

The shadows that sprang up to crush the light in Wabi's eyes sent the muse soaring up through Francisco threatening to rip him apart with music.

Transformer
Rose Garnett

The loud, hysterical screaming from the bathroom told Portia Douthwaite-Hodges that all was not well with her new boyfriend, Simon. She sat up in bed, clasping the duvet to her chest.

Either his luxuriant, blond coif was not quite to his liking, or, it was happening again.

She knew better than to investigate—not after last time, when she had nearly been trapped in the spare bedroom with her ex, Jason, and...*it*.

The shrieking stopped. She tilted her head, straining to hear in the sudden, crushing silence. An enormous crash, pounding feet—and Simon burst into the bedroom, gibbering.

"What-the-fuck-what-the-fuck-what-the-fuck."

"Simon, darling, are you okay?"

She switched the bedside lamp on, and by its rosy glow she saw that Simon was most definitely not okay. One eye was swollen shut, a mask of blood covered his face and the top of his head was a flayed mass of raw flesh, leaving only a fringe of blood-soaked, blond hair around the sides. He began to stagger around the room, arms flailing, a bloody gouge carved down the length of his back revealing rocky outcrops of the bone beneath, as though he had been mauled by a wild animal.

Maybe he had.

"Can't...I can't...oh, fuck," he keened, snatching his trousers from the floor.

A low, rasping noise issued from the toilet, as though whatever was in there was trying to speak. Freezing for a second, eyes popping, Simon screeched and dropped the garment, running nude out of the room and down the narrow hall. The door slammed, and Portia, leaping out of bed for the window, was treated to the sight of her injured lover pounding, still naked, down the High Street and into the night, the sodium lights turning his blood-stained flesh piebald, as though he was shedding his skin.

At least Jason had stayed long enough to put his clothes back on. This was a new low in a two year spate of them since this whole thing had started.

From past experience with all the other guys she'd lost before she'd loved, this was the last she'd see of Simon. She couldn't even call him to check if he was okay, because he'd left his mobile on her bedside cabinet. He'd surely turn up at some point to retrieve it and all the rest of his belongings, so she'd just have to wait.

Such a waste. She'd been quite into him too— handsome, smart, funny and not interested in the usual tedious, I-only-like-you-if-you're-unavailable, game-playing bullshit. She had been in this surreal, unendurable situation so many times, however, she was hollow, as though the part of her that could feel had been scooped out and binned.

"Oh, Simon…" moaned the thing in the bathroom, panting. A girlish giggle, high, teasing, was accompanied by rhythmic banging. "Oh, oh, *oooooooh,* give it to me good, yeah baby, harder, HAAAARDER." it squealed. "What do you mean, 'it's like a sausage up a close?'"

Enraged, she flung on her dressing gown and stumbled on leaden legs towards the source of the sound, punching open the bathroom door and snapping on the light.

"Fuck you," she shouted. "I won't let you ruin my life."

But the intruder had gone, leaving only the usual carnage in its wake—the mirrored cabinet on the wall, now smashed on the floor, contents vomited all over the sink. Blood was spattered on the cream tiles like a Rorschach test and there was a viscous, dark pool of it surrounding the toilet. A sharp pain underfoot from the glass shards, and her own blood bloomed outwards to meet Simon's, like the unfurling of the petals of a dark, exotic flower. At least they'd shared some bodily fluids after all.

It was as well she didn't have any flat-mates to disturb at this ungodly hour. Ironic really, as daddy had bought the one-bedroomed flat so she could complete her English degree at Edinburgh University in peace, without others bothering *her*. Another plus, on the strength of past visitations, was that the creature had done its worst and wouldn't show up until the next time she attempted to have sex.

Wincing, she picked the shards from her feet and padded back to the bedroom, putting on a pair of shoes. She fetched a brush and pan from the small, tidy kitchen and started sweeping up the worst of the debris.

There was a small, dead rodent on the cistern and she poked at it with her brush, leaving a bloody smear on the white, ceramic surface. Something golden gleamed amongst the blood and mutilated tissue and she touched it again, with more care this time.

This was no rodent—it was Simon's missing scalp and hair. Not knowing what else to do, she put it in the pocket of her robe, unwilling for the moment to throw it out with the rest of the rubbish—after all, they could reattach these things, couldn't they?

After achieving some semblance of order, she climbed into the bath and rinsed her feet with the shower head, watching, emotionless, as the bloodied water gurgled down the plug hole. Retrieving a tube of antiseptic from the floor and smearing its contents on the cuts in her feet, she decided to leave the rest of the clean up until later on, when she'd had some sleep and it was light.

Despite her screamed defiance, her life *had* been ruined. She never had a boyfriend beyond the first time they attempted to have full, penetrative sex. Because it, whatever the hell it was, always attacked him—and it didn't matter where she stayed, her house or his, wherever, it just appeared. On two occasions, she'd even tried telling the bloke in advance, but that had backfired as both had scarpered, clearly under the impression she was a fully-paid up, card-carrying mentalist.

But the violence against her boyfriends was definitely escalating. The rumour-mill at uni was working overtime with wild stories, all concluding that she was a sadist who got off on it. She kept having to look further and further afield to find guys who hadn't heard about her. It didn't surprise her that she got the blame, though, because who was naive enough to tell people they had been attacked by a monster and then expect to be believed? Perhaps some of them even convinced themselves she had attacked them—it was a damn sight more comforting than the truth.

The whole fucked up mess had started soon after she had broken up with Bryan. He took it badly and even stalked her for a few weeks—on one memorable occasion hiding in her bedroom closet to watch her undress—until she finally got the police to him. She heard from mutual friends that his parents had come up from Hull to collect him, and she hadn't seen him since, not even at uni where he had been doing a degree in business studies.

They had only been together for a few weeks and Portia never understood why or how he had become so attached to her. She had initially been attracted to him because of their differences—but therein were sown the seeds of the relationship's destruction. She eventually had been forced to dump him, unable to bear the weight of the chip on his shoulder about her family's wealth and inability to live up to what he perceived her expectations to be.

The truth was she had envied his closeness with his parents, his ability to talk to them about his problems and actually have them listen as though they were interested. Her own parents, more focused on each other than their only child, had dumped her in a series of boarding schools from as early as she could remember, and she barely knew them. Her father, Adrian, was a workaholic banker and her mother, Sophie, a bored housewife who had swapped Portia for charitable causes and long, boozy lunches with the girls.

Worst of all, it was the Friday of the long Easter weekend and all her close friends had scattered to various parts of the globe—some on skiing trips, others visiting family—leaving her here alone, trapped in her flat with an unknown entity that wished harm to the men in her life.

Tying her long, blond hair up in a pony-tail, she sat down at her dresser and removed her make-up. She looked like her mother—the same huge, grey-green eyes and dimpled chin. Unedified by the comparison, she threw her dressing gown by the bed and got into her favourite pair of pyjamas—fluffy, white, cotton decorated with red love-hearts. She was damn well going to have a real, live fully sexed-up valentine for next year, if it killed both of them.

And that was another thing. She knew her unwelcome, no sex guest was changing her, skewing her perceptions—and not for the better. A few months ago, she had watched, *It Follows*, about a murderous entity passed on by sex, like a supernatural STD. Instead of just enjoying the pre-packaged thrills and chills like everyone else, she was furious that the lucky cow of a heroine had at least managed to go the whole nine yards with a living, breathing partner and the inevitable consequences had been a small price to pay. Jammy bitch.

Putting her Lou Reid cd on, she flopped into bed and snuggled under the duvet, expecting sleep, like her would-be lovers, to elude her.

But come it did, and with it, the revenant that haunted her.

***

The sultry night air wrung beads of sweat from her as she waded out into the lake, the long dress clinging around her hips, like the arms of a fevered lover. The warm water was almost at her waist and the tips of her unbound hair floated behind her. Somewhere in the distance, an animal shrieked and a full moon, half concealed behind fitful ochre clouds, limned the water with silver. A welcome chill caressed the back of her neck and she smiled, relishing what was waiting for her.

Raising her right hand to brush some stray strands of hair from her eyes, it was covered in a viscous substance that dripped into the lake in slow, heavy drops. Revolted, she rubbed the hand on her dress, but the heavy material was already saturated in it.

A disembodied head surfaced inches away from her, decomposed eyes a milky white, swiveling from side to side, as though worked by an unseen ventriloquist's hand. The nose was gone and the skull, peeking out beneath the rotting layers of flesh, grinned wide. More heads popped to the surface, and sibilant, urgent whispers rent the suffocating air.

Something clawed at her ankle and she turned back for the shore, tripping and falling in her panic. Strong arms held her under the surface and old, clot-filled blood filled her nose and mouth. A heavy burden compressed her chest as though she had consumed her weight in stones and she knew she was about to die. Raging, she lashed out at her oppressor, legs kicking...

***

She woke, gasping for air and hysterical with relief that it was finally daylight and she was back in familiar surroundings. Her skinny jeans were slung over the armchair in the corner where she'd shed them the night before. A spring sun streamed through bamboo blinds, turning the room a warm, familiar amber and casting intricate patterns on the stripped floorboards, large red rug, and prized picture of her current Hollywood crush, Zac Efron. But it was her precious plants that calmed her the most—two six foot tall Swiss cheese plants, three asparagus ferns, and a Busy Lizzie, laden with fat, pink buds sitting with pride of place on the windowsill.

And then she spotted it.

A leprous shape moving around by the side of her bed, illuminated by a single ray of sunlight that had escaped the confines of the blind.

"You never learn, do you?" it rasped, rolling around like a dying fly on its back.

It was pale and hairless and about the size of a border terrier. The head was canine too, with a long snout and longer, floppy ears. There the mammalian resemblance ended, with four crab-like legs and two smaller, pincer-shaped limbs just under the shoulders that were more like vestigial arms—all of which were thrashing around as it tried to right itself, like a giant beetle that had been flipped onto its back. Two Xs were carved into the jelly of its eyes, a bright blue iris rolling around in each of the eight v sections that made them up, all of which were now fixed on her.

Had it been squatting on her chest, drooling over her face as she slept? She jumped out of bed, happy to do a Simon and sprint out of the flat in just her pyjamas, never to return.

"We need to talk about Simon," it said, wheezing.

Had it read her mind? More to the point, what was it still doing here?

"Get away from me," she said, inching towards the door.

"Okay, if you insist—how about Jeremy then? Or Hugo? Now there was a *real* man. Although there was that unfortunate business with your best friend Camilla."

Mention of Hugo and Camilla, now a loved-up item of an epic two months, made Portia's lip curl.

"Look can you help me up, I'm struggling here."

She had obviously lost her mind, brought on by the shock of last night and not helped by the prospect of finals in less than a month—stronger souls than her had been known to succumb for less.

She looked at the still straining creature.

"Why are you still here? What do you want with me?"

"Want?" With a mighty effort, the thing righted itself and pattered closer on six pincered feet.

"Get away! What the fuck are you?" she screamed, raising her hands in front of her face.

"Calm," said the thing. It tsked, waving a censorious forelimb.

A wave of nausea hit her and the contents of her stomach spattered on the bare floorboards. The creature ventured closer still, eight cross-stitched eyes still trained on her. The mouth opened to reveal tiny, serrated teeth, and a long, pink tongue unfurled, picked its way through the chunks of soupy vomit. Finally, it found a piece to its liking, and flipped it into the oversized maw, groaning in satisfaction.

"Waste not, want not," it tittered, munching with its mouth open.

Her gorge rose again.

"I'm going to be sick," she said, hand to her mouth and making for the door.

Quick as a flash, the creature blocked her passage, grinning up at her, needle-sharp teeth gleaming.

"While that sounds delicious, we should talk first."

She had seen first-hand what it could do. If she could just keep it together, she might outwit it and get out of the flat in one piece. Fucking baldy Simon clearly hadn't bothered to alert anyone to her peril—he wasn't to know it usually disappeared after attacking the current man of the moment.

"Let's go into the kitchen, get a seat," she said, running a shaking hand over her hair and putting on her dressing gown. Surely to God this was just another nightmare and she'd wake up soon.

"Here's just fine," it said, grooming long whiskers with a claw and drawing blood from the misbegotten face for its pains.

"What are you?"

"What do you mean? I am…me."

"You're not human, so what are you?"

"How would you answer that question? If I asked you what you were, what would you say?"

"I'd say, 'stop attacking my boyfriends, you total arse-hole and I'll think about telling you.'"

"Ooh, single-minded. I do like that in my women."

The monster skittered sideways over to the nearest asparagus fern and began to chew on one of the feathery fronds. Portia threw herself forward, her toe connecting with the scaled back-side, so hard, she felt a *crack* and a blinding pain.

"You can do what you like to me, but touch my plants and I'll fucking kill you. And I'm not your woman."

"The lady doth protest too much, don't you think?"

"What?"

"I said—"

"I heard you. You said you wanted to talk. So talk."

Four pairs of eyes narrowed. Was it finally upset?

"Easter is a time of transformation, Portia," it lectured in a high sing-song voice. "Barren winter into fertile spring, the dead into the living, you know, the whole Christ is risen thing." The eight eyes all rolled around in the monster's head, as though independent of each other.

Portia imagined a loaf-like, freshly baked Christ, but bit her tongue, sensing from the creature's change in tone that this was not the right time to interrupt.

"The resurrection being the reward for all that nasty crucifixion stuff, even if that's not how the bloody Christians tell it."

It unleashed the tongue again, this time flicking it in her direction, as though tasting what she was made of. Although it had surely already done that by supping up her vomit.

"Mmmm, sugar and spice," it said, as though reading her mind and licking its mouth. "That's what my little Portia's made of."

"I'm not yours. Now fuck the fuck off out my life."

"I'm afraid that's not an option," it said, pursing a pair of red, remarkably human lips in the canine snout, and blowing her a kiss.

Her index finger came into contact with the pocket in her dressing gown containing Simon's scalp. A tear trickled down her cheek. Images of her and Simon, holding hands in the Meadows, gazing into each other's eyes over drinks and kissing for what seemed like hours on end, so absorbed in each other, they were unaware of anyone else. How had it come to this?

"Did you know that 'Portia' means an offering in Latin? Did you ever wonder why your parents called you that?"

"Did Bryan send you?" she asked, ignoring the bait.

"Bryan?"

"Yes. You just appeared in my life after I dumped him. Did he hex me? Is that what this is?"

The creature laughed as though she'd just told the best joke in the world. It laughed so hard it fell over and almost rolled onto its back again. A gelatinous substance oozed from the deformed, spider-like eyes.

"You really are priceless," it rasped, trying to compose itself. "Okay. Here's the thing. I don't know this Bryan character. Although if he's anything like the other dweebs and idiots you've gone out with, I won't have missed much."

"Then why are you ruining my life?"

"Don't be so dramatic. I'm not here to hurt you—not yet. Think of me as the ultimate safe sex method—no diseases, no unwanted pregnancies. No muss, no fuss."

This rang a faint bell in the deep recesses of Portia's memory.

"For how long?"

"For as long as you are capable of conceiving."

She fell silent, the full horror of it sinking in.

"What if I swore I'd always take precautions."

"Precautions fail. Besides maybe I prefer keeping you to myself."

Winking, the creature skittered without warning up the wall and hung, bat-like, from the lampshade, swaying to and fro in a shower of plaster.

"Why don't you come down from there?" she said, trying to sound friendly, with a queasy, churning sensation in her gut.

"Why? Missing me already?"

"I've got something you might want to see," she said, smiling and patting her pocket.

"Yeah, like what?" it asked, like a sulky child, interested despite itself by an obvious bribe.

"Come on down and see."

Without warning, it dropped from the ceiling, landing on its back at her feet, rolling around, momentarily disabled. Without pausing to think of the consequences she whipped Simon's scalp out of her pocket and, with one foot pressed down on the creature's chest, bent down and thrust the flayed flesh onto the thing's own head. But the monster thrashed around so much, the flesh wouldn't stay on and she had to snatch it back before she lost her grip on it.

"What the fuck do you think you're doing," it snarled. "Don't make me hurt you, Portia, or we'll both regret it."

"I only wanted you to look nice," she said, assuming a hurt expression and pushing out her bottom lip. "Don't you want to look your best for me?" She looked at it sideways from beneath her eyelashes.

"I didn't know you cared," said the creature, frowning.

Beneath the sarcasm, Portia detected something else, a hint of *yearning* that she couldn't quite put her finger on.

"Oh, go on, please. Just for me. You'd look ever so fetching in it," she held the scalp out to the creature. "I've got a thing about hair. I think this would really, ah, bring out your eyes."

"If this is a ruse to trap me—"

"It's not, I promise, it's not. I'm just tired of this fighting. And while I hate to admit it, I'm also lonely— and I think you are too. Why don't we just try to get along a bit better and see how things develop, shall we?"

"Develop? With me, you mean?"

"Why not? It's not like I'm going to get a chance to do that with someone else. No, wait, I didn't mean it like that," she gabbled as the creature's expression darkened.

"What I meant was, I've been increasingly drawn to you over the past couple of years. I think," she sunk her teeth into her lip, gathering herself, "in fact I know, that I have feelings for you."

It had come out in a rush, and not a believable one at that—had she blown it? She crossed her fingers behind her back, hoping that if there was a Supreme Being, she'd be forgiven for the lie.

"Go on, sweetheart," she stumbled over the endearment, "put it on for me, will you? Anyone would think you didn't want to look your best for me and that can't be right, can it?"

She held out the scrap of bloodied flesh, the golden hairs glinting in the filtered sunlight. Seconds passed on tiny, pincered feet. Then, slowly, a claw extended and took the proffered present.

"Hang on," the creature bit into the scalp, spitting out pieces of flesh, grimacing, and then stuck it on, long ears appearing through the two newly made holes.

Simon's thick, golden hair, with the somewhat deflated, but still intact coif, now decorated the creature's grotesque head, silken strands hanging down on either side of its face. The long ears became erect, quivering, making it resemble, for the few moments that it managed to hold the pose, a mutilated, myxomatosis-ridden rabbit. At least it was seasonal.

"How do I look," it cooed, fluttering stubby, crap-encrusted eyelashes at her.

"If I wasn't in love with you before," she smiled through gritted teeth, wondering how the hell this creature could ever think it had a chance with her, "I am now."

Bloody men, in the ego department they were all the same, human or not. She paused for a few beats, giving herself some extra time.

"Let's start over, shall we?" she said in a cold voice.

The creature looked up, startled.

"What do you mean, honey bunny?"

"I ask the questions. What are you and why are you here?"

"I'm an incubus," the creature began, unable to stop the words spilling from its malformed lips. "What have you done to me, woman?"

"I've bespelled you, or at least the vaudun priestess I hired did. I set the whole thing up, and you fell for it. I arranged to have Simon over, knowing you'd appear. She told me all I had to do was give you a present of flesh and have you accept it—which you did—and you'd have to obey my every command. No, don't bother trying to get it off, it's too late. You belong to me now. You didn't think I was just going to take this lying down, did you?"

"I was only doing as I was bid."

"By whom?" Portia started pacing the room, face flushing.

"Your parents, of course."

"The truth, godammit," she raised a threatening hand, although what she would have done, she couldn't have said.

"It is the truth, I swear. It was your parents—they conjured me and forced me to be their slave. I'm a sex demon, for Beelzebub's sake," it spluttered, outraged, as though that explained everything.

"Why would my parents summon a sex demon. Hang on, you don't mean they wanted you to have sex with me? That's gross."

"No, child, not in this case." The incubus looked almost sorry for her. "They wanted me to guard you from the attentions of other men, to guarantee you would never become pregnant."

"But why?" All her certainty, all she had ever believed about the world, began to drain away. Feeling faint, she sat on the bed.

"You were an accident—they never meant to have you."

"So? Surely they've gotten over it by now? Why stop me having kids?"

"It was prophesied a long time ago, if your mother bore a daughter, that child would give birth to the antichrist."

"And they believed this appalling *Omen* style bollocks?"

"It happens to be true."

Her head was swimming. "But don't I have to have sex with the devil to have a little Damien? The way I feel just now, I'd actually settle for that—at least I'd get a shag out of it."

"That's just movie nonsense. You come from a long line of witches and dabblers in the occult. Why do you think your family's so fabulously wealthy—financial astuteness?" The demon gurgled like a drain and she realised it was laughing.

"Any child of yours will end the world—your parents were very foolish to let you live. That's why I have been appointed your personal demon, to make sure you never mate and so trigger Armageddon. Or so they believe."

"I can't believe this is happening."

"It's not so bad. I'm here to protect, not harm you."

"By making me celibate?"

"There are other things you can do."

"But I want children. I want a normal life," despite herself, she heard a note of pleading creep into her voice.

"I'd say you were way beyond normal."

The demon stared, uncharacteristically sombre for a moment.

"What do you mean?"

"You invited Simon, who you've professed to care about, here tonight, knowing, no, banking on the fact that I was going to hurt him. Now you're throwing around a piece of his head as though it was an old sock. You might as well be Leather Face from the *Texas Chainsaw Massacre* for all the regret you feel about what's happened to him—or any of them for that matter. Yes, yes," the demon flapped a claw, "I've watched your extensive collection of stupid horror films in the time I've spent with you—didn't have much choice, since I'm bound to you, and you do little else.

"You're a monster, just as much as I am. In fact, you're worse—I'm only a lesser demon on a very long ladder, but you…you are the destroyer of worlds."

On reflection, Portia thought the demon could well be right. She had caught Simon texting an old flame last week and had decided to go ahead with her plan in that instant, using him as bait.

"Is there no way to lift this…this curse?"

"It's not a curse, it just is. And I'm your personal demon, for better or worse. For ever and ever, amen."

It bared its teeth in a grimace.

"Don't you have a name?" she asked, too shell-shocked to be interested, but asking anyway, as though a semblance of normality would stop her being pitched, screaming, into a void of her own insanity.

"Well, actually," the bewigged wretch lowered his eyes, "Back home, I'm known as the Transformer. Want to know why?"

It grimaced again.

"Go on then, why?" she sighed.

"Because, well, I can change form."

"Yourself, or others?"

"Myself, of course. Isn't that enough?"

Woman and demon stared at each other.

Portia walked over to the far wall and, with the utmost care, took down the picture of Zac Efron, returning to where the Transformer crouched.

"Prove it," she said.

"How? And more importantly, why?"

"Because I'm the boss of you now. And anyway, I think you're as sick of the way things are as I am. I mean, you're a sex demon doomed to a life of enforcing the chastity of another. It can't be much fun."

The demon considered this.

"Put like that, even if I wasn't compelled, I'd be happy to be at your command, my lady," the creature said, trying to bow.

"Change into this," she said tapping the picture. "And I don't mean the picture itself, I mean, I want you to change your physical form into this man, Zac Ephron, down to the last detail."

Portia wasn't an expert on demons, but she knew she had to be as specific as possible to avoid disaster.

The Transformer studied the fine cheekbones, chiseled jaw, and sultry, blue gaze for a long moment.

"Really - this guy? What about Simon? I mean, look, I've already got the hair down," the creature thumped itself on the head.

Portia shuddered, "God no. And hurry up, before I get the idea you can't do it."

The Transformer stood up straight and held its breath. At first Portia didn't think anything was happening, but gradually the outline of its body began to waver, as though she was looking at him from a distance through a heat haze. The revolting hybrid disappeared, to be replaced by a dark haired human male, broad shouldered, six packed and toned, with long, muscular legs.

There, standing in front of her, stark naked and misty-eyed, was Portia's ideal man.

"Hold on, that's too small," she said, pointing.

"What is, darling," said Zac the Transformer.

"Zac, I mean, you're only five feet eight in real life and I'm a couple of inches taller. Stretch," she commanded.

The Transformer stretched.

"No, that's too much, back a bit, back. There! That's perfect."

She traced a finger along the line of his perfect jaw, the curve of his neck and down to his shoulder.

"I'm beginning to think the Easter weekend won't be such a wash out after all," she said, tilting her face towards his.

"If you force me to mate, I warn you there will be a child that none of us will survive," said the Transformer, breathless with rising excitement. "Are you so quick to die?"

"Come on, how can little old me having sex bring about the end of the world? It's too stupid. And anyway, can't you use protection?"

"I have enzymes on my skin that drive my lovers wild—there is no protection against that."

The Transformer's lustrous skin gleamed and his eyes blazed sapphire. Portia stroked his chest and shuddered, as caught in the demon's thrall as he was in hers. The Transformer took the tie from her ponytail, running his long, tanned fingers through the lustrous fall of her hair and they launched themselves at each other, somehow making it back to the bed despite their animal frenzy, ripping Portia's dressing gown to shreds.

Unseen in the corner, Portia's plants were rippling over the floorboards, walls, furniture, like a green tide.

Thick aerial roots from the Swiss cheese plants forced their way under the window pane, opening it a few inches. The Busy Lizzie had fallen off the sill and was now the size of a large shrub, huge, pink flowers the size of dinner plates, blooming, dying and blooming again in the space of seconds.

And from under the burgeoning canopy of plants, the sounds of consumption reigned.

**

No one heard from Portia over the next couple of days. Eventually, Simon became worried enough to risk a visit to her flat on Easter Monday when she wouldn't return his calls.

Touching the enormous bandage on his head, as though it was a good luck charm, he rapped three times on the front door, his stomach clenching with fear. Was it his imagination or was there an expectant hush, as though the world was holding its breath?

"Portia," he shouted. "Are you okay? Open the door darling, or at least shout if you're able."

He listened at the door and fancied he heard someone giggling.

"Portia," Simon called again. "Are you there? I'm sorry I ran away."

He turned on his heel, about to leave, when the door opened. The room beyond was dim, and the stench of rotting vegetation and corrupted flesh assailed his nostrils. A flicker of light and motion from the television in the corner of the room, and Mia Farrow burst on screen, clutching her pregnant belly, screaming. Why was Portia watching *Rosemary's Baby*? She'd seen it a million times and it wasn't exactly Easter fare, was it?

As his eyes acclimatised to the gloom, he made out the figure of a tall, slim woman standing in the middle of the room, the bright gold of her hair glimmering in the tainted light. How had she opened the door?

"Oh sweetheart, thank God, I thought something had happened to you. Are you okay? I've been worried sick."

He made to go in, but she was at the door, before he even saw her move. The meagre light from the stair landing shone on her face.

"Are you hurt, darling? What has that creature done to you? Here, let me see. Oh Christ," he screamed. "Look at your eyes! What's happened to your eyes?"

She put a clawed hand around the edge of the door, lop-sided grin on a wet, red mouth.

"They say, I've got my father's eyes, Simon. What do you think?"

Simon froze, mouth opening and shutting, a stream of urine running down his leg to pool on the floor. Behind the woman, two mummified corpses gutted from sternum to pubis lay propped against a huge flowering shrub which had wrapped itself around them, green shoots and massive pink blooms exploding from their wounds.

"Tell you what," said the woman, plunging the nails on both thumbs into the jelly of his eyes and flaying the skin from his body in seconds, "why don't you change into something more comfortable."

Minutes later, the woman and the newly made red man, stripped down to the bare essentials of muscle and bone, left the tenement for the street, trailing screaming, bloody murder in their wake.

And over it all, a hot sun beamed down from a cobalt sky as though this was a spring day like any other. The tinny strains of *Satellite of Love* ventured forth from the partially open window of Portia's flat, only to be swallowed up in the jumble and carnage of the brave, new world outside.

The dread Messiah had risen.

Dumpster Princess
Matthew Gillies

= I =

They swarmed the bar with rabid animosity. These vile creatures wielding dual lives. During the day, they shielded their true nature beneath a thin veil of fraudulence. But as the sun waned beneath the horizon, swallowed by the sea, darkness soon spilled its shadow upon the city. It was then, and only then that these creatures – these contemptible and repulsive beings set forth into the night... true Dr. Jekylls and Mr. Hydes.

Loud... obnoxious and belligerent. They congregated at the edge of the bar, their faces flushed with intoxication. Sweat glistened against their flesh like an oily film as they swayed back and forth, barely keeping their stance as they drowned themselves against the rim of their bottles.

Oh, but it was the noise. The foul chatter of slurred bantering filling the depth of the bar with a heavy resonation that weighed densely in the air. The noise... that horrible sound of undecipherable speech... that sound of a hundred voices molding into one torturous rumble of white noise – it was almost a new language... the sound of a hundred conversations turning into a singular phonetic syntax.

But then, in one instant, everything stopped the moment the door opened. For that moment, it was as if all sound had been vacuumed outdoors – the bar now vacant of voices as every person stopped mid-action to gaze upon the figure standing by the entrance.

She was tall. She was beautiful. She was glamorous. She did not belong in a place such as this – a place of men and women, marinating in the humid aroma of lingering sweat and stale beer. Or did she?

Everything about her appearance was equally as fraudulent as the personalities of the bar's current patrons. She didn't have the same flawed complexion, hardened features, and sleep deprived exhaustion as those in the room. No. This was a woman who was at the peak of perfection. Her hair was styled elegantly. Her dress no doubt designer – her face tight, almost swollen, as if ironed of all wrinkles. If she had smiled, there would be no way to tell from her sore and pained expression – she was a cold, dead woman.

Yet, there she stood, wearing a dress so tight her thin frame was only accentuated, despite the small bump of a potbelly protruding from her stomach.

"D'you know, I fucked her once," one patron murmured to another.

"Who hasn't," replied the other.

"Oh my GAWD, look at her dress," said a woman at the other end of the bar.

"It doesn't suit her," replied her friend. "I mean, look at how her stomach swells in it. That's just disgusting. You can almost see her flabby handle bars."

"As if *she's* here," said a man in the distance. "I thought she was some A-lister from Hollywood."

"I heard she's in rehab," said another.

"How can she be in rehab if she's here?"

"Isn't that what happens to all those Hollywood starlets? They start off as hot shit, make their money – then they crash and burn and have nervous breakdowns before doing a successful comeback."

"Sometimes they come back."

"Yeah, sometimes they go into hardcore porn."

"Isn't that…?"

"Natasha," shrieked a dwarfish woman whose ugliness was unspeakable. She crossed the room with incredible speed on stubby fat legs, her pear-shaped body swaying from side to side as she pushed through the crowd. "Oh my GAWD, it is you! Natasha! We went to high school together. Remember? I'm Gretchen. Oh, you might not remember me; you were a year ahead of me. But now look at you. You're famous, Natasha."

Lowering her sunglasses, the woman tilted her head slightly so as to gain better visibility of the homely looking woman that stood before. These were the patrons of the *dive*. Their hideous appearances were things of solitary folklore. The woman smiled widely, her mouth a crater of jagged yellow-stained teeth, her lips chapped and split and marred with red blemishes. Her skin was sickly, with large pores and acne scars.

"Lilith," said the woman as she scowled at the grotesque monstrosity that stood before her.

"Lilith," Gretchen echoed with unsure understanding.

The beautiful woman sighed noticeably annoyed. "My name is Lilith, now. It's my stage name. Lilith Narcissus. Sounds like a flower if I do say so myself. I find it suits me just wonderfully. It's quite divine as a matter of fact." Lilith leaned in closer to the ugly woman. "So don't... fucking... call me... Natasha... again," she said.

"I'm so sorry," Gretchen began to plead, but before she could finish, Lilith was already pushing the woman aside and crossing the room toward the bar. She moved as though she owned the place. Heads turned subtly as the attendees tried to steal discrete glances of the starlet.

Across the room, two butch women dressed in biker leather watched as Lilith planted her arms on the barstool and with the flash of a crisp bill in her hand, waved down the bartender. Her presence alone was enough to send coos of whispers to float amongst the patrons. Her life was a slow train wreck of *rumours* of house arrests, car crashes, ingested white powders, public outbursts, celebrity feuds, and televised breakdowns.

"Look at that tramp," said one to the other. "Such a shameless slut."

"I know," said the other. "It's disgusting. I heard she slept with every stage hand, producer, and director just to land the best roles. But I suppose that's how you rise in Hollywood."

"She probably offered her cunt on the catering table with a sign that read *all-you-can-eat for deep divers.*"

The two women started to laugh before turning to look back at Lilith.

"I thought she was hospitalized for exhaustion because of her last movie," said one to the other.

"Exhaustion is Hollywood speak for gonorrhoea," said the other.

"That's not it," said a lone voice. When the two women looked up, the bartender was standing before them, two opened bottles in hand readying to replace the empty ones in front of them. "Exhaustion is Hollywood speak for substance abuse. It's been well covered in the news tabloids. Lilith Narcissus caught on video smoking crack. Lilith Narcissus charged with DUI. Lilith Narcissus fired from set for erratic behaviour and failure to attend meetings. She's a train wreck."

"If that's the case, why is that prissy little bitch here, then?"

"Apparently we have the best *Rehabilitation Clinic.* All of them Hollywood agents send their clients here. Though, by the looks of it, a lot of good it did her."

Suddenly, the bar fell silent once more as Lilith climbed onto the bar table. With a fierce whistle, she directed the attention toward her for a brief moment and then scanned the crowd with great difficulty. This was her limelight. She was the centre of attention and she commanded it with a natural ease.

"Listen up, bitches," Lilith shouted with a stuttering slur. "I need a stiff drink and a whole lotta coke, so who's going to ante up and be my cabana bitch for the night?"

Without hesitation, a group of sweat soaked men with flushed faces clambered toward the bar wildly, with drunken lust and hormonal conquest festering in their minds. It didn't matter to them what sordid tales of lewd perversions stemming from the tabloid magazines had starred Lilith. Her body could have been an incubator to the vilest venereal diseases known to humankind, and yet, these men fuelled by a hedonistic urge flocked to hear like the blind leading the blind.

= II =

Her journeys to and from the washroom were becoming more frequent as the night wore on. Each trip marked a further spiral into self-destruction. The white stains powdering her nose became less discrete. Each step was a struggling stagger as she swayed toward the bar, ready to embrace her adoring *fans* with snide derision and unconcealed contempt. Oh, how she basked in the attention; the compliments and the praise; the eager desperation of wanting to impress; the doe-eyed hopefulness of ogling men and women enthusiastic that she, Lilith Narcissus, would soothe the fiery desires swelling between their legs. The attention fueled her ego. They fed her bottle upon bottle, and slipped baggy upon baggy of fine white powder into her clammy palms. And without dispute she accepted everything with a gluttonous welcome.

With the night well underway, the bar had grown louder, the crowd thicker and the stench bitter. Lilith sat hunched on the stool, her head hanging low, her stomach bloated and distended against her thin physique. Shifting her weight awkwardly her stomach rumbled with a noxious discomfort. There was a churning weight pushing against her intestines and smothering her bladder, but she did her best to fight through the twisting of her innards.

Glancing downward, Gretchen stared at Lilith's stomach, her face shifting from overzealous to suddenly concerned. Beneath Lilith's dress, her stomach seemed swollen and rock hard, yet there seemed to be a peculiar movement of something bulging slightly before ebbing away.

"Lilith, your stomach," Gretchen yelped, her face streaked with a cross-eyed drunken dismay. "What have they been feeding you at that clinic?"

Clumsily, Lilith placed a hand on her stomach and moaned drunkenly before pinching a roll of skin. She burrowed her nails deep into the tight fatty flesh, viciously so, and gave her stiff belly a harsh tug. "Fucking greasy-assed bar food... that shit goes right through me," she said with a belch. "There's nothing like a good binge before a colonic purge, though. That's how I keep this incredible figure."

Again, Lilith's stomach grumbled an unsettling gurgle. Only this time the bulge in her stomach seemed to spread out with a ripple of smaller bulges, as if something were trying to force its way out of her. Lilith grimaced as her face twisted with pain, her fingers dug deeper into her stomach, nails burrowing into flesh, drawing blood. But the bulge reacted more violently. It shifted aggressively, forcing her stomach to stretch wider.

Lilith stifled a cry and punched her lower intestine.

"Are you sure you're okay," Gretchen asked.

"Never better. But speaking of colonics," she said with restrained pain, "I have to use the tinkle room. Be back soon, BITCHES!"

= III =

She didn't waste any time making her trek to the washroom. With elbows propped, she charged through the dancefloor, pushing through the orgy of sweaty bodies swaying hypnotically and grinding against one another. She didn't care who got in her way. If a body came into close proximity of her arms, she forcefully drove through them, knocking bitches to the floor and pushing drunken men aside.

When one woman attempted to confront her, Lilith spun around. As if possessed by a demon, her once fraudulent celebrity beauty was the thing of the past, replaced now by a horrifying monstrosity. Sweat layered her face like a secreting mucous clinging to putrefied flesh. Mascara ran down her cheeks, a heavy smear of black accentuating the tight lines on her face. Her eyes bulged and hung low. With a fierce snarl, Lilith barked at the woman who tried to confront her.

"Bitch, I will tear your intestines from your anus so bad, you'll wish it was just prolapsed."

"Fuck. Chill, you crazy cunt," the woman said, throwing her hands in the air with defeat.

Lilith didn't waste any more time with the woman. The pain was gnawing away at her stomach with increasing distress. All she could do was scuttle through the bar, her body hunched with agony.

Up ahead, the washroom was overflowing – a line of chatty women huddled from leg to leg, clasping their fingers tightly as they struggled to keep from pissing themselves. Lilith had no intention of waiting. Let the bitches flow a river of gold on the floor if they must, she was too important to stand in a line. Without so much as a glance, she cut ahead of the growing line that extended well along the far wall and forced her way into the washroom.

Inside the brightly lit room, a row of women stood in front of the mirror, each one touching up their makeup like clowns before a performance. With their cosmetics sprawled across the counters, they stared at their reflection, their noses inches away from touching the mirror.

She stood there; toe tapping the ground impatiently, arms bent outward, hands gripping her bony hips and she waited a moment, fighting through the pain of the protruding bulge within her stomach.

When no one paid her any attention, she coughed slightly, clenching her body out of fear before shouting, "Out! All of you cunts, OUT! Don't you know who I am? I'm Hollywood fucking royalty and y'all will be sorry if you don't get the FUCK out NOW!"

Instantly, the women stopped what they were doing and turned to face Lilith. The women made to protest but thought better of it. Gathering their makeup and shuffling it into their purses, they made their way out of the washroom, exiting one by one. When the last one had made her way through the door, Lilith threw herself at the door. Fumbling for the handle, she frantically locked the door, twisting the bolt in place.

Sighing with relief, she began her quick inspection.

Step by step, she crossed the length of the washroom, pushing in stall doors, ensuring no one was squatting over the toilet. This was important to her. She needed privacy. There couldn't be a single person in the washroom with her in that moment.

Satisfied she was alone, she stepped into the last stall. It was by far the cleanest. No driblets of piss or flecks of shit icing the toilet seat. Quickly, she slipped out of her panties and hung them to the hook on the inside of the stall door. Then, hiking her dress up, she stepped onto the toilet seat, fastening the pointed heels of her stilettos against the rim of the bowl and squatted awkwardly.

It felt like a practiced routine. Her balance was impeccable in spite of her inebriated state and with the grace of the starlet that she was, she squeezed her arms together, holding the edge of her dress tightly between her constricted torso and pushed.

The veins on her neck swelled – they were thick tendrils that threatened to tear through her thin flesh at any moment. Snorting wildly, she clenched her jaw, forcing her joints to pop unnaturally as she gnashed her teeth.. Her stomach rumbled loudly in the quiet washroom and, for a moment, she felt as if she was going to keel over. The pain was excruciating. It moved through her lower abdomen like a spiked ball, heavy and piercing. She wanted to scream out, but fought back. The last time she screamed, a bouncer nearly tore through the door to make sure she was okay. That was a close one. She didn't dare think what would have happened if she had been caught. Oh, the scandal it would have caused.

"C'mon, you persistent motherfucker," she said with a strained grimace. "You're worse than the others."

Her stomach rumbled loudly, a painful gaseous gurgle. As if her innards were shifting and settling, her stomach bulged and twisted, the flesh expanding and contracting lower as she strained an uncomfortable push.

"Come on. Come on. Come on, you little bastard. Come on. Come on."

Her face swelled with discomfort. She could see the world fading around her as she exerted herself beyond what was natural, but she pushed and pushed and pushed until a heavy gush of thick, gooey liquid splashed into the toilet.

She exhaled a long breath as her face eased and relaxed.

When her stomach grumbled once more, Lilith pressed her palms against her belly and massaged the flesh downward, feeling the hard bulge within her stomach. As if fighting against her motion, the obstruction refused to move, but Lilith was persistent. She pushed and massaged it downward. Again, the lump resisted. Annoyed, Lilith balled a fist and struck her stomach, once… twice… three times. The bulge slackened and then a loud plop splashed into the toilet. For a brief moment she stood there, feeling a calm release wash over her.

Taking a deep breath, she reached between her legs, nimbly feeling around until her fingers found the slick cord dangling from her vagina. With a tight grasp, she pulled downward, feeling her stomach drop slightly. Once again, she pulled, but her fingers slid with no conviction.

Irritated, she coiled the oleaginous cord around her hand and pulled and pulled and pulled until she heard the gentle release of a supple squirt followed by another splash. Easing her fingers, she let the cord fall to the ground, where it bounced against the linoleum floor with a gentle wet smack.

Spreading her arms, she used the walls of the stall to brace her body as she stepped down from the toilet. The last thing she wanted to do was touch her dress. No amount of money could wash away the vile stains of what she had just endured.

When she was firmly planted on even ground, she turned to the toilet and reached down, picking up the umbilical cord that hung over the toilet seat. At one end, the bloody placenta lay splattered against the floor, pooling a filmy plasmid goo onto the stained linoleum.

On the other end, floating in the tainted toilet water was a curled up creature of unimaginable hideousness.

Carefully, she hoisted the creature from the toilet while keeping her arm outstretched. It was smaller than she expected. Holding *it* in her hand, she studied it with curious yet repulsed eyes. Its skin appeared scaly, tight and leathery. Folds of flesh seemed to dangle from its neck. Its nose was upturned and crusted, its eyes large, red swollen slits. It didn't make any sounds, but its clawed fingers widened slowly before clenching shut. When it opened its mouth, a row of fanged teeth protruded from its thick gums.

"You're more hideous than the others," she sneered with disgust.

The creature made a noise – a gurgled whine. The sound was enough to incite a disapproving grimace from Lilith. There was no maternal instinct. No desire to comfort. Instead, she held the repulsive creature a good distance away, opened the stall door and marched toward the trash bin.

"Nope. The last thing I need in my career is another scandal."

Opening the trash bin lid, she dropped the monstrous newborn into the cushion of tissues, tampons and panty liners. As if it were a stone being dropped into the ocean, the creature sank down, disappearing within a sudden avalanche of used papers.

= IV =

Darkness was a comfort the creature was well acquainted to. Swimming within the sea of tissue paper, it groped through the abyss, seeking and searching until the poignant flavour of iron bated its lips. It had sniffed out the aroma and, suckling the blackness, soon found the soggy substance of its meal in the form of a tampon.

For what seemed like an eternity to the creature, it suckled away until the flavour was no longer there. But it wasn't enough for it. No – an unquenchable hunger tormented its belly for a more filling substance

Twisting and turning in the cushioning, the creature was becoming entangled by a thick cord. The more it moved, the more the cord seemed to twist tighter. Frustrated by the constriction, the creature reached out, pulling at the fleshy tendril, until it groped something squishy and large.

As if on instinct, the creature greedily pulled the placenta towards its lips. It could smell the aroma surrounding it. This was food. It had to be. It smelt like food. It tasted like food. The creature took a bite. And then another. Instantly the burgeoning discomfort within its stomach began to ease. So it ate, chewing with ravenous lust, devouring every last bit of the placenta until all that remained was a severed umbilical cord flopping from its belly like a misplaced tail.

With its belly full and unsure of what more it could do, the creature rested.

= V =

The lid of the trash bin opened and closed periodically. Flickers of light drifted in and out as paper towels piled on top of it. But the creature didn't seem to mind. Peacefully it lay, resting in a nest of damp cloth and used tampons.

Without warning, everything changed. There was a motion – a sudden elevation. The creature sank deeper down, until its body pressed against the plastic lining of the garbage bag. It hung there, suspended in a peculiar weightlessness. Then the bag fell, landing hard against uneven ground. With a swing and a sway, the creature struggled against the motion.

No, the newborn didn't like this. Its body was twisted and uncomfortable against the surface and when it tried to howl, its voice was smothered by a rush of paper towels.

= VI =

The janitor hated cleaning the women's washroom the most. Of all the things he had to do, he dreaded the moment he had to enter the women's washroom. So, he left it as his final task for the evening. But the moment he stepped through the door, Hugo couldn't help but grimace. The women's washroom was the most unhygienic cesspool he had ever known and it was enough to turn him away from the *fairer* sex.

Shit and piss stained the toilet seats and the surrounding floor from drunken hovering and poor aim. If these women had been hired to drop bombs on foreign countries, judging by the aim of their own excrement, he was convinced they'd have bombed everyone but their intended targets.

But the shit and piss wasn't the worst of it. It was the tampons. Bloody spatters painted and dripped down the walls of the stalls in some kind of abstract art piece. It was as if these women had been throwing their tampons to see how well they stuck. It was enough to drive the man insane. Even the toilets were watery graves of clogged filth.

His was a grimace the moment he stepped into the washroom. But he made sure to clean it quick. With rubber gloves and a can-do attitude, Hugo hustled about, spraying down everything with disinfectant and bleach before taking the garbage to the dumpster. And even the trash bin was a nightmare. Overflowing with paper towels and used panty liners bunched up in the plastic wrapping film.

Hugo sighed quietly and shook his head. His shift was almost done. A quick glance at his watch was all the more confirmation he needed. All that was left was tossing the garbage, and he did this hurriedly. Lifting the lid, he pulled and tugged the plastic bag, letting all the contents settle below. When he pulled up, he noticed an awkward weight fall to the bottom.

Strange, he thought, but paid the heftiness little notice. It wasn't his job to sift through the trash. No, he'd leave that to Chumps, the local bum who slept in the alley. As the saying went, one man's trash is another man's treasure. And god bless Chumps for the treasure he may find in this bag.

Carrying the bag out of the washroom, Hugo made his way to the back of the bar. He gave a firm wave to the bartender who scrubbed the counter of spilled alcohol, a smile to the waitresses who counted their tips, and nodded to the cooks who had gathered around the back door, smoking their cigarettes and laughing about the successful sabotage of bar food served to the patrons.

When they saw Hugo approaching, they cleared a path for him.

"You missed out, Hugo," said one cook.

"Yeah, man. Lot of fine looking ladies. In fact, we had someone famous here today," said another.

Hugo smiled quietly.

"Fine piece of ass on that one."

"You kidding? She had the ass of a little boy."

Hugo stepped into the dimly lit alley, letting the cooks banter on. He didn't care who was at the bar. After the sight he had just witnessed, staring at a woman's ass would have plagued him with horrific memories. He would have been happier being ignorant to the activities of women. But such was not the case.

Making his way toward the dumpster, he surveyed the alley for Chumps. If the man was out there, he was hidden in the shadows.

Without wasting further time, Hugo tossed the bag into the dumpster, bidding the evening of fecal displacement a joyous farewell.

= VII =

Through a thick fog, he watched Hugo the janitor. Hugo had thrown the last of the bags into the dumpster and was scanning the alley, no doubt searching for Chumps. But Chumps waited patiently in the darkness, camouflaged in a black garbage bag and seated against his flattened, discarded boxes. This was the time of the evening he most looked forward to. The cooks had tossed their cigarette butts and the janitor had just filled the dumpster with a fine shipment of… well… whatever he could find.

The moment Hugo made his way inside, Chumps was already on his feet. Let no man of longing linger lest he wish to starve, he thought. The words weren't so much a mantra as they were inspiration. His last meal was stale bagels and moulded cheese cream. Most people would have scuffed at the fuzzy gelatinous cream, but not Chumps. No sir, he found something rather endearing about the foamy texture dissolving on his tongue. The thought was enough to send his stomach into a frenzied grumble. He hustled over to the dumpster, licking his lips and rubbing his hands together with unrestrained greed.

"What have we here," he said quietly. Caressing his beard, he eyed the contents in the dumpster. Mountainous bags piled one on top of the other, his mind was a flurry of eagerness. He could just imagine what he would find; half eaten burgers, some chicken wings with meat still clinging to the bones, carrot and celery sticks with a cup of fresh dip. The thought of food made his stomach rumble with eager anticipation.

Climbing into the dumpster, he tore through the plastic bags, sifting through the remnants of discard, fishing out what little he could find that resembled something edible. What he did find, he tossed into a tiny tin tray he had salvaged weeks ago.

It always surprised him how little food people ate even though they were paying for it. He imagined they led luxurious lives where food was so plentiful it was disposable. He couldn't fathom such a life. He had been homeless for too long. How many years had it been now? More than he cared to count. More than he dared to count. The life of a vagabond was all he knew and, while others would look at him both with pity and contempt, it was a life he was well accustomed to. This was freedom. But it was not without its burdens. He had performed acts out of desperation. Perverse and depraved acts. It was a means to an end, he supposed – when times were hard, he had to turn to something, even if it meant degrading himself.

But those were the old days. He tried not to think about the past. It saddened him. Those were the days when he didn't know how to forage and survive off the land. The days when he relied on the generosity of others – though that generosity was often self-serving. Not now, though. Those days were long gone. Now, he had only himself and that meant being self-sufficient. He knew the best places to go. Which were the best dumpsters for food and when the best times were to be there.

Shuffling the bags, Chumps came across one that was soft, yet slightly heavy. As an expert garbage picker, he could tell what was inside a garbage bag simply by touch. Weight spoke volumes of what hidden treasures lay within. But this particular bag was odd. It was heavier in the bottom, as if someone had discarded something in haste.

Ripping through the plastic, tissues and tampons poured through the opening as if being expelled from some severed body. The sight was enough to bring a smile to his aged face. He salvaged a bundle of tissue paper. No doubt, he'd be able to make use of these.

When he had collected enough tissue paper, he snatched a lone tampon. Bringing it close to his nose, he moved it from nostril to nostril, savouring the scent as if it were a cigar. It was a nice find in his opinion; still fresh and heavy with its flavourful smell. He pocketed the tampon, knowing he would find use for it later.

Turning his attention back to the bag, Chumps drove his arms deep inside as he groped around. He felt like a surgeon, delicately searching – feeling around for that special something – until his hand pinched something soft and fleshy.

"What is this," he asked to no one in particular. His mind was a flurry of thoughts as his imagination ran wild. It felt like meat – fresh meat. Could it be a rotisserie chicken! It sure felt like it. The body was round and pimply from where the feathers would have been plucked out. It was slick and greasy, as if it had been slathered with a tasty glaze.

Without further hesitation, he pulled the weighty ball of meat up and out of the bag.

Chumps shrieked loudly. Dropping what he had thought to be chicken, he scurried backward, his eyes fixated on the unmoving monstrosity.

Pointing a long finger at the *thing* he cried out, "What the fuck is that?"

When the creature didn't move, Chumps leaned in, mustering up all the bravery he could. It was hideous beyond words. There was no other way to describe it.

Whatever *it* was, it looked alien and otherworldly – almost reptilian.

Wait!

Could be? Was this proof of the reptilian species that was living amongst humans? He had known – always known that the human species had been infiltrated by a race of reptilian creatures. They were the ones who controlled the government. The ones who masterminded assassinations on political figures. Yes, the reptilian race was alive and well and now… now he had proof!

Chumps leaned in for a closer inspection. The creature didn't move. Instead it lay there, curled in a tight ball. It must have died. The mother reptile probably decided it was of no use and instead of eating its own younglings the way they were supposed to, it had just abandoned it. It made complete sense.

Grabbing the creature by the arm, Chumps lifted it up. Instantly the creatures body unfolded, revealing a deformed and disproportionate body. Its head was large and oddly shaped. Instead of a neck sprouting from the centre of the shoulders, the left half of the head seemed to blossom from the left shoulder, while a soft narrow bulge stretched toward the right shoulder in what appeared to be the neck as an afterthought. The creature's face was passive and somber. Its swollen eyelids remained tightly sealed.

For a moment, Chumps considered what he was going to do with the body. He needed to somehow preserve it. He'd wrap it in newspaper and store it in a cardboard box. Then he would go to the local newspaper. Yes, an ambitious journalist would pay good money for an exclusive story.

Just then, the creature's eyes shot open. Small black eyes stared ahead, gazing upon the startled expression of a frail old man.

Chumps released his grip, dropping the creature once more. Again, he scurried backward, but this time with more conviction and desperation. The creature was moving, twisting its body and clambering over the bags of garbage with a speed that seemed unnatural for something its size.

Kicking his feet, Chumps struggled to find his footing.

The creature was on him now. Its tiny, clawed hands digging deep into his ankles as it climbed. But Chumps wasn't going to give in so easily. He kicked with his free foot, bashing the creature with enough force to send it on a retreat. Yet the creature didn't seem fazed. Instead, it appeared aggravated and annoyed. Each time Chumps threatened to hit it with his foot, the creature hissed and bared its small, fanged teeth.

Chumps wasn't intimidated, though. He didn't care how sharp the beast's teeth were. All he wanted was to be rid of the creature. And it soon came to fruition. In one final kick, the creature released its grip, letting its body be thrown into the cushion of garbage bags.

Wasting little time, Chumps hoisted his body onto the edge of the garbage bin and rolled off. He fell with a heavy thud, his head striking the ground hard. It bounced against the impact, stunning him. His reckless attempt to escape was an action he soon regretted. The throbbing was excruciating. It blistered and swelled in the back of his head with built up pressure yearning to be released and it clouded his judgment. He struggled to rise to his feet.

On all fours, he pushed his body up, tumbling into the garbage bin and falling over. Realizing his pain, he tried to call out, but his voice had become lodged in his throat.

A shuffling clamber from above gave him a sudden burst of motivation. He forced his body back, using the garbage bin as a brace for him to walk himself upright. Little did he realize the creature was already climbing over the edge. Pulling its body up, it spotted Chumps, staggering and wildered. He moved like a wounded gazelle and the creature saw an opportunity.

Diving down, the monstrosity latched onto the homeless man's shoulder. With its claws burrowing into Chumps' flesh, it climbed with incredible dexterity until its eyes settled upon his neck. In one fluid motion, the creature lunged forward, its mouth widening, its teeth barred.

Chumps finally found his voice. But it was too little, too late. Instead of being able to cry out for help, the sound that emerged from his lips was the gurgling cry of a man drowning in his own blood.

The creature worked the homeless man's throat with ravenous ferocity. Biting down against flesh, it tugged and pulled, shredding the man's neck until it came to cartilage and bone. But even that did little to slow the creature. Without showing any signs of tiring, the creature continued to burrow its head into the gaping hole in the man's throat.

After a few minutes, the creature leaned back, letting a pool of blood spill from the shredded wound. Not quite satisfied, the creature reached out, forcing its arm into the cavity. Twisting and pulling it pushed its arm up the man's esophagus, until those tiny clawed hands found the inside of the mouth. Carefully the creature stretched its arm until its hand gripped the homeless man's thick tongue. With one mighty pull, Chumps' tongue was torn from his mouth and extracted from his throat.

But it didn't matter much to Chumps any longer. He was long since dead, and the creature…well… she feasted like royalty. A buffet fit for a princess.

A Piece of Good Luck
Tracy A. Cross

Hugh and Floyd sat in the dive bar, drinking. They were excited to be out of prison, but happiness did not describe their new living arrangements. It seemed while they were going in and out of prison, time had moved forward and things had changed. Perpetrators of violent crimes were sent to specific sections of the country and locked behind walls and gates called Quads. There were eight Quads; the higher the number, the richer the Quad. Middle-class people lived in Quads 5 & 6; the rich lived in 7 & 8. The criminal Quads - 2 and 3 - were filled with abandoned warehouses converted to apartments. Some warehouses were the only businesses in the Quad assembly lines. Within the Quad, each person was given a small efficiency apartment to live in with a bed, night table, one light bulb, one lamp and a kitchenette. Everything else they needed was gotten on a barter system at the weekend markets.

Once every few months, there was an opportunity to earn extra money: a race through

their Quad. Winners became police officers. If they made it through to the end. If a racer was able to capture a competitor alive, they would receive credits. Credits allowed them to buy or have nicer things sent from other Quads, like better food or nicer clothes. Buying nice things was also dangerous because people robbed each other in the streets. Delivered packages were always stolen.

Hugh and Floyd always had a way with bad luck. Before the Quads, they had lived near each other in the countryside. They were the "bad boys" mothers warned their children about: stealing cars, smoking weed, drinking, and hanging out with the bad girls from a town or two over. By the time they graduated from high school, they'd spent most of their free time locked up or sent off to juvenile centers. They earned half their diplomas "on the road," as they would describe with a hearty laugh. They would escape the juvenile centers, come back to what they knew, and picked up where they left off.

Hugh'd left, hoping to find employment in the big city. He had no luck finding a job, except as a handyman of sorts. He lived in the worst part of the city, in a rundown hellhole and tried not to commit crime. But the rent was due. Working as a handyman in exchange for a portion of rent was his saving grace. Also, being the only handyman in town didn't hurt his opportunity. However, eventually, there was nothing for it. Needing to pay his rent, he robbed a convenience store.

"Hey, Hugh! Remember that botched bank robbery years ago that you did? Man, when I heard about that madness, I was almost committed to the looney bin for laughing for days."

Floyd tossed the remainder of his beer back and beckoned the bartender for another.

"Man, looking back, it was not funny then. But now that we're older...yeah, I could see how amusing it was shooting myself in the foot, having the getaway driver leave me, and having the dye packs explode as I walked out of the bank. Yeah, that's real funny." Hugh tapped the counter acerbically before the bartender walked away. His mug was refilled. The bartender left the pitcher.

"Hey, Floyd, whatever happened to that drug you made...HPF?"

"The drug I made? The one I called HNFP: Hugh and Floyd Productions? Even when you were locked up,

I thought of you." Hugh turned to Floyd and jokingly pointed a finger in his face. "Well, those were the days of making some of the best stuff ever. Now, this synthetic crap they're making these days has nothing on my stuff."

"All right," Hugh leveled his hands and turned back to the bar, "Come off the soapbox, man. They make what they can with what's available."

"I guess." Floyd sighed, "Anyway, I was making insane loot and no one knew my formula, but it was inevitable that some chem grad would figure it out. And when they did, their stuff was so pure, like manna from heaven! My stuff became the crap stuff, so I switched and ran drugs for the new guys. And even after being a drug runner for those shits, they still set me up."

"Sucks, man," Hugh shook his head, "really sucks."

"Heeeeyyyy, this guy got a life sentence, beat that! Technicalities got me out. Then, I was put in this shithole 'Quad'. I had no clue what a Quad was."

They nursed their watered-down beer at the long, stained bar. The bartender flung a towel over his shoulder, walked over to the television and turned up the volume, "Hey, check this out!"

"Good news for the residents of Quad Three! Edward "The Sphinx" Maccoli made a successful run through 'The Gauntlet' and is now an Official Police Officer. He made it through Quad Three with Christina Vasquez of Quad Four and..." the voice continued as pictures of the new recruits flashed across the screen.

"Sphinx! That's Joey Maccoli's kid! Is he a cop now? Damn, I taught that kid everything he knows. But look at his face. Looks like it was smashed into a brick wall." They both paused and looked at the TV. "Well, with a man 'inside', maybe we won't get jacked as much. You know, things will get easier."

"Things will be easier!" A voice yelled from across the room.

"Yup, shoulda thought of that before you tried to kill him. 'Sphinx' don't forget a face."

Another voice yelled.

Floyd and Hugh looked at each other, paid their tab, and left. They walked out of the basement bar and up the stairs to Hugh's apartment. Hugh opened the door and flipped on the light. Floyd's apartment was across the hall.

"I can't believe it. I taught that kid everything he knows." Hugh sighed as he flipped on a lamp. He'd managed to procure some nice artwork and a plant for his apartment. He also had a small table and two chairs next to the window. He'd made them while he was in prison. It was the one set of things he kept when he was released. He walked over, sat down, and shuffled a deck of cards on the table.

"Hey, bud, you look lower than a bowlegged toad, what gives?" Floyd asked as he sat

across from him. "Maybe that kid will come to town and remember you and help you out or something."

"Doubt it. What we need is a piece of good luck, like a four-leaf clover or something."

"What we gonna do with a piece of good luck? We are two old guys from a past that doesn't exist. We lucky to have these crap shacks the 'benevolent government' has given us."

"No, man, look, we get us some good luck and maybe we can get out of here and move into one of the nicer Quads." Hugh walked over to the sink and turned on the tap. "Water?"

Floyd shook his head.

"Look, all I'm saying is things are bound to change for us. We are due." Hugh tossed his

water back.

Floyd scratched at his graying stubble. "Like a genie's lamp or somethin'?"

"I'm thinking bigger!"

"Two four-leaf clovers?"

"Don't be a dick, Floyd. The bigger, the better - and the more luck! Okay, so imagine something with a lot of good luck symbols on it." Hugh held his hands up for emphasis. "We can pull it out, rub it, and ba-boom! We got good luck! I'm telling you, I'm so sure we are gonna get lucky that I put in an application to move Quads. I've been checking in with my parole officer and I did some community work with the delinquents here. All good things. All I need to do is get this one piece of good luck and I'm moving on up!" Hugh spoke with a twinkle in his eye.

Floyd sat back and rubbed his stubble. "Sounds like you've got a plan and you've been working it." He pushed back from the table. "We can talk about it tomorrow. I gotta get some sleep; work tomorrow at the factory. I'll see you at the bar at about six? We can talk about luck."

"Uh, I may be a little late tomorrow. I'm gonna go for that luck and I just feel, once it's in my hands, I'll get the letter moving me to a better Quad. Things will change for me, you'll see. Man, I'm going places." Hugh clapped his hands and stood, "Things are about to change for this old man."

"Good night, 'Lucky'." Floyd walked over to the door. "Just remember me when ya get it and don't be disappointed if you don't."

"Yeah, yeah." Floyd heard Hugh lock the door behind him as he left.

###

Floyd worked the assembly line on one side of one of the nondescript warehouses in the

Quad. His job was simple: some days he sorted things like circuit boards or bolts, some days he drilled. He never knew where the things he was working on would go but he was glad to have work.

He met Hugh for lunch. They both carried the standard issue metal lunch boxes or they

could eat the standard lunch from the cafeteria: cold cut sandwiches, an apple, milk, and a bag of chips. They joked the food they were fed at the warehouse was the same in prison. They never ate the standard issue lunch.

Floyd looked around. "You ever wonder where that meat comes from?"

"Oh no, not the 'soylent green' business again!" Hugh laughed.

"It's always the same every day. It's a good population control technique." Floyd swirled his ramen in his thermos. "So, Hugh, I've been thinking about this luck. What's the deal?"

"Lean in," Hugh whispered, "it's gonna blow your mind."

"Dude, as long as no one gets hurt, I got your back. You know this, right?" Floyd slurped some of his ramen broth from the thermos he bought from home.

"Look at where we live, man. Felons, thugs, rapists. Do you think any life is worth anything in this Quad? As soon as one of us 'passes on', their apartment is emptied, scrubbed clean and set up for the next person, okay?

"Remember how there was a library here years ago? Folks got too smart and started breaking out; faking IDs to get into other Quads, or making bombs. The powers that be in the Eighth Quad decided it was enough and the library was gone. We are meant to stagnate here.

That's why I'm getting that luck! I'm not going to just live and die here, like nobody." Hugh sat back in his chair and nodded at Floyd.

"Do what you think is right. Just... no one should get hurt in your quest, Lancelot." Floyd slowly stood and gave him a pat him on the back.

There was an announcement for an extra four-hour shift. Hugh and Floyd looked at each other.

"Guess I'll see you at the bar in four hours," Floyd laughed.

Hugh gave him two thumbs up and walked away.

If he had not promised Hugh to meet later, Floyd would have gone home and passed out.

His body was too old to continue working twelve-hour shifts, but he enjoyed getting the
paychecks.

He punched out and joined the drones as they left the warehouse, each heading down their separate paths. Tonight was particularly loud. There were lots of street workers for pay, lots of gambling, and in some alleys there were robberies. Floyd held his lunchbox handle and strolled past the women, down the streets with the crumbling warehouses with signs that promised new apartments or new places of employment. Floyd laughed to himself. The signs were so old, they were yellowing and falling off. There were sounds of kids playing among the rubble of bombed out warehouses. He never saw them, only heard them, like they were ghosts of the past. He walked by the enclosed areas where the gardens were kept by the gardeners. There was always one living in the shack on the land with a shotgun leveled at anyone that tried to climb over the gate. Floyd remembered turning them down when they asked him to join. He didn't have as much of a green thumb as he thought.

Surprisingly, some streetlights were lit as he neared the central area of town where most of the shops and bars were, and the Quad looked alive. He checked his watch. It was almost seven. He had a few minutes to run up to his apartment to get a quick shower and leave his lunchbox. As he strolled inside the building, there were old mailboxes along the wall. He ascended the steps and heard a few televisions blasting, babies screaming, and ran into a few kids playing in the hall. Ironically, he'd never seen the kids outside the apartment building. Once, he spoke to one of the mothers and she told him that it was simply not safe for them to go out.

"Good evening, Mr. Floyd." A little snaggle-toothed girl with two pigtails walked up to him and sang as he put his key in the lock.

"Look, Cindy Lou, don't try to rip me off today. I'll give you a piece if you leave me alone. Next time your ma wants money, have her come get it from me." He laughed and flicked a silver coin in the air.

"My name's not Cindy Lou. It's Rebecca." She tossed over her shoulder as she caught the coin.

He made it inside as he heard the little girl's footsteps race down the hall and another door slammed shut. He had to stop giving his money away like that. "They will all look at me as some idiot donor. I'm not rich." He laughed as he took his clothes off and jumped in the shower.

He bounded down the stairs and headed to the bar to wait for Hugh. He held his finger up for one beer. The bartender limped over with a glass. "Evening sir, where's your friend?"

"Late, I guess." Floyd looked around and didn't see Hugh. "Just one tonight, Damon. I think he should be here any minute."

"Sure, Mr. Floyd." Damon wore a white apron and had a heavy Irish accent. He also had a pronounced limp. When he returned with the beer, Floyd asked him how he ended up here in the Quads.

"Well," he leaned back and wiped his hands with a towel. "Everything was fine with me wife and such. Kids were grown and off to school, ya know. The wife asked if her mum could stay in the extra room we had. I wanted wifey happy, so I agreed. But I'll tell ya', damned if her mum didn't ride my ass everyday about any and everything. 'Dayyy-mon' is how she said me name, 'Oye need...' and it just went on. I mean, I tried to talk to her but I may as well ha' been whistlin' jigs to a milestone. So, one day, the wife goes ta work and I'm alone with this old bag.

She asked me for one simple thing. I can't remember and I walks out to the yard, gets me favorite axe, come in and chop her up. I had her buried and the house cleaned before the wife came home and oh was she a mess when I told her. But let me tell ya' boy, she looked relieved, she did.

There was a twinkle in her eye and she smiled a little before she called the coppers. Visited me ev'ry day in prison too until she died some years later. Rest her soul."

Hugh stormed in like a tornado and pulled up a stool next to Floyd, "Aye, one for me, Damon. How's it goin'?"

"Slow and steady, sir. Was just chatting with yer bud here. I'll get that beer for ya."

Damon limped away as Floyd whispered, "I like Damon and his Irish accent. The other bartender, I don't like as much." Floyd took a huge gulp of his beer

"So, I found it." Hugh leaned in, "and I wanna show it to you." Hugh took a swig of beer from the glass Damon set down.

"What'd you find? This piece of luck?" Floyd finished his beer and took out a few bills to pay for it.

"Yep, and we're going to see it tonight. Right now," Hugh turned up his glass and poured the beer down his throat, "after I finish my beer of course." He put the glass on the bar and left a few bills, "Let's go."

As they left, they saw "Sphinx" on TV talking about how rewarding it was being a police officer after his rough childhood and hard work. Everyone in the bar applauded except Hugh. He was headed straight for the door. Floyd felt his muscles ache as he tried to catch up with Hugh.

Hugh led them down a street and around the complex maze of warehouses to a tattoo shop. The shop was above ground and well lit; it occupied one of the nicer locations in the warehouses.

Hugh opened the doors and a friendly girl with a high black Mohawk and golden brown skin walked over, her arms covered in tattoos.

"What's the good good, Hugh?" She smiled behind the counter. She wore black leather pants, biker boots, and a black shirt that stopped above her pierced navel. She had perfect white teeth and a happy demeanor for a girl living and working in such a bad place.

"Hey, Terra! This is my friend, Floyd. He's my best buddy. We've been buds forever."

Hugh took off his green baseball cap and rubbed his salt-and-pepper hair with his dirty, tanned hand.

"Are we still talking about 'luck'?" She smiled, put her elbows on the counter and cupped her face in her hands.

Floyd noticed the tattoos covering her body, excluding her face. "So, uh, what's all them tattoos stand for?"

"Well, my left arm," she extended, "is like all the evil and bad I've done. See, here's a gun

- held up a liquor store. Some dudes I beat up - those are the Day of the Dead faces with the mouths stitched. Snitches," she snorted. "Some chick I didn't like, so I took care of her: the doll with the sewed up mouth. But this, this one is my favorite. My spider web on my elbow. If you know what that means, well, you wouldn't want to mess with me outside these walls, you know?" She winked.

"What's the spider web on the elbow mean?" Floyd leaned in closer to look at her arm.

"Mmmm," she hummed, "I killed someone in prison. But don't tell them that, I could lose my job." She laughed.

Floyd pulled back, intrigued, "But the other arm, what's that all about?"

"See, with everything that is good, there is bad and vice versa. These tattoos on my right arm are my good luck symbols. For every bad tattoo representing my past, I got a good one representing my future. Like the Buddha, his hands, some Tibetan script, koi swimming upstream, and my favorite that my boy just finished: a hamsa on my inner arm with the warning eye. It's for protection and good luck." She held her arm out and outlined it for them.

"So, all this good luck negates the bad luck and bad things you've done?" Floyd asked as he tilted his head to look closer at her tattoos.

"You could say. I mean, I'm trying to bank on some good karma as well. Good deeds and all that. Hey, Hugh, decide on some ink yet? I'm always ready to get started."

A tall white guy lumbered up behind her and smacked her on the butt. His face was a series of ridges and tattoos. His arms were as thick as baseball bats and covered with tattoos; he had the same spider web on his elbow like Terra. He shot a quick glance at Floyd and Hugh. He grunted and stood next to Terra, "You gents lookin' fer something particular?"

"I think we found it. Terra, have a great night." Hugh smiled and backed out the door, followed by Floyd.

They walked along in silence until they got to Floyd's apartment.

"So, ah," Floyd began, "we are getting all sleeved up for luck? This is your idea of good luck? I think I'll take my chances with a rabbit's foot or something. Besides, I tried to get some tattoos in prison and almost had my arm amputated because they got infected. India ink and a needle, my ass."

"You just don't see it, do you?" Hugh held his head down and laughed. "We ain't getting'

tattoos. We takin' 'em."

Floyd's eyes were noticeably larger than they'd been a second ago. "Wait, what?" He

thought for a moment, "No, not what I think. We could...we could...man I just..."

"Pal, let me show you something, over here in my place. I've finished it today, worked on

it for a while."

They walked across the hall to Hugh's place. Hugh flipped the light switch, "Bathroom."

He pointed.

Floyd walked into the bathroom. It was covered in plastic drop cloths, "We're taking that chick's arm and we're gonna skin it. See, I've read about how these

Japanese people sold their fully tattooed skin after they died. Like, willed it to someone. It was treated like a prized possession. So, when they died, it was part of the will for them to be skinned and the skin was sold and preserved. It's a black market thing now, but it got so popular they - the Japanese - were making offers to bikers, here in the US. Or what was the US. Now, we steal that chick's arm and skin it. How else are we gonna get that much good luck?"

"You can't be serious."

Hugh pulled a chainsaw from behind the curtain in the bathtub, "Did you think I was joking? I told you, man, one way or another, I'm getting out of here." He laughed and started the chainsaw. "Purrs like a kitten."

"Really? You are going to take some girl's arm? That has to be the stupidest thing I've heard! Think about it. I mean, what are you going to do, whip out her arm when you're buying a lottery ticket and start rubbing it? This is some serious shit, man! I do not want to have someone looking to exact justice on me in this Quad. Lives here are worth nothing. But you do that and your life will be less than nothing. You may even be moved into a worse Quad, and I don't think you'd survive there at all."

"So, now you don't support me in my endeavor?"

"Why would I support murder? Sure, her tatts were cool. Sure, she was a nice looking girl who wouldn't give an old man like me the time of day, but this is wrong. Besides, did you see ol' boy standing behind her? He looks like he eats guys like us for breakfast, lunch, and dinner!"

"Meh, I'm not worried about him. I just need to get her alone and get it done. So, again,

I'm asking if you are going to support me in my endeavor of acquiring some good luck." Hugh stood up straight, lifted his chin and crossed his arms.

They stood face to face. Hugh firmly held his ground. Floyd sighed and shook his head.

He stepped out of the bathroom. "Good luck with that."

He only saw Hugh one more time.

Floyd sat in the bar after another shift at the factory, days after he'd tried to convince

Hugh he was wrong. The idea was ludicrous, but every time he knocked on his door to talk about it, Hugh was never home or didn't answer. He couldn't find him at work. Eventually, he gave up trying.

After a few hours of TV and small talk with Damon and the other patrons, he settled his tab and walked home. He went inside, flopped on the couch and turned on his new, very small, black market, black and white TV and watched the news. He decided he would watch until he fell asleep. At the site of Hugh's face, Floyd sat up and leaned forward to turn the TV up. He managed to hear the word 'murder.' He focused on the screen. Even though they lived in one of the worst Quads, there were reporters from the richer Quads that would sneak in and film footage, just to show the world how awful the people in the poor and dangerous Quads were. The hope was to abolish all the dangerous Quads because the rich were running out of space in theirs.

Hugh's face was on the screen and there was a voiceover. They spoke about the murder.

They'd managed to get into the apartment the night of the murder and filmed it.

There was blood all over the bathroom. There was Terra, one of her arms handcuffed to the shower curtain rod. Her legs were spread and cuffed to something unseen. She had on her leather pants and black shirt. The only odd thing, excluding the blood all over the walls and floor, was her missing right arm. There was a bone and some muscle in the bathtub and Floyd heard the word "skinned". He shook his head and mumbled beneath his breath that he couldn't believe his friend actually went through with a plan so macabre. He sat up, put his head in his hands and shook his head. "I can't believe he was that desperate. He actually did it. Damn, Hugh."

He thought back to that last night he saw his friend. It all began with a banging on his door. He looked through the peephole and saw Hugh, grinning. He peeled the door open and began to speak before Hugh cut him off.

"I did it! And I brought something over for you!" Hugh looked antsy as he pushed his way into Floyd's apartment.

"Man, is that why you weren't at work today? You didn't do it, did you?" Floyd closed the door as Hugh giddily paced around with a small folded item in his hand. He looked at Hugh's shoes and they were covered with blood. He felt his stomach drop and his skin lost all color.

"I can't believe you did it." He felt as though someone punched him in the gut. Hugh had the eyes of a mad man.

"This is for you." Hugh held the small folded item out and motioned to Floyd. Floyd stood by the door and slowly locked it. "Come closer," Hugh beckoned.

Floyd stepped back. Hugh lumbered over to him and pushed it in his hands. Floyd slowly opened the layers of plastic and tissue paper. Inside was something small and very oily.

Hugh nodded with approval, like a mad scientist. "Luck will change tomorrow! I promise you that! I told you I would do it!" Hugh walked around in circles, tapping his fingers together.

"I gotta get back, and it's all still fresh. Gotta start saving it, preserving it. Not a lot of books on preserving this type of thing, but I think I got it figured."

Just like that, Hugh was out the door.

Living in such a dangerous Quad, justice was handled internally. No court or trial. For Hugh, justice meant two fully tattooed guys with baseball bats kicking in his door a few days later. Floyd heard a loud boom as they kicked Hugh's door in. One of the guys was the bald guy

from the tattoo studio. There was a big brown skinned guy, covered in tattoos, bald and stocky and wearing sunglasses that stood in front of Hugh's door. The big guy had to sense something because he held his finger up and shook it very slowly from side to side, saying "No" towards Floyd's peephole. Floyd nervously stepped back, his heartbeat so hard in his chest, he was sure the stocky guy heard it.

He walked to his sink and grabbed a bottled water. He ripped it open and drank it. Part of the problem with these old buildings was that some of the apartments were soundproof and some weren't. Hugh lived in an apartment covered with brick walls, so any sound coming from within was muffled. Floyd dropped the empty bottle when he heard noises in the hallway. He ran over and peeked out the peephole and saw Hugh trying to run. Someone grabbed him from behind and Hugh held onto Floyd's doorframe with all the strength he had as someone yanked him away.

The door closed, and then there wasn't any more sound.

Ironically, the guy at the door pulled out a bottle of cleaning solution and a towel. He sprayed and wiped the bloody handprints on the door frame. He put the bottle on the floor and folded the bloody towel and put it in his pocket.

Floyd sat on the couch in a daze. He heard thumping sounds and knew things were not going in Hugh's favor. Petrified, he looked out the peephole to see women standing outside the door. Once the other guys left, the big guy at the door nodded and they rushed inside with their elbow length gloves and plastic suits to clean the apartment. The next day, the local news reporters asked Floyd and his neighbors if they knew what had happened in the apartment. Later, they broadcasted the footage, "We have obtained exclusive footage from inside the killer's apartment. We believe he was practicing some type of voodoo ritual..."

A knock at his door snapped him out of his thoughts. Floyd walked over and looked out the peephole. There was a man in a suit. He nervously looked around as the two very armed police officers stepped back and blocked the hall with their stature. The knock was persistent.

Where was his good for nothing lawyer now?

"Yes?"

"Sir, would you please open up? It's of a personal nature."

"What kinda nature?" Floyd asked.

"A monetary nature. Now please, open the door or these two lovely officers will kick the door in. Trust me, sir, I don't want to be out here in as much as you want me out here broadcasting your news to your neighbors."

Floyd undid the chains and opened the door. The man fixed his tie and walked in. One officer stood at the door and another came inside and closed the door. The man in the suit walked over to the table in Floyd's apartment and sat down. He was sweating profusely and had a nasty comb over. His suit was a work of art, brown and polyester. Floyd thought the suit looked like something his father wore. The man smoothed his hair down, took a deep breath, and pulled out a folder. He opened it and put a pen on the papers. He motioned for Floyd to sit down.

"Sir, Mr....ah..." The man shuffled the papers, looking for a name.

"Floyd. Just Floyd."

"Yes, then...ah Mr. Floyd, I'm not sure if you knew, but you were the prime beneficiary of a Mr. Hughefort Neville. Please sign these documents and I will have the credits transferred to your account immediately. Because of your exemplary behavior and high work ethic, we are offering you a one-time transfer to the edges of Quad 5. It's a lower middle class place, but there is a small house on the edge, near the perimeter fence that needs to be fixed up. A person like you doesn't deserve to be in here. You've paid your debt to society. And to be frank, you're old. Who are you really going to harm?" The officer laughed a bit.

"What about work?" Floyd looked at the paperwork and put the pen down.

"I'm not sure you saw the insurance amount." The man's tone changed, he lowered his voice. "You don't need to work anymore. You can spend your last years in peace, living on that small plot of land, fixing up the shithouse in a halfway decent Quad, or you can stay here with your credits and get robbed or killed. The choice is yours. News like this travels fast in these parts. You know, with you not opening the door and all."

Floyd looked at the paper. He hadn't seen that many zeroes in a while. He laughed a bit and signed as the man pointed to certain spots on the papers. He also had to initial here and here and here. When he was done, he put the pen down and asked, "When do I move?"

"The officer will be stationed outside your door tonight. There will be two more downstairs, so we can move you whenever you are ready." The man looked over the paperwork, stacked the pages together neatly, and put them in a briefcase. He pulled out a device and clicked a few buttons. "Money is in your account. I'd like to thank you for your time, Mr... Floyd. I imagine you don't have a lot of belongings. Hopefully, you can leave tonight. Remember, word travels fast around here. Have a great night." He stood and extended his hand.

Floyd shook it and the man was out the door. The officer stood outside and asked Floyd if he knew when he would be ready to go.

"I need about a half hour, is that okay?"

The officer nodded and Floyd closed the door.

###

Floyd exhaled. For the first time, he smiled. What luck! He was getting out! He walked into his bedroom and sat on the edge of the bed. He opened the nightstand and pulled out his Bible. Inside was something wrapped in plastic. He pulled it out and peeled the plastic open. It was the hamsa from Terra's arm. "I don't know if this works. If Hugh was onto something, or maybe it was just my time. Either way, thanks for the luck, baby. Tomorrow's gonna be a better day."

He wrapped the tattoo and put it back in the Bible, grabbed his bag from beneath his bed, and packed his few belongings.

Harvest Moon
Ken Goldman

The citizens of Durney County crowded into the huge red and blue striped circus tent whose American flag-topped spires rose three stories above the dark sod of Corney Adams' field and pointed toward a purple twilight sky. The tent sat upon eight acres of land that had once boasted the tallest corn stalks in the county back in the days when old Corney used to work the soil himself while perched upon his John Deere like a proud sea captain. Now it took four farm hands to do what he used to, and that spread the money considerably thin. Still, Durney's soil always seemed to know the right way to treat those who invested time and sweat plowing it.

An inspection of many of the town residents' fingernails might have revealed crusty dirt still embedded from the recent June harvest. Nature had smiled upon the small hamlet during the past spring, and the old girl had again seen fit to nicely sweeten the county's fertile earth. The corn had grown tall and proud since the spring planting and throughout the months that led to summer. Now that the cultivators and threshers were hosed off and shedded, tonight's full moon would shine down upon an equally proud little burg that finally had some loose change to spend.

On the eve of another bountiful harvest, Corney Adams joined the people of Durney gathered beneath the colorful party-striped canvas. Seated ringside and alongside Durney's mayor, Corney hoped to watch his neighbors part with some of that change while catching a glimpse of what the whole town had been buzzing about since the handbills had passed through every mailbox in the county. Rumor had it that the Malvolio

Thrill Show boasted a finale that was a real show stopper.

Of course, two weeks earlier, old Corney had harbored his suspicions concerning this three-ring dog and pony show. He listened as the stranger who called himself Mr. Ambrose Malvolio promised the county's mayor that the good people of Durney would witness performances inside his tent that none would likely soon forget. When the lanky visitor met with him and the honorable Nathaniel P. Withers to close the deal in the mayor's office, the man wore a seer-sucker sports jacket that would have appeared ridiculously out of date anywhere else. Although Malvolio's words seemed more like a sermon than a sales pitch, he did not have to say very much to convince Withers to sign on the dotted line. Adams proved a tougher sell, and the old farmer's eyebrow remained arched throughout the slick huckster's entire sales pitch.

"I won't mince words, gentlemen. The Malvolio Traveling Thrill Show considers it a point of honor to deliver to every man, woman, and child of Durney County the kind of spectacle that folks used to call 'a real barn burner.' You'll not see its match anywhere else on this green earth."

Although the man might have more appropriately uttered his lofty words through a megaphone from center arena, he had managed to capture the mayor's interest. Since Corney and he were kids, Nathaniel had been an easy mark, the kind who would be first in line to whitewash Tom Sawyer's fence or to purchase himself a genuine divining rod from any grade school pitch man who desired a few extra coins in his pocket. While Withers sat rubbing the smaller of his two chins, Malvolio removed some papers from his seer-sucker and flattened them upon the mayor's desk.

"Kids 'round here ain't never seen a circus come to Durney," Withers mentioned almost sheepishly to his old pal without a glance at the official looking papers before him. He turned to Corney seated across the desk, knowing his friend owned the town's largest tract of land. Without his consent Mr. Malvolio might just as well move on to the next county. "Might be a good idea at that, Corney. Circus comin' to town might put somethin' back into Durney's coffers."

Circus.

Malvolio actually blanched at the word. He ran a perfectly manicured hand through a head of thick black hair that looked like it had been recently lubricated with motor oil, then leaned back in his chair as if rehearsing the next words he wanted to say.

"Gentlemen, I am not a man who is given to understatement. Would you call the soil of Durney County that is its lifeblood dirt? Would you remember your most bountiful summer harvest as a simple perk of the seeds you have sown? Perhaps you misunderstand that what I offer to you today is a celebration of life, so much more than--"

He stopped himself and looked into Withers' eyes, then Corney's, and for a moment the man seemed ready to close the books on the whole deal. The smile that smeared his face seemed an afterthought, a studied attempt to reclaim lost dignity. He placed three rolls of hundred dollar bills on the table before the two men.

Oh, this guy is good, Corney thought. Let some other brainless yokel blow a day's pay on ten jars of snake oil that cured baldness or provided rock-hard erections; Corney no longer had much use for hair, and his Josephine could care less about the endurance of the stub inside his pants. Skepticism cost nothing, and it had been quite some time since the old harvester had last fallen off the turnip truck. But it couldn't hurt to listen to what the stranger had to say.

"Count the money if you like. That's three thousand dollars in exchange for the use of Mr. Adams' eight acres, plus a guarantee of twenty-five percent of the take. Should that twenty-five percent fail to exceed two thousand dollars apiece, I am quite willing to place that amount in escrow this very moment. In cash, of course. That's at least seven thousand dollars, gentlemen. So you see, Durney's coffers shall be filled despite whatever your bottom line shows."

If money talked, then the tall stranger's cash was speaking volumes. He leaned forward on his elbows as if about to share a secret. Both Withers and Corney instinctively did the same, like two puppets on a single string.

"There is one thing I must insist upon, however. I prefer to keep mum about our main attraction so as not to spoil it for our paying customers. I'm sure you understand ..." He placed another four rolls of fifties and hundreds alongside the contract and held out a pen. "Now, do we have a deal, gentlemen?"

Corney and Withers stared at the bills in front of them, then at each other. Corney tried to exercise a little mind reading. Ambrose Malvolio seemed mighty intent on pitching his tent in Durney.

"Hold on for just one minute, Mr. Malvolio," Adams finally said. "Just what sort of 'main attraction' might you be talkin' about? We got kids comin' to your show, for Chrissake, and ours is a God fearin' town. All those dead presidents don't impress me one lick if you're talkin' about some sort of girlie show with titties hangin' out--"

Malvolio raised his hand and the old man shut up as quickly as if his tongue had been cut out.

"Mr. Adams. This is not some cheap corn whiskey burlesque act. I would sooner sell one prayer book than a library of filth, and I admit I have done both. But I am also a businessman, and I am talking about a genuine twenty-four carat show stopper! Why, anyone who has ever enjoyed the sensation of sitting on the edge of his seat with his heart clamped between his teeth knows exactly what I mean. The good people of Durney County expect that heart-stopping final act, and once they fill our tent they shall have it."

He flashed a smile that showed more teeth than seemed necessary.

"Of course, sustaining the secrecy of our main attraction is of the utmost importance. You see, it is a specialty act that is best performed after dark, and only once per night. Understand that there are some secrets we in the entertainment business prefer to keep close to our chests, for professional reasons. After our first show, the word will spread, of course, but until then -- well, you understand."

"A real barn burner, eh?" Withers added.

"Exactly."

Ambrose Malvolio had put his money where his gonads were. But none of Malvolio's hyperboles seemed to reach Nathaniel Withers' brain so much as the stranger's can't-lose guarantee, and even Corney understood election day was not so far off that Durney County's voters would forget who had brought this show to their town. If Malvolio's mysterious once-a-night final act sold more tickets, so much the better. Corney knew the advantage of having hizzoner in his own pocket when time came to determine whose stalks got selected every summer for those huge Durney barbecues at the mayor's mansion. Besides, who wouldn't be curious to see just what Mr. Malvolio's main attraction was all about? Withers caught Corney Adams' eye and the old man nodded his consent.

With handshakes all 'round and a few strokes of Malvolio's golden Waterford that bore the A.M. monogram, the three men sealed the agreement that same minute...

***

The people of Durney County came to see a show stopper, just as Ambrose Malvolio said they would.

Inside the colorful tent, a variety of smells immediately assaulted the senses with a strange co-mingling of the pleasant and the putrid. In the mixture rogue scents of popcorn, peanuts, and corn dogs combined in an unlikely stew with the raw odors of hot animal fur, shit, and sweat.

Corney Adams and Withers sat together at ringside with their wives, each woman in a flowery summer dress and straw hat, each man a portrait of self-satisfaction. The stands behind them swarmed with people clear up to the tent's multi-striped canvas. It seemed that every citizen of Durney had turned out to see tonight's opening show, and there would be much pressing of the flesh later if the rest of the night went as well.

Corney called to the kid selling cold beer, Withers sprang for the first round and some corn dogs, and the men clicked their plastic cups together like two college kids. From the center arena, Ambrose Malvolio, wearing the bright red long-tailed coat and silk top hat of the ringmaster, saw the toast and pantomimed a raised glass back to them. Corney noticed Malvolio's eye caught the women's, and the ringmaster toasted them also.

Josephine Adams immediately looked away, her face crimson. Corney saw his wife shifting in her seat. "Josie, you sittin' on a beehive I should know somethin' about?" His wife forced a smile but said nothing.

"Where are the clowns?" Elvira Withers asked her husband.

"What?"

"Clowns. I don't see any clowns. A circus is supposed to have clowns."

"Haven't you heard, 'Vira?" said Corney, wresting the last of his corn dog from its stick. "That man in the funny hat down there in the center ring says this ain't no circus. So there ain't no clowns."

"Why, that's plain foolishness, Corney," Josephine chimed in, clearly relieved that the subject had changed. "'Course this is a circus. What else could it be?"

"Damned if I know," the old man muttered. "But I'll tell you what I do know. 'Cept to deliver this overgrown tablecloth we're sittin' under, I never even seen any other trucks or trailers pullin' up to my place with the Malvolio logo. God knows how that man managed this menagerie without a whole army." Again, Josephine Adams fell silent, her complexion bearing a close resemblance to old man Bryant's tomato patch. Corney wondered if maybe his wife was experiencing a little gas.

Their attention focused upon the center ring where two dwarf jugglers warmed up the audience while dizzying calliope music swirled in the background. Noticing the over-sized bulbous nose of one performer and the floppy elephant-like ears of the other, at first Corney had almost added "There's your clowns, 'Vira." But he quickly stopped himself when he realized neither of the two dwarfs wore painted faces. They simply were ugly.

One man juggled five corn cobs. His partner tossed five short-handled hooked sickles into the air, the kind farmers used for cutting tall grass. The men lobbed the objects at each other and juggled them back and forth to the audience's polite applause. Pretending to be distracted by the crowd's approval, the big-nosed juggler did not seem to notice his partner had tossed two hooked blades at him. Missing a beat, he grabbed too late at them as each sickle sliced neatly through his wrists. Both hands plopped into the dirt and lay at his feet, caked in soil. For a moment, the dwarf looked blankly at his two bleeding raw stumps, then ran screaming from the center ring.

His big-eared partner hesitated a moment. He picked up the two severed, blood drenched hands and dusted them off. Then, along with the five corn cobs, he juggled the lot of them high into the air as he walked off.

No polite applause this time, only dumbfounded silence followed by a few uncomfortable murmurs. Whispering had always been the small town's primary language, but before any of its citizens could respond further the house lights dimmed. A sudden drum roll almost caused Corney to spill his beer. Slicing through the darkened tent, a blinding spotlight washed over the center ring to reveal a large cage. Inside, a lion paced restlessly. Alongside the cage stood a tall, shapely beauty whose butterscotch tresses rivaled the mane of the beast stalking at her back. The woman could have passed for one of those big-haired bar flies that frequented Bill Dunlap's Tavern, the kind who would go home after last call with whoever sprang for the most beers, except this one seemed to have all of her teeth.

The cat kept its distance from behind the bars, but it did not take its eyes from the object the woman held in her hand. She cracked the whip to the accompaniment of the animal's thundering roars, and the crowd gasped with each snap of the lash. The roars continued even as the cat withdrew from the long-legged tamer who stood facing its snapping maw outside the cage.

Malvolio's voice came on the public address system.

"The Malvolio Thrill Show presents ... Selena and the jaws of death!"

Short, simple, and trimmed of bullshit. Corney saw Withers smile, and the expression proved infectious. The old farmer had to respect Malvolio's sense of showmanship.

The community fell into a dutiful dead silence as the long-stemmed beauty bowed, unlatched the door, and stepped into the cage. Stopping in its tracks the cat stared at the woman dead-on, clawing at the air inches from her face. She cracked the whip again and the beast cowered in the corner like a frightened kitten.

"Hey-ah! Hey-ah!" the woman screamed at it.

Corney again looked over at his grinning old friend, wondering if the lovely Miss Selena had simultaneously managed to pacify the animal while giving 'hizzoner' a hard-on.

Without losing her toothy smile, the woman suddenly tossed the whip over her shoulders through the bars of the cage. It landed in the soft dirt, out of reach and useless. She turned her back defiantly on the cat and pulled a large ear of corn from behind her cape. Sinking her teeth into it the tamer seemed oblivious to the menacing creature behind her. She tossed the chewed cob aside and threw her arms high in the air to receive the crowd's applause, following this with a deep bow to the stands closest to her. The lion stared at the shapely ass she had pointed directly at its face, cocking its head one way and then the other as if drawing a bead on the tamer's firm buttocks. The woman continued to bow with her back turned as if taunting the beast to act.

It did. In one terrible instant the cat lunged forward, knocking the woman completely off her feet before she had any chance to turn or utter a sound. The animal fell on her and she seemed to disappear beneath it, her head and torso lost somewhere under its great mane, her long legs covered by the animal's rope-muscled haunches. Growling and snarling, the lion lowered itself over her and swiped a paw at the woman's golden tresses. The great cat opened its mouth wide and brought it down in a sudden fury directly at the woman's neck as if it were gnawing at a cob of corn.

Withers took to his feet. The entire crowd followed. Several women screamed.

Corney remembered what Malvolio had said about having his heart in his mouth. He was practically chewing on his, watching in numb horror as the great cat rolled over upon the woman while she twisted and turned beneath the beast like a broken doll.

"Jesus, oh sweet Jesus!" Withers groaned more to himself than to the people who stood slack-jawed around him.

And then, as suddenly as it had begun, the struggle inside the cage ended. As if an electrical cord had been pulled from its socket, the cat flopped on its back and lay without moving, one of its claws still dangling a large swatch of sequined blue silk from the woman's jumpsuit. The beautiful tamer also lay motionless and blood-soaked alongside the animal.

Somewhere in the audience a child had begun to cry. The crowd in the stands stood frozen in the phantom illumination of the naked spotlight.

"For God's sake, somebody do something!" a woman called out.

"Turn off the goddamned spotlight, for Chrissakes!"

"Call a doctor! Jesus, will somebody help her!"

Screams. Cries. Shouts. In the center arena, a grotesque still-life remained under the blazing circle of light.

... and then the woman tamer jumped to her feet, her blood-soaked tresses bouncing like a cheerleader's behind her in the spotlight. With a neck still leaking blood, she turned to face her audience and threw two smeared arms into the air, this time not as a gesture of defiance but of triumph. The lion remained completely motionless at her feet lying in a slowly expanding puddle that dripped from the cage and seeped into the dirt floor.

A thick stream of reddish gore trickled from the woman's mouth, and the spotlight that washed over the animal revealed blood oozing in thick gouts from the lion's throat. Standing in center arena, still smiling, the woman licked her lips.

The spotlight snapped off, leaving the center ring in total darkness, and Corney in stunned bewilderment. Someone in the back of the tent clapped and quickly stopped, the hollow sound smothered by the audience's befuddled silence.

"What in hell was that all about?" Corney whispered.

"Must be some sort of trick," Withers answered. "Not in real good taste, that's for damn sure."

The mayor of the township looked at his wife who stood alongside him in the grey light of the grandstand. Elvira's mouth had not closed for the last three minutes.

Corney looked at his wife too. "Are you feelin' okay, Josie?" he asked.

Josephine Adams looking back at her husband could mime only her befuddlement and disgust with wild eyes and trembling lips. Her mouth formed words that did not seem willing to come. Finally, she managed to spit a few out.

"That woman ... I think that woman just killed that cat. Just bit into its neck, killed him, and took her bow! But she was mauled! I saw it! My God, Corney, didn't you see what just hap-?" Josephine looked like she was about to woof up her inner intestines.

"A trick, Josie. That's all it was. That's what it hadda be--"

Before Corney could say another word, Josephine pushed her way past him and through the crowded stands. He noticed that she was not alone as she beat a path toward the exit. More people than Mrs. Josephine Adams had already seen enough of the Malvolio Traveling Thrill Show.

"Let her go, Corney. She'll be all right. We can't leave," Withers insisted. "I'm sorry ... but how would it look? Jesus, that could be our asses down there floating in that pool of blood with that lion."

Corney nodded, but he turned again to watch his wife head toward the exit. Elvira Withers stood in place as if she had been planted by her husband's side. When Nathaniel Withers again took his seat, Corney and Elvira followed his cue. Corney knew the mayor fervently hoped that the hundreds of paying customers who remained in the stands behind him would do the same. Every Durney citizen walking out now would cost the man at least one vote each come November.

Twin spotlights flashed on, this time focusing upon two platforms connected by the high wire above the center ring. Malvolio again spoke into the microphone, but his workman-like introduction to the next act revealed nothing. It was as if the last ten minutes had not happened.

"Ladies and gentlemen ... Cacilia and Gregor Hieronymus defy death high above the big top! Notice there is no net ... and if you will direct your attention to the arena directly below the wire ... "

Had he been seated elsewhere, right about now Corney would have been through the exit. Instead, he considered discussing with Nathaniel the merits of seeing this ringmaster tarred and feathered in the village square. The spotlight below again splintered into two beams. The bright white circles revealed a large rectangular platform from which protruded at least a hundred sharpened wooden stakes, each honed to two prongs pointing straight up directly beneath the high wire like huge skewers for cobs of corn grown to man size. There were enough of them to gore at least a dozen men with plenty to spare.

Again the crowd gasped, and Corney felt his mouth go dry. Withers was already mopping his forehead. Malvolio's thrill show was living up to its name, all right. In spades.

And in stakes.

From opposite platforms, clutching long poles for balance, the handsome couple inched toward each other upon the high wire above the upright spikes. When they met in the center, each threw the metal poles aside, allowing them to thud into the soft dirt below.

"... And now begins the kiss of death!" Malvolio announced crisply into the mic. With knees buckling for equilibrium upon the wire the couple embraced high above the platform of spiked prongs, maintaining a precarious balance that seemed not only to defy gravity but to insult it. They pulled one another closer. They kissed tentatively, passionately.

... and then they fell.

Their bodies briefly pressed tightly together, then Cacilia and Gregor Hieronymus toppled separately through the air to the pointed spikes below. The woman hit the spikes first and, pressed by the weight of her mate who fell upon her, three prongs passed neatly through her back and one impaled her through the neck. The stakes crunched through tissue and bone, emerging as bloody stalks through the man's buttocks and shoulders. Skewered in a twisted missionary position, slowly each body slid down the length of the sharpened poles, a meaty human kabob locked in a lovers' embrace.

They remained gored in the naked spotlight. Corney watched the audience take to its feet, its stunned silence quickly inverting itself into a confused gibberish of gasps, screams, and curses.

This time, the people of Durney were more decisive, and most of the crowd pushed, jabbering for the exits. Parents quickly ushered children out, many shielding their eyes or holding them in their arms. The spotlight lingered on the bleeding flesh of the performers who still lay impaled upon the spiked platform. The remaining people in the stands stood waiting in mute silence as if unsure what to do while the tent emptied.

Malvolio paused until the last person filed through the exit before he spoke into the microphone again. His voice revealed nothing of the events that the people of Durney County had just seen. The ringmaster turned to the nearly empty seats, proclaimed "Ladies and gentlemen... Once again... The kiss of death!" and stepped back into the shadows.

Gregor and Cacilia Hieronymus, although blood-soaked and impeded by the shafts that had passed through their bodies, slowly twisted and writhed upon the wooden prongs. As they strained to reach for one another, Corney felt an icy chill. If this were a trick, this was the best fucking illusion on the planet.

It was also the most revolting.

Gregor eased his body even further down the stakes to press the lovely Cacilia's lips to his and, sopping with the same scarlet gumbo as her partner, the woman arched her back to join herself to him. The man had reached the woman's dripping thigh just before the spotlight again snapped off.

Behind Adams someone gagged. Withers turned to where moments before Elvira had risen to her feet, suddenly noticing she no longer stood there. He looked at Corney watching him. The old man's eyes already spoke the only words he could think to say.

"We've got to close this show, Nat. Goddammit, we've got to close it right now before that bastard puts this town through any more of this!"

Withers turned toward the stands behind him. Although the crowd had noticeably thinned, at least a hundred Durney diehards remained, some babbling amongst themselves, others standing alone in either confusion or white-hot expectation.

The mayor's expression revealed the face of a man witnessing his political career dissolve before his eyes.

"Malvolio, you lying son of a bitch!" he called out in the dim light of the darkened tent. "Close it down! All of it! Right now!"

Ambrose Malvolio stepped out of the shadows and stood before Nathaniel Withers. He still wore the clothing of the ringmaster, and his voice revealed no change of expression despite the evening's grue .

"Why, Mayor, how could I possibly allow you and Mr. Adams to leave without seeing our main attraction? You and the remaining stout-hearted souls of Durney County represent a highly select audience. Any businessman worth his spit knows how to target his paying customers, and you and Adams here, among all the others, have a definite taste for death. We crave such an audience for our closing act."

"What in Christ are you talking--?" Corney said, turning to leave. "You don't have to show me the exit, you cheating shit. I ain't buyin' another bottle of whatever marmalade you're sellin'!"

Malvolio grabbed the old man by the arm.

"Not yet, Mr. Adams. You came tonight to see a show stopper, and you shall see one!"

Withers tried to push past him. "I'm closing you down, you stinking rat bastard! You got snakes chewing through your brain if you think you're getting away with any more of this--!"

A blinding spotlight snapped on, forming a ring around Malvolio and the two men. Malvolio clicked on his hand microphone and faced the mayor as he spoke.

"Ladies and gentlemen of Durney ... the Malvolio Traveling Thrill Show presents our main attraction ... To you people we dedicate our final act. You have harvested more from the soil of Durney County than you could possibly ever know! "

He shut off the mic and stepped forward to speak privately to Corney Adams and Withers. "It's harvest time, gentlemen. Time to reap what you have sown. You take from the soil, the soil expects payment back. And there is more than one kind of fertilizer, my friends."

The arena's floor heaved and swelled, buckling and blistering beneath the stands. Inside the tent, the earth spit dusty brown dirt like an oil geyser.

"It's a dirty business, gentlemen, but as they say, somebody's got to do it..."

The ground split open, a festering wound that oozed green stalks of corn like pulsating tumors pushing through the brown earth. Massive weed-like stalks in fast-forward motion rose and twisted through the stands, encircling those who sat in them, dragging them thumping and screaming down the long rows of seats to the soft dirt in the center arena.

Ambrose Malvolio stepped between Corney Adams and Nathaniel Withers. His grinning face, suddenly pocked and blistered, turned a jaundiced yellow. Grasping each man by the neck, he pulled them kicking like wicked children to the center ring, and dropping them there with the others in the dirt. He hovered over them. He still smiled, but where there had been teeth Adams saw there were now only kernels of corn.

The arms inside his long ringmaster's coat suddenly fell limp and his sleeves hung loose at his side. Great leafy stalks pushed their way through his chest, popping the buttons from his shirt and shredding his clothing. What remained of him fell laughing upon Withers first, and Malvolio's face fragmented like a grotesque jigsaw. The laughing did not stop even when the face no longer was there.

"A real barn burner, gentlemen! A show stopper to end all show stoppers!" he shouted. His voice now came from a large green stalk that still wore the silk top hat.

Malvolio approached Adams next, falling upon him like a deranged lover while particles of the ringmaster's shredded face found their way into Adams' mouth. Gagging on the fleshy debris lodged in his throat, the old farmer realized what it was. Something that tasted so familiar, so damned familiar...

Sweet corn.

From somewhere high above, a spotlight filled the tent with glaring light. Corney Adams forced himself to look up. The entire top portion of the canvas had opened, and through the tent flaps the dazzling harvest moon shone through. The Malvolio Thrill Show performers stepped into its shimmering light ... the two ugly little jugglers, golden-haired Selena, the Hieronymus couple still oozing fluid from every pore, even the kids who had sold Withers the corn dogs and beer.

They each bowed. Corn spilled from their mouths.

A moment later, undulating stalks stood where they had.

Something tugged at Corney's feet. The soil loosened beneath him like a thin fabric about to give way. His foot became tangled in vine-like ropes that had crept along the dirt floor of the arena, pulling him down to a soil-filled undertow below. He looked at Nathaniel and knew he had read the man's mind as he sank neck-deep into the soil. A fistful of soft dirt filled his mouth. It packed itself under his lids, burning his eyes, and he remembered. He remembered well even as the soil swallowed him.

Ambrose Malvolio had said it himself.

It was harvest time.

***

Josephine Adams waited up past midnight for her husband. Sleep would not come easy and she chose not to even try.

Well, she could take a little upset like tonight; considering the harvest Corney and his hands had just hauled to market. Of course, maybe she deserved a little credit for that herself.

That old prayer book Ambrose Malvolio had sold her last winter had sure done the trick. The man had come selling those books door to door, and he had explained to her all about the 'corn psalm' she ought to recite over the field.

Growth to the stalks that come from below. Growth to the earth from whence they come. Growth to all things beneath the soil. May they rise to the kingdom above ...

It was more like a chant than a psalm, but with Malvolio's prayer book in her hand Josephine had recited it all spring, and every word of it had proved true. The corn on those eight acres had grown like a weed.

Naturally, Josephine could not tell her husband about any of that, considering what she had paid Malvolio for that book. She felt mighty surprised when Ambrose Malvolio returned to town to pitch that traveling road show of his, and even more surprised when he picked Corney to do business with. Fortunately, the man had kept his little commercial transaction with her a secret from her husband.

She looked at the outer field from her kitchen window. It sure didn't sound like any thrill show was going on anywhere nearby. She wondered why the tent pitched across Corney's land had gone so quiet. Considering what she had seen under that canvas earlier, maybe she didn't really want to know.

"Shoulda figured somethin' was wrong when 'Vira didn't see those clowns," she told herself. She understood Corney had to stay at that awful show, but there was no reason that she had to without being hog-tied. And, if truth be told, that Ambrose Malvolio made her feel damned antsy.

Josephine looked through the kitchen window across the moonlit inner cornfield toward the huge tent. For a moment, the realization did not register. She had been so used to hearing the rows of corn stalks rustling like crunched paper out there in the field, it was as if they were not there.

But they were out there, taller than they had ever grown before, stalks that she had seen cut down for harvest all week. They were out there, all right, out there in the field by the hundreds yielding to the warm breeze in the great spotlight of the full moon. Josephine had to rub her eyes, certain the stalks would be gone when she looked again.

She looked again. The stalks remained.

That prayer book may have worked too good, she thought.

A knock on the door. More of a thump than a knock, really. Had her husband forgotten his key again? No matter. He would explain what in blazes was happening out there in the corn field tonight.

Josephine went to the door.

"Corney? Is that you?"

Scorned
Timothy McGivney

1. Hell Hath No Fury…
Sunday June 30th, 1995 5:54am

Kevin opened his eyes and squinted: 5:54am. Good morning, Sunshine. He tapped the alarm before it had a chance to go off and sat up. The alarm was a necessary precaution, allowing him to sleep peacefully, confidently. But he always woke up without it—vigil and alert. A man on a mission. Raising arms above head, Kevin inhaled deeply, then groaned into a stretch, the steady hum of the air conditioner drawing his attention. Perturbed, he jumped from the bed and tiptoed across the cool parquet flooring to turn it off. Absolute silence was vital.

This was it. This would be the last time. The last pair. But Kevin knew it was a lie. He couldn't help himself. They were only good for a month, maybe? At best.

Kevin touched the front door with both hands, one wrapping around the door knob, the other resting higher, just below his jaw and pressed temple against door. Eyes shut, he concentrated on the silence, willing his ears to pick up on that one special sound, the tantalizing signal that would tell him the time had come—that the coast was clear for takeoff. Heart hammering, Kevin held his breath and waited…

…there…yep, there it was…faint, but gradually growing stronger…the sweet, swooshing, smacking, clickety-clacking sound that could only be made by a pair of flip flops. The sound gave him an instant hard on, and he reached down to squeeze his tiny dick, the whole of it no bigger than a baby's pacifier. Wait for it. The flip flopping acoustics faded into the distance as Kevin cocked his ear, straining...

...there...the muffled sound of a door closing caused a Pavlovian reflex in Kevin's wrist, a quick flick of it unlocking the front door. And we're off.

Driven by a sick compulsion beyond his control, Kevin moved with a cat-like grace down the open hallway of his condominium complex, the warm tile slick with summer rain. He heard the washing machine before he saw it and knew every last second was precious. Move, damn it. Careful not to slip, he tiptoed down the stairs, taking them two at a time. Tiptoeing was for Sundays. And Sundays were laundry days. Kevin lived for laundry days.

At the bottom of the stairs waited a makeshift laundry room, one washing machine and a dryer crammed into an outdoor closet. Almost there. With bated breath, he reached for the lid of the washing machine and flipped it open. Praise Jesus. Right on top sat an unsoaked pair of baby blue boxers. Kevin scooped them up and brought them straight to his face, inhaling sharply, deeply, the fresh, potent scent of man juice—a blissful concoction of semen and piss. Eyes rolling back into his skull, Kevin let out a groan of ecstasy and inhaled once again, noting the intoxicating, familiar musk of the boxer's owner. It was especially strong today and Kevin lifted the boxers away from his face, holding them up for inspection. Crusty jizz stains were more than prevalent. He must have shot directly on them! Kevin let out a squeal of delight and brought the boxers to his open mouth, tongue and lips eager for a quick taste.

"What the fuck are you doing?"

Kevin froze. Oh, shit. His back was to whoever had caught him, but he knew that voice, knew it with the familiarity of the boxers in his mouth. It was their owner, the Italian God himself, Franco Lombardi. Sheer terror wiped all thought process from Kevin's mind as he slowly turned his head in Lombardi's direction, eyes locking with the smoldering beast. At six-foot-four and two hundred twenty-five pounds, Lombardi had the giant, hairy physique of a hard-working lumberjack. "Answer me, you sick fuck."

He opened his mouth to speak, but no legible words would come. He couldn't breathe, couldn't move, but was keenly aware that the boxers were hanging from his blubbering mouth. Light-headed, Kevin's vision turned fuzzy; he could tell Lombardi was only wearing boxers—and the two military dog tags he always wore around his neck—but otherwise, he was at the mercy of Lombardi's furious gaze.

Lombardi tossed something into the washing machine and stepped back. "Close the fucking lid and never touch my shit again."

Kevin managed to pull the boxers from his lips and extended them forward, almost as a peace offering. Lombardi winced and the fury in his eyes momentarily turned to pity before settling on disgust. "Keep 'em." He turned around and started up the stairs. "You pathetic fucking troll."

Kevin watched Lombardi's beefy calves ascend the stairs, flip flops clickety-clacking with each step. He blinked once and breath returned to his lungs in a sudden rush, as if he'd been brought back from the other side. Drained of all energy, he turned toward the washing machine and flipped the lid down. That's when he noticed the boxers clenched in one fist and his hand began to shake, nerves of fear and humiliation giving way to anger. Who the hell does he think he is? A dark, spiteful rage poured over Kevin like black tar from a boiling cauldron.

"You'll pay for this," he whispered, nostrils flaring.

Franco Lombardi.

Kevin open his clenched fist and stared down at the dirty boxers. He felt nothing, no stirring of excitement, no forbidden cumlust. Nothing but contempt. He tossed them in the garbage and took to the stairs, no need for tiptoeing, not ever again.

2. The Feminine Mystique
Friday February 3rd, 1995 5:23pm

"We have to have each other's backs. That's what she meant. On the edge of each other's battles. We have to stand up for all our sisters, Lauren. We can't pick and choose."

Here we go again. Leah wanted to roll her eyes, but sighed heavily instead. Sitting in the middle of the back seat, she had a clear view through the front windshield of the lonely highway they traveled, headlights barely penetrating the vast darkness of the desert. They thought she was listening to her CD Walkman, but it was just a ruse to stay out of the conversation. She was so sick of debating and dissecting the essays and poems of radical lesbian feminists she could vomit. One more semester and she'd be a free bird—a college graduate with a worthless degree in Women's Studies. Yippe-ki-yay!

Was it her fault nothing interested her besides comic books? Music maybe, but she was tone deaf and didn't have the discipline to learn an instrument. And horses. She did like horses, which was partly why she agreed to this trip. And she really was trying to make an effort to be more social and make genuine connections with people, but it was hard. She had zero self-esteem and no friends. No true friends.

She was also cursed with eczema. Majorly cursed. As camouflage, Leah always wore long sleeves and pants, no matter the weather. It helped with the itching, too, which she learned to control over the years. But there was no masking the fact that, naked, she looked like a walking pathogen. Countless dry, red, scaly patches covered her entire body; oval in shape—like a pressed penny—they showed mercy only to the soles of her feet, the palms of her hands, buttocks and genitalia.

Her face was spared from eczema as well, but acute acne took its place—forehead and cheeks an oily battleground of moist white heads and hard, stubborn boils.

Being slightly overweight and of Filipino descent didn't help her social game either. Leah knew the world was made for Barbies and Kens, which was why she was so taken aback when Kate and Lauren befriended her. Lauren, a cheerful, pink-frosted lipstick lesbian with long, pin-straight hair and her best friend, Kate, militant in personality and piercings, but a softie at heart; they both were a different kind of cool. Perfect models for a Queer Barbie line? Leah grinned at the idea. She didn't care that they were gay; they were cool, the closest she'd ever felt to being cool, too, and she wanted them to like her, even if she wasn't so sure she liked them herself. They exuded such a strong sense of self-worth and purpose that it was hard not to say yes to them. She'd been saying yes ever since they first met at a Women's Studies recruitment seminar two years ago, and the rest, as they say, is "herstory."

"And we have arrived. Red Rock Ranch." The Jeep Wrangler began to slow and Kate turned off the highway, onto a wide, dirt road. Leah sat up to get a better look but still couldn't see much, only dirt and the usual desert foliage. "Thanks for coming, guys." Kate turned to Lauren and smiled before looking back at Leah. "You're gonna love—"

Something hit the front of the Jeep, head on, splintering the windshield like cracking ice on a frozen lake. Lauren screamed and Kate slammed on the brakes. "Holy fuck."

Leah's mouth hung open, eyes wide with shock, her facial expression mirroring the other women.

"What was that?" Kate whispered, unbuckling her seat belt as she opened the driver's side door.

"No, wait. Don't go out there," Lauren pleaded, grabbing Kate's forearm.

"I have to see. Let go," she said, pulling away and stepping out of the car.

Lauren turned around and grabbed Leah's hand. "Can you see anything?"

Leah shook her head, trying to pierce through the darkness, the taillights giving off the dimmest of glows. She thought she could see Kate's back, crouching over something.

"We should get out too." Leah pulled away from Lauren's grip and reached down for the flashlight she saw earlier. "Kate's always prepared." She turned it on, shining a strong beam of light on the Jeep's floor.

"I'm scared." Lauren brought her hands to her chin, eyes welling with tears.

"Come on, get out." The stern tone in her voice surprised Leah, but she wasn't the mothering type. Did they hit an animal? A wild coyote, maybe? She unfastened her seatbelt and followed Lauren out the door. It always amazed her how cold the desert could get after the sun went down and tonight was as crisp and cold as ever, with overcast skies masking the stars and allowing for only a sliver of moon.

"Wait." Lauren grabbed Leah by the bicep and pulled her close. It felt strange to be taking the lead with Lauren, but not entirely unnatural. With flashlight in hand, she spotted Kate twenty feet behind the Jeep. Oh, no.

She was standing over a body. We hit someone.

"He's dead." She said it without looking at them, head bowed.

Leah pointed the flashlight at the man on the ground, starting at his knees and moving up. He lay on his back, in a Y formation—arms spread wide above him, legs pressed together. She'd never seen a dead body before and hesitated at his face, unsure if she wanted to see it, but stepped closer, shining the light dead on. Leah gasped. A Filipino man. His eyes were open but vacant and stared indifferently into the flashlight's beam, a thin trail of blood glistening from nostril to lip. He was dressed for a day in the sun, a tank top and cut-off jeans.

"I don't recognize him. Maybe he works for my Uncle?"

"We have to call the police." Kate nodded in agreement and reached down, lifting up the body by the ankles.

"What are you doing? Don't touch him!" Lauren shouted.

"Can you grab him by the arms?" Kate was looking at Leah, who stared blankly back, but only for a second, before passing the flashlight to Lauren, who took it meekly, cheeks stained with mascara.

What would he feel like? Would he still be warm?

"What was that?" whispered Lauren, her stance frozen and alert, neck craned, like a deer in the woods. Leah and Kate turned toward the Jeep, in the direction Lauren was looking.

"Help!" someone screamed, the terror in their plea causing the hairs to rise on the back of Leah's neck. It sounded close. Kate dropped the body and headed toward the Jeep.

"Give me it," Leah grabbed the flashlight from a trembling Lauren and followed Kate, coming up behind her in front of the Jeep.

"Hello?" Kate yelled, stepping up past the glare of the headlights. "I can't see anything, damn it." Leah joined her, aiming the flashlight straight ahead, its beam suddenly hitting the figure of a running man.

"Get in the car! Get in the car!" he shouted, bony chicken legs sprinting at full force. Leah could see him clearly now—a platinum blond, scrawny little man in a sequined, fuchsia pink tank top, his perspiring, overly tanned face an animation of terror.

"What's wrong?" Kate asked, stepping closer.

"Go back! Get in the—" A garbled yelp of surprise erupted from the man's mouth and his neck snapped violently back as his arms swung out behind him, back arching impossibly forward, like he'd been hit by an invisible locomotive. Leah heard herself gasp and shut her eyes, just missing the sight of the man belly flopping onto the ground right in front of them, landing with a definitive thud.

And then came the screaming.

Leah opened her eyes expecting to see a hysterical Lauren, but it was Kate who was screaming. Kate?

No, not just Kate, Lauren too, the two of them now huddled in a desperate embrace, Lauren pointing to the man on the ground.

Leah slowly looked downward and saw what she had failed to see before—the head of an ax, and its long wooden handle—sticking straight out of the dead man's back.

Leah joined her sisters and screamed.

3. Ribbit
Friday February 3rd, 1995 5:23pm

The hay was stacked into steps, eight bundles high. The huntsman stared up, to the very top, and smiled at his prey. Like it had a chance.

Through wide-set, red-rimmed black orbs the size of eggs, the prey stared back defiantly. Squatting like a puffed-up Buddha, its green, spindly legs splayed wide, four-pronged orange hands caressing its bloated, freckled belly. This one was multi-colored in a rainbow of neon hues. It was still wet from fleeing the hot springs, water dripping from its white, double chin. It was a frog.

A human-sized, six-foot frog.

Was this a test? Another trial from the Gods? Orion didn't know, but he was prepared for anything and had felled most of the giant amphibians all at once, slaughtering half a dozen congregating by the pit of fire. Plotting. This one was part of a different group—a copulating triad mating in the springs, the other two now an eviscerated orgy of floating carcass.

The demon frog opened its mouth and emitted a high pierced shriek, its pink tongue protruding with a shrill battle cry. Not to be outdone, Orion beat one fist onto his massive chest and roared back. The creature shrieked again and then leaped in a zig-zag fashion down the bales of hay before springing outwards and up, straight at Orion in a feeble attempt to clear him completely. Death to you now.

Orion had come across Poseidon's trident resting at the entrance to the barn, and he wielded it now with the ease of a warrior well trained, piercing the unnatural fiend's belly in one swift, upward motion, the tips of the three-pronged spear jutting out from its back in an explosion of showering frog-innards. He grimaced at the fresh rankness, but watched his prey struggle against the throes of death without judgement, its legs and arms thrashing valiantly, like it could swim, or even fly away. Enough.

Tossing the trident straight up into the air, Orion flipped the palm of his hand over and caught it between thumb and forefinger and with the grace of an Olympian athlete hurled it like a javelin, carrying the skewered frog back the way it had just jumped, the three prongs of steel pinning it to the top of the haystack.

Gratitude for your trident, father. Orion would return for it later. The kills were of little challenge and he would use his hands to extinguish the last two demon frogs. Smaller than the others, they were the first to flee, abandoning their army when he'd first attacked. Orion had no doubt they were cowering behind a rock somewhere, or perhaps under a vehicle.

Exiting the barn, he gradually made his way across the flat, desert ground, bare feet plodding through dirt, beginning to drag...

...the night seemed to turn in on him suddenly and he swayed forward even as he felt himself being pulled back and under, a white wave of excruciating pain pounding into the back of his skull, threatening to bring him to his knees. Teeth clenched, he growled through it and steadied himself. Had Hades cursed him from the underworld? Drenched in sweat, he fought to steady his breath, chiseled torso glistening, heaving in exertion. A loud clanking sound pulled him from his torment and he looked up, toward where the sound originated—a row of ten double parked cars.

"Ribbit."

Foolish beast. Wiping sweat from furrowed brow, Orion narrowed his eyes and moved toward the vehicles;

the sound came from beneath a black Chevrolet C/K pickup 2500 series, fully loaded.

Orion faltered, unsure of himself.

The truck seemed familiar somehow.

He reached out his hand to touch it, but stopped short and bent over instead, peering underneath. Two obsidian black globes lined in yellow stared back at him. Gotcha! He snatched the demon frog by a skinny green arm and yanked it out into the open where it thrashed and shrieked in vain, its gangly legs kicking at Orion's thighs as he lifted it off the ground, holding it out at arm's length.

Pathetic. He eyed it with disdain. This was a poor example of a demon frog. At five feet, it was the shortest yet, and sported a weak armor, the sheer, protective covering highlighting its protruding belly.

From his peripheral vision, Orion saw the second demon frog leap up from the bed of the truck.

It held an ax.

Releasing his flailing captive, Orion turned to meet the armed enemy head on and was surprised to see the ax already swinging his way, the demon frog's eight-pronged grip steady and sure. If Orion was at full capacity, he would have easily dodged the strike, but he was slow and faltered, the ax cutting into his shoulder blade, half an inch deep. The demon frog shrieked triumphantly, letting go of the ax and leaping over the top of the truck and onto the hood, before escaping into the night.

Cursing the Gods, Orion pulled the ax from his shoulder, releasing a stream of warm blood. The cascading rivulet bathed his bicep and forearm in a coat of crimson red, the sight of it igniting a murderous rage. Death to the enemy. With ax in fist, he took off at a trot, following in the direction the demon frogs had fled, letting the cool evening air guide his way along the dark road, oxygen filling his lungs, reenergizing him, until…

…a glint of color…of movement, appearing in the distance: the pink, shining armor of the demon frog who had drawn first blood. Orion's heart began to quicken in anticipation of the kill. With the strength of all the Gods behind him, he raised the ax up high and stopped in mid-stride, torso torquing forward, the full weight of his body moving into the launching of the weapon.

Artemis guide my aim.

And he released it, watching blade and handle whiz round in rapid succession, hurtling into the night's black void. A faint cry could be heard in the distance, and Orion smirked in just acknowledgment that he'd hit his prey, smug satisfaction cut off by a cacophony of hysterical shrieks. By the Gods, what now?

Hazy beams of light appeared on the desert's path and he stopped abruptly, studying the possible new threat. Headlights. Crouching close to the desert floor, he moved cautiously forward, eyes widening at what he saw—three demon frogs congregating around their fallen comrade—Orion's ax protruding from his target's back. The trio of demon frogs were unarmed and… and different from the ones that had come before…these ones were female.

Demon she-frogs.

4. Intersection
Friday February 3rd, 1995 5:40pm

Get in the car. Get in the car. The dead man's words kept repeating in Leah's head and she obeyed them without another thought, rushing back to the Jeep as Lauren and Kate piled in from the other side.

"What's wrong?" Leah asked. Why weren't they moving? She'd taken the shotgun position and looked over at Kate in concern. The car was running but Kate sat there, hands on the wheel, immobilized, staring straight ahead. Leah followed her gaze out the front windshield and gasped. A naked man, covered in bright red blood stood over the dead man on the ground, his face obscured by a wet mop of tangled curls. He appeared to be looking down at the body, studying it.

The mysterious stranger was built like a bodybuilder, the Jeep's headlights highlighting the defined musculature of his body, and Leah couldn't help but look past the surreal, blood-soaked like effigy that stood before them, to the monstrous erection jutting out from the man's pelvis. She'd never seen a penis in person before and, even from a distance, was startled by its foreign virility. Untouched by the grisly streaks that painted his body, the thick appendage seemed to take on a life of its own, throbbing rhythmically against the man's bloody torso.

He suddenly bent over, breaking Leah's hypnotic gaze, and then stood back up, wrenching the ax from the dead man's back.

Oh my God. Lauren screamed from the backseat and Leah jumped, cupping hands to ears, but never once taking her eyes off the man on the road, who now ran at them, in a savage, dead sprint.

***

Lauren's scream snapped Kate into action and she gunned the Jeep, her only intention to get away, but the mad man was headed straight toward them like something out of a crazed Conan the Barbarian film, and her gut told her to hit him...and Kate always followed her gut. You got this, girl.

Shifting into third, Kate shouted, "Hold on!" and braced for impact, ramming the Jeep right into the ax wielding psychopath, the steely blue of his eyes bulging out of his blood mask and locking with hers for a split second before he smashed into the windshield, barreling over it and out of sight.

The front, and then back wheels bounced over what felt sort of like a speed bump, but Kate knew it was the body of the man who had warned them to run, and Lauren screamed again, twice, as if to emphasize this fact. Let her scream. Kate though, was through with screaming. She was going to get them all out of here alive. No more victims. She glanced in the rearview mirror and shifted into fourth. "Do you see anything?"

"Can you see, Lauren?" Leah asked, turning in her seat. "Lauren!"

"Don't make me, don't make me look."

"Come on, Lauren." Leah started squirming her way into the back, trying to force Lauren out of the fetal position.

Kate looked in the review mirror again and her blood turned cold.

***

BFGoodrich.

The bold white letters curved around the spare tire and Orion stared at them as he found his bearings. Motionless and secure, with cheek resting against hard rubber, Orion steadied his breathing as he held his pelvis against the metal rim, inner thighs and forearms squeezing the outer edges of the tire, allowing for firm purchase.

He still held the ax. And it was time to use it.

Hoisting himself upwards, Orion straddled the tire with ease, the wind freeing a blood caked mat of hair from across his face. He peered through the back window and spotted his next kill, a demon she-frog cowering within. A weak, spineless species.

With the balls of his bare feet planted firmly on the back bumper, Orion stood up, heedful to keep his body pressed to the outer shell of the Jeep, which appeared to be gaining in speed. Gripping the roll bar at the roof's corner edge with one hand, he raised the ax with the other and swung downward, the blade easily slicing through the Jeep's vinyl covering and into the bottom of the backseat, narrowly missing the demon she-frog's skull. He heard it shriek and nearly lost his balance, toppling into the vehicle, but he steadied himself and cursed the Gods for the second time that night as he yanked the ax free and swung it back upwards...

***

...Leah could only watch in horror as the ax swung down a second time, and then a third and fourth, each time making direct contact with Lauren's head. The second strike had killed her instantly and Leah found the subsequent blows of overkill to be perplexing. Did he really have to keep killing her? Mouth agape, she faced the senseless carnage head on, knees pushed into the bottom edge of her seat, her back pinned against the Jeep's console, with one elbow on the dashboard and the palm of her hand swiping at the windshield, as if she could phase through it, like her favorite of the X-men, Kitty Pryde. What would Kitty do? Would she sit here and watch a friend get butchered? Beautiful, sun-kissed Lauren, with her button nose and Colgate smile, now obliterated beyond recognition.

The monster dropped the ax and smiled at Leah; his teeth gleamed pink from blood splatter and his maniacal eyes promised she was next. No, please, no. She shook her head and cried out in revulsion as his fist pushed down into the center of Lauren's face—bone and cartilage collapsing inward like an overworked pumpkin on Halloween. He then thrust his fist upwards, lifting her into a sitting position and flinging her up and out through the top of the Jeep, like a defective blow up doll. She'd seen enough. She knew what Kitty would do. Kitty would phase away, live to fight another day.

Without another thought, Leah lunged for the door handle and pushed it open, falling forward and into the night.

***

Kate threw the stick in neutral and slammed on the brakes, chancing a quick peek behind as she opened the door and jumped out, frantically turning around and back-stepping away. Where was he? Where was that motherfucker? Panting rapidly, she stood facing the driver's side of the Jeep, eyeing the scope of it, but seeing nothing, no one.

"Leah?" she whispered, hoping for a reply.

Dead silence.

Ruby. She needed to get Ruby. Kate eyed the back of the Jeep, where she kept her shoulder bag and swallowed nervously, too scared to move. What if he was hiding on the other side? She looked to her right, out into the pitch-blackness of the desert and saw nothing, then to her left, where she could see the barn, and next to it, the backside of her Uncle's million-dollar ranch. It was built in the adobe Pueblo style, with the typical flat roofs and thick, rounded walls made of sunbaked mud. As a kid, she always called it the Play-Doh house. It looked empty. No lights shined from within, but the swimming pool was lit and the fire pit ablaze, the smell of BBQ in the air... And what was up with all the cars lined along the driveway? Was her Uncle throwing a party? He hadn't mentioned anything to her. Maybe he forgot they were coming? But where was everyone?

She looked back at the Jeep, anxiously clenching her fingers. Move your ass, girl. "Go!" she shouted, forcing herself to the Jeep, where she pushed down the top of the front seat and snatched her shoulder bag from the back floor. It was wet and sticky, and she tried not to think of Lauren as she snapped it open, revealing the black leather satchel's true purpose: to conceal Ruby, her beloved .38 Smith and Wesson Special. The revolver was small-framed and easy to handle, and she carried it with her everywhere, having purchased it after becoming another rape statistic. Kate always kept it loaded and sighed in relief as she cocked the gun and smoothly pulled the trigger, firing into the sky. "Uncle Mel, it's Kate! Are you here?" Holding the gun out in front of her, she slowly made her way around the Jeep, making sure to clear herself from all sides as she vigilantly moved toward the back patio. "Somebody call 911. It's an emergency."

Please help me.

***

Orion heard the thunderous boom and stopped momentarily, wondering if the Gods were calling him home. But then the demon she-frog shrieked and he knew it was most likely her doing. Crafty creatures. He'd slightly underestimated this unnatural species and could see now they were more capable than previously thought. Except for the demon she-frog before him... it was wounded, a true and easy prey. When it had leaped from the moving vehicle, he was swift to follow, slightly amused at its feeble attempt to outrun him. The Gods were no doubt delighted as well.

Headed for the springs now, one of its thin, gangly frog legs dragged brokenly behind it. Orion would relish an easy kill and slowed his pace, deciding to play with it a little, for sport—make a wish, and snap it in two.

***

Leah wanted to shout back at Kate, to let her know where she was, but she was too afraid. The monster was behind her, she could feel it; he was stalking her, hunting...

And her leg was all messed up. She was sure her ankle was broken. It hurt so bad. Pure adrenalin must have fueled her escape from the Jeep, but she could no longer run. Hopping along on one foot was all she could manage, her arms propelling her forward with each movement, pumping circles in the air like a wounded bird, trapped on the ground.

She'd made it to the pool's edge; kidney shaped, it glowed an eerie aquamarine. A foulness permeated the air and she wrinkled her nose in disgust. It smelled of shit and piss and blood... of death...

The bubbling sounds of Jacuzzi jets drew her attention upwards and she looked out across the pool, but promptly squeezed her eyes shut and jerked her head, brain refusing to register the atrocity she barely glimpsed.

HIDE.

Overcome with a renewed sense of urgency, Leah hopped toward what looked like a bunch of photography equipment. A photo shoot? Surrounded by several soft light boxes and photo umbrellas was a rustic, porcelain bathtub, a white backdrop perched behind it. Leah hopped over to the muslin sheet and struggled to get around it. Was it see-through? She wasn't sure, but it would have to do. Suddenly cold, she began to shiver, the stench of urine assaulting her senses. Did she wet herself? Teeth chattering, she clutched her chest and tried not to cry.

Why did she say yes to them? She could have been in her dorm right now, reading the latest batch of comics, without a care in the world. This is what she got for trying to be a social butterfly.

***

A puff of air made a popping noise from beneath Kate's sneaker and she jumped, stepping off of something soft and squishy—a bag of marshmallows. Pull it together, girl. Annoyed, she kicked the bag down a travertine stoned path that she knew would first lead her to the fire pit and then to the pool area and on into the house, where hopefully, she could find Uncle Mel, or a phone at least.

She came across a box of graham crackers next, followed by king-sized chocolate bars, all strewn along the path, culminating in an array of eating utensils and plastic cups, all capsized at the foot of an overturned table. Not a good sign. Moving closer to the fire pit, she noticed a slickness to the stone tiles, her sneakers sticking with each step.

Blood.

And she knew it to be true without even glancing down, for all the slaughter lay before her—an abattoir of headless corpses. Holy hell. Discarded around the fire pit, some bodies still sat in the chairs from which their heads were first severed, others had fallen to the ground, redwashing the stone patio in buckets of blood.

No heads. Kate counted seven headless bodies, but no heads. Uncle Mel? Was he amongst the dead? She couldn't tell. She didn't want to know. The fire sizzled and crackled and her eyes were drawn to its gleaming flames. The pit itself was a circular wall of stones, four courses high and large enough to sit on, and what she'd failed to notice before, she clearly saw now—the decapitated heads—roasting within. Charred black and smoldering, they were stacked closely together, in a pyramid fashion. Human BBQ.

Kate wretched and turned her back to the ungodly sight, the sounds of splashing water drawing her attention toward the pool, which appeared to be empty, but then a gut curdling screamed pierced the night. Leah.

***

It tried to leap away but Orion grabbed the demon she-frog's thick boiled neck with one hand and slammed her into the chamber trough, holding her under the dark liquid waste as it thrashed and kicked, its orange-pronged fingers slapping feebly at his arm. Drowning was too merciful. He lifted it up and released his grip.

***

Coughing uncontrollably, Leah grabbed her throat and struggled for breath, her eyes and throat on fire. Mama! She couldn't see a thing, her eyes and nose burned with ammonia, and a saltiness she somehow knew to be urine dripped from her open mouth. She was immersed in a tub of urine.

***

You're mine now, motherfucker. Kate pulled the trigger and watched the psychopath's ear explode from the side of his head in a flume of red. Fuck. She aimed for his head again and missed, the bullet tearing through a sheet-like background, which he'd already managed to throw at her, the squared backdrop flying at her like an out of control, over-sized kite. She tried to duck as it smacked into her, firing blindly into it once, regretting the shot instantly. What if she hit Leah?

All at once, two giant hands wrapped around her throat and she fired at the killer's face, the bullet only grazing a cheek. She missed again? Unbelievable. With an unnatural ease, he lifted her from the ground and, despite herself, Kate dropped the gun, the constriction around her neck unbearable. Suffocating, she clawed at his face, her feet kicking air with the frantic will to survive. Stick thumbs in eye sockets. The self-defense tactic flashed through her mind as a ringing sound began to consume her... why couldn't women be as strong as m—

***

Orion felt the creature's neck break between his fists and dropped it to the ground. One more... there was just one more... one more thing to do...

The side of his head suddenly burned raw with a pain he never knew possible and he screamed out in agony, his voice lost to him in a soundless, vacuous void. What was happening? Where was he? Taking a slight step backwards, he looked up into the night, an overwhelming feeling of confusion enveloping him. The stars were dim and scarce and far away, and he felt small and alone. Abandoned. Looking down at his naked body covered in blood, he began to tremble. Was he alive?

Panic-stricken, he wheeled around, almost bumping into a girl. She was soaking wet and holding a gun. He looked at her quizzically.

"Who am I?"

The girl pressed the muzzle of the gun to his chest and pulled the trigger.

***

Leah stood naked between the two bodies, a piece of overturned photo equipment shining a harsh spotlight across them. Kate looked as if she were asleep, but Leah knew she was dead. Everyone was dead.

"And all because of you." She looked down at the monster with venom and spat in his face. She had watched him bleed to death as he cried like a little boy and begged for her help. She showed no mercy.

What's your name, monster? Crouching beside him, she picked up one of the dog tags knotted around his neck and flipped it over. The oblong-shaped metal was light and warm and stained with blood, she wiped it with her finger, revealing the name: Lombardi Franco L. The name meant nothing to her and she dropped the tag coldly. Standing back up, she rubbed the tips of her thumb and index finger together, making tiny circles with the dead man's blood. "Fuck you. Franco Lombardi."

Turning her back to him, Leah faced the swimming pool. She had always been too embarrassed to wear a swimsuit, forget about skinny-dipping, but she knew her life would never be the same. She was alive.

Taking a deep, cleansing breath, Leah dived head first into the pool.

5. ...Like A Woman Scorned
Friday February 3rd, 1995 5:00pm

Come on, Alvin. You're really going to take a piss now? Beyond exacerbated, Kevin bit his lower lip until he tasted blood; the anticipation was killing him. Hurry up, goddamn it. They had just completed filming Cock of the Gods II: The Trials of Orion, and Kevin couldn't believe that his moment of retribution was about to be fulfilled. If this silly queen would only finish pissing.

On loan from the Piss Play Society, cast and crew alike were encouraged to use the abused tub as a public urinal. It was rusted a dark gold, like someone had sandpapered brown sugar into it. Earlier that day, they had used it in a photo shoot and for a water sports scene, which wasn't exactly Kevin's cup of tea, but he wasn't one to judge, especially here, for he knew his place on the totem pole and fully understood that his acceptance into the world of gay pornography, albeit behind the scenes, was absolutely contingent upon his oral skills...

Poor dental hygiene and a decade lost to cheap Vodka had culminated in Kevin waking up on the side of a curb, covered in bird shit, with the majority of his teeth knocked out. The traumatic event managed to sober him up, and he used the mishap to his advantage, doubling down on his greatest gift. Blessed with no gag reflex, Kevin could easily take a 10x6 penis to the base without even wincing, and harnessing the talent wisely, soon built a name for himself within the porn industry—his toothless, gummer blow jobs becoming legend. From blackout drunk to fluffer of the year, everyone wanted to fill Kevin's plush velvet throat—everyone but Franco Lombardi.

Up until a year ago, Kevin hadn't seen much of Lombardi. At least not in person. He had, however, been spanking the monkey to his films for years. Building muscle and losing fat, Lombardi had sculpted his body into Herculean proportions, growing a long, wild mane to match. And with an inflated ego the size of his mammoth dick, it came as no surprise to Kevin that Lombardi felt no need to use a porn alias. Everyone in the gay community knew his name. He'd become, without question, the biggest sensation in porn.

Franco Lombardi.

Franco Lombardi was all Kevin had thought about for the past ten years. Whether he was busting a nut to one of his films or reliving the harrowing experience of being caught sniffing Lombardi's underwear, the love hate obsession had turned all consuming, eventually culminating in Kevin weaseling himself into a fluffer position for HardAss Productions, Lombardi being one of their featured, exclusive stars. But his plan had backfired. When on set, Kevin wasn't allowed to speak or even make eye contact with Lombardi. Being able to watch him from a distance was better than nothing, though. And, of course, he was grateful for all the manly meat he got to nurse in-between takes, but no one measured up to Lombardi. Literally.

Did he want to have sex with him, murder him? Take him out, like Sharon Stone in Basic Instinct? Kevin honestly didn't know. It was Alvin who had first suggested putting a curse on him. She had this witch doctor of an aunt, a mangkukulam, who practiced kulam, a form of black magic. Kevin didn't believe in the supernatural, but he agreed to visit her, if only for a cheap thrill, and while he may have left with nothing but a rag doll full of pins, the voodoo session had rekindled the bitter flames of resentment trapped within his cold, black heart.

Cracking his knuckles, Kevin looked out across the patio apprehensively, eyes furtively darting from the threesome forming in the hot tub, to Lombardi holding court by the fire pit, and back to Alvin. There she was, finally.

Finished relieving herself, Alvin strutted down the length of the pool, like she was showing off her hideous Daisy Dukes on a runway in Milan.

"I really like that tank top." Kevin ignored the compliment.

"Did you give it to him? Did he drink it?"

"Every last drop. Can you make me one of these?" Alvin touched the hot pink sequins on Kevin's tank top and he scowled at her, swatting her hand away.

"He didn't complain about the taste?"

Alvin shook her head. "Chugged it like always."

After every wrap, Lombardi drank a fruit smoothie loaded with natural supplements that supposedly not only sweetened and whitened his load, but enhanced the powerful multi-cum shots he was so famous for. It was Alvin's job to make the smoothie, but today, Kevin helped too. "Maybe this was a mistake. What if he freaks out?"

"That's exactly the point." Kevin squinted his eyes and frowned. The ranch handler they had rented the property from had joined Lombardi's posse and was showing him some fancy Samurai sword. The old perv had been drooling over the actors all day and was laughing with them now, like he was one of them. We'll see who gets the last laugh.

Kevin had spiked Lombardi's smoothie with more than a few drops of liquid PCP. Alvin's cousin said the drug worked fast, but Lombardi looked unaffected. Still eating up all the attention, he now proudly posed with the sword, his thick, spent dick swinging freely between his thighs.

"And we're going to need more Bull Frog for tomorrow's shoot. We're almost out and you know how Franco gets if…"

Kevin drowned out the incessant chatter. Shut up, bitch. The fireworks were about to start and he had front row seats. Maybe he'd make a S'more? This was going to be epic. Franco Lombardi was going to lose his fucking mind.

Unfunnytale
-
Pigtails and Ponytails
Brandy Delight

Mud pies and golden straw pigtails,
flip flops and sundresses,
are summertime innocence.
A vacation in imagination insanity,
interrupted by a word through a wooden fence.
"Hello…"
A simple greeting from a stranger,
the little girl paused and listened.
"Hello little one…Do you like ponies?"
Wiping her muddy hands
on her floral smock,
she approached the fence,
yet unable to see.
"I had a pony once. I called him Brownie.
I liked to brush his mane and tail."
"Well," the old lady replied,
"I have two ponies. Would you like to see them?"
The little girl did want to see them,
so very much,
but she was sure Mama
and Her Ever Watchful Sister
would say "Nay!" to her inquiry.
"I have to go now."
The little girl skipped away.
flippity flop…flippity flop….

The following day…
The little girl waited by the fence
hoping the old lady would appear.
She picked honeysuckles from the vine

and sipped the nectar from each delicate stem.
"Hello little one,"
the voice bellowed through wooden slats.
Just then the Ever Watchful Sister
Joined in the strange gathering.
"Who goes there?" the sister demanded!
"Oh hello," the old lady replied friendly.
"I have some ponies in need of grooming.
You may ride them too if you wish."
"Your offer is thoughtful and kind,
But we must respectfully decline.
I am doubtful Mama would allow
Just such a visit." big sister responded.
Twirling her pigtails
and kicking at the mud,
the disappointed little girl
heaved and sighed.
Sloppity slop…sloppity slop…

Another day has come and passed.
More conversations with the old lady
through the fence with
The Ever Watchful Sister
always close behind the little girl.
"The ponies' names are Flash and Star.
They are so beautiful!
I do wish you can see them."
The Ever Watchful Sister
Looked down at the sad little girl.
She missed her pony,
as every little girl would.
Mama couldn't afford to feed him
anymore.
"Okay, we can come see the ponies.
But we must be back before the first
Hint of dusk."

With glees of laughter
the two girls skipped away,
hand in hand, step to step,
all the way around the block.
They stopped at the front gate
where the old lady dwells.
The vines and moss covered the house,
making it ominous and uninviting.
Overgrown trees cast gloomy shadows
across the windows and yard.
"Welcome children! Come, Come!
Let me show you the ponies."
She was hunched and grey,
wore a dusty, tattered dress
and pointy black boots.
She led the girls to a small red barn,
nestled behind the old weathered house.
Once inside, it became clear.
There were no ponies here.
No manes, no tails;
just a trap door under some straw
in an empty pony stall.
The old lady pushed the girls
Down the deep, dark hole,
eight feet down they go.
There were no ponies there either.
Clippity clop... clippity clop...

No ponies, only children;
Various ages, races, shapes and sizes.
Fifteen I counted, one young as three.
They huddle in a group,
Vacant and empty looked thee.
A small boy approached
The Ever watchful Sister.
He reached for her hand

in panic struck desperation.
"How long have you all been down here?'
she asked the frightened boy.
"Days, weeks, perhaps months,
Please help before they come again."
"Who is coming?" she asked,
Her ever watchful eyes
turned to ever frightful eyes.
She withdrew her hand in retreat.
No answers came, just silence
and staring and silence some more.
The little girl with the golden pigtails
Curled in a fetal ball on the dirt floor
At her sister's feet, and sobbed.
Sobbity sob…sobbity sob…

An unknown time came and went
when suddenly a ladder dropped
from the hole above.
One after one, two after two,
freaks, weirdoes, perverted injustices
climbed down into the hidden cell.
They were all in grand costume
and hid their shameful faces.
A sick display of improper indecency.
Leather bond and on a leash
A masked man licked at the ball gag
tied in his mouth.
All the while his Mistress,
with large bobbing phallus,
blew lollipop kisses to
all the frightened children.
A well-dressed couple,
in eighteenth century grandeur,
hid their faces behind feathered fans,
as small penis' grew hard under

petticoats and skirts.
Rudolph played Reindeer games
with Smokey the Bear,
stroking and fondling fuzzy coats.
A Catholic Priest scratched at his balls
and fingered his ass,
as he sized up the flock before him.
Two evil dwarf clowns
made obscene balloon animals
and sang and clapped their hands.
Clappity clap… clappity clap…

The old woman appeared
and the auction began.
The smell of fear, urine and sex
filled the hot, moist air.
"Five hundred for the darling with the golden
pigtails!"
Shouts and squeals rose from the crowd.
The children stood frozen and numb.
"She's fresh, untainted, virgin meat!"
The dwarf clowns won the bidding
And paid in large bills
and IOUs for circus favors.
A small pink poodle
danced on its hind legs
around the curious crowd
barking and yipping.
Yippity yap… Yippity yap…

"Nay, take I in place of my little sister!"
demanded the Ever Watchful One.
"You can fuck me little daddy,
while the little mommy watches."
she cooed at them with pouty lips,
squeezing her tits and wiggling her ass.

"I would like it so much,
and I am better than a virgin,
tight as one but experienced."
"You can even beat me,
call me names, just take me
instead of my dear little sister."
she pleaded.
The little clowns grew angry
and the Ever Watchful One
grew restless, spitting in
their little painted faces.
Little clown arms and legs erupted
in a fighting display
kicking and punching.
Slappity slap… Slappity slap…

The dwarf clowns with painted frowns
grabbed the little girl by her pigtail hair,
dragging her across the room.
Screams of laughter and terror rang out.
"We must pass on your offer,
although it was so very sweet of you.
But you are old and all used up.
We have no need for you."
Hate flushed The Ever Watchful Sister's face.
"Fuck you! Fuck You!" she screamed
and lunged at them
with all her might and all her fight.
She knocked them to the floor,
just as they were climbing the ladder.
The little clowns went tumbling and bumbling.
Boppity bop… boppity bop…

The Ever watchful sister swooped up
the little girl with golden hair
and pushed her up the ladder to safety.

Scrambling behind in hurried escape
she managed a breathless command.
"Run little one, do not stop
until you are safe in Mama's apron strings."
When The Ever Watchful Sister
emerged at the top of the ladder,
there stood, in that empty pony stall
the old lady from behind the fence,
golden pigtails in one arm
and a shotgun in the other.
A flash of white, then good night.
Nighty night... nighty night...

Trusting Garry
Jaap Boekestein

"Do you love me?" Louise asks. They are in bed, sweaty, glowing, happy. How long do they know each other now? About six months.

"I love you," Garry answers. He kisses her on the forehead.

"With all your heart?"

"With all my heart," he assures his sweetheart. "You are the love of my life." He isn't lying, she is the joy of his life, his sunshine, his soul mate, the woman he wants to spend the rest of his life with.

"You would die for me?" Louise sounds a little bit surprised, a little bit excited. What is he going to answer? Would he really be willing to die for her? That would be real, true, complete, total love.

"I would die for you," Garry says, meaning every word.

"I love you!" Louise says, and she embraces him. She really does.

#

Would you die for me?

Louise's words bounce back and forth in Garry's head while he drives to work.

"Yes," he says. He meant it last night, he means it now. "Yes."

Yes, he is willing to die for Louise.

If he is strong enough, that is.

#

The usual lunch break chatter. Garry participates on full automatic pilot, but his mind is somewhere else.

Would I be strong enough? If I had to choose, really had to choose, would I die for her?

Garry knows he is willing, now. But those are just words, intentions. If he really, really had to die, would he dare to?

Am I just a braggart with big words and good intentions but nothing else? Do I really have the guts and character to die for Louise, or am I weak, flawed?

People say you can only judge a man's true character in times of great stress.

What if I fail? If I break?

Doubts.

Handle doubts, or they grow into something bigger.

Something darker.

#

Handle doubts?

That is nice self-help crap, but how can you test a life or death situation?

You can't. Not realistically. Unless you start behaving like a psychopath.

Garry isn't a psychopath. He isn't going to put Louise and himself in some sick, weird situation where he has to choose. Psychos are willing to take the risk, Garry isn't. He is a regular guy.

So the doubts stay.

And start to fester.

They turn into fears.

#

Fear does strange things to people. They start to obsess.

It influences the way they think and behave.

Fear can turn regular guys into psychopaths, to some extent.

Anyway, fears can get unhealthy.

You can start to think strange things, to do strange things.

So, handle your fears.

If you can.

And if you can't... No, it is much better you do handle them. Try, at least.

Try as much as you can.

Please.

#

Wednesday night, two more days and it is weekend. Working is fine, not having to work is much better. Garry and Louise are sitting in the living room. He is watching sports, she is busy on her tablet. Just a regular evening.

The fist pounds on the front door, loud and demanding.

"Open up!" shouts a harsh bully-voice. "Open up!"

What...?

Who, what, why?

Again and again the fists pound on the door. The sound is brutal and invasive.

"Open up! We know she is here! Open up!"

Louise jumps up, fear is on her face, in her eyes.

"They have found me!" she whispers urgently. "Don't tell them I am here, or they will kill me."

"Open up!"

Louise takes two steps, kneels down in front of the television, and touches the wall underneath. On the big screen, beautiful young women are singing about the delights of some shower gel. A panel comes lose and reveals a space just big enough for a small woman to hide. Louise is small enough. She slides in and with a last desperate look at Garry, pulls the panel close.

The door flies open, forced by boots and shoulders.

Men in long leather coats burst in. They wear old fashioned hats and round metal framed sunglasses.

They work Garry to the ground, start tearing up the place.

Garry protests, which earns him a kick in the belly.

Kneeling with tears in his eyes, he fights for breath. His arms are held up behind his back, a heavy boot on his shoulder keeps him down. The pain is infuriating.

"Where is she hiding?" a voice asks harshly. Garry can't see the face the voice belongs to, he can't stretch that far.

"We know she is in the house. Where is she hiding?"

"You can't..." Garry wants to say. Somehow the words never come.

This isn't possible! The police wouldn't...

"You are wasting my time. If you don't tell me where she is, I will shoot you in the face."

An unseen hand grabs Garry's hair and pulls his head back much further than he thought possible. The boot on his shoulder doesn't move an inch.

Even with the tears in his eyes, Garry recognizes the gun pointed at him. The muzzle is two inches from his eyes.

The sound of a hammer cocking.

"Where is she hiding?"

Time to die for your love, Garry. Time to be a man.

"Under the television. Louise is under the television," he croaks.

Aaaaaaaaaaaaaah!

Fucking weakling!

Fucking Garry! She trusted you.

I would die for you

Fucking bollocks!

You are weak Garry. Weak, weak, weak!

A failure, a fraud, a liar.

But how weak are you really, Garry?

You know you are weak. You have always known you are weak. Otherwise, you wouldn't have doubted yourself. You were flawed from the very first moment. That you knew.

But do you know how weak you really are? How deep you can sin?

You will find out.

…

The leather coats – Police? Army? Secret service? Gangsters? – pull Louise from her hiding place. She kicks, she screams. They beat her and laugh.

Garry is forced to watch, a boot on the shoulder, the hand still pulling back his head.

"You betrayed me!" Louise shouts. "You said you loved me!"

"You did the right thing, Garry," says the same voice, the one that threatened to blow his face off. "The cunt isn't worth it."

The voice walks away, Garry's arms are cuffed behind his back and he is dragged outside. He sees how Louise is thrown in the back of a black van. Garry is put in the back of another black van.

He lands on the steel floor and immediately it gets dark: someone has thrown a blanket on top of Garry. Boots keep Garry down and keep the blanket in its place.

They drive. How long, where to? It is impossible to say. Bumps in the road, the van takes corners with screeching tires. If it wasn't for the boots, Garry would have rolled all over the floor of the van.

Finally, they stop.

The door of the van opens, the blanket is pulled off, but Garry is blinded by harsh lights. Two pairs of hands grab him and pull him from the van.

They, the leather coats, don't bother with walking. They just drag him along and, after a few doors and corridors, throw him in a small, empty cell.

The massive steel door closes with a bang.

#

Gray concrete walls and floors. A bunk, a single light. Nothing else.

Garry's arms are still cuffed behind his back. The steel cuts into his wrists, the muscles in his arms and shoulders keep sending pain signals to his brain.

Garry is in shock. This can't be real, this isn't happening. It is Wednesday night! Louise is a normal, regular woman. They can't be looking for her. It is all a mistake!

But the walls are the walls, the floor is the floor, and the handcuffs are the handcuffs. They don't lie.

Not them. Do they, Garry?

How weak are you really? Now that is an interesting question.

Garry is sleeping, or at least dozing off, when the cell door opens.

"So, Garry." It is the voice again.

Garry looks up. The voice wears black boots, leather overcoat, fedora, round sunglasses. His skin is gray-white. The man looks like an evil Nazi from some low budget movie. Or something from a nightmare.

Maybe it is all a nightmare. Maybe he is dreaming all this.

Maybe, Garry.

Maybe not.

The voice smiles. It is a kind of friendly smile, which of course makes it a sinister smile. Context is everything. "You can see Louise now."

The man doesn't wait for a reply, he just leaves.

Other leather coats come in, grab Garry by the arms, and drag him off.

Gray, anonymous corridors, sickly fluorescent lighting, and finally a room with a big window.

On the other side of the window sits Louise, chained to a chair. Dried up blood under her nose, bruises on her cheeks and forehead, a swollen lip. She has put up a fight.

It takes Garry a moment to realize the window is a one-way mirror, just like the cop shows on television. He can see Louise, she can't see him.

"We finally have her," says the voice somewhere behind Garry.

Garry turns around, his head full of questions and demands. Who the hell are you? What is happening? This is illegal! You can't do this.

Again, no word comes from his lips.

He can't. He doesn't dare.

You weak sack of pussy shit, Garry.

"We need your statement," says the voice. "We have enough to put her away, but things look better with a statement, with reliable witnesses. So you are going to sign a statement, Garry."

"What kind of statement?" whispers Garry. They are his first words in... hours, at least.

"The statement we will provide," the voice answers with a smirk. "Enough to get her convicted. Nice and legally."

"But..."

The voice puts his finger – leather gloves, of course – to Garry's lips. Garry shuts up.

"I know what you are thinking, Garry. Truly, I do. You are thinking 'But I haven't seen my sweet Louise do anything illegal. I don't think she is evil. She can't have done all those things she is accused of. I love her.' But, Garry, let me assure you, you are wrong. That piece of filth there," the voice points to Louise in the other room, "is guilty. As guilty as night and day. Now, we want to do this nice and legally, with little fuss. But if that isn't possible, we will do it less nice and less legally. So, Garry, you see, no matter what you do, you can't save Louise. She is going down. But you can save yourself, because if you don't sign the statement, I will blow your brains out, here and now."

The voice pulls his gun and puts it to Garry's forehead, in a nonchalant, routine fashion.

"So, Garry, help us to convict Louise, or say die."

Choices Garry.

You are a coward, you already know that.

The question is: how much of a coward?

How far will you bend?

How little will you do to save your loved one?

Choices.

"I will sign," Garry cries out. "I will sign the statement!"

Someone was taping the conversation and now replays the last sentence.

"I will sign the statement!" says Garry's voice, in both rooms.

"I will sign the statement!" says the voice again.

Louise looks up.

She breaks, hope leaves her face, her eyes, her posture.

"I will sign the statement!"

"I will sign the statement!"

Garry, Garry. Hell has a special collection of tortures waiting for you.

You had the nerve to say you loved her?
Sick bastard.

#

Garry has earned his freedom. Or at least, the freedom of his hands. The leather coats uncuff him, but he is still in the bare cell.

They feed him, he pisses and poops in the bucket that is provided. Garry sleeps, the light is never turned off.

Nobody talks to him.

Garry listens at the door, he hears nothing.

He has cooperated! He deserves better! An explanation, a lawyer, something.

Ask for it, Garry.

Ask for it. Have the guts.

No, you don't.

You stay quiet in your cell.

Garry, the hero.

#

"We need a confession," the voice says. The man stands in the door opening of the cell.

Garry doesn't dare to look at him. He looks at the floor. "I have signed a statement," he says quietly.

What kind of statement, Garry doesn't know. He never got to read the paper he signed.

The voice laughs. "Garry, Garry! I don't mean you! We need her statement. Just to wrap it up. The last dots on the 'i', the finishing touch, so to speak. We like things nice and neat."

The voice shuts up, gives Garry time to think.

Garry still doesn't dare to look up, but he knows an answer is required. He can't stay quiet, he really can't.

"What... What do you want?"

"Good boy!" The voice chuckles. "Help us get her confession. You know the consequences if you don't."

The voice pulls back his leather coat. The gun is on his belt, he doesn't even bother to draw it. They both know how the game is played. They both know who will win.

It ain't Garry.

"I will help you to get her confession," he says, tired and nervous. Is it the right answer?

Garry, Garry...

You... Ah, why bother? Never mind.

#

I will help you to get her confession.

You said it, Garry. What did you think? That you would talk Louise into confessing? Hold her hand, convince her?

Naive piece of shit.

You will help them to get her confession.

Louise is strapped in a kind of dentist chair. She is blindfolded with a dark blue sleeping mask. She has lost weight, she looks terrible.

Garry is alone with her in the room. On the small steel table, there is an assortment of all kinds of nasty looking tools and instruments. Drills, curved knives, needles, hammers, wires... Evil.

"Confess." The voice comes from a speaker. He sounds smug.

Louise clenches her teeth, shakes her head, and tenses in anticipation of the awful pain.

"Confess, dear. Or our man will have to hurt you."

Sweating, Garry looks around for a way out. Does he have to witness Louise's torture? Please, God, no! He wants to beg, to cry, to pound with his fists on the locked door, but he doesn't.

What if Louise would hear him? Know he is there with her?

What if he angers the leather coats? He has been cooperative, he doesn't want to throw away the goodwill he must have bought. Surely?

So Garry stays quiet, while the woman he said he would die for is about to be tortured.

Garry, you are despicable.

"Either you confess, or you don't," the voice continues. "In the end, it doesn't matter. You will only make things so much simpler for yourself if you confess."

"Nnnggg!" Louise shakes her head again. Her frail body rocks in the chair which doesn't move. It is bolted to the floor.

Confess! Garry begs her in his mind. Confess, Louise, and all will be over. Please! I don't want you to be tortured.

What Garry means, of course, is that he doesn't want to watch, hear, and smell it.

Torture is a very messy business.

There is a way out, Garry. Several ways, actually.

You can set Louise free. Just take one of the knives and cut her throat, swift and merciful. Or plunge it in her heart.

You will be doing her a service.

And if you are quick enough – it doesn't take long – you can kill yourself.

Slash! That is your own throat. Don't mind the spraying blood.

Or.

Stab! That is a knife in your heart, or somewhere nearby. It will hurt, but you will be free.

Kill your love, and kill yourself. It is dramatic, but it will be your redemption.

You will have beaten the leather coats, the fucking smug voice who thinks he owns you.

Do it, Garry.

Do it!

But Garry doesn't.

Nope.

He backs away, looks nervously at the door, expecting some torturer to come in. Will he wear a long leather coat?

Most likely.

Only... The door doesn't open. Nobody enters.

The voice speaks again: "Dear, you brought this upon yourself." He actually sounds a bit sad. The voice continues: "Sir, you can start. We need that confession."

Garry looks around. Who...?

It takes a full second before Garry realizes who the voice is addressing.

He looks at the speaker. No!

From the speaker comes the sound of cocking the hammer of a gun.

No! No! Please!

Desperately Garry looks at Louise. Confess! Confess bitch! Do it!

Nope.

She has balls, Garry. You don't.

Garry takes a step toward the little steel table. He hesitates, looks at Louise.

Time to be a hero, Garry.

Garry takes a set of pliers, very useful for pulling out nails, twisting fingers and toes and such. Absolutely no help at all in killing someone quickly and killing yourself.

Garry has made his choice. He is going to get a confession from Louise.

#

Garry doesn't eat. He feels sick, he doesn't want to sleep. Images of what he has done haunt his dreams.

That's good, Garry.

It means you are not a psychopath.

You have empathy. You feel.

They say a sadist has to have a lot of empathy. How can he otherwise know what his victims feel?

Anyway. Garry succeeded. He got Louise to confess.

Did she know it was him? Did she recognize her lover's touch? His smell? The tiny characteristic sounds everyone makes?

Probably.

It didn't matter. In the end, she talked. She gave names and dates and places.

It didn't mean anything to Garry, but the voice seemed pleased.

The door was unlocked, and Garry was escorted (not dragged) back to his cell. Clean clothes and warm food was waiting there.

In the end, Garry eats and sleeps. A body can only endure so much before it shuts down.

It is probably somewhere in the afternoon when there is a polite knock on the steel door.

"Garry?" It is the voice.

The man enters, looking the same as always.

Garry doesn't say anything, just waits for whatever the voice wants from him now.

"It is time, Garry. Time for justice."

The voice turns and leaves the cell.

Garry follows.

Corridors, a big room this time.

For one moment Garry thinks there will be another bout of torture. This time, Louise is strapped in a heavy wooden construction, not unlike a kind of throne. Then Garry sees the heavy wires running to the straps around her forehead and chin, her wrists, her heart, the gag in her mouth.

Garry recognizes the thing for what it is. It is an electric chair. An execution chair.

"Louise will die," the voice speaks. "The evidence is overwhelming, with your statement and her confession. Execution is the only option."

"Yes," says Garry. What else can he say? Louise confessed. She did things – Garry doesn't know what exactly. She made choices.

He trusted her! He damn well trusted her! He loved her, was willing to die for her!

And she betrayed him. Lied to him. Tricked him. She used him.

Louise has to die, there is no other option.

Garry almost believes it himself, but deep in his heart he knows all of it doesn't mean shit. He is weak. That is why he is here with Louise.

There is only one to blame.

"Garry, I want you to do the honors."

The voice nods in the direction of the single button on the desk. Garry doesn't need an explanation.

Would I die for her?

No, Garry, you wouldn't.

Would I kill for her?

Most likely not, because that would be putting yourself in danger, Garry.

Would I kill her?

We are about to find out.

Garry looks at the voice. "Really?" His eyes do the asking.

The voice nods, fatherly.

Garry reaches out and pushes the button.

The electric chair is a horrible way to die. One isn't killed instantaneously. Oh no, definitely not. The current fries the body, makes it dance, burns away tissues. Smoke rises, the generators buzz, electricity cackles. Louise's eyes are almost popping out, her mouth is twisted into a permanent skeletal grin.

It does take twelve minutes before she is dead.

…

Well, that settles that question. Yes, you will kill her, Garry, if need be.

#

Garry is alone in his cell. He is alone in so many ways. No more Louise, no more love of his life. No more self-respect either.

You did what you did to survive, Garry. An explanation is unnecessary. Really.

Betray the woman you love. Trick, torture, and kill her. It had to be done. Not because you wanted it, or liked it, but because you had no choice. It was life or death, you or her. Love is fine, but survival is the only thing that really matters.

You will live another day.

Or maybe not.

The cell door opens. The voice enters. Strange, he looks a bit like that other voice, like Frank Sinatra. Garry only notices now.

I did it my way, plays in the back of Garry's head. He knows he is getting hysterical.

"Garry, I am quite pleased with you." The voice smiles. "We got off on a rough start, but I think we really had a productive relationship."

Are you nervous, Garry? You should be. This is the part where the voice will pull out a gun and shoot you.

Do you think they want witnesses? Even now you are being naïve.

Goodbye, Garry.

"Of course you are free to go now, Garry." The voice smiles.

He is waiting for you to walk out the door, Garry. He will shoot you in the back. 'Prisoner shot down during an escape attempt', that will be in his report. Come on, Garry, smile, say thank you, think you are free. You will be dead in a few moments.

Not that it matters, of course.

Garry rises, oblivious to what is waiting for him: bullet in the back, a one-way trip down to Hell.

"But I think it is a waste to ignore someone with your talents," says the voice.

...?

The voice steps aside and one of his henchmen enters the cell. In his arms, he carries a long leather coat, a pair of boots, a fedora, a pair of round metal framed sunglasses, and a gun.

"I would like you to join us, Garry. I think you will be a valuable asset."

What?

Garry... Please don't!

Not even you can be that...

Garry smiles, friendly, sinister. "Yes, I will. I would love to. Thank you so much!"

He takes the coat, and everything.

#

Doubts can become fears, and fears can do strange things to people. Their mind wanders, they start to fantasize, to dream.

Was it all a dream? A thought experiment?

Maybe.

But it doesn't diminish any of the horrors.

Garry thought of it. Thinks he is capable of doing those things.

He is not sure, he has doubts. He hopes he won't do them, if he ever has to make those choices. But the fact is that he entertained the possibilities.

He didn't do those things.

He didn't intend to do those things.

But he thought about them, and on some level, feared he could do those things.

Garry, Garry.

Maybe you aren't weak and evil, but you could be.

Go on, live your life. Pray you will never have to choose.

#

Garry strokes Louise's hair. They are on the couch, watching television.

Would I die for her? Garry quietly asks himself.

He knows - no, *suspects* the answer.

I will try.

It is the best he can do. He is only human. He would try.

Garry kisses Louise's hair. She is so lovely.

The fist pounds on the front door, loud and demanding.

"Open up!" shouts a harsh bully voice. "Open up!"

Garry is paralyzed. This can't be true. How...? No!

Doubts.

Choices.

Time to stand up, or break.

Again and again the fists pound on the door.

Now.

Or never.

Louise jumps up.

"He is here! The bastard is here!" she shouts. "Get him!"

She looks him in the eyes.

She knows.

She knows he is weak. She knows he is faulted. She knows.

The leather coats storm in, grab him. They shout and hit him. Louise laughs and laughs.

Beaten, bleeding, dizzy, Garry is dragged to the waiting black van.

He knows what will happen.

He knows Louise will be present, laughing, jeering, participating.

He knows he deserves what he will get.

He deserves it.

Because he is weak.

He knows he is weak.

Suddenly, Garry feels at peace, for the first in a long time.

Scream Through the Stitches
Kane Gordon

Christ's Church
Luton Village
Chatham, Kent
September 5th, 1914

I had marked the ending of this day with her blood on my coat tails.

The moon energized the ichors, gave them late evening sparkle.

Warden Wickens, rotund, standing at the lych gate, the only witness. His vision poor, impossible at such late an hour to determine shadows from reality. Eyeballs clouded by cataracts.

What he could not see, however, he had certainly heard smelt.

The firing of the musket; the spent gunpowder.

The warden stepped away from the gate. Moon doused him in shade.

His silhouette came toward me like a heavy broadsword. "It's Warden Wickens. Do not hide from me!"

I looked behind, around. Seeking a route out.

Gravestones. At angles. Sunk into the earth. Moss-tipped obstacles to avoid. Caskets buried deep, decayed bodies turning. Skinless fingers scrabbling for attention on coffin lids.

At ten years old, hurting someone didn't scare me. Being dead did.

"Got you! Urchin!" The musket grasped, pulled from me.

The warden clawed my throat with his free hand. A paperback copy of Dracula, carried with me to the churchyard, spilled from my coat pocket. "No. Damn! Get off me!"

"Will, let the poor boy alone!" Mrs Wickens. Cheeks puffed. Came into the dimming air. Drying her hands on her housecoat. She pressed them to her hips. Her stance forceful. Demanding.

The warden relinquished his hold on my throat. I wheezed.

"Urchin child. Miserable scallywag!"

"Oh, you desperate thing." Mrs Wickens again. Her sentence aimed not at me but towards my sister. Skirt fanned across her felled shape, face mottled black and crimson by the night light and bullet--the shape and colour that best suited the fifteen year old hag! "What have you done, Will?"

"What are you talking about, woman?" The warden looked perplexed. Scratched his head. Shook it.

"The girl. What have you done?"

I used that moment of confusion in the man to make a run for it. If he gave chase, the likelihood of him tripping was high because of his eyes, tipping escape in my favour.

Making damn sure the paperback got retrieved, I ran, ran hard, and hopped between the headstones, staring but not stopping at the ring of flints encircling and marking the pagan burial ground of the village's blackest past, a coven.

"He stole the musket!" Warden Wickens' voice followed after me but quickly grew distant, which made me confident he had not followed.

Yes, and stolen for good reason! "Should've finished you off, Willoughby. Little bitch sis! Should've buried you in a ditch!"

*

"Little sister, little sister
Eating boys for tea,
Little sister, little sister,
You will not eat me!"

*

She would be after me soon. Vengeful. The lines rattling like a quiver of septic words in my head. Made up to cope with the night she became lost as my part of the family.

*

Where to hide?
Where?
Nowhere local would prevent her finding me. My heart and head in agreement with that. This was a village small enough that we both knew the best places to remain from view.
Distance, "You need distance, Stanford Cal!"
The dusking hours had spun my breath into cottony vapours that stuck to the air and seemed to curl behind and mark me out amid the deepening of the day.
What to do?
A plan formed as my predicament forced me between houses and alleys. To dip from view. Cautious. On edge. Fretful. Locals would be out drinking. Public houses filled. Smoke and beer a fixture of the atmosphere. The river had to be my destination. Take a boat out to the Isle of Sheppey. To Sheerness.
Waiting for dawn, shivering, in the grounds of another church, curled into a bush, sleep put me into a dreadful place.
Into the realm of the unthinkable.
Where my sister chatted to the dead.

Chatted to the possessed.
The sinister presence that owned our home.

*

After father had broken his leg and could no longer work portering patients up at The Naval Hospital, paying rent on a sparse tenement in the heart of Chatham had been difficult. To compensate, we lived on a small holding on land at the end of a road occupied with Victorian red brick housing. Half hour's walk from the centre of town.

Lilli Campbell had taken us in. She had been a childhood friend of mother's and had bought the holding with her husband, Levi, shortly before he died of influenza.

Mother commented how "She could do with our help," and it was "God's blessing," she and mother had remained in contact over the years. "Else we would be street paupers." We heeded the declaration. Tried. Living with another woman watching, interfering with what we did or said, had subjected us to unwanted pressure.

Lilli had a fearsome demeanour. She hadn't liked me the moment we arrived and I had to shake her warped hand in greeting.

She startled me with her sucked-in cheeks, moth brown skin. One of her eyes had bulging veins, discolouring the white of the eye. The prayers she spoke, which never said anything good about the Lord Jesus.

Willoughby and I spent our evenings playing with the free roaming chickens, ducks and calves. Enjoying each other's company. Filling the log stack with twigs and branches from the pair of dying oak trees that grew to one side of the garden. A chicken wire fence divided the dwelling from that of the nearest property.

At my tender age, I could tell my position in the woman's affections matched that of the crows that nested in the oaks. Good for nothing vermin.

Any chance of telling mother how scared of the woman I was found me hurried from room to room, pushed into the corners like some ill-disciplined dog. It caused a churning in my stomach. Nervousness; a foreboding.

I could not inform her that Lilli showed over fondness towards Willoughby. That their closeness caused me to feel jealous when watching them dance off into the shadows, to laugh, and sing silly rhymes.

Unusual, menacing verses for a ten year old schoolgirl to learn.

During our first winter at the small holding, as her bond with the woman grew much stronger, the change in Willoughby happened.

Late, into a snowy Sunday.

*

Mother and father had been deep asleep but my slumber had been disturbed by the squeals. Happy sounds then echoes of pain.

As I went to the window, grabbing the hard-backed chair mother sat upon to read me bedtime stories, I sought out Willoughby only to find her bed empty.

The laughter outside distracting me from wondering as to her whereabouts.

Below, cavorting across the whitened back garden Lilli, naked. The shock of seeing a naked woman pinched my eyes alert. She held a calf locked by its neck under her arms. I stood on the chair to improve my view.

Holding its tail, also naked, Willoughby. Her smile out of place with the scene.

Snow light heightened everything into the finest detail. I became held in a magician's trance. Unable to go waken my parents. What the pair was doing could have been a game. Acting out a nursery rhyme.

Until the calf's throat was cut by a scythe the woman took from the top of the wood stack.

Lilli turned the jerking animal towards Willoughby so the blood covered her small body in a dress of thick red juice.

Black, winged creatures swooped and cawed. The crows in flight. Lilli swiped at them, with the scythe.

I blinked. My breath steamed the window pane; I hurriedly rubbed it clear with a pyjama arm.

The sudden appearance of the fat naked man looming out from behind the stack gave the occasion added revulsion.

His presence appeared to come at me, big shady hands to reach through the patch of glass I had cleared to enclose my mouth as he took Willoughby by the hand, led her to the bottom of the garden.

The squeals that then followed left me in no doubt something bad had happened.

Had there been an accident? Had Willoughby suffered an injury? Had she died?

She reappeared, palms pressed to her stomach, not more than one or two minutes later.

Lilli knelt to lick slithers of blood from her cheek, the dress smeared. From up in the bedroom, I thought it had been smeared in only certain, private areas.

I watched on. Waiting for the fat man to follow. Watched. Waited until my body succumbed to exhaustion.

To dreams. Dreams that wrecked me with their violence.

Crows the size of oak branches, perched around the border of the small holding. Worms between their beaks.

No, not worms, snakes. In whose wide jaws are children, clinging to their fangs. Is me.

My head slid against a pane, bumped down the frosted glaze. Time appearing not to have moved yet.

Willoughby tapped me on the shoulder. "Good morning, sleepy!"

I must have frowned as she stepped back. Looked at me. Afraid?

Her eyes narrowed. She hissed.

Not afraid. Not afraid, at all!

She made me tremble. Stood tall over my small frame like a crow from my dream.

"Mother said to hurry up or you'll miss breakfast."

I stared. Grabbed her face, squeezed. Searched for sharp, serpent's teeth. Ruffled up her dress, looking for something but I wasn't sure what. Her body clean. Unharmed.

Willoughby's voice constricted with my squeeze, sounded reedy. "You are hurting me!"

"What did he do to you?" I asked. My pyjamas were soaked with sweat. Or had I wet myself. An area of liquid around the feet of the chair told me the dreams had terrified me into urinating.

"Who?"

"The fat, naked man. What did he do?"

"You stink!" she said. Then added, "Not for little boys to know!"

Willoughby pushed herself back and danced towards the bedroom door.

Behind her, disturbing lines trailed "Not for little boys to know what the old man did; down by the shed, you'll never know 'what' we did!"

After that night. My relationship with my sister deteriorated.

She would sit away from me at the table.

Poke fun at me.

Call me names.

Speak verse that turned more and more unpleasant with each new day. Phrases that conjured shadows into marionettes, made dead bugs convulse.

Trapping me inside those verses. Rolling me in blame for the death of the calf. For befriending a fox. Allowing it into the garden. A lie. A lie everybody believed. Accusing me via one phrase of having "Little boy fantasies."

Then, one evening, she had it arranged for her, mother and father, to visit an aging uncle; leaving me at home, alone, with Lilli.

An evening when, Lilli showed me the attic.

Introduced me to the hanging men.

Turned off the gas lamp.

Locked me inside.

*

1921.

After nearly seven years.

She had found me out.

*

Lilli told me the men were former husbands. Three men. "Preserved and prevented from temptation."

How had they remained alive? Bound in hessian rags. Rags that smelt old. Eyes rigid yet watching. Fingers free at the nails. Twitching. Mouths stitched to stop whispers and cries. Death scared me. This sight disturbed me anew.

Shut inside with them, they seemed to emerge from their bindings. At least found a way to release their voices.

They got inside my head. Mocked me for being weak. Jostled me with unkind comments. Screamed through their stitches at me to get out. "Get away!"

I was too young to understand.

"He had been a curious boy to go up into the dark room on his own," Lilli told mother when she opened the door, some impossible time later. My first thought had been to jump into my mother's arms but Lilli stood between us, blocked me finding the comforts of a mother's love.

Willoughby scolded me. Called me a silly little brother. I snarled. Leapt at her. Father hobbled, trying to pull me back. Stumbled, damaged his leg further. Ended up in hospital. Caught an infection. Died.

Willoughby blamed me for my anger taking her sweet, loving daddy from her.

Mother took a "brave decision" said Lilli, to send me to the Rag-Edged School. "He would learn discipline."

Lilli and Willoughby waved me off with sniggers as the school's warder hauled me from the small holding. There had not even been time for me to go to court to defend myself. Father had taught me about justice. He had once worked as a court clerk. Told me about trials. How courts could decide a man's fate.

With father dead, there had been no trial.

Only punishment. My punishment.

Mother looked on, tried to prevent them taking me. Lilli locked her by the neck in the same manner as she had the calf. Enough to still rather than kill her.

I wanted to be with my mother. So wanted to stay and protect her from this woman.

Snow fell full and heavy that night.

It felt as if it snowed daily. Snowed forever during my stay at the Rag-Edged.

Five years, I had to spend incarcerated at the school. With boys who had been older. Brutal. Wise. Cunning.

Over time, I grew up physically. Adapted. Defended my name with honour. Despite my palms transforming into fleshy wood bark, fungal infected, cracked.

We were never allowed visitors. Were stopped from reading. Being educated. This was not an educational school.

A kindly old neighbour took pity. Sneaked in books for us to read. I was happy to receive a paperback version of Dracula. Some of the boys were illiterate. Others able to read me the tale. I looked at how they mouthed the words, copied. My way to rebel. To become literate.

Filled my nights with another dubious world, one of fantasy; a world far beyond this harsh one in which I had been imprisoned.

Lilli passed on by with Willoughby every few months. Each of our cells had narrow window slits through which we could see the changing seasons. The pair had been deliberate. Spoke to the warders. The older children mentioned that I had not been the first little boy she had gotten sent to the school. Lilli likened to an illegal copper. Able to pull the youthful squalor off the streets. Clean Chatham of juvenile criminals.

I feared she did not like males.

Willoughby appeared to be growing larger each visit. Around her belly. Surely, not old enough to be pregnant?

When she became suddenly thin again, Lilli could be seen besides her pushing a pram.

*

I saw nothing of my mother. Wondered if she had been tortured, made to spend time outside the warmth of the house.

On my tenth birthday, they let me out of the school. A treat. To collect coal for the furnace.

The neighbour watched. Smiled. Cheered as I used his diversion of talking to the warder assigned as my escort to run.

I had never known how much running would be required of me.

For revenge.

Being in such a place like the school, for five painful years, had given me inner resolve.

Every weekend, we had been forced to walk to Christ's Church for Sunday Evensong. I had often noticed the warden. His wife helping him practice shooting with his ancestor's musket, before disappearing into the kitchen. Her words of "Don't sleep too long, dear," imprinted on my mind.

Each Sunday, as we left evensong, I would note the gravestones. Drift slightly from the group. Taken by the stone ring. The warden's voice warning me not to stray too far into the burial ground. Should my footfalls drag them to the surface. "I'll bring you your new companion, soon," I said. Spat into the ring once the warden's head had turned.

*

The day I ran, there had been only one thing on my mind. Lure out Willoughby.

Get her to the church.

Shoot her dead.

Pull her past the flint ring. Shovel up earth. Toss her body on top of a coffin. Stamp the soil down hard. Real hard.

Baiting her had been easy.

Getting the warden's gun had been easy. There were boys in the School with tips on how to steal.

My time there had come with many benefits.

How to commit murder and get away with it, for one.

I almost stopped the plan. Almost.

Looking through the front window of the small holding, Willoughby sat with someone. An infant girl of about four years old, hugged to her breast. Feeding from her breast.

She turned sharply. Sneered. Blood trickled from the girl's mouth.

In both, the same features. Willoughby and daughter? The idea struck like a hot iron.

I pulled back. My head filled with guilt for wanting my sibling dead and denying the innocent mite a mother. No. This must end. I could return for the little one later.

Gathering my thoughts, I felt Lilli was to blame. She, too, would need to die!

The window flew up and a stick cracked me on the forehead. "I'm gonna kill you, brother!"

How to entice, without even bothering to try.

Willoughby reached the front door as I rubbed my head. She may have been young, too young to give birth but the cry of "Mummy!" answered that horrifying question. Prevented her coming out with the knife, allowing me an opportunity to straighten, twist and be gone.

"Stay, Dolores!" An angry blast. I did not look back.

The front door slammed.
Wickedness filled Willoughby's eyes.
Her chase that of the incensed.

*

Warden Wickens had been snoozing. Evensong finished. I had reached the church far ahead of my sister. Affording myself a good five minutes to commit crime number one.

A tiny knife honed from a spoon handle in the depths of many sleepless nights in the school, allowed me easy access past the warped windows of the warden's cottage. I saw Mrs Wickens in the kitchen garden. As expected. According to plan.

The musket rested to the side of the hearth. Shot and gunpowder side by side on the stone floor.

I crept in.

Collected the gun. With stealth.

The warden's eyes opened, closed. His booted feet rolled apart, preceding a gravelly snore confirming he was asleep.

The warden had lost much of his sight a year earlier. It had been difficult to judge if he had seen me but a risk worth taking.

Once back outside, my fingers prepared the musket. Hate may have filled my soul but incarceration had taught patience. Perhaps, time inside the establishment of the Rag-Edged had been of use. A coarse learning in survival.

Night-time had pulled in fast. Extra fast. Added atmosphere. Coldness.

In the churchyard, amid the graves, enraged, Willoughby. Her scream baleful, that of a wild woman. Still in her adolescence but already with a hollow face; her nostrils pinched, fingers around the hilt of a bread knife, crooked, flesh raised and barbed. Hair sooty.

"You came back! The dead do not return—you will not return, ghost brother!" Spittle flew from between her scratched lips.

Two things gnawed at my brain, where was my mother and was Dolores truly my kith and kin? None of the answers would be forthcoming as Willoughby launched her attack.

I raised the musket. Fired. The shot kicked blue sparks into the air.

Willoughby fell. A bullet to the skull. Slivers of bone cutting into the night like glassy, jagged blades of moonstone.

As she was spun back, it became clear my aim had been off, her head had lost part of its temple bone but she showed no effects of being dead.

I had marked this lateness of the day with her blood.

Not her life.

*

In the morning, my legs had stiffened but would not stop me reaching the docks. Sheerness would hide me. The docks would give me work. Lose me in its crowd of waterside labourers.

Keep me safe.

For nigh on seven years.

Then they came.

*

I found work as a wharf rat, graduated to be known in less menial terms as a stevedore. From sweeping to helping load and unload the boats. Be on hand. A butler to the most precious cargo, passengers.

These passengers arrived on a small ferry out of Gillingham that I had helped rope safe.

Clothes without fancy, charcoal fabrics. Dusty cream bonnets loosely tied. Each carrying an unopened parasol. The ferryman an unsmiling assistant, guiding them individually dockside before returning for their luggage.

The ferryman, George Loader, and I had drunk together on many occasions. He looked uneasy, directed raised eyebrows towards me. He had reason to show concern. My nod acknowledged as much.

Perhaps it was the scar on the side of Willoughby's head which first caused his concern. It caught my attention. Followed by the gutter sluice texture of her skin, the posture hunched. The girl showing similar disfigurement.

Dolores had grown into a diminutive replica of her parent. Their connection too strong to deny.

I had often considered my reaction if this moment ever occurred. That my legs would decide my fate. They chose not to run. They chose to keep me here, to face a providence that had been impossible to avoid. Always expected.

Willoughby became aware of me straight away. I'd taken to wearing a cross. Grabbed at it, prayed for help. Shuffled nervously. Careful of stepping from the edge of the dock. Pleasant weather today. Clouds high, sweet white lace swirls across a light blue.

Her hand curled, raised itself, a finger pointed. A word mouthed. The expression on Dolores boiling; her skin turning purple. The bruising associated with an uncontrolled temper.

The pair had begun walking towards me, slow, mannered then with lengthier strides. George Loader unloaded three suitcases. A sewing box. Several loose needles thrown onto the lid. My friend keeping a respectful distance. He went back on board. Searched around. Picked up a long pole. Began to get off the ferry. I lifted a hand to stop him. Unhooked the ferry, waved him off. Checked for other workers. We were alone. "Safer to be alone," I whispered.

It was time to worry. At sixteen, I had already both a wife and son, Hawk, mere weeks old. They should not be part of this bile towards me. George should not become embroiled. His safety could not be guaranteed. Something told me these were not objects of beauty, delicate ladies. Easy to hurt. They would be the opposite.

Sheerness Docks covered a vast space. Filled with hiding places only an employee would know of and, yet, it suddenly became impossible to think straight, to get back into that child version of Stanford Cal that had eluded this deranged person for so long.

Marrying Albert Cannell's only daughter, a teacher called Ella, had softened my resolve. The birth of Hawk had mellowed that softening further still. Left me vulnerable. Weak.

Dolores had me by the neck, chubby, fingers applying enough pressure to bring me to my knees in agony.

"Good girl, good girl!" said Willoughby. "There. We will do it there!"

Dolores deliberately bent my neck, forced my eyes towards a group of stacked, broken tea chests piled at the entrance to a warehouse. Warehouse Four. It would be empty. Hardly ever used.

Willoughby had me by the arms and dragged.

My head thudded across the tarmacadam, the pain extreme.

Unconsciousness followed. A brief respite from the torments.

An abomination of cries, ululations greeting me on re-awakening.

*

The men in the attic.

I hanged amid them.

Wrapped.

How long had I been here?

What had she done to me?

The room had been lit with multiple gas lamps. Three, perhaps four.

Willoughby and the girl were sat on tattered green leather chairs. Usage long gone to age.

"Hello, brother."

I thought of my wife. Worried she did not have me to protect her. I worried for Hawk. His father not there to read to him.

Willoughby got up from her chair. She struggled. Dolores leaned over to help.

My sister appeared pregnant. She shuffled towards me. Adjusted her gait to let my fingers brush against the bump.

I remembered. A scattering of abusive visions.

My trouser belt slid free. Breeches tugged down. A hail of words. Latin? An older, ancient script? I thought of the bodies buried in the churchyard. Imagined Willoughby in league with their spirits. How she had served the infant with blood milk. Remembered her hands touching, grubby, rough, rubbing me erect.

An act so impossible even blinking did not remove it from memory.

Willoughby lifting her dress, stepping over. Lowering.

A coupling happening despite attempts to prevent it. No signs of assistance from the girl. She had been banished from viewing. Told to keep watch.

Around me invisible ropes.

I should not have released inside her and yet did. There had been an unhealthy language flowing through my head, injecting me with illicit lust.

"Bad added to bad makes better bad." Willoughby had shouted at the time. Time carouselled. My body turned, turned again. The strength of my sister beyond measure. How had I been transported to here? Brought up into the attic. Pictures of what happened shimmered. George Loader helping? Willingly?

I repelled the revelations but the effect encouraged a sensation of sickness of which I could not be rid, so gulped down. Choked. "There, there brother." She patted my back. "You will not be dying anytime soon.

"Of course, I wanted you dead when you were five, but then I had greater plans." Willoughby sighed, breathless from her condition. "And now my family is soon to be complete." She twisted her head to sneer at my hanging companions. Their eyes upon her. Looked away. At me. "Death is too good for you. You should be in an institution. Forever. But this will suffice."

Willoughby shuffled back. "Sweet, Dolores, this is your uncle Stanford. His is the father of your long-awaited baby Queenie."

Queenie? It would be impossible to tell whether it would be a boy or girl!

Dolores called me uncle. It removed me from being an older brother. Many families had families within their group. None, I bet, through such corrupt, vile means.

How long had this captivity had me at its mercy? My mouth felt dry.

It would take many weeks before Willoughby could be seen as pregnant. Had they kept me here that length of time?

Dolores sidled towards me. "It is my kindest pleasure to meet you, dear Uncle Stanford." She stopped. Grinned. "Such funny sewing, mother. I so like what you have done." Tiptoed, kissed my tightly closed lips.

"We will be going now." Said Willoughby. "Dolores, please turn out the lights."

She skipped to each gas lamp and lowered its light until it faded. Leaving me alone in the darkness.

I thought again of my wife and son.

Of my sister—lost.

Whom she now bore, my offspring...my daughter?

Of mother; of Lilli. Where had Lilli gone?

I thought to retain my sanity.

Considered these concerns, questions that yearned answers.

Had to block the unrest they caused.

Willoughby imparting further retribution.

Without killing me. Through reflection.

In the form of never knowing why things had happened.

What things might have happened.

I could do nothing but endure.

Confined in the attic.

With Lilli's husbands. Those poor men who clung to life by unknown, unknowable means. Like me.

Waiting for them to get in my head.

Issue their warning.

Only this time, I would scream back at them through my own stitches.

Other HellBound Books
For You To Enjoy

All available now in paperback and eBook from Amazon, iBooks, Barnes & Noble, Kobo etc. For full details, visit our official website

www.hellboundbookspublishing.com

Or
Download our App from iTunes / Google Play – or simply scan the QR Code below

Demons, Devils and Denizens of Hell Vol. 1

A hellish collection of short stories from some of the best in the business - compiled by the award-winning author P. Mattern.

Featuring tales from the darkest pits of Hades by Tania Hagan, Lily Luchesi, Jay Michael Wright II, Ken Goldman, Sergio "ente per ente" Palumbo, Emery LeeAnn, Crystal Barnard, James H Longmore, Toneye Eyenot, James Richardson, Lori Fontanez, Marcus Mattern, Lance Tuck, L. Ashby, P. Mattern, Elizabeth Cash, Bryan A. Tann, Elizabeth Zemlicka, Michael Sutton, Thomas S. Gunther, Feind Gottes, and the incomparable Nik Kerry

Blood and Kisses
By
James H Longmore

The definitive short story collecting from James H Longmore - an eclectic mix of dark horror, bizarro and Twilight-Zone style tales of the downright disturbing.

Welcome to the long awaited collection from the writer of horror novels *'Pede* and *Tenebrion*; a forword by Richard Chizmar (co-author of *Gwendy's Button Box* and author of *A Long December*), 18 short stories, 5 flash fiction and even a poem - all skin-crawling, soul-shredding tales of terror, of the darkest things that skulk amongst the night's inky shadows, and of the everyday gone horribly awry.

Discover the alternative implication of technology becoming self-aware, enjoy the acquaintance of a charismatic new pastor who promises his flock a brand new place in which to worship his God, and spend a little time in the company of a nice young man who is inexorably caught up in his home town's terrible secret. Then there is Cupid's revelation that personally he has never experienced love, yet we discover that very emotion alive and not so well amongst the ruins of a post zombie apocalypse world, and we bear witness to a childhood innocence forever destroyed in a war-torn city. There is more, Dear Reader, much, much more; for within these pages we have devils, demons and ghosts, lycanthropes and demi-gods, all rubbing nefarious shoulders with vilest of Hell's offspring who have slithered from the netherworld to doff their caps and wish us all the sweetest of dreams…

No Rest For The Wicked
By
Pamela Morris

Every ghost has a story. Not all of them want it told.

From beyond the grave, a murderous wife seeks to complete her revenge on those who betrayed her in life; a powerless domestic still fears for her immortal soul while trying to scare off anyone who comes too close; and the former plantation master - a sadistic doctor who puts more faith in the teachings of de Sade than the Bible - battle amongst themselves and with the living to reveal or keep hidden the dark secrets that prevent any of them from resting in peace.

When Eric and Grace McLaughlin purchase Greenbrier Plantation, their dreams are just as big as those who have tried to tame the place before them. But, the doctor has learned a thing or two over his many years in the afterlife, is putting those new skills to the test, and will go to great lengths in order to gain the upper hand. While Grace digs into the death-filled history of her new home, Eric soon becomes a pawn of the doctor's unsavory desires and rapidly growing power, and is hell-bent on stopping her.

Worship Me
By
Craig Stewart

Something is listening to the prayers of St. Paul's United Church, but it's not the god they asked for; it's something much, much older. A quiet Sunday service turns into a living hell when this ancient entity descends upon the house of worship and claims the congregation for its own.

The terrified churchgoers must now prove their loyalty to their new god by giving it one of their children or in two days time it will return and destroy them all. As fear rips the congregation apart, it becomes clear that if they're to survive this untold horror, the faithful must become the faithless and enter into a battle against God itself. But as time runs out, they discover that true monsters come not from heaven or hell…

…they come from within.

**A HellBound Books LLC
Publication**

www.hellboundbookspublishing.com

Printed in the United States of America